# THE
# SPANISH LADY

## by Maurice Walsh

# THE
# SPANISH LADY

## Maurice Walsh

CHAMBERS

This edition

Printed in Singapore
by Tien Wah Press (Pte) Ltd

ISBN 0 550 20419 9

# CONTENTS

## PART I

### THE SOWING

## PART II

### THE REAPING

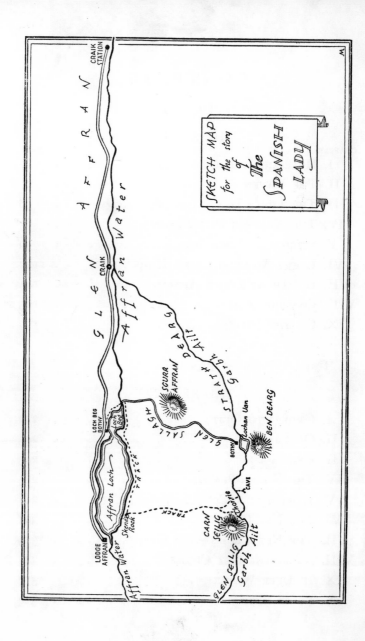

SKETCH MAP
for the story
of
The
SPANISH LADY

# PART I : THE SOWING

## CHAPTER I

### HOLE-AND-CORNER

I

DIEGO USTED was the only passenger that got off the train at Craik Station, but, then, as far as he could see, there was no reason in the world why anyone—even himself—should get off at that station in the portals of an empty mountain wilderness.

He had left six people behind him in the compartment, but who they were and where they were going he did not know and did not care. He did not care at all. In fact, he had not a care in the world. All the way from London he hadn't had a care, not even when half a score of passengers crowded into the compartment at York, and a stout person, probably female, edged him into the corridor. For hours he had stood there, his hands on the rail across the window, looking out at the fattish, flattish, tameish, leisurely English landscape sliding by and showing little or no sign of the *blitz* that might go on for ever and ever and ever. He could be leisurely, too, in the same stolid, enduring, toneless way, a way that was beyond hopelessness and underneath despair.

He did not remember much about that long train ride. At the beginning of it he had set his mind in what he called stoicism without knowing much of the real doctrine of stoicism. But all the time he had been conscious of an emptiness somewhere about the pit of the stomach, not hunger, but a vacuum in which there was no pain. He was pleased about that, that is he was pleased there was no pain, that the vacuum did not break down into that persistent, weary, mind-destroying, just-bearable gnaw that he had known for so many months. He had used his ration book hardly at all. Probably, in spite of his spurious stoicism, he was afraid, though he would not admit fear; but somewhere, deep down, he was afraid to stir again into life that patient, ravening gnaw. At York he had had some weak tea, and at Edinburgh, where he stayed the night, some soup and milk pudding off the scanty menu; and all next day, through a country that was often desolate and sometimes ugly and always strong, he had not eaten at all until reaching Inverness —full of soldiery—where he had stayed another night.

Here now, in the April afternoon, he was at his destination, his very final destination on top of earth, the spot from which he hoped to step off into another dimension —if any. For he told himself that another three months —or six—would see the end of the entity that was Diego Usted. He would go out with the fall of the year. After five years of very savage warfare he wanted to die in a hole-and-corner. That was the Latin blood in him, or the Gaelic.

He took the awkward step down to the platform, pulled his old leather bag after him, and looked round. Yes, he was the sole passenger getting off at Craik; and there was no one here to meet him, though he had written three days previously. He felt a small touch of disappointment, for he was not yet the lone wolf he thought he was.

There were only three persons on the platform: the guard, the station-porter, and a postman, all oldish men, manhandling a few parcels from the van at the other end of the train.

Diego felt stiff after the long constraint, and stamped up the length of a carriage and back again. He was not cold. The air here had not the dank harshness of the London atmosphere that had done its worst on him

8

during four wintry months. This air was brisk and had a feeling of youth in it, and the April sun was shining as if it had never known treachery. He did not stamp about for long, for his legs had lost much of their pith, and too much activity might start that old gnaw nibbling, and he felt as empty as a drum. He went across and sat on the iron seat between the windows of the solid, stone-built, one-storeyed house that was ticket-office, waiting-room, goods-store and station-agent's quarters. In due time the porter would come along, take up his ticket, and give him a few route directions. He found the ticket and slipped it in his cuff in readiness. It was a single ticket.

He sat there quietly, stolidly, legs out, hands deep in pocket, his eyes on the battered bag lying forlornly on the wide spread of packed gravel. All sounds were muffled in the bright but fragile sunshine. The engine, conserving its steam, was softly hissing to itself. The driver leant out of his cab, looking down the platform to where the guard, the porter and the postman, having finished with the van, stood gossiping amiably. The murmuring soft draw of their Highland voices just reached Diego. And then one of them laughed. They were in no hurry. This train was at least three hours late, so why trouble about another five minutes? And, then, a wisp of green waved, a door banged harshly, the engine gave a husky snort of whistle, puffed heavily, thutthered rapidly like a machine-gun, and went back to slow, laborious, steam-jetting effort; and the train snailed out of the station, the curling puffs of steam fading quickly into the thin, blue, spring sky.

It was then that Diego Usted felt marooned in his hole-and-corner. Any place he went from here he would go on his two feet—or with his two feet first. He did not mind which.

Now that the train was gone he could view the prospect

across the double line of rails. There was no platform on the other side, only a bank wisped with bleached grass, a white paling, and beyond that country, country, country. There was not a house anywhere, not a friendly tuft of smoke anywhere, just empty upheaved country.

Diego knew something about desolate landscapes, but this one was new to him. Beyond the paling was a sea of red-brown grass humped with grey-green islands out of which grey stone ribbed. From beyond came the cold sound of water strong-running, but he could not see where it ran; and beyond that hidden water the land lifted slowly and was clothed in wood. He could see the brown trunks of the first ranks of trees, and then nothing but a sombre, dark green mantle lifting upwards, flowing over, and again lifting upwards. He tried to remember the names his Highland mother—she was now with God —had given to the Highland trees: birch, rowan, alder, and the conifers, spruce, larch and pine. In his own mind he always confused the spruce and the larch. One remained dark green all the year round, the other put forth a tender green in spring and cast its needles in the fall. This was spring, but there was no shade of spring green relieving that sombre mantle. He did not know that May was the burgeoning time in the Highlands.

He lifted his eyes above the trees and looked upon the Highland hills really for the first time. Yesterday, coming up through Perth and Inverness, he had seen the Grampian Mountains, but mountains seen from a train are like mountains seen in a moving picture; they do not touch one intimately. In the country where he had been reared and grown to manhood the nearest mountain was five hundred miles away. He had, of course, seen rugged and serrated mountains in Spain, but had been too busy fighting and hiding to notice anything but their forbidding harshness and brittleness. Now the mountains were awesomely all around him.

Beyond the wooded slopes facing him, the great breast of a hill heaved upwards clad in the rusty grey that he knew must be heather. High up it was buttressed with bare rock, and between the buttresses and hooding the long ridge of the summit was the appalling white of snow in shadow, for this face of the hill was turned away from the sun. But that was only one hill and not the biggest. Beyond its shoulders was the gloom of distance out of which rose massive peaks; slopes glistened in silver; blue chasms cut sheerly into the white ridges; and far away over a snowy pass lifted one conical peak tinged with gold and faintly washed with rose. And the sun, bright and brittle, marched along the summits.

Like any man who looks, for the first time, at the big hills so close at hand, he felt a touch of awe. He felt minute and unimportant in the hollow of those huge, dreaming, aloof masses. They were not dead masses. They had a life and awareness of their own, different from his life and awareness, not evil, not inimical, just in a different dimension that belittled his. He wanted to grasp hold of something to hold himself in time and space, for he had that sensation that a man gets who loses his head on a cliff and has an abandoned desire to let go all holds in a reeling world. He could still feel; these mountains that his mother had known moved him.

The porter, having arranged his parcels in a neat pile, was coming up the platform, buttoning his jacket. Some distance behind, and more slowly, came the postman, a slack grey bag over one shoulder.

When the porter got nearer, Diego saw by his cap that he was more than a porter. He was the station-agent also. In a universal war all the able-bodied men would be with the Forces, and wayside stations like this would be run by the old or the unfit. This man was old but hale, of good girth, smooth ruddy face, and nose suspiciously ruddier. He turned towards Diego and spoke in his easy Highland voice.

"A fine day in it, sir! A touch o' frost come evening —too clear above the hill." He tipped a hand, half in salute, half in request for Diego's single ticket.

Diego had been brought up amongst a courteous people and would not stay seated while any man on his feet spoke to him. He rose and tendered the agent his much-punched ticket.

"It is a fine day, sir," he agreed, and stopped himself inclining from the hips.

The agent examined the ticket back and front, and looked up at the tall dark stranger interrogatively.

"You'll be for Craik, sir?"

"Am I not there?" There was no signboard or anything else to indicate the name of the station, but a ticket collector had assured him that this was Craik.

"Craik Station, sir—the township, I mean."

"There is a town, then?"

"Ach no! A bit of a township—eight mile up the Affran Water."

"In Glen Affran?" He knew of Glen Affran.

"The very place. The mouth of the glen this is. You'll see the gap of it out front." He gestured a hand.

"Will you please tell me if a gentleman by the name of Hamish McLeod lives at this end?" He spoke very good English but used it formally.

"Hamish of Loch Beg Bothy?" There was now a live interest under the agent's lifted brows.

"That is he."

"Goad be here! You'll no' be his foreign nephew, James, up from London."

"I am, sir." In his own place he was called Diego, and that was not London.

"Gi'e us your hand, Mr—Usted, isn't it? I'm an old friend o' the family. Ross—Peter Ross the name. I heard of you often from Big Ellen, and Mairi, your mother—God be good to her—I knew her since she was that high."

He shook Diego's hand warmly, and the foreign man bowed over the clasped hands.

"You're longer in the bone than the uncle," Peter Ross said, his chin up. "You'll be taking after the father's side?"

"That is so, Mr Ross." But not quite so. His father, though of a tall race, had been short and dark and wirily lean. He himself was dark and lean, but tall—almost too tall—and once, not so long ago, he had been wiry as steel is wiry; but the steel wire in him had sagged down to that internal malaise.

Diego was not a talker, and Peter Ross was. In this empty land one would either possess oneself in silence or dam up a spate of talk ready for bursting.

"Ay, man! a strange thing your Uncle Hamish is not down to meet you. But he'll be, never you fear. The up-mail was a bit early for once—not more than three hours late anyway. He knows you're coming?"

"I wrote my aunt three days ago."

"Three days! That's no' muckle these evil times." He shouted over his shoulder at the postman, who was only three paces away: "Hey, Wally! come here! Do you know who we have? This is Wally McKenzie the Post, Mr Usted, another old friend."

Wally the Post was a small, hardy, weather-beaten man, but one would not know he was weather-beaten till he removed the uniform cap that came down to the tip of his nose. A walrus moustache hid his mouth and most of his chin. As he said later, he sported that moustache to stop the winds of the glen blowing his "fawsers" down his gullet.

He came forward and gave Diego a surprising hand-grip, and blew through the hairs covering his mouth.

"I heard you, Peter. You're welcome to Glen Affran,

Mr Usted. We're a' friends—most of us—and any friend of Hamish and Big Ellen's is double welcome."

There were courteous and friendly people in this stern mountain land, and Diego's heart lifted at the thought.

"Mr Usted wrote three days ago," said the agent. "Did you take the letter up, Wally?"

"No, then, I didn't. I took two up from Ian and young Larr." He twirled the grey bag off his shoulder and slapped its slackness. "Three days, you're saying! It'll be in here among the King's mail, and I'll mak' sure in a minute."

He broke the postal seals with a jerk, thrust in a hand, and brought forth a fistful of mail, mostly in buff. He shuffled through it expertly.

"A' for the General, Head of the Home Guard—On His Majesty's Service. Ah! what did I tell you? Here we are!"

He held up Diego's letter addressed to Mrs Hamish McLeod, Loch Beg Bothy, Glen Affran, by Craik. Apparently she was known locally as Big Ellen.

"I ken your hand-of-write well's my own," said the postman. "You write Big Ellen once in the two months —fine newsy letters."

Wally was being merely polite. Diego Usted did not write newsy letters. The deadly work he had been engaged on could not be given in news to a woman. The postman thrust the letter back in the bag with the others.

"I'll deliver it myself the morn as in duty bound," he said.

"If you gentlemen will tell me where my uncle lives——"

"Losh! 'tis a long step, sir," said the agent. "Glen Affran is a gey long glen. Eight miles up to Craik, and six more to Affran Loch, and four beyond to Lodge Affran where the road ends."

"And Loch Beg?"

"The name we have on the near end of Affran Loch. The head-forester's bothy—your uncle's place—is close on the shore of it, fourteen, maybe fifteen miles from where we stand, a good road all the way, but stiff."

"I could hire——?"

"No' since the war. But it'll be a' right, Mr Usted. I've an old boneshaker of a bike you could manage, and we can send up the bag in the Lodge car to-morrow or——"

"Hist! speak o' the devil!" interrupted the postman. "Hear ye that?"

That was the smooth powerful purr of a motor-engine coming up to the station and stopping outside the far door of the waiting-hall. The postman waddled quickly into the hall, and was back almost immediately. He was frowning a little.

"Ay! the Lodge car! the General and Mistress Ann. We'll manage you a lift all right, Mr Usted."

But there was no confidence in his voice, and Diego wondered at that. Surely, amongst a kindly people where cars were few, a lift would be given as a matter of course. Or did the people of Lodge Affran hold themselves aloof from the Glen?

The agent, moving down the platform, gave Diego a wink over his shoulder. "The General, he's thrawn. He'll be wanting them parcels double quick."

The postman moved to a red bicycle propped beyond the door, and began strapping his mail-bag on the carrier. Diego sat down again and restored his hands to his pockets. He might not get a lift, he might not take one grudgingly offered, but he could if necessary cycle fourteen or fifteen miles, in spite of the vacuum at his middle. Not so many months ago he had walked and run and hid and killed for twenty miles in the dark on the rocky coast of Brittany.

15

Footsteps sounded in the hall, and two people came out on the platform. A man as tall as Diego was in the lead, and the young woman behind him was also tall. They did not see Diego, for they turned the other way at once. The man said:

"See that old dodderer has all our things, Ann."

The young woman was already long-striding down the platform. Passing the postman, she flung him a fine free gesture of a long arm. "No news for me to-day, Mercurio," she said in a deep easy voice. The postman lifted his peaked cap, and his smile was warm.

The man's back was to Diego, a long straight back with great width of shoulder under rough tweed, and his legs were so slender and short that he looked top-heavy. Judging by his upright carriage and smooth red neck he was a man in his prime; but his hair belied that judgment. His head was bare and he had a fine bush of curled hair, but the hair was white, not white as snow, not albino white, but creamily white all over, like hair that had once been red. That curled, creamily-white bush was startling above the smooth red neck. He took a pace forward and spoke to the postman in a cultivated but light voice—too light for his big torso.

"Any letters for me, McKenzie?"

"They'll be in the bag, General." The postman blew through his moustache.

Diego caught the change of inflection in the postman's voice. It was coldly respectful.

"I'll have them, please." That was an order.

"The seals of this bag are not to be broken but in the privacy of my own Post Office," said the postman firmly, and added, "Them's my regulations."

"Damn your regulations!"

"Surely, General! But who'll be the first man to report me if I break them? And I won't either."

"Oh, very well!"

The General turned on his heel and saw Diego. The postman winked behind the turned back. The seals had been broken for Diego without a thought of regulations, and there were many buff letters for this General. Evidently Wally the Post was a man of independent mind, and owed no friendly allegiance to this tall soldier. Yet he had smiled warmly to the young woman.

The soldier looked at Diego, and kept on looking unwinkingly as he walked the four or five paces between them.

And, then, Diego saw that he was not a young man, or a man in his middle years, but a man who would soon be old—if not already old. He was sixty, he could be seventy, he might look no older at eighty. He seemed youthful, but the set of his eye-sockets and the fine mesh of minute lines between his full cheeks and flat ears told the tale of many easy years. He had a short upper lip, and his under lip pouted roundly. He had no eyebrows, and his light eyes had white lashes. They were ordinary, slightly protuberant blue eyes, and yet extraordinary, for they were without expression and did not once blink. Then or later Diego never saw a trace of feeling in those unwinking eyes, neither anger nor affection nor fear nor cunning, nor anything. They were just to see out of.

The lower lip pouted, and the light voice spoke.

"Who are you? Are you a soldier?"

There was something intolerant in the voice, and Diego did not like it. Though the eyes showed nothing, Diego could read the thought that prompted the two quick questions. The unblinking eyes were looking down on a youngish, lean, dark, foreign-looking man in old tweeds, and such a one in wartime had to be questioned by men rightly set in authority. But this man-in-authority had no manners, so Diego did not rise to his feet. He had to lean his head back to look up soberly at his questioner.

"I am not a soldier," he said quietly. That was true. Diego Usted was not a soldier any longer.

"Why not?"

"Because I am no damn good."

"You mean——?"

"Just that."

"What is your name?"

"Consider, sir, before you ask that."

"What the devil do you mean?" His eyes did not warm, but his lip pouted some more. "I am Head of the Home Guard in Glen Affran. I ask you your name?"

"Then you will consider your manners."

"Look here!" He brought a forefinger smartly into one palm. "I am Major-General Charles Harper——"

"Enough! I am Diego y Hernandez y Mendoza de Usted."

"Ah!" The explanation exploded, and he turned a supple neck to look down the platform where the young woman and the old railway-man were gathering and checking parcels.

"A Spaniard? A Red?"

"Paraguayan," Diego told him.

"What are you doing in Craik?"

"Visiting my uncle."

"Who is he?"

"Hamish McLeod of Loch Beg."

"Why, he is my head-forester!"

"And my uncle."

He kept on looking down at Diego. Would his eyes never blink? Evidently he lived in a world several planes above that of his head-forester, for he had never heard of Diego y Hernandez y Mendoza de Usted. Moreover, he probably did not believe this dark foreigner, and was considering some more authoritative questions. But this dark foreigner had answered all the questions that he would answer, and rose so abruptly that even a General had to retire a step. Their eyes were level, the dark deep-set ones and the light expressionless ones.

"You will ask many questions, sir, and I answer thus: 'Go thou to hell!'" That formal way of putting the direction made it uniquely expressive.

Indeed, coming of a courteous race, Diego should not have said that to a man so much older than himself. But, though old, the man was mighty, and could have broken Diego in two in his then physical condition. He did not try to, and Diego knew that he would not. The men of this Britain, brave enough, had got to that state where they no longer thought it worth while to react physically to an insult. That is why they had become so abusive to each other. The General stepped back another pace, and did not ask any more questions.

"You will be investigated," he said shortly, turned on his heel, and stamped out in his top-heavy way to the motor-car at the entrance.

The postman was grinning at the other side of the door. He clasped one hand with the other and shook hands with himself.

"Tell me, Mr Usted, did you make him blink?" he whispered across.

Diego shook his head. No, he had not blinked once.

"You will some day. Dom! but you shut him up. You were welcome before, but now you're twice welcome. Weel! I'll be off. See you the morn. You'll find Hamish and Big Ellen the best in the world."

Peter Ross was coming up the platform heavily laden. Behind him strode the tall young woman, a parcel under one arm and another, and a heavier, bearing down a shoulder. There was a soldier out there, but he was not a soldierly man to let one of his women bear heavy parcels. Diego's duty was plain. He met the lady half-way, his hand horizontal below his left breast.

"Señorita?"

Her black eyes crinkled at the word and she yielded up her burden. "Thank you, señor," she said, and, surprisingly, she gave the word *señor* the proper little castanet slur.

Outside the station door on the curve of gravel was a long, blue, open car, and the General sat in the front seat next the driver's, looking straight ahead. Diego put the two parcels on the back seat, lifted his hat to no one in particular, and turned back into the station, not hesitating. He did not want to give any impression that he was hoping for a lift.

He sat down and waited for the agent and his cycle. He was finished with these people of Lodge Affran. The man was ill-bred. And the young woman? He had not come to this place to be concerned with woman, but he was slightly intrigued all the same.

Voices came through to him, but not the words. There was the quiet draw of the Highland voice, and the high pitch of the soldier's, and the woman's voice that was deeper than the men's. Now the Highland voice had stopped, the soldier's voice was almost petulant, but the woman's voice strengthened angrily and held the field. Had her lord told her that he had been consigned to hell, and was she resenting that insolence? Came silence, and quick light steps came tapping through the hall. The woman was back. She came round in front of Diego and he felt the angry aura of her. He rose to his feet to face the storm, and looked at her really for the first time.

She was young and tall and slender, but nobly breasted. Her thrown-open, tweed coat showed a tartan skirt, mostly green with small red checks, and a dark-green pullover that outlined her firm breasts. A bright green

20

ribbon held her hair, and her hair was the reddest and livest that he had ever seen. No hair is ever genuinely red, but that hair had more of red than yellow in it. It was the red that is sometimes seen amongst the black-haired breeds—Latin or Semite. But for the holding ribbon it would toss about her head, not in a nimbus but like the locks of that snake-woman of old. Her face was broad above and tapered rather quickly from wide-moulded cheek-bones to a firm chin. Her mouth was full and shapely, and just red enough to make one wonder if she used lipstick. Her eyes, wide but deep-set, were black, not shoe-button black but lustrous damson blue-black, and her lashes showed no trace of red, nor did her eyebrows that had the devil's upcurve of thought and temper from each side of a tempered line between her brows.

Most men would call her exotic, and some men might call her beautiful, but to Diego Usted she was only dangerously bad-tempered. She was certainly in a temper now, her eyes hot and her nostrils flaring at each side of a small nose down-tilted; but though she was in a temper there was no tinge of red in the smooth matt surface of her face that had the lovely tint of old ivory.

She was engaged in gaining control of her vocal cords before using them on Diego Usted. He got the first word in, which was unusual for him.

"But, señorita, I told your father where to go only once."

"But for the mercy of the good God that is your road and my road too, señor," she said deeply and surprisingly, and lifted her hands in a gesture that was all easy grace. "You are Diego—James Usted, the nephew of Hamish McLeod?"

His bow admitted it.

"It is my regret that you should be questioned with

rudeness in this glen where your people live who are my friends."

She had a voice of low pitch indeed, but of good resonance and that small sibilance of breathing that a foreigner uses in speaking English. And her hands were expressive.

"I ask your pardon, señorita." He was asking pardon for the thoughts he had had. This lady might be warm-tempered, but she was not bad-tempered, and she was not ill-bred, and she was not British. What she was he did not yet know, but he was tempted to try Spanish on her.

"And I yours, señor," she said. "Your people are not expecting you. Hamish was in his wife's garden as we came down. May I give you a lift to Loch Beg?"

"But your father——?"

"General Harper is my husband, señor."

"Your pardon again, señora." He felt something that was more regret than disappointment. And then he remembered that the postman had called her Mistress Ann. Mistress Ann Harper, wife to Major-General Charles Harper the Head of the Home Guard and Lord of Glen Affran by Divine Right.

"It will please me, Señor Usted, if you accept a drive in my car. Is that your bag? Let us go, then."

She turned before he could say anything. But he must accept that invitation, divine right or no divine right. He strode across for his bag, and followed her out to the car.

The station-agent was holding the door open for her. She slipped under the wheel, and he tried to close the door softly.

"Bang it, my Saint Peter!" she said, and banged it herself for him. Her husband was sitting up stiffly, and did not turn head towards Diego.

Peter Ross had stowed the parcels in a corner of the

wide back seat, and there was plenty of room for Diego and his bag. Diego's hand moved tentatively towards a hip pocket, but the old man moved a forefinger rapidly and banged the door on him.

"See you Sunday, Mr Usted. That day I often go up to Loch Beg on the boneshaker."

He had to lift his voice on the last words, for the car was already on the move.

III

The three in the car spoke scarcely a word all the way up long Glen Affran. Diego mused on that with some astonishment. He was an incomer from the great, shattered, struggling world, and these two people lived secluded amongst mountains. Surely, then, in any society worth the name, the three of them would be communicating intimately and naturally. Had the civilisation of this insignificant planet developed so, into watertight compartments, that the only hope for man was such a complete shattering of organisation as would compel the surviving remnant to begin over again? Possibly a few here and there were beginning even now; and Diego wondered if he could be one of them. He knew that he could not. He had too many inhibitions of his own breed and caste, and, moreover, time would not be given him. If this empty-feeling middle of his started again to gnaw he would have time for nothing but steeling himself to fortitude till release came.

It was evening now, and they were going westwards in long curves, so that the sun low-shining through a gap in the mountains sometimes troubled the lady at the wheel. The road had a good surface, but was barely wide enough for the big car, and it had an ugly ditch, now at one side, now at the other. At every furlong there was a small bay to enable conveyances to pass each other.

23

They were going deeper and deeper into broad-based, snow-topped mountains, and Diego felt smaller and smaller. In places the sides of the glen narrowed in to rugged buttresses, and the road hung over a strong torrent that shouted at them over the purr of the engine. The water was not peaty but very clear, and ridged and torn by white-seamed quartz rock. Sometimes the glen opened out, the slopes were easier, and the level straths, through which the stream ran fast but smoothly, were verdant even at the end of the hardest, longest winter in living memory. On the braes were brown spreads of withered vegetation that Diego did not recognise as bracken, and scattered graceful pale-trunked trees with a close network of slender red branches that he did not know were silver birches; and by the course of the stream were squat leaning leafless trees with dark trunks that he did not know were black alder. Sheep, ragged and small and with black faces, were everywhere, but there were no shepherds and no houses though there were many ruined walls. Diego's mother had told him the tragedy of these ruined walls. A telephone wire looping on wooden posts was the only evidence of modern communication with the outside.

Eight miles up they passed through the township of Craik. Here the strath was fully a mile in length and half that in width, and the slopes rolled over in green pastures that carried many sheep. There were no cattle, for at this season cattle would be in byre. All along that mile of strath, on the stream side of the road, was a scattering of houses, mostly one-storeyed and grey-slated, but there were some ancient squat buildings with insloping walls of unmortared stone, deep-set, foot-square windows, doorways not five feet high, and thick felts of thatch round black vents. Many of the houses were empty and falling into ruins. There were old men and women and many children about the houses and gardens, there were no young men and girls. Adolescence everywhere was out at war for an ideal that had been falsified by the older generations.

The evening was still and clear and cloudless, and a blue film of peat-smoke drifted from the low chimneys and vanished; and it was then Diego's nostrils caught a strange odour that he was to live with for many a day. It was a pervading, dry, burnt-earth sort of odour, not a perfume, but not pungent, and not unpleasant. He had not experienced it before, but he knew at once what it was. The one nostalgia his mother had had in the hacienda of San José in Paraguay was for the scent of peat-smoke in a Highland glen. This was the scent of peat-smoke, and those dark-brown clamps at gable-ends were peat-stacks.

Two miles out of Craik the car slowed and stopped before a many-barred gate closing the road, and a high wire fence ran straight up the breast of the slopes on either hand. This was the boundary fence of the great deer-forest of Glen Affran, but there was no forest. There were bottom-lands of sound grass, and slopes of heather and grass, and above them the snow-fields seamed with grey and blue rock; and there were side glens impressively lonely, with slopes and bluffs and cliffs glooming off into blue distance; but there were very few trees that Diego could see.

Diego had his hand on the door to get out and open the high gate, but the General with youthful energy beat him to it, as much as to imply that he would not take or yield a favour to a man who had consigned him to Hades. The car slipped through, and the gate clanged smartly behind. The woman spoke in her low deep voice:

"When one is old but strong one grows petulant at his own centre."

"I shall remember," murmured Diego.

25

In another two miles the road took to the slope to lift above a crag that breasted into the torrent of Affran Water, and the young woman, whose live red hair was stirring under its green band, lifted a gauntleted hand off the wheel and pointed ahead. Diego looked and in the near distance saw the evening sheen of lake water. So that was Loch Beg, which in Gaelic means small lake. It was a small lake, an oval not more than half a mile in length. The station-agent had said that it was the lower end of Affran Loch, but Diego could not see any water spreading away beyond it, for the shore lifted suddenly into twin bluffs that curved towards each other and hid the further prospect. But beyond the bluffs he could see that there was a great hollow in the hills lipped with cliffs that swept round and made an end of Glen Affran. The loch would be down in that hollow, and at the far end of it would be Lodge Affran where General Harper and his wife lived.

And then, as they got nearer, Diego saw the house, and wondered if it was Loch Beg Bothy. It was on the near side of the slope and between the road and the water. In the distance he took it for an oblong white rock, for it was lime-washed, and the grey slates toned into the bluff behind. Nearer, he saw that it was not a bothy at all. He understood that a bothy might be anything from a hut to a one-storeyed but-and-ben. This was a real house of two storeys, a bow window, and four good-sized windows along the length of the first floor. The white of it stood out strongly against the crag behind, and against the crag itself were lean-to sheds.

But it was Loch Beg Bothy and the end of his journey. The car stopped before a high wooden gate set in a frame in a low drystone wall.

"That is your uncle in the garden," said the lady. "You and I, we meet again soon."

"God is good," said Diego.

He got out and pulled his bag after him, banged the door, and lifted his hat. But no more words passed between them. The car moved on up the slope, she lifted her right hand off the wheel, and her slow gesture of fare-you-well had a unique grace and charm. Her husband did not even turn his head.

## CHAPTER II

### THE HAVEN

I

DIEGO USTED, standing there on the roadside, was sorry for himself for half a minute. The leather bag dragged at his arm, and he let it drop at his feet. He was spent and empty, his thighs trembled, and for a moment the world tilted, so that he had to brace his legs to maintain his balance. He was no good any more—never any more—but he must not fall down before his uncle's door. He shook his head clear and looked about him to get his bearings. That was a habit he had acquired on hard campaigning.

The white house stood end-on between road and loch. Fronting it was a good-sized kitchen-garden divided into four sections by paths edged with white stones, and there were many small fruit trees and berry bushes just beginning to bud. Before the house was a patch of green grass starred with shaped flower-beds, where daffodils "hung down their heads as they burned away," and tulips stood up gracefully tall, not yet flaunting their colours. The garden sloped down to the loch, where a short pier jutted out of the shallows into deep water and a small coble was tied to a mooring-post; and beyond the quarter-mile of sheening water a brown hillside lifted in slow folds to a ridge of snow. A low drystone wall enclosed the garden and house on three sides, and strung along the top of the wall was a wire netting. At the moment a black-and-white cock and his numerous harem were balanced on the coping, poking silly heads at the netting. No doubt there were worms in the dark soil that the man in the garden had been turning with a digging-fork.

The man had stayed his digging as soon as the car stopped, and was now walking down the path towards the gate, his thick, bowed, short-gaitered legs moving sturdily, not slowly, not quickly, just steadily. Diego picked up his bag, clicked open the garden gate, and went to meet him, controlling his movements carefully so that his weakened legs would not stumble. Over the man's shoulder he could see the bow window on the near side of the open door. It was lace-curtained and one of the curtains was pulled aside as if a hand held it.

The man approaching was Diego's blood-uncle on the distaff side, but in no feature was he like Diego's mother who was dead. She had been tall and lissome and fair and lovely and joyous. This man was short and squat and dark and ugly and unsmilingly grave. He had truly remarkable breadth of shoulder and depth of chest, and big incurving hands hung to his knees at the end of bent arms. A massive neck supported a massive wide head under a brown two-peaked cap, and his black straight hair, not a white hair in it after sixty years, showed about his close-set pointed ears. His small black eyes set deep in bony ridges were strangely hazed with blue, and his face was one smooth, sallow, blood-less tint. His colouring, the shape of his eyes, the bosses of cheek-bone, the uptilted nose with open nostrils, the straight mouth, were queerly Mongolian in a Highland-man and a McLeod.

He was indeed an ugly gorilla of a man, but he was not repulsive. There was a dry clean savour about him. All the same, if he had beaten the big drum of his chest and roared, Diego would not have been surprised. Instead, he spoke in the quiet, slow, husky way that a man has who is not accustomed to using his voice. He said:

"You are my sister's son, James?"

"I am, Uncle Hamish." He could not bow very well on these unsteady legs, with the bag dragging at his shoulder.

"I see her in you. You are welcome, boy." His right hand, hard and dry, reached for Diego's and pressed once. His other hand possessed itself definitely of the bag. And Diego wondered where he saw his lovely mother in his own horse-headed darkness.

"Big Ellen, the wife, is within the house," said the uncle, as if stating the one important thing.

That was all. He made no fuss of his nephew from foreign parts, but led up the path, the heavy bag nearly touching the ground, his arm bent and his shoulder straight as if the bag had no weight. The curtain of the window had dropped back into place.

Hamish McLeod was on the step of the door when he moved aside with surprising nimbleness to give room to a tall woman who strode as if straight through him. She stopped short in front of Diego, and her fierce, intensely-blue eyes took him apart feature by feature. He inclined head and shoulders, and wondered what she was going to strike him with, tongue or hand.

"'Tis himself, Big Ellen—James—our nephew—all the way from London," introduced her husband.

"Sure, I know that well, Cuchulain. Haven't I eyes in my head for this tall and gallant man?"

That was the richest voice that Diego had ever heard, a leisurely, vibrant, effortless, deep bell of a voice, rising and falling in cadences easy as breathing. That woman was a complete surprise to him. He had often in the last year pictured the type of woman she must be, and he was good at picturing. Some time after escaping out of Spain into England he had written this uncle whom he had never seen—and who was surprising too— and the reply had come from his wife, a picturesque, impressionist letter so full of imagination as to be almost incoherent without being ungrammatical. Every month or two after that they had exchanged letters, so that he had a background for his picture. He knew that she was Irish, and so he had seen her in his mind's eye as a small, voluble, volatile, light-voiced, warm-hearted slattern; that is, exactly what many Irish women are supposed to be. He was mostly wrong. Talkative she was but not voluble, for her talk was eloquent; and she was not small and not light-voiced, nor was she slatternly, but whether her heart was warm he did not yet know.

She was a very tall woman, and she had the erect figure and carriage of a caryatid, head, neck, shoulders, and the flowing line that a blue-and-white check apron could not hide. Her strongly-carved, clean-boned, aquiline face was strangely touching, for it would be melancholic, almost tragic, but for the fierce blue eyes that made it alive. And with the blue eyes went the black Irish hair, flowing back from her forehead, with a thick plait of it folded round her head. She was one of the ageless ones; her fifty years had left no mark on her; she might be a matron with babies about her knees. She was the first woman that Diego had met to whom the name matriarch might be applied. Not that he believed in matriarchs. There were none in Paraguay, nor even in Spain. The Spanish people, with the possible exception of the Basque, permit no woman any pedestal but one.

"I am sorry that I come like this, my aunt," he spoke carefully. "My letter, it has not arrived."

"What other way could you come that would be better? Give me your hand while my mind is open."

There was something sibylline in her without the frenzy. She took his hand in both of hers, and her cool fingers smoothed the back of his brown, bony claw. He felt her vibrancy coming through, and her fierce, wide-open eyes were almost hypnotic.

"You have the big Scottish bone under your Spanish leather, and room for a little flesh between." Her voice deepened and at the same time softened. "You come of a good stock, and there's iron and honour in you. But your hand is hot and dry, and there's an old fever somewhere, and your eyes are hurted. Who's been doing things to you, my little lad?"

And like a little lad he shook his head.

"So you are one of the silent ones too. That's right!" She nodded her head and smiled, and her eyes were no longer fiercely intent. "Not many men get room to talk and Big Ellen McCarthy with her mouth open. Listen! it was myself drew you to this Glen of Affran, and I saying to Hamish that if you had the right drop in you I would make the Glen draw it." She patted his hand and drew him forward. "I have not welcomed you at all, and you are welcome." Her hands were on his shoulders and her lips touched the hollow of his brown cheek. He felt the clean dry odour of her, and again his heart lifted. "Come into the house now, *alanna*, and never mind my talking. You'll be weary to the bone, and small wonder. The last time our Larry was up from the south he slept for three days between meals and after that went on eating."

Diego could sleep for three days too, but he knew that he would not. He had not slept soundly for months, and he had not eaten soundly either. She drew him inside the door and towards the foot of a stairway at the back of a narrow passage. His uncle was already clumping up ahead of them.

"The west room, Cuchulain," she called, and spoke to Diego over her shoulder, not lowering the bell of her voice. "Don't be minding him, the poor fellow. He has only the use of a hundred words of his own, five at the one time, but anything you say to him he can repeat at the end of a year and a day. 'Tis what is called a boomerang, and you with your mind changed maybe."

Diego went slowly up the stairs after her, his hand heavy on the banister to help his unsteady feet. This big aunt-by-marriage was wise, and her voice was oracular. Her foremother might have talked to Aeneas at Cumae. She knew. And she would go on talking. The only thing he could do was to let her go on talking, and nurse his own silence. Perhaps that is what his uncle had been compelled to do after many defeats. She was talking now.

"You will be surprised at the fine house that's in it. Sure, the luxury of it isn't good for man or beast. You see, it was the gents' shooting-lodge till they built the big ugly place at the head of the loch. Look! there's a bathroom in there with hot and cold water and a cake of soap with a carbolic flavour. And this is your room."

The bedroom—the west room, the ceremonial room which is sometimes south but is always called west, and is never to the danger-point of east—was conventionally furnished in dark oak, with an island of carpet round the white-counterpaned, brass bed. And there his aunt left him, saying quickly:

"I will now go and wet the tea. You will come when you are ready."

II

Diego sat on the side of the bed, and put his head in his hands. He was, indeed, weary to the bone and very empty, but he was not hungry at all. He felt that never again would he be hungry. But he had to get this evening over somehow, and lie down, and gather a little resolution about him for another day—and another day after that. All he had to do was to sit still and be silent with his silent uncle while the Irishwoman's voice poured over them like a 'cello. She had some soothing power in her, and her voice helped his weariness.

He went into the tiled bathroom, and found the water in the hot tap boiling. He soaked himself in hot water for five minutes, felt too deliciously drowsy, and waked himself up with a brief cold douche and a brisk rub that made his heart thump. Then he donned a soft white shirt and his best blue suit, and looked at himself in the mirror. He was too thin, and there were hollows below his cheek-bones, and his skin was surely Spanish leather, but he could see no pain in the dark of his eyes, though there was a line between his brows and a grim line to his mouth. He had to admit that there was a quality in his looks that might be called distinguished, but it was not the quality of good looks, for in his own way he was as ugly as his gorilla uncle.

He went downstairs then, treading softly, and his aunt hailed him from down the passage.

"Come you in this way. This is the place we live—Hamish's but-end."

He went into the big kitchen-living-room, an admirable cavern of a room, but before he could take it all in she directed his gaze to the window. She had pulled aside the curtains, and he could see miles down the glen to where it narrowed to a gorge. The grass plot and the garden patch were already in shadow, but an orange glow lit the valley to a lurid glory. The glow seemed to flow upwards over the brown of the heather and lighten as it lifted till it struck gold off the quartz rocks and tinted with yellow and pink fire the snowy peaks that marched down the glen.

"That's the best you'll see it," his aunt said at his shoulder, "but it'll break your heart if your heart wants breaking. I am drawing your attention to your uncle."

He was back at his digging, turning the heavy dark soil with an easy flick of the wrists and breaking the clods with a deft side-knock. But he was no drudge. Every four or five forkfuls he squared up his massive head and shoulders and looked down the glen for half a minute. Smoke drifted about his ears.

"That's his method rain or shine," said his wife, musing sonorously, "but he covers a power o' ground in the length of a day. Gardening he does not like, for it is not in his blood, but he has the growing hand with flowers. A shy, ugly sort of a man and deep as a well, and a comfortable sort of a man to have in the house with a woman talking. Do not you be thinking that he is giving you a cold welcome, for deep down he is as happy as the day is long that his sister's son is in the house with us. Seeing his blood is in you, you ought to know that?"

"What I do not know my aunt will tell me," murmured Diego.

"Ha-ha!" There was a quick happiness in her chuckle. "That is one of your uncle's back answers. I'll talk because I can't help it. Come you over here to the fire, and don't be caught by the lonely end of the day."

He turned into the room that by contrast with the stern grandeur of the glen was full of dusky comfort. His aunt was bent at the fire building up the peat-sods with a long tongs, and the glow from the licking flames was already stronger than the dying day.

"I see you're sniffing," she said. "The peats you're smelling, but you'll not notice it after a while. The sods we have throw out a stronger perfume than my

34

own Irish turf. Sit you down here and let me get a word out of you. It was myself sent Hamish to the digging, for I wanted to find out the man you are, so I could compare notes with him in the heart of the night. I'm telling you that, for my heart is drawn to you already, quiet man."

The peats were now blazing brightly on the open hearth that under a head-high mantelpiece filled two-thirds of the end wall. The walls were done in a cream wash, and the rather low ceiling was black-beamed. Brown flitches of bacon, solid-looking as oak, hung from the beams. There was an oval white deal table at mid-floor, and a small table with a red cover in the bow window, and on that table books were scattered. Indeed, one of the first things Diego noticed in that room was the number of books and magazines. There was a glass-fronted press of them by the side of a pine dresser gleaming with blue and brown delf, and there were piles of them stacked on the mantelpiece—all sorts of books: school books, text-books, second-hand library books, cheap prints, and monthly journals. There was at least one reader in this house.

At one side of the doorway was another tall glass-fronted press holding rifles, fowling-pieces, cased fishing-rods, and all the paraphernalia of head-forestry. There were a few coloured prints, mostly religious, on the walls, and under one of the Sacred Heart a small red lamp burned. And over all the ruddy glow of the fire washed and pulsed.

Diego went across into the pleasant diffused warmth of the peats, and the tall woman had to press him down into an armed straw-bottomed chair. He did not want to sit while she stood. There was a big iron kettle hanging from a crane, and he looked into the glowing peat-coals below it; and the patience that was in him was near content. She placed a hand on his shoulder.

35

"That is your chair from now on. What is weighing in your mind, son?"

"I should not have come until I had your permission." He was merely avoiding the answer to her question.

"You had a reason of your own for coming, so you came—and why not? Well?"

"Your letters to me were splendid. They drew me here."

"They were meant to. I'll try again. Are you out of the Army?"

"For the time."

"You were on Commando?"

"I could not stay that pace—a decadent son of the sun."

"As we all are. In your last letter and the one before I saw that you were sick in mind, but it was your body?"

"Yes."

"Your stomach?"

"Yes."

"I thought so. You see, I have a son a doctor, and I used be reading his books till I had every disease that was ever known or imagined, and I stopped for the sake of my sanity when *Medical Jurisprudence* began to give me nightmares. Ulceration?"

"They told me so. But there is no pain now—only emptiness."

"Ah, indeed!" Her fingers pressed his shoulder, and her voice mused. "Yes—yes! he was not sure but it might be worse—something malignant—and there we are! The young are sentimental as well as the old, and one likes to die amongst one's own. So he came up to look around and find a corner to die in."

And there was his secret in her hands. And he had said so little too. He was strangely troubled and afraid.

"How did you know——?"

"How couldn't I, and the eyes you have in your

36

head? Your uncle, for devilment, tries to keep a secret from me once in a while, but he's no better at it than his nephew. But I will not trouble you any more now." She bent down and looked into his eyes. "I know all I want to know, and I am happy that you are in this house. You will leave yourself in my hands, and you will forget that you have anything down below the palate that savours your food." She straightened up and ran her hand down his short hairs, and he felt the soothing hypnotic tingle. Her voice flowed comfort into him. "Your colour is right, and I smelled sound blood under the tan, my nose against your cheek. You will go my way as long as you can stand the wagging of my tongue, and when you can't there are the bens and the glens and the waters running. From now till October you'll get no grander place than Glen Affran, barring one place I know. Go out into the sun, and if you have to, find your hole, find it, and die in it, and we'll bury you decent. But don't be sorry for yourself any more."

"I am glad that I am here," he whispered.

"Then we are all glad."

The lid of the kettle thutthered, and with remarkable ease she moved the crook aside on the crane.

"What do you eat?"

"Anything—or nothing."

"That's right, you have your lesson. Leave it to me."

She gave his shoulder a friendly push and went out into the passage. He heard her voice lift.

"Come you in, Cuchulain! I'm getting the tay drawn." Why did she address him by that strange name, Cuchulain?

III

Feet sounded in the passage, and after a pause heavy boots clumped as they fell. And then slippered feet came

37

shuffling, and Hamish entered the living-room, still smoking. The long northern twilight was darkening now, and the light of the fire shone stronger. The glow lit up the dusky pallor of his face, and his eyes in the bony ridges looked darker than ever.

"Take that dhudeen out o' your gob till the viands are et," Big Ellen ordered, "and draw the curtains. We'll not light the brass lamp, but, this being a ceremonial occasion, we'll have a light on the table."

Diego noted that she used dialect or chosen English just as the words fitted. She lighted two candles in old brass candlesticks on the dresser, while her husband pulled heavy dark curtains across the bow of the window, for even in this remote glen the black-out regulations must be obeyed.

"The devil sweep this war!" she grumbled feelingly. "But for it we'd have the electric down from the Lodge—and the poles up ready. The paraffin we get is only enough for the cooker, and mostly we sit in the light of a bit of bog-deal."

Hamish swung a chair lightly to the other side of the fire and sat down. He looked across at Diego, nodded his head, and put a big thumb over his shoulder.

"She talks, that woman. Thirty years, and I don't know her yet."

"It is a high compliment that you pay, Uncle Hamish," said Diego.

"Man, oh man!" came her rich voice, "aren't fine manners fine in themselves? Not that I have any use for them—no woman has."

She turned to the table, and for the next ten minutes was extraordinarily busy with her hands as well as with her tongue. There was a back-kitchen or cooking-place, and she was in and out and about almost without pause, and the flexible organ of her voice lifted and lowered so that ever the same volume of sound reached the

38

men's ears. She was talking to herself as much as to them.

"There's a regular diet, I know, and I'll have to look it up, so as to forget all about it. To-night he'll have to take a small bit of a risk. There's no wine, and a small drop o' the craythur——"

"There's a bottle ben the house," hinted her husband.

"Late you minded it. No, we'll not touch alcohol for a month." Her voice came from the back-place. "Say, young fellow, what name were you known by where you were reared?"

Diego realised then that not once had she called him by his name, though he had signed his letters James Usted. He smiled to himself and waited till she was in the room.

"My baptismal name is Diego y Hernandez y Mendoza de Usted."

"The Lord protect us! A hidalgo handle like an engine shunting trucks."

"The first and the last count. Diego is James. I am James Usted."

"Your mother—God rest her—what did she call you?"

"Jamie when I was young. When my father—who is also with God—died she called me Diego."

She nodded her head, and a smile lit the carved gravity of her face.

"I like Diego. It reminds me in a strange way of a lean romantic man I read about. I think that I will call you Don Diego." She turned to her husband. "Cuchulain, I might change your name to Sancho— only you are not handsome enough."

"Something is burning, woman."

She fled, and the odour of frying rashers came into the room. Then Diego knew that much of his emptiness was plain hunger, and his mouth watered. If she served him that bacon he would eat it, and probably repent it to his dying day. But he would not be valetudinarian any longer, and damn the consequences!

In fifteen minutes supper was ready, and the table shining in linen and silver under the soft light of the candles. Diego did not get fried bacon. First he got a deep plate of creamy soup.

"'Tis the bree of a two-year-old hen that signed her own death-warrant by laying only two eggs a week. 'Twon't hurt you. Try a small corner of toast with it. And after that you'll have cold the back of a young rabbit I cooked a way of my own."

That was the nearest to a full meal that he had eaten for months, and he refused to entertain forebodings. He finished with scones and two cups of tea mostly cream. His uncle worked steadily and neatly through a great platter of rashers and eggs. His aunt ate hardly at all, sipping tea and nibbling at a buttered scone, and talking most of the time.

"The tea is not what it was when I was young where real tea was drunk four times a day, but I do be having an odd cup to myself all the same. Cuchulain, what name have you for my Don Diego?"

"His own name."

"We'll be seeing."

"Aunt Ellen," said Diego, "you call my uncle—how do you say it?—Cuh-hoolin. Is it in his name?"

"You know about the great Cuchulain?" She laughed, but stopped short at the shake of his head. "What? You never heard of Cuchulain—or Fyoon MacCool?"

"But you will tell me?"

"I will so. The two were the greatest heroes of antiquity, and like Neil Gunn up Caithness way I can't make up my mind which was the greater. Finn, as he calls him, had the cunning, but Cuchulain had the sword hand. Let me see, now, can I remember my book larnin'? You heard of Lame Timor the Tartar?"

"Tamerlane, yes."

"You would, and he only a foreign man. And Saladin the Turk?"

"But not a Turk."

"You can have him, as well as Richard he walloped. And the Cid and Gil Blas?"

"The Cid lived."

"And Bayard, and Roland for an Oliver? Yes! Well, Cuchulain was the whole of them rolled into one, and one or two besides. He was a Pict."

Diego's mother had told him about the Picts and the Scots.

"And there is a Pict for you at the end of the table. Cuchulain was a Pict out of Ireland."

"He was in Scotland as well," rumbled her husband.

"We loaned him. The red Milesians who were top dogs when sagas were sung made the legend that he was tall like themselves with red in the gold of his hair. But an older legend has it that he was a small dark grave man—not small, short, and wide as a door. He was a Pict, and the Picts came out of the butt-end of Caucasus Mountains. They had Tartar blood in them. Look at him!"

Diego did not look at his uncle, but he knew that she meant him to note the unmistakably Mongolian cast of her husband's features.

"Cuchulain's real name was Setanta, a man of Leinster, and he became Cuchulain, which means the Hound of Ulster."

"He got his learning in Skye," said her husband.

"As much as you have yourself and all you need." She chuckled in that deep way she had. "Hamish McLeod, do you mind the first time I called you Cuchulain?"

"A sad day for me," said Cuchulain, cocking one shaggy eyebrow at his nephew.

"It was then. Don Diego, you asked me why I called him Cuchulain, and you'll be wondering how a Highland McLeod from Glen Affran met one Ellen Honora McCarthy from the borders of Desmond in Cork. And I'll tell you, for a reason of my own and to show you the sort of foolish people we were—and are still. But sit you over here by the fire, and if you fall into a drowse I'll not blame you."

Diego sat in his own chair at the left of the fire, the glow and warmth of it agreeably on his face. He was no longer empty, and he was only pleasantly weary, not bone-weary. He had this hour at least, maybe two, and he would no longer think ahead. His uncle sat back in his chair at the other side of the fire, a quiet and grave man, glancing underbrowed at his nephew and at his wife, smoking an old wooden pipe with a plug in the bottom of it. And the tall woman moved about the table and in and out of the back-place, her voice lifting and falling like the sea. Diego felt himself a-rock on the waves of it, and could barely follow the story of youth she was unfolding for a reason of her own.

IV

"Thirty-two years ago come August," said Big Ellen, "and in the County Cork it was, convenient to the Orange town of Bandon. Hamish McLeod, an old bachelor of thirty and not near as handsome as he is now, was no more than under-bailiff to Sir Myles Appleby of Knockeenbegbrowadra House. Old Myles, a black Protestant, wouldn't employ anyone but Scotch stewards and keepers, and he wouldn't employ Hamish if he knew beforehand that the same Hamish was a Scotch Papist—and that's next door to a Calvinist. But, having got the job, he held it down by dint of saying nothing and doing his work, and belting the daylights out of

42

five or eleven wild lads he caught torching salmon in the dark of a harvest night."

"Two it was," corrected Hamish. "I didn't mind the poaching, but not on the spawning redds. That's dirty work."

"At the same time I was a telegraph pole of a girl just out of College. You wouldn't think to hear me that I got a sort of half-education——"

"She was a B.A.," amplified her husband, "and a Secondary teacher."

"Ay! I was teaching in the town and cycling home twice a day past the house where under-bailiff McLeod was lodging with the head-keeper. The first time I saw him I got the fright of my life, for there was word of an ourang-ootang that had escaped from Bostock's Menagerie. And, maybe, he took me for the Thin Woman out of one of the side-shows. I'll not deny that I was a lath of a girl, and I'll not deny that I was fond of the boys, like all my sex; but devil the boy would look at me straight or crooked, for I had a quick hand, and my tongue was limberer than 'tis now——"

"Goad be here!"

"—and no boy likes to stand on his tiptoes to steal a kiss. So there I was, and like to be an old maid at the end o' the day——"

"Tell the truth once, Big Ellen! Every boy in the parish was through your hands."

"What good, and myself and yourself frightening the life out of them. You see, Don Diego, one Sunday walking home from Mass, a venturesome boy at my left hand, I noticed himself here keeping the far side of the road a step or two behind us, his nose to the sky in its accustomed fashion. Not a word had ever passed between him and me, and didn't then—not for three Sundays, and there he was every Sunday, as near as he dared and as far away as the road would let him. And

43

the fourth Sunday I was alone, the venturesome lad doing his month in jail——"

"Don't listen to her, Jamie!" Hamish was rubbing his hair exasperatedly. "That was not why he was in jail. He was one of the two I caught at the poaching——"

"And isn't it poaching he was?"

"Go on! Go on!"

"Hold your whist, then! I walked on, not too fast, wondering would he pluck up courage to pass the time o' day, but there he was, dumb as a post, his black beads of eyes watching up at a lark soaring. I couldn't stand it any longer. 'Where are you going, Hamish McLeod?' I said. 'Home to my dinner, Miss McCarthy.' 'It'll be cold on you,' I told him, 'and you taking the long way round.' So he was, for his lodgings were two cross-roads away. He made no attempt at an excuse, being a half-truthful man, and to his dinner he was going right enough. So I took pity on the both of us. 'Come over here a bit closer,' I said. 'There's a cold wind from the south'—and the crows with their tongues out in the heat of the harvest day—'you'll be as good as a half-door anyway.' And he sidled across at a long slant that took him half a mile, and kept his distance a yard off, his head no more than up to my shoulder. I talked to him. He was a good listener, I'll say that for him, and is to the present day. For two Sundays I talked to him, and if I got a word out of him I don't remember it."

"You couldn't. What chance had I?"

"And after a time, learning of his prowess amongst the poachers, and the way he beat the nation bowling the iron ball, I put the name Cuchulain on him. I knew all about the great heroes that used be in Ireland before Saint Patrick softened them and the Danes hardened them and the Normans robbed them. I couldn't call him Fyoon MacCool for he had no cunning, but I took it into my head that if Cuchulain was dark and short he must have been as wide as a barn door to do the things he did to the men of Connacht. The very spit of my quiet man, Hamish McLeod. So Cuchulain I called him.

"And then one great Sunday he found his tongue at last and talked me into the ground. 'Why do you mis-name me, Miss McCarthy?' says he. 'My name is not Cuchulain.' 'It is so, Cuchulain,' I said. 'Wasn't he the greatest of them all—with his hands? And what's more, he could twist any woman round his little finger.' 'Any woman?' 'Every dang one o' them.' 'The one he wanted as well?' 'That one too,' I said, leading him on. 'Thank you, Miss McCarthy,' said he, and not another word. And I hadn't anything to say either, for it was in my mind that it was myself had done that bit of courting, if courting you'd call it.

"But the following Sunday, and we approaching my father's, he says, 'You were not joking about Cuchulain, Miss McCarthy?' 'I was not, Mr McLeod.' 'In that case,' says he, 'I'll call in and talk to your father.' And my heart nearly leaped out of my mouth. 'What in the world will you talk to him about?' I asked him. 'About the two of us.' 'You're a quare Cuchulain,' said I, hoping to damp him. 'How?' 'He never talked to a father.' 'I'll try the Christian way for a start,' says he. 'Look here, my poor fellow,' I said then, 'my father is a strong farmer with the grass of fifty cows, and he is descended from the great McCarthy Mor, Prince of Desmond and Carberry. Who are you to talk to him?' Being a respectable girl, I said nothing about a drop of Spanish blood in us flowing down from a gay lad of a Spanish hidalgo who fought at Kinsale. 'I'm a McLeod,' says he, 'and once we kept our own Piper.' 'Another thing,' I said; 'my father has a thousand pounds fortune for his daughter, and whatever about the daughter, he'll not hand over a thousand pounds to a Scotch under-bailiff, piper or no piper.' 'It would come in right handy for the bairns' education,' says he, and I not knowing where to look. 'And moreover,' I said desperately, 'I have two brothers, namely men, and you fined Garret two pounds for coursing a hare out of bounds. They'll throw you out on your ear.' 'You called me Cuchulain,' says he. 'Here's the gate.' And in he turned, calm as the day, and I trailing behind him, my heart in my mouth. I was just reaping what I had sown, mind you, but I was afraid the crop wasn't ripe.

"My father and my two brothers were sitting impatient at the kitchen fire waiting for their dinner. And listen! Without as much as 'God-save-all-here,' Hamish faced up to my father, and says he, 'I want to marry your daughter, Mr McCarthy.' No more and no less, just as if he was offering to buy a heifer. Before my father, a quiet man and sparing of words——"

"In that house," said her husband.

"Before he could open his mouth—or rather before he could shut it—my young brother Garret, a hot-tempered, whalebone lance of a lad, was up on his feet roaring, 'What's that you're saying, you Scotch bustard?' And it wasn't bustard. 'Your father I am addressing,' says Hamish peacefully. 'And I am addressing you. If you think that yourself and that long weed can insult the McCarthys in their own house you are mistaken. Get out or I'll throw you out.' Cuchulain pointed a thumb at him, taking time to remember a few more words, but before he could get one out, Garret jumped in at him and gripped him by the collar. That was a strategic mistake on Garret's part, for he was now employing the one language that Cuchulain could talk turkey in."

"I never hit the boy," protested her husband.

"No, but you started to take him apart in an expert manner. My big brother Larry, six foot two in his soles, and not a cross man, jumped in to separate ye, and before you could wink there were the three of ye

46

on the floor and all over the floor. The fat was in the fire sure enough.

"There was my father in the corner by the hob yelling for peace in the name of God, and there was myself out of harm's way on top of the table, not wanting peace just yet and looking for a back to plant my feet on. The three of them were tangled like eels or like octopuses, tentacles flailing, and four brown plates fell off the dresser, and a round-bellied pot walked out the door on its three legs, and the tongs fell across the fire and sent a red spark into the top of my father's brogues. To hear him then you'd think he was fighting the three of them. And there the tangle hit the table and I fell off on top. Maybe it was myself won the victory, for I fell hard on top of Garret. Anyway, Cuchulain rose out of the tangle and pulled me after him. And Larr rose up, pulled Garret to his feet, and held him. Larr nodded at Cuchulain. 'We will resume on a fitting occasion, Mr McLeod,' he said meaningly. 'Every Sunday from now till Shrovetide if you want to,' says my bold Hound of Ulster. His eyes were like two lit candles, and his nostrils flaring red; and without another word he picked up what was left of his hat and marched out the door and down the path, his shoulders filling the sky. He was a warrior again and had forgotten the cause of the quarrel—myself."

"Be fair, Big Ellen!" urged her Cuchulain.

"I'm fair enough. You did forget for a while. Young Garret, having made sure that Cuchulain was gone, made a pretence to go after him to bring back his liver, but Larr threw him contemptuously into a chair, where he yelped at me, 'You broke two of my ribs, you straddle-shanks. If you bring that baboon into this house Sunday or Monday I'll put a double dose o' buckshot in his carcase.'

"Big Larr was wiping the blood off his nose with a

47

towel hanging at the end of the dresser. 'You will not,'
he says, 'and I've a damn good mind to warm your
hide for you. I ought to have more sense than go
between fighting men—or fighting dogs. The only
blood spilled was my own, and it was the leg of the
table spilled that for me.' He looked around the floor.
'Hamish McLeod and myself are bulky men; we'd
need more room. I wonder now if I had him where I
could use my feet——?' 'No—no, Larr darling,' I
stopped him, and he grinned over the towel at me. 'Is
that the way, Ellen Honora? Very well so! Do you
want to marry him?' 'If I don't he'll kill one or the
other of ye,' I said, and he laughed. 'My darlin' sister,
ready to sacrifice herself to save a brother's life.' He
shook his head at me, an understanding man. 'You
started this in divilmint, but you've met your match.
'Tis for my father to say.' He went across to the old
man, who had his shoe off and was rubbing his instep,
but I knew he was considering things in his own mind.
'Padraig McCarthy,' says Larr, 'these two might have
their minds made up to marry each other, but the
McCarthys can prevent them. I am only warning you
that it will be an ugly preventing.' 'It won't take me
long,' shouted the young fellow. 'Shut up you!' ordered
my father sternly. 'Larry and I will deal with this, and
for a beginning I'll not have one other word about it
till my mind is made up. Ellen Honora,' says he to me
in his quiet way, 'the spuds are in *brusker* and the goose
a cinder in the bastable.'

"And not a word was said by anyone all that week,
and on Sunday Hamish came to my side as usual.
There was no sign of the Cuchulain in him anywhere.
'I am sorry about last Sunday, Miss McCarthy,' he
says. 'In that case,' said I to him, coldly as you like,
'you had better go home to your dinner the shortest
road there is.' 'I will,' said he, 'after calling on your

father.' And my heart troubled me. 'Maybe you are not so sorry after all,' I said, 'and 'tis no use trying to prevent you, Hound of Ulster.'

"When we were approaching the house I was in a fret and wondering if Larr had hidden the gun, and the sort of humour he'd be in. I needn't. For there was my father leaning over the gate, a fine hale man with a pleasant smile. 'A fine day, Hamish McLeod,' said he. 'Won't you come in and have a bite of dinner with us?' And there was my bold Cuchulain with his mouth open, for 'twasn't a Michaelmas goose he was looking forward to, but, as the song says, a hot breakfast of powder and ball. Before he could shut his mouth the old fellow got in his second shot. 'You'll be welcome, and we'll have time enough later to talk of—other things.' And what could Hamish say? A wise man my father. He established a truce by evading the gage of battle, and gave himself time to discover what sort of lad this was who had to become either a casualty or a Benedick—one and the same thing you'd say. Sure, there is not much more to tell.

"During the harvest and winter my father, for some reason beyond me, got to like my man from the Highlands—Larr liked him from the beginning—and before he went back to the University in October young Garret spent all his days shooting rabbits with him. It was a pleasant winter in one way and another, and before the end of it I had doubled the poor fellow's vocabulary, and he used whisper most of it in my ear on occasion. So, to make a long story short, I took pity on him at long last and married him on Shrove Tuesday. He got my thousand pounds as well, and maybe it was that he was after all the time. Am I right, Cuchulain?"

"You have a fact here and there, but you made up everything that was said."

"And you could repeat every word. But the heart

of the story is with me all the same, and maybe Don Diego knows us a little better. And he will note that I still call an old fellow, Cuchulain."

V

All through the telling of this, her love-story, the housewife had been clearing the table and in and out of the back-kitchen; and Diego had been listening to the flexible cadences of her voice as much as to the story. And sometimes she paused at his side and put a hand on his shoulder, and he knew what she wanted. She wanted to draw him into the family life of this house from the very start; she wanted to show that her silent bear of a husband was a man of parts, that she herself had attracted men in her youth, and that he had won her from the best of them in spite of the handicap that he was a penniless outlander in a land of family pride where a marriage portion—for male as well as female— was more essential than love.

Hamish was filling his old plugged pipe with black tobacco sawn off a stone-hard junk of twist, and Diego wondered when again he himself might roll a cigarette. But he must not think of tobacco just yet. He said:

"You stayed on in your own country——?"

"Not for long," said his aunt. "There was nothing in Ireland for us but my thousand pounds. Old Myles Appleby wouldn't promote a Papist anywhere short of hell, and Hamish would not take to farming, for he was a hunter by blood. It takes me all my time to get him to dig my patch o' garden. So Scotland it was for him and me."

"It was you persuaded me, mind?" said her husband.

"I had to. First down Beauly way, and then here in his native glen as stalker, and now he is at the top of his job, head-forester of fifty thousand acres. It was

50

here in this glen that our children were born, not that he was much good to me in the matter of children. Six is all I had, and I still a young woman."

"Big Ellen!" protested her husband.

"Forgive me, Aunt Ellen," said Diego. "I did not ask for my cousins."

"What chance had you? They are all in the hands o' God, for evil men are seeking to do their worst on them. There is Hector—after Hamish's father—the engineer, and he is a prisoner in Hong-Kong; and Padraig the tall one, after my own father, and he swam the sea to Java and is now in Australia; and Ian, who is little, is a doctor in the Canal Zone; and our baby Larry is in the R.A.F., his life in his hands on the South Coast; and the two girls, Helen married in Glasgow with two grand-daughters for me, and Mairi after your mother—God rest her—teaching her squad of evacuees in Cornwall, and nursing in her spare time. Scattered far and wide on the face of the world, but under the mantle of God's Mother all the same."

These two while still young had had six children about them, and now, growing old, they were alone in one of the loneliest glens in all the Highlands. Diego mused on that. Alone and often lonely! A mad, creaking, moloch-owned world had wrested their children away; and if one remained alive when the slaughter was over, that one might be happier dead. But meantime these two would carry on, and hide their hurt.

"Sure, we could not keep them in this place all our days," the woman said, reading his thoughts uncannily. "Many a generation has gone since this glen kept a clutch from baptism to matrimony, from marriage to death. It might again, but not in our time. We only breed the wandering ones, but haven't I my own at the end of a pen?"

"You write letters as you speak, Aunt."

"I'm well practised. Six letters I write in the round of the week, more sometimes, and Wally the Post up from Craik cursing myself and the weather. Wait now! light is scarce, and we'll not be wasting it. A skelp of bog-deal will do to light our talk."

She moved towards the table where the candles burned, and Diego said:

"A candle for a moment, Aunt Ellen?"

He took it and went upstairs to his west room, and returned with his two small parcels. His aunt was sitting low on a big straw hassock at the fire-front staring into the fire. A gnarled knot of bog-pine was beginning to flame, and when he blew out the candle her shadow leaped on the beamed ceiling, and the big room was a ruddy cavern of security and ease. He placed one papered box on her lap, and put the other into his uncle's hands.

"Only a small token."

"Bless us!" said his uncle, startled.

"Oh, my dear!" said his aunt. She folded her hands over her box, and looked at her husband's fumbling fingers.

"Your turn first, Cuchulain. I can guess what it is, but let us look."

Diego was glad that his uncle's pipe looked utterly unsmokable. His present was a case of briar pipes and a carton of strong tobacco.

"Too much altogether," he said, a big thumb caressing a polished bowl.

"Maybe you'll smoke a decent pipe at last," said his wife, chuckling softly.

"Ay, will I! I'll break one in on the hill to-morrow."

He gave Diego a nod, rose to his feet and placed the case carefully on the mantelshelf, and then sat down to refill his old pipe from the carton. Diego did not know that his uncle already possessed a dozen unsmoked pipes —presents from men who had stalked with him—too beautiful to be desecrated with twist tobacco. Then or later he never saw him smoke anything but that ancient plugged cherry-wood.

His aunt unwrapped her parcel, being careful not to shake it. Inside was a box of African black-wood inlaid with Cordoban scrolls in silver. The lid opened to a spring, and she lifted a pad of cotton-wool and paused.

"Your mother's?"

"To the matriarch of the family."

His mother's trinket-box and trinkets. Not many, for his mother was Scottish and did not care for the massive gold of the Paraguayans. A ring or two, a wrist-band, a few brooches, and mantilla combs.

"There's one I'll wear at my neck going to Mass on Sunday. And what have we here?" She picked up a plain band.

"My mother's wedding-ring."

"Just so. We keep that carefully." She wrapped it softly in cotton-wool and stowed it in the corner of the box. "Lad, you were kind-thoughted, even and all if my old hide won't stand bedizenment."

"Permit me, Aunt Ellen?" He picked out a comb of red coral and set it aside in the thick coil of her hair, and at once it glowed in the rich darkness.

"Uncle, could a queen wear it any finer?"

"Losh, but it's neat," understated his uncle.

The blood touched the strong bosses of her cheeks, and her woman's hands patted the hair about her ears.

"Cuchulain, 'tis well for you that I am growing old and this gallant hidalgo in the house."

"I am glad he is in the house whatever."

"Good man! And he will remember that the house is his."

At that moment a bell thrilled in the passage and Diego started. Anywhere else but in this fastness he would have known it for a telephone bell. It was.

"Lodge Affran is connected with all the bothies by private wire," his aunt explained. "That'll be for you, Cuchulain?"

Hamish shuffled out into the dark passage, and in a little his voice came back. "Loch Beg. . . . Yes . . . yes, sir . . . I'll be there."

That was all. He came in and nodded to his wife. "That was the General. He wants me up-by the morn."

"It'll be about the heather-burning."

"He didn't say."

A thought struck Diego. This General Harper who lorded it over Glen Affran might have something to say about a foreign man in the Glen, and it would be necessary to hint as much to Uncle Hamish.

"It is possible, Uncle, that he will speak to you about the rudeness of your nephew."

"Glory hallelujah!" chanted his aunt. "Of course! of course! He would show his power and glory by asking you a lot of cross questions. He did?"

"Within his rights."

"And you up and told him go to hell?"

"Only once."

She chuckled deeply. "Do you know, Don, I was afraid for a bit that you might carry your politeness too far. The poor man! his eyes like glass marbles and his under lip stuck out. Did you make his eyes blink? No! Don't be bothering your head. The old soger's teeth are too soft to bite Cuchulain's iron. And didn't he give you a lift?"

"His wife insisted."

"Ann would. Did she talk to you?"

"A few words. You were her friends."

"We are. Did you have a good look at her?"

"She is not British?"

"You had a good look, then. Her name is Ann with a longer handle than your own, finishing in Mendoza.

54

She is not Spanish of Castile, she says. She is Basque and proud of it."

The Mendoza were Basque, and Diego had Mendoza in his family line going back four hundred years to that Pedro who founded Asuncion.

"You will be wondering how she got into Glen Affran? Aren't you in it yourself? And amn't I? Faith, she got in much the same way as myself—only dam' different."

"Talk English, Big Ellen," her husband advised her. He relit his pipe and looked down at his wife's hair with the red comb jaunty in it. She had gradually worked her straw hassock nearer him so that her hand rested along the arm of his chair, his wrist against her fingers. She brooded into the fire and her voice made patterns for them.

"There is no great harm in the General unless you are under his thumb, and we are not. And there is no harm in Ann Harper and she is not under his thumb either, though he thinks she is. But they might do harm enough to each other before all is done. She is not happy, I think, but unhappiness is not deep in her— yet. She is in a strange land, and she is young, and she is tied to an old man, and she has not known any man to love him—I think that too. That's her unhappiness. A girl's unhappiness. It does not canker, and she can still say her prayers. She is a good Catholic. The Basques are, so I'm told, though they were on the side of the Reds in that civil war."

"The Government side, Aunt," Diego corrected. "I was on that side too."

"I know, boy. I'm not holding it against you. You were not at a place called Guernica?"

"I would not be here. That was where the Germans tried out bombing-planes to find out what they could do. They found out."

55

"Ann Mendoza was there, and she is here. Her father was there too, and her mother and two of her brothers, and they are not anywhere any more—not on this side. The girl was a prisoner for a while, and after that became a refugee. That is how she met the General. He was a British agent over the border."

"I know. A non-intervention agent throwing loaded dice for the butcher."

"It could be. But he saved the girl anyway, if you'd call that an act of disinterested virtue. She is a girl would be easy to save by putting your arms round her. She had nothing, and was at the end of her rope, and he offered her honourable marriage. What could she do but accept? And if either of them repent it I haven't noticed."

"You would notice, Aunt."

"I would. I notice more than is good for me often enough—and see things that I do not want to see."

"She has the second sight," said her husband.

"I have not. It is not prevision. I only know. And I know now that it is time for Don Diego's bed. He'll be stifling a yawn in my face."

"Not while you talk."

"Then I will not talk, and I will warm a panny of new milk to make you sleep easy. Let you and Hamish go out and look at the night."

Diego followed his uncle out into the starlight. There was no moon, but the night was frosty and clear, and in that clear frostiness the stars multiplied themselves and scintillated. The floor of the glen was dark, the skin of the loch was a wanness in that darkness; and the dark bulk of the hills loomed above. And above the dark bulks the snow peaks were phantom-like and withdrawn, in a faint light of their own, apart from this dark glen that remained dark under all the brilliancy of the stars. There was no breath of air anywhere, near or far, and the silence was of old time. One could hide oneself in that silence and be not afraid, unless one had fear in his own heart.

The old man moved along towards the garden wall. Under the cover of the dark speech came to him more easily.

"Watch your feet. A still night, but not always. The water has a tongue most nights, and there's a cock grouse betimes, and the roaring of the stag in the fall. You'll not be too lonely, Jamie?" So he would call him Jamie.

"Loneliness does not hurt."

"No, then. Big Ellen is lonely sometimes for the tumbled bits of hills about Inchageela. We used go to her brother Larr's place once in a while before the war."

"You will again."

"With the help o' God." That was his wife's Irish. "You'll be liking her?"

"I only hope she likes me half as well."

"She does then from the start. If she wants to know a thing she knows it, and sometimes a thing comes to her she hates. I often wonder why she married me."

"She told me why."

"That was her way of telling a story."

"True in all essentials."

After a silence he said, "I would want you to be at home here, Jamie. The hills are free to you twenty miles any hand."

"Your General Harper——?"

"Forget about him. I mind when I was a young lad I wanted no one to show me the hills but myself. You could try that. If you're lost I'll know where." This was an understanding uncle. "Do you fish or shoot?"

"Fish, no. I have used a rifle—but not in sport."

"Just so! I'll teach you to throw a line——"

"Will you teach me to dig?"

Diego heard him shaking with quiet chuckles. "The first thing, and I hope you'll take to it. True for the wife, I hate the dom' digging."

"I have got myself a job," said Diego.

"A job it is. Come in now and try the warm milk. We keep three cows, two of them calved. Maybe a spark of something in it would make you sleep sound. We go to bed early and up with the sun."

Perhaps in this quietness Diego too would be able to woo sleep in the dark of the sun. He felt sleepy now, comfortably sleepy. They went in and had their warm milk. Hamish had a full-sized spark in his, but his aunt would not allow Diego any. Then Diego went to bed, while the old people stayed behind to smoor the fire and talk quietly of this new nephew.

Diego slept. He forgot to say his prayers. But that is not correct. He had got out of the way of saying prayers. But there was one prayer he should have said that night, the one prayer that a man should say, the Prayer of Thanksgiving.

## CHAPTER III

### THE LION'S DEN

I

DIEGO slept and did not waken with the sun—his first good sleep in months. As was his habit, he had unblinded the window before getting into bed, and it was the sun on his face that awaked him. He rolled out of bed and went across to the window that looked down the glen. The sun had topped the crown of the gorge, and spread spring's fingers over this secluded bowl. The grass was thrusting up its first green shoots, the birches on the slope wore a ruddy veil, the waters of Loch Beg were wrinkling in gold and silver to the brush of a breeze, and all the snowy peaks were etched clearly as in a vacuum against the thin blue of the sky. The world was young again, and he was not old either.

There was no sound in the house or about it. The garden below was empty, but the digging-fork stood upright on the edge of a newly-turned patch of soil. His uncle, who had promised to teach him the simple art of digging, was probably now in the living-room at his breakfast. Diego dressed quickly in his comfortable old heather-mixture and went downstairs.

His uncle was not in the living-room, and the table was laid only for one. That big room was full of light and air, and already the tang of the peat was pleasant in his nostrils; the flames of the fire were pale in a shaft of sunlight, and the table shone in linen and china and stainless steel.

His tall caryatid aunt came to the door of the back-place rubbing her hands in a clean check apron. Her fierce blue eyes were on him, intent and unsmiling.

"You slept!"

"Like the dead, Aunt."

"You haven't an ache anywhere?"

"Unless hunger is one."

She smiled now and her eyes softened. "Then I bid you good morning."

"Good morning, Aunt. You should not let me sleep——"

"Isn't it sleep you want? Hamish was at your door twice in the night, for, to tell you the truth, I was afraid we were taking too much of a risk with the back of a rabbit. I'll take no risk this morning, so you are getting a light breakfast."

"But, Aunt, I am all hunger."

"I'll keep you that way for a week yet."

"I would like to eat with you and Uncle Hamish——"

59

"I know. You don't want to break the routine of the house, like the courteous man you are. We'll see! Sit you down! The porridge is hottering away on the stove."

That breakfast consisted of a deep plate of brown porridge with a bowl of cream, a brace of brown eggs lightly boiled, buttered scones the necessary one day old, a pot of tea, and home-made marmalade. His mother had taught him how to deal with porridge. He did not reach for the sugar-bowl, nor did he pour the cream over to make a soggy mess, but dipped a half-spoon of the firm porridge into the bowl and, so, got all the flavour. The oatmeal of that porridge had been ground from grain toasted in the kiln to a fraction of a degree of brownness. It had none of the usual insipidity of porridge.

"Aunt," he wanted to know, "if this is a light meal, what is it that you call a square one?"

"You'll know the morning you break your fast with your uncle. We are early risers. There are the cows to be milked and redded, and the hens to be fed, and the pony watered—and the hearth swept clane, as the song says."

"And some digging?"

"A thing he doesn't like, for he comes of a pastoral people—hunters and killers. But dig he will as a discipline. He did a bit this morning, and is away up to see the bould soger boy at the Lodge."

"I was ill-mannered——"

"What harm? The General is as pompous as a bladder o' wind, so let him have his blow off. He can't hurt Hamish, and Hamish can hurt him but will not. Four of the stalkers are in the Army, and there's only old Donald Gunn over at Strath Dearg and two men back from retirement at Craik, Long John the blacksmith and Piobar Maol Tam our piper. Mind you, if a thing happens that the General has in mind—and that's the break of the entail and a sale—we have other plans.

We are our own masters, and as for gear—as Hamish calls worldly goods—we have more of it than grace, and more than we want. Now, go you out and greet the morn, and I'll wash up the few dishes."

Outside, the morning felt as fresh as it looked, briskly fresh, not yet softly fresh. The currant and berry bushes had burst their buds, but the apple trees had not. The spring cabbage he identified as brassica, and a long row of oval-leaved plants might be of the bean family, and he guessed that the beds of bulbs with pointed green shoots were of the onion. They were shallots and potato onions. He owned a hacienda of many thousand acres, yet had himself never planted a vegetable or digged a sod.

He moved across towards the freshly-turned soil. The digging implement was a four-pronged fork, with blades of a flat triangular section. He handled and hefted it and found it unfamiliar. It lacked balance. At least, it had not the balance of a good rifle, or of the thirty-two-inch rapier that he could use expertly. The weight of it dragged to the point, but that was only reasonable, for the point was eager for the soil. Probably some little skill was required in the use of this implement; but why use it at all for digging? If one needed to turn the soil, why not use a broad-bladed spade and rude country strength? And yet, his uncle had been using it as a spade, and in his hands it had efficiency.

He set the four prongs in the soil and pressed. With just that much pressure his rapier would have pinked a man. But this soil was packed after winter, and the points went in only an inch or two. He applied more force, got the prongs three-fourths home, and got them all the way home with a drive of the heel. But this was waste of energy: three separate efforts to imbed four sharp points in the soil. His uncle had done it in one smooth motion that was continued in the easy turning over of the loaded fork. Right! he too would turn over this forkful. He learned then that even plain dark soil has a ductile resistance to being torn asunder. With an effort he wrested that forkful free, but, once free, it surrendered all its ductility and broke away between the prongs. This surely was one poor instrument for delving—or he was a poor delver. He set the end of the handle against his breast, rubbed the back of his neck, and considered the problem. His aunt's rich chuckle came across from the door. She had a nicely-turned walking-crook in her hand and shook it at him.

"Nephew to his uncle! He'll do. Already you have his very way of resting before you begin."

He would never see that woman stroll lazily, and yet he would never see her move awkwardly or hurriedly. She was at his side, swishing through the berry bushes, took the spade out of his hands, and thrust the crook into them instead.

"An instrument of precision requires delicate handling, and you'll learn in time that real land-work is skilled labour same as carpentry or smithery. A machine-tender or even a fitter of standardised parts is nothing—not even a labourer. He is one of the main reasons for assuming that man has not an immortal soul. Hamish had to search near and far to get this worm preserver into the Glen. Look! 'Made in Canada,' where they have long backs and don't like to bend 'em—same as in Ireland, where they are supposed to be lazy in addition. Now in Scotland they use a short handle with a cross-grip, for they like to bend over their work, faces to the soil, which, indeed, is a proper attitude for men who do not own the soil yet are bond to it. Over in Ireland Hamish got to like the long-handled spade—I mean tolerate it, for he doesn't like any spade at all. 'Tis called the lazy man's spade, because it keeps your back straight and tempts you to pause and look at the sky. And isn't it well known that the toiler must keep his head down lest he suspect that he lives in three dimensions and, maybe, begin to speculate on a fourth? Now that is the way a digging-fork is used."

During this lecture she was driving in the fork smoothly with arms and foot, and turning over forkful after forkful from the leverage of her thigh.

"A matter of persistence of force. Where you took three bites to your cherry I take a gulp. The arms and the wrist, and the turn off the knee, that is all. Try it again some time. And now you might take a walk over the rise for a peep at the Affran Loch. That crook is to help your feet. Dinner at one and any time after."

She straightened up and looked down the glen, thrust out her long chin and swore.

"Dammit! where's Angus the Bobby bound for this morning?"

Diego followed her eyes and saw the approaching cyclist, a big man pedalling solidly against the rise in the road. He was near at hand, and Diego could see the policeman's cap with its black-and-white check band.

"He is coming here—to investigate me," Diego said.

"Isn't that what I'm saying? And what'll I be doing? Driving the four prongs of this pike through his gizzard, and wishing it was mister bloody General Harper."

The big policeman dismounted at the gate, leant his cycle carefully against the wall, and opened the wicket.

"Get off my premises, Angus Campbell, you fat hound!" boomed the Amazon, and forthwith swept across the garden, the fork at the attack. Diego, aware that the Irish had little respect for law and order, grasped his crook and hurried after. He did not want homicide done on his behalf, though he did not like policemen. He had seen the Civil Guard at work in Spain.

But that policeman imperturbably turned his back,

shut the wicket leisurely, and faced round again. The sharp prongs were within a foot of his adequate girth. He ignored them, taking off his cap and rubbing a palm over a warm forehead. He was a well-fleshed man with a round and ruddy face. His light blue eyes glanced at Diego and away again.

"Dom! the heat has started a'ready," he said.

"A bit blood-letting is the thing for it." Her fork was six inches nearer.

"Guidsakes, Big Ellen! Gi'e us another six months to see my pension!"

"What are you doing here?"

"What am I doing here any time?"

"Drinking Hamish's uisgebaugh. Was it our tin-god sent you to pry?"

"Couldn't I call myself in a friendly way?"

"God give me patience! Did anyone ever get a straight answer from a crooked-mouth Campbell?"

"Permit me, Aunt Ellen," said Diego. "I think I can satisfy this gentleman."

"Don't miscall him," said his aunt. "He is not as bad as that, anyway."

Diego had moved close to her side, his shoulder against her arm, so that the prongs no longer threatened disembowelment. From his pocket-book he had extracted a light buff document, and tendered it to the policeman.

"That, sir, is a certificate of my identity."

The light eyes were scrutinising Diego, and did not leave his face as a big hand fumbled for the paper.

"Aunt Ellen! Aunt Ellen?" he ruminated. "Gosh be here! Don't tell me this is Mairi's son from the Paraguay?"

"Didn't your General tell you that?" enquired Aunt Ellen scathingly.

"The dom'd auld cuddy! bringing me all the way from Craik. Ah well! I'm glad I came."

64

He thrust the certificate back into Diego's hand, and caught the hand in both of his.

"I was in love with your mother, sir—everyone was. You are right welcome to the Glen, Mr——"

"Usted—James Usted, Mr Campbell."

"Plain Angus I am—and a Campbell too, cocks o' the West, and the North forbye. Put away that bit document, I 'm no' looking at it." He spoke seriously to Aunt Ellen. "A prod was coming to me, Big Ellen, but I didna know."

"And you'd have it, only you remembered your manners in time." She dropped the fork carelessly and took the document from Diego. "And now you'll do your duty, Angus boy. Have you your glasses?"

The paper was under his nose and he steadied her hand with his.

"Ay! Captain James Usted—hack—hackiendo San Joes, Asuncion—that's the capital of Paraguay, only I always mixed it up with Uruguay and Monte Vidayo— mother a British subject—a Highland lassie she was— age 28—uh-uh! that's a good likeness of you, Captain. And that's all! I ask your pardon, both of you." This big policeman had none of the Civil Guard in him.

Aunt Ellen folded the paper and presented it to Diego.

"And now that the dirty work is over, any news o' the bairns, Angus?"

"They were a' fine last we heard, Big Ellen. Peter got a bit knock at Tobruk, as you know, and was in a rest camp at a place called Timsah on the Canal. And that reminds me, Aelec is in Ireland this minute."

"What place?"

"His boat was sunk off the west side some place, and he got to the shore in his drawers, himself and his mate an Irishman; and the Irishman took him off to his own place for a rest—a toon on the coast—Ballybunion. A postcard we had. That was it, Ballybunion—they'll ha'e bad feet."

"Bad every way. That place is in Kerry, and everyone knows the likes o' Kerry. But they'll treat Aelec well—if he has a head."

"Ay, has he. Torry is in one o' them Commandos rampagin' up and down the coast o' France—worse than the Black-and-Tans and the I.R.A. you do be telling us about—desperate hand-to-hand, close-quarter work, but the Campbells were aye handy wi' the sgian. Torry will be all right."

Torry was all right the last time that Diego had seen him, for, strangely enough, Torry Campbell was Captain Usted's top sergeant. But Diego had not known that Torry came from Glen Affran, nor had Torry known that his Conquistador—as he called him—had an uncle in the same glen. One does not talk much of one's antecedents on Commando. Torry was a tall blond Highlandman, and had spent three years reading Presbyterian Divinity, so he took to Jahveh's work like a duck to water. The sgian was his weapon, as the rapier was Diego's. Torry was a metaphysician and argued everything from first principles, and he had a habit of lifting his left hand and counting his points with a thumb on his spread fingers. Diego did that now without thinking. He raised his left hand, fingers spread, and counted his fingers with his thumb.

"Goad be here!" cried the constable, startled. "That's Torry. You know him, Captain?"

Diego dropped his hands quickly. That had been a foolish thing to do.

"I know him," he said briefly.

But the policeman had straightened up and was staring at him.

"By the Lord!" he said in an awed voice, "you are his officer, and isn't that the strange thing! The tall man of Spain that he called Con—Conqustodore, and using a thin bit of steel like a sallagh with ten points——"

"We don't talk about it, Mr Campbell," said Diego. Torry Campbell had talked too much.

His aunt noted his restraint, and took her cue.

"Wait you, Angus! we'll put our thumb on that." She patted Diego's shoulder, and gave him a firm shove. "You go off your walk—Conquistador. Angus and I are going to have a good old gossip about the weans. Come on in, peeler! You'll be needing a buttered scone and a glass of—buttermilk."

She strode off up the path, and the constable, giving the full military salute, followed her. He spoke in a low voice over his shoulder.

"Hurt a fly she wouldn't, Big Ellen. I'm proud to know you, Captain."

Diego knew that he could rely on his aunt to put her thumb on the policeman's desire to talk. She was throwing words back at the big man, and he was nodding his head amiably. Some few minutes ago there had been dangerous steel between them. But, of course, it was not in the least dangerous, and both of them knew that. His aunt's gesture with the fork was only an urgent request to the man to show the quality that was in him. And he had. No doubt his aunt meant it for his own enlightenment.

II

Diego went through the wicket and faced the brae that broke down into a cliff fifty yards behind the house. The road, sandy on the surface, curved steeply to avoid the cliff, and Diego went up slowly, aiding himself with the crook. Half-way up he paused for a rest, his heart pounding. He certainly was in poor condition. Not so long ago he had taken the rocky ridges of the Sierra de Gredos in his stride, and sighted a steady rifle after a hard climb; and still more recently he had played hide-and-seek with death along twenty miles of the rocky coast of Brittany;

67

and here, now, was his breath coming short on the smooth tilt of a brae. Six months of starvation and pain had done that to him; but now the pain was gone, and there was no longer that wasting feeling of emptiness. Perhaps, after all, life was not as desolate as he had thought. His own entity was again in control, and he would no longer yield to an obsession that was not part of him. He drew in a long breath, stamped the ground firmly, and went upwards, no longer using his crook.

The road curved over, flattened out and went downwards in an easy gradient. And he was looking up the length of Affran Loch. It lay there shining and wrinkling in the morning sun, a long oval, possibly four miles in length and a mile in width; just a big oval pond resting in the hollow of the hills, and from where he stood his eye could sweep round the whole curve. Here and there along the margin was the warm gleam of sandy beaches. Except at the far end the whole sweep of shore was heavily wooded in pine and spruce, and the dark green mantle spread smoothly upwards for half a mile to the base of a cliff of grey rock that followed the contour of the shore and broke down into the craggy notch of a pass at the top end. Amongst the crags he saw the white sheen of a torrent. Above the cliff the hills sloped upwards slowly, and on the southern side were dominated by a cairn-like peak, its head cowled in snow.

At the top end the shore levelled out to a good-sized spread of bright green grass, scattered with the bare bulks of deciduous trees, and far back on that green lawn Diego saw a house of grey stone. That would be Lodge Affran.

The whole scene gave him a sense of remote seclusion touched with something akin to sadness. There was a feeling of somnolence over this sheltered hollow where the gravity of the pines swallowed the sunlight. And then it was that Diego noticed the silence. It was a real silence, the brooding silence that one finds in the heart

68

of a summer day. And yet the base of that silence was one even sigh that was just within the compass of hearing. That was the eternal sough of the pines. Living here, life would go inwards and silence become a habit. One would grow quiet with the quietness, or one would eat one's heart out in loneliness.

Diego felt the quiet, and he had as yet no cause for loneliness. And lacking that cause he had no deep experience of life, for one has not tasted of life until he has experienced the things that thereafter bring loneliness. He had fought and killed and felt fellowship with soldierly men, but he had never known the real love of women. Would he ever know now? Was the basic fear in him the fear that he would never know? What experience of life and love could he find in this remote glen, listening to the organ of an Irishwoman's voice, nursing silence with his blood-uncle, eating and sleeping, wandering amongst the hills and hollows, leaving youth behind him for ever? What he needed was an anchorage to which he could always return. There was his own hacienda of San José, but his father had died so young that he himself had had no time to acquire a national consciousness before going to Spain to complete his education; and his nostalgic Highland mother had imbued him with a sense of her own race without making him of it. If he was to have any life at all, all life was before him.

His uncle had gone up to Lodge Affran to beard the lion in his den, and Diego decided to go part of the way and meet him. The road slanted down towards the loch, and in a few minutes he was amongst the trees in a shadowy tunnel turning this way and that for easy gradients in the folds of the ground. The trees were close-planted and straight-trunked, and between them he could see the clear water rippling in sunlight, and the reflections wavering on the brown boles. There was no undergrowth, but the eye going uphill was soon denied a further prospect by the closing in of the trees. Here and there the sunlight came through and shone richly on the matt of brown needles, and that golden gleam relieved and accented the solemnity of these deep woods, where the sough of the pines was the very undertone of sadness.

He did not meet his uncle, and he went on and on. He was in no hurry, and the road dipping and tilting and turning drew him onwards. In an hour the wood thickened into a new plantation and the road turned away from the water and went steeply uphill. He paused amongst the spindly trees and considered whether it was worth while going on, and then decided to walk to the head of this last rise to see how near he was to the end of the loch. He must have done nearly four miles, and his legs and his heart were better than when he had set out. He toiled up to the last tilt and came out surprisingly into the open. All the solemn trees were behind, and the prospect opened out before him.

He was at the head of an easy slope grown with withered bracken. Below him and to his left the shore curved round the end of the loch, and a boathouse jutted out into deep water. Half a mile ahead was the ragged notch of the pass, with the head-stream of Affran Water cascading down from a wilder glen. Below the pass, on the near side of the cascade, was a belt of pines, and below the pines the green, tree-dotted demesne of Lodge Affran. The demesne was surrounded by a wall, but from the eminence where he stood Diego could see over it to the grey house not more than a quarter-mile away. It was a solid ugly house of grey granite. The middle portion was of two storeys, steep-roofed and step-gabled, and, right and left, a long one-storeyed wing ran out, with crenellated parapets hiding a flat roof. Fronting the central part was a big glass porch or sun-parlour.

The road Diego was on ran straight down the slope,

through an open gateway without a lodge, and curved across the lawn to a bay of gravel fronting the sun-parlour. And that was the end of that sixteen miles of road from Craik Station. But outside the wall a pony-track branched off and crossed the torrent below the cascade by a wooden bridge.

There was no sign of Diego's uncle anywhere, but a tall man was strolling back and fore on the lawn in front of the house. At that distance Diego took him to be General Harper. He stood watching him for some time, nodded his head at a thought of his own, tucked his crook under an arm, walked steady-paced down the slope, through the open gates, and across the grass towards the man who so leisurely strolled.

When he got near he saw that this man in brown tweeds was not General Harper. He was equally tall, and with the same high width of shoulder, but he was longer in the leg, and leaner and much younger—a man still in the prime of life, but not for much longer. He was bare-headed and his hair was dark grizzled-red and straight and worn rather long; his eyes were deep-set and grey, his deeply-bronzed face was aquiline and strongly carved, and his long jut of chin was deeply slit. Diego would give a good deal to be as fit as that man looked. He turned as Diego approached and put a hand to the pipe he was smoking.

"Well, sir?"

The enquiry was casual, yet there was a trace of superiority about it, and Diego checked the inbred inclination to lift his felt hat. The self-conscious British always misunderstood that gesture of courtesy between men. He made only a small hand-movement of salute.

"Could you tell me, sir, if Hamish McLeod is here?"

"Hamish? No. He was here but went home by the south side—oh, an hour ago." He had a good voice, but rather harsh in timbre.

"My thanks. May I ask if General Harper is at home?"

"In the house somewhere. You want to see him?"

"If I may."

"Why not? Come this way."

He walked slowly towards the sun-parlour, and then Diego noticed that he had a barely perceptible limp. He had not asked for Diego's business or name, and Diego remembered then that he should have given his own name.

"My name is James Usted," he said. "Hamish McLeod is my uncle."

"I had guessed that. We heard about you last evening." His voice showed no feeling.

He paused to relight his pipe, turning towards Diego to avoid the drift of air, but his deep-set eyes did not look up.

"You rubbed my brother on the raw, it appears?"

"I had a raw edge too."

"Charles would find it."

He turned and walked across the gravel, Diego at his shoulder. He was completely casual, and Diego got the impression that he was not interested in Hamish McLeod's nephew, and not courteous enough to give his own name in return—but this might be merely the British carelessness of manners. The man had called General Harper his brother, but he was of sterner stuff than the General.

The sun-parlour had a side-door, and Diego followed the tall man through. It was a big room with a tessellated floor rug-scattered, pot shrubs, and wicker chairs silken-cushioned: a pleasantly warm room on an April day. In one corner was a huge elephant's foot, knee-high, holding walking-sticks and half a dozen fencing-foils, and by it stood a padded fencing-dummy on a weighted hemispherical base. Diego saw those foils first thing, and he wondered who was the fencer in this house.

There were two people already in the room. A young man in red dressing-gown and slippers lay flat out in a wicker chair, and Diego noted that he was short but massive in build. He had a dark sullen young face, strong enough, but with the hapsburg lip that betokened kinship to General Harper. He was not reading or smoking; his hands were behind his head, propping it forward, and he stared sullenly at his red toes. For a moment he lifted his dark dream-hazed eyes at Diego, and again resumed his sullen staring.

A female, elbows on the arms of a straight-backed chair, was mostly hidden by the newspaper she was reading, and newspapers and journals were scattered on the floor about her. She wore a short tartan skirt, and her crossed knees showed a long shapely silken leg from knee-cap to brown brogue. As the door closed behind Diego she said in a pleasant half-Highland voice:

"This war is getting dam' dull, Pop. I don't think I'll go back."

"Your uncle about, brat?"

That gave Diego the particulars of relationship. This man was her father, and the General was her uncle. Who the sullen young man was he did not yet know.

She lowered the paper, and Diego saw that she was young, not much, if at all, out of her teens. But even at a first glance he was able to gather that in her own mind she was a girl no longer. Here in this remote glen on an April morning she was as carefully made-up as if about to embark on a kick-over-the-traces party. Her lips, full and shapely, were outlined in colour that was nearer orange than red; the touch of colour on her cheeks was surely counterfeit; her fine flaxen hair had been recently and expensively waved; and her eyebrows, that might be lighter than her hair, were plucked to thin dark curves. She had needed to do nothing with her eyes. Under the mask of that make-up Diego could not tell whether she was vivacious or dull or sophisticated or plain stupid. And yet, underlying it and not at all accented by it, was that quality of good looks that is called bonniness.

She looked at Diego interestedly out of a fine pair of golden-grey eyes, and he could read the speculation behind her look. Her eyes crinkled to his hat-in-hand bow.

"Your uncle, Hett?" said the man she called Pop.

"In there." She moved her paper towards the glass-panelled door to the inner hall. "Pin-pricking his maps—he has to pin-prick something—blast him!"

The tall man was already limp-striding towards the inner door. He opened it and glanced through. "There he is," he said, and gestured to Diego. Diego went through, and the tall man shut the door between them.

The room, or hall, he entered surprised Diego. It was an immense room, filling the shell of the two-storeyed part of the building. The ceiling was the pointed cavity of the roof lined in red pine and with heavy pine collar-braces. Indeed, all the walls, between the high-set windows, were lined in red pine, which is a raw wood, lacking the dignity of oak; but the rawness in this case was toned down to that polished brownness that comes with many years of peat-fires. The floor was parqueted and thickly scattered with an archipelago of the skins of beasts: deer, bear, lion, tiger, leopard, and some that Diego did not recognise; and all the walls were decorated with trophies of the chase and of the sporting rifle, not only of native beasts but of all the antelopes of Africa; and amongst the trophies, arranged in saltires, were most of the deadly weapons used by aboriginal races in ancient and modern times, not excluding the British and the

74

latest rifle. There were no pictures and no hangings. It was the hunter's room, and completely barbarous.

An open fireplace with a brazen canopy filled a third of the far wall, and a fire—big as a bonfire—of bog-pine and peat gleamed on polished fire-irons. On the wall, left of the fire, a place had been found for all the war-maps that were; and General Charles Harper was leaning towards a map of Europe, shifting position-flags here and there. He would derive no satisfaction in shifting them in the direction that present circumstances compelled.

Diego was beginning to be sorry that he had set foot amongst these people who had their own insular ideas of manners—or was it their own notion of caste? If it were caste and he cared to consider it, what with Mendoza on one side and McLeod on the other, he might not let the Harper even kiss his feet. But perhaps he would not be so indifferent to caste if he could not claim it.

General Harper heard the door close and turned round. He recognised Diego at once, and straightened up stiffly, but made no move forward. As lord of the manor he waited with dignity. Diego strode carefully. The parquetry was polished, and one of those unnecessary skins might slide from under him, to the loss of the dignity he was trying to imitate. So, holding hat and crook firmly under one arm, he tacked by-and-wide amongst the islands and brought up on an even keel facing the General. He noted how strangely the man's creamy-white bush of hair stood out against the coloured maps.

The expressionless eyes were slightly disturbing. Were they intentionally meant to hide a warm temper, or was it only that the hairless eyebrows and eyelids were somehow non-flexible? He waited for Diego to speak, and that was not the proper way to receive a caller. Diego controlled his voice carefully.

"I regret, General Harper, that I spoke with rudeness

to you yesterday at the Station of Craik. My rudeness, it was not necessary—in the circumstances."

The moment he had spoken he was sorry he had used that addendum. The General seized on it at once, his lip pouting.

"I stand rudeness in no circumstances, sir."

Diego let that go. He could imagine circumstances in which it would be easy to be more than rude to General Harper.

"It is due to my uncle and to myself," he said evenly, "that I show no disrespect to his employer."

"Your uncle spoke to you?" He meant spoke in reprimand.

"He speaks little. He does not know that I am here."

"You are discharged from the Service?"

"For the time."

"For reasons of health?"

"Yes."

"You might have so informed me. If and when you are fit again you will take service in the Home Guard." That was not a suggestion as much as information from Headquarters.

"If and when I am fit I go back to my own unit," said Diego quietly.

"What unit is that?"

Diego hesitated before he replied, and then said briefly :

"Commando."

"Oh!" His voice lifted but his eyebrows did not. "You were on Commando?"

"We do not talk about it."

"What is your rank?"

But Diego was perverse and would not tell him that he held the King's Commission. He said, "General Harper, we do not speak at all about Commando, and I will not waste your time further. You will accept my regrets. Good day, sir!" And he knew that nothing he had said had in the least mollified General Harper.

He was about to turn away when a green-baize door opened at the right of the fireplace and the lady with the red hair came through. He had heard her before she entered. She was singing, and he knew the air but not the words, for the words were Basque, of which he knew little. The words, he knew, were satiric.

"Grey falcon, in my wrist do you dare set a claw?
                    Claw then! claw then!
Don Cupid, to my heart your arrow would you draw?
                    Draw then! draw then!
For my hand is cased in leather 'gainst claw and wind and
        weather,
But my heart is soft, unguarded, unwise, unware, un-
        warded.
                So I laugh then, and I fall then."

Her voice was contralto inclined to huskiness, but it had a gay quirk in it to suit the satire of the air.

She saw the visitor, stopped singing, threw up a hand in that fine, free, foreign gesture of greeting, and came straight at him. She had come straight at him yesterday too, but this time her hand was out, warmly, impulsively, welcomingly.

"It is Señor Usted. How good of you to call, and so soon!"

Diego took her finger-tips, bowed slowly, and brought his lips lightly to the back of her hand. Her hand was warm with life, and he felt one finger-tip twitch. She would know the salute of her own breed.

"I regret, señora, it is not a call."

She looked at her husband and laughed, a pleasant chuckle of laughter with a little lift at the end.

"Come off your high steed, my Carlos!" she urged him, strode to his side, faced round, and looked up at him, her eyes crinkling. "Are you on your feet, Major-

77

General? No! But how many times do I not tell thee thy destination?" She shook his arm.

"This is business, Ann," he said, his lip pouting and his voice going high.

"Business! Business! Do not make me angry. No, I will not be angry. I will laugh at you two fine gentlemen who bristle . . ." And she laughed that chuckling laugh, and brought her hand chidingly on her husband's shoulder.

Diego had it in his mind that this young wife was not happy. Yesterday she had begun in storm and ended in silence. But to-day she was the pleasantly imperious young housewife, the housewife in control within the doors of her own house as the Basque housewife is. She had come from the working quarters of that house, and a leather-covered housekeeping book and a bunch of keys hung from her waist-belt. As the Spanish saying puts it, "Give the woman many keys or one lover." She had the keys, and probably loved her husband. Her heart-shaped face might be one to win love, might be more beautiful in unhappiness, more poignant in tragedy; but to-day it had pleasant lines, her black eyes sparkled, and her mouth, suited to woe or laughter, was now laughing. Her live red hair was held down by a black ribbon, and her belt-strapped, long-fitting black gown showed up the splendid proportions of breast and hip. Diego wondered if she was yet a mother. Few Basque wives are not.

"Hamish, your great uncle, but not in speech," she said in her deep voice with the correct sibilance of correct English, "he was here, but is gone to see that the wicked little roe have not eaten of his young tree sprouts. They will have. And you, señor, you will stay to eat with us? Henrietta will talk to you for two hours, and there will be lunch."

There was no condescension in that invitation, and he might have accepted it; but the thought of talking to whoever Henrietta might be for two hours appalled him; and again, this General would not care to sit at food with his servant's nephew. Diego bowed.

"My thanks—madam—but, to-day, you will excuse me?"

She looked from Diego to her husband and back again, shook her head, and moved one hand pityingly. "There it is, the one thing I cannot break. It is not pride, it is worse, it is hauteur." She shrugged shoulders. "You will not even take sherry? Ah well! time is my help-mate. Another day, and often, you will come and dip your fingers, señor. The invitation—the first one—will be very formal, and you will be formal too; but you will come, Señor Capitan?"

"With great pleasure, madam. Good day, madam! Good day, sir!" He would not call her señora any more.

He pivoted carefully on the polished floor. The General did not return his parting salute, but Diego found the woman walking at his side.

"You will mind these skins so devilish," she said, putting a graceful impulsive hand on his arm. He felt the warmth tingle through his sleeve. "Or have you tumbled already?"

"You have not tumbled, Mrs Harper?"

"But every day in the beginning. Oh! the words I got penance for!" She chuckled. "But now I am the acrobat, and no longer blue—in places." That was the frank Basque girl talking, and Diego was beginning to feel his kinship with her. "My poor Hetty will be so in grief that you did not fall down. This floor it is her source of income, but to-day she has only three peseta—that is half-crowns—two of which she owes me, and now young Carlos will take the other."

He opened the glass door and she went through before him. The three were still in the sun-room. The tall man, back-turned, was looking down the length of the loch; the young man in the chair still stared at his toes; but the girl was not now reading, and, as soon as the door opened, turned her eyes on Diego with new interest. Ann Harper's free swinging arm took them all in.

"These are my people, that in idleness suck my blood. And this is Señor Usted, my blood-brother of lost Spain, and his blood you will not suck."

Her voice was pleasant even in badinage, but Diego sensed the challenge in it, a pleasant challenge, but a challenge all the same, and on his behalf. Somehow his blood stirred to it. She was telling the Harpers that they would not ride roughshod over Diego Usted. That went.

The sullen-eyed young man levered himself belatedly to his feet. He nodded casually at Diego.

"Captain Usted and I will meet again," he said, and his voice was not sullen but Highland. "I'll throw on a few duds." He yawned unconcernedly, and Ann Harper pointed a finger at him.

"That youth whose tongue you have seen is brown in the morning is my nephew-in-law Charles—Charles Harper, the second-lieutenant and the second Carlos—which he regrets so much."

The young man flushed and the young girl snorted shortly.

"Cheese it, Ann!" he said, and moved towards a curtained door on the far side of the room. "Thanks for the half-dollar, Captain," he said, and disappeared.

"You will think that the boy from his manners is not half of your mother's race," said the lady, "but he is, and he is not a bad boy notwithstanding his sole parent whose back is not now turned to us. That is Arturo—Major Arthur Harper, hunter of big game—but a hunter also."

This young woman could use steel, button on or off. She ruled this house with the sword of her character and the sword of her tongue. She would not be dominated, because she would maintain the initiative. Silence for her would mean defeat among these islanders so insular who used silence sometimes as a weapon, sometimes as a cloak to emptiness.

Major Arthur Harper had turned from the window and leant easily against the sill, a half-frowning glint of speculation in the eyes moving back and forth between Diego and the woman.

"Mr Usted and I have met already," he said; and then he looked down, and one foot—the sound one— tapped thoughtfully on the tiles.

The girl with the waved flaxen hair and orange mouth was on her feet.

"You are forgetting the baby, Spanish Ann?" she said.

"The manners I am learning. You will forgive me, my darling who should be first. Señor, this is Henrietta, Hetty, the last of the Harpers, the very last of the Harpers, because, alas! I am without children. She will now proceed to take you away from me."

"Like hell she will, you Spanish vamp!" said the girl warmly.

She slouched lazily forward and reached Diego her hand, but the grip she gave was not lazy. She held his hand, and her golden-grey eyes searched his face with interest, but he had no inclination to lift her fingers to his lips. She was a tall slip of a girl and shapely, and the white, heavy-collared pullover outlined her firm buds of breast. And then she smiled, and Diego realised that, in spite of the make-believe sophistication, she might be quite a pleasant girl.

"You and I have to get acquainted, Captain James Usted," she said. Her neat nose crinkled at him. "You looked so absolutely dead certain for half a dollar or even five bob. You see, I have a standing bet with little Charlie that no one gets safely across that blasted floor first time. Half-crown for a slip, five bob for a full-lengther, and a whole quid for a broken limb. Haven't got the limb yet. How did you know?"

"Brought up on parquetry, Miss Harper," Diego told her.

"But so I was," cried the lady-of-the-house, "and look at me—or, rather, please do not look at me."

"If you will now excuse me," said Diego, bowing, and took a step towards the outer door.

But Major Harper came across the floor, his limp very evident, as if his mind, somewhere else, no longer controlled it.

"We are a barbarous people, Ann," he said, "and you are losing your sense of hospitality amongst us. Is not Mr Usted staying to lunch?"

"Not to-day, Arturo. It is arranged, another time, between the señor and myself." She said that as if already there was a confidence between herself and the man of her own breed.

Young Henrietta strode across to the elephant's foot in the corner and plucked out a walking-stick.

"You will notice my seven-league brogues, Captain," she said. "It is necessary that I walk and talk with you, as the song has it."

Diego could do nothing but bow the pleasure he did not feel. Her long legs looked limber for walking, and talk she would beyond doubt.

"You will be careful, Señor Captain," warned the aunt-in-law. "She is a vampire this one—but there are ways with vampires."

"Fat chance I have to vamp anyone with Spanish Ann getting her dirty work in first. But, by gum! I have a claim to stake here." The girl was warm about it.

Ann Harper went outside the door with them, and in her own impulsive way put her finger-tips on his wrist.

"You will be at the Mass on Sunday, señor—or do you follow the fashion of our men?"

He knew she meant the fashion of her and his countrymen, who seldom went to Mass any longer.

"I shall be at Mass on Sunday, madam," he said, who had not been at Mass for five years.

She nodded her head, and her red hair tossed under its band. She had been in full control of the situation this morning, and he was proud of her; but he was not sure whether it was a personal pride or a mere pride of race.


# CHAPTER IV

## THE HARPERS BY HEARSAY

### I

HENRIETTA HARPER was a good walker, too good for Diego Usted just then. Not talking at all, she went off at a hip-swinging pace across the lawn, through the gates, and up the slope towards the definitely marked line of sapling conifer. He was still young enough not to like lagging behind a girl, and his breath was hissing through his nostrils by the time they got to the top of the rise. But once amongst the trees, out of sight of the house, she slowed down to that easy stroll that makes for confidences, and edging a little closer, turned head to him. The flow of air had thrown her fine flaxen hair backwards, and the delicate flush on her cheeks was in strong contrast to her orange mouth. It was a good mouth, and there was a good chin below it.

"Sorry!" she said, strangely considerate. "You are in pretty poor shape?"

"I am."

"They chucked you out, the Army Johnnies?"

"On my ear—is it not?"

"Couldn't stand the racket?"

"Some of me."

"Yes! there are some bad pushers. I was in the A.T.S., Hamworth way, and don't I know! What was your unit?"

He hesitated, and before he could answer she laughed at him.

"Don't you tell me. You keep pretty dumb all of you, don't you? Wading in blood up and down the Bay." She opened her yellow-grey eyes at him. "Whatever drove you into Commando?"

Diego would not tell her what had sent him into Commando—the things that had been done to so many of his friends from Alcazar to Gijon, a boyish desire for vengeance—other things. That was all wrong, of course, for the men they killed were good men condemned by a mad world to holding the wrong end of the stick; and how wrong he wasn't even sure.

"How did you know that I was in Commando?" he asked her.

"My dear man, I have been reading every letter you wrote to Big Ellen this year and more. Very formal, proper sort of letters too, a bit like yourself." She looked aside at him. "Big Ellen did not say anything about me?"

"A pleasure to come."

"Bosh! You ask her about Hett Harper—'Etty 'Arper, her baby of the Harpers. I'll not spoil her stroke." She lifted a slender column of neck out of her high-collared jumper and laughed with some chagrin. "Hell! my technique is rotten. You will think me an unmitigated young rip."

That is exactly what he was thinking, but he did not say so.

"I think you are young," he said quietly.

"Touch. Do you fence too? Do you know what I am trying to do?"

"Giving me the false impression."

"Nice of you to say that. I am trying to stake a claim on you."

"I assay base metal."

"Most men do. You will be staying some time in the Glen?"

"Some time."

"Then let me tell you that we shall be seeing a good deal of each other. You ask Mother Ellen if I haven't business with everyone at Loch Beg."

They were strolling easily along the winding narrow road, the trees closing in on them, and sunny glimpses of lake water shining up at them between sun-flecked trunks. She moved closer to him, and sometimes her shoulder brushed his. She had stirred his curiosity. Apparently she had a claim on him because of some relationship with his people at Loch Beg. His aunt would tell him, and he would do no prying now. He turned to her and saw that she was frowning at some thought of her own.

"Wrinkles come easily, and go not at all," he quoted.

"Yes! I was just wondering how Spanish Ann puts her hooks in all you men. She's one dam' bitch with men."

"Your tongue, young lady!"

"Damn my tongue! I don't mean that she makes a dead set at you. She doesn't need to. The lift of a hand, the crook of a little finger, the stir of her hair, and there you all are at her feet." In those few words she had actually summed up the strange charm of that woman. This was no dumb modern empty-headed wench.

"All of us?"

"Every darn one! There was our tin-god the Major-General. Buried two women already—and a pot of

85

money with each. I mean he buried the women but scooped the money—and knows dam' well what to do with it, or, rather, what not to do with it. She hadn't a peseta, and he retrieved her from between the yawning doorposts of a brothel in Biarritz. Blast my tongue! She didn't say she was on the street, but how do I know? What else for her in that hell?"

*What else indeed.* But he did not say that aloud.

"And he married her without a cent, and cherishes her like—like a green bay tree; though, mind you, he would like to treat her like the walnut tree, only she'd slap him down like one o'clock. I have heard her threaten to do so in one of her tantrums. He loves to put her in a rage, and then beg his forgiveness, remembering what he saved her from. The old tyrant! I could cut his liver out sometimes, and some day I will. Curse him!"

She spoke with a vindictiveness that was astonishing in one so young and modern.

"You do not love your uncle?"

"I do not—though I bite the hand that feeds me."

"Nor his wife?"

"There you are wrong." She paused and frowned. "She could make me crawl on my knees if she wanted to, but she doesn't want to. Perhaps I am only selfishly grateful. You see, she makes life possible for us in that stone prison—for Charles and me, and my father too. Yes! my father too."

She glanced aside at him, but he did not rise to her bait. He would say nothing about that strong man her father. She laughed scathingly.

"Oh! he's like the rest of you. A real good scout too, but he's a man and a widower. I guess he made a pass at our Spanish lady combing her hair by candle-light. He might be making a pass at her yet for all I know. They can be secret devils both of them."

"Woe to the scandal-monger!"

"A foul mouth, haven't I? If you are staying on at Loch Beg you'll hear all about us, and I'm getting the first naked word in."

"Naked, yes!"

"And I am just warning you. 'Ware red-heads! You are one of the middling young ones. Just above Charlie's class."

"Your brother too?"

"Head over heels in love with her, and the heels showing for all the world to see. In the old days—the very old days before the war, three, four years ago—before the Spanish invasion, Charlie hated that ugly house back there. Now we can't keep him away, and he has only two desires in the world. One is to cut his uncle's throat—and you can guess the other. He's stationed over Tain way with his Seaforths, and sometimes brings some of his push across—just as a cover—and then he can't get near his Ann for all the bees round the honey-pot. And, you know, she treats him and me like children. Puts me sitting on her knees sometimes, and she'll take on Charlie at fencing, and he's good at it. She's strong as whalebone."

An old Spanish saying came into Diego's mind: *A virgin: lukewarm water! A courtesan: strong wine!* But he did not say it aloud. Instead he said:

"You suffer from jealousy, Miss Henrietta Harper."

"Of course I do—sitting my lone in a corner. Ach! Let's forget it." She threw her stick in the air and caught it neatly. Then she put a hand on his arm and chuckled. "I knew that you were our crowd when I heard that you told the old owl go to hell. Don't tell me you came up to apologise?"

"I did. I am sorry for that man, your uncle."

"You will not be."

"But, behold! His wife twists him round her little

87

finger, his brother would steal the wife, his nephew cut the throat, his niece merely carve the liver. That is what you tell me. He is not blind?"

"Not him. He is only cocksure. And we are only his goods and chattels to be teased and made feel impotent. We are poor as church mice, and haven't enough guts to be poor and free—not even my father, who is something of a man. Say! when you told him to go to hell, did his eyes blink?"

"No."

"Keep on and they will. Kissing her hand as if it was the Pope's toe. I saw you through the glass. You did not kiss my hand?"

"Not your hand that would be kissed."

"Do I look that easy? I suppose I do. You try, and see where it gets you?"

That was an indignant warning and not a suggestive dare. She stopped suddenly and faced towards him.

"I talk too much, and I am not Big Ellen. I have to let off steam once in a while, you know, and you may as well see me at my worst, for you will see a lot of me. Thanks for listening, and giving me a prick occasionally." She grimaced chagrinedly. "I am a bit of a beast. Of course, you and Ann being of Spanish blood——"

"She is a Basque," he corrected.

"All the same."

"Like the Scot being an Englishman?"

"So he is mostly, the renegade! And what are you? Gaucho?"

"Nothing so definite. Scot and Paraguayan, and a trace of the Guarani; the tribe the Conquistadors could not subdue."

"I see! A touch of the tar-brush! You are dark enough."

Diego thought he was old enough and disillusioned enough to have got rid of race prejudice. He was not.

88

He could stand being called "dago"; it was not quite as bad as being called "gringo"; but the implication of the negro tar-brush made him suddenly hot under the collar.

"You young jade!" he said warmly. "You a man and I a real Gaucho there would be a carving of the liver most intimate."

She was embarrassed and angry with herself, but tried to carry the thing off in bravado. "Come on! Forget my sex. Here is my sword, same like Alan Breck."

She stepped back and brought the stick on guard like a foil.

"Just so!" said Diego softly.

His crook engaged her stick, and the moment it did he knew that no longer had he the iron wrist of the fencer. But he had skill enough for the occasion. He played the crossed weapons head-high, tapped the stick smartly to loosen her grip, and, then, binding it in *flanconade*, whipped it out of her hand and down amongst the trees.

"Blast!" she said.

"Not yet," said Diego.

He reversed his grip, deftly slipped the curve of th crook inside the collar of her pullover, and jerked her close to him with the necessary explosive force. One hand went over her shoulders, and he brought his mouth down on hers. She laxed and stiffened, but before she could struggle he released her, and propped her off with the curve of the crook under her chin.

"That is now a Gaucho," he said.

She stared at him out of wide-open wondering eyes, the young blood suffused her cheeks, and a hand came for a moment to her smeared orange mouth.

"You astonishing hellion!" she whispered. There was dismay in her eyes too.

She lifted her hands and cautiously loosed the crook from the neck of her jumper, her eyes watchful on his, then stepped back quickly, poised and ready for flight. He grinned at her, and she grinned back with some difficulty.

"Don't tell Mother Ellen," she said, turned on her heel and went away at a rapid walk. She had forgotten her walking-stick. A down curve of the road soon hid her, but, before disappearing, she lifted her right hand above her head and clenched it. Was that a declaration of war? He had certainly astonished her, and frightened her too, so probably she was not so sophisticate as she had made out.

He wiped his mouth, and shook his head distastefully at the orange-red stain on the white of his handkerchief. He was not sorry that he had kissed her, but though her lips had been warm his blood was not the fraction of a degree warmer than usual. That kiss had been the most condign punishment he could think of at the moment.

He walked on. She was an astonishing girl, and had none of the reticence that her class is supposed to have. Not that he had found the British—especially the South Britons—in any way reticent. They would speak of their loves and their difficulties as readily as any of the Slavs he had met in Spain. But he understood that a certain caste amongst them had made a cult of meiosis until it had become a fetish, often enough cloaking inarticulateness.

Young Henrietta Harper was not inarticulate, and though some of her talk had repelled him with its skeleton-baring, she was not vapid, and her vocabulary was vital enough and with some allusions to show that she had been reasonably educated. But why had she talked so freely to a stranger and a foreigner? Did she really want to stake a claim on him? Probably he was a fool to kiss her, even in anger, for once kissed she would kiss again, and he was not amenable to that sort of philandering—not with a girl. Also there seemed to be some traffic between her and his Aunt Ellen—the reading of his letters, for instance—and he was to ask his aunt about it? . . .

That household back there was not a particularly pleasant one. It had not the wherewithal that makes for happiness. Trouble could breed in it like a yeast. But that was no concern of Diego Usted's. And yet he was intrigued by the Spanish-Basque lady whose last name was Mendoza. She had the spirit not to be defeated by that house, the debonair spirit. She had the temper and whip of a good rapier, his own weapon, and used it as it must be used by her, in attack. What her relations were with the men in the house he did not know. But that was no concern of his either. Good luck to her all the same! . . .

## II

When he got back to Loch Beg Uncle Hamish was digging in the garden. His uncle did not like digging, but he made it look easy. Diego went across through the berry bushes to his side, and at once he drove in the fork and leant an armpit on it.

"A nice daunder, Jamie?" Evidently he had chosen the name Jamie.

"Right along to the Lodge."

"You'll be needing your luncheon, then."

He was. He was as hungry as a hawk. A real hunger, no longer the empty gnaw that called for easing with food. And then he noted that he had not remembered to be tired. He had walked some eight miles and was not leg-weary. The clean air and the balsam of the pines and the sunlight were already doing their work on him, and he even now wondered at the gloomy forebodings that had possessed him only yesterday. Strange how a malaise of body could cloud the mind. Surely the spirit could not be in a citadel of its own aloof from the body; perhaps it was not an entity at all but a mere functioning of the body. But that was a speculation for philosophers.

"I hoped to meet you on the road," he said.

"Eh, man! I'm sorry I didn't know. I came down the other side and had a take over into the Sanctuary by Scurr Affran." He pointed across the loch to a fold in the hills.

"A sanctuary?"

"A deer-sanctuary, I mean. You see, it's this way. You must give the deer a confidence in the hills or they'll just about die out on you. So in most forests there is a hill or the face of a hill—a good easy slope, ridge and hollow, good cover and good grazing—and that's the Sanctuary. You ken? The deer are safe in it."

"Not shot at?"

"Losh, no! Not ever. Even with a beast sair wounded you put him over the border before easing him. And the deer get to know it. The stags'll just lift head at you and go on browsing, and moving quiet you'll get right up to a hind and her fawn, and she'll just stamp a hoof and order you off." On his own subject he was quite fluent.

"And how are your deer this morning?"

"Fine. The young buck coming along nicely. They wintered well—a long winter too, but Donald Gunn over at the Strath had a good stock of hay. There'll be a head or two worth getting come September—and not many to get them. Big Ellen should be calling us to our meat any minute." He was hungry too, and stepped back from his enemy the fork. Diego pulled it out of the ground.

"Look here, Uncle Hamish! You don't go at this the best way. You dig by numbers—for the numbers come. Thus! One—in goes the points hand and foot. Two—you lever it to break contact. Three—over it goes on the fulcrum of the thigh. Four—No! that did not turn over like a squad. We'll try again."

"Goodness!" exclaimed his uncle. "This is no' the first time you handled a digger?"

"Certainly not. Had my first lesson this morning."

Hamish slapped his thigh. "Man, has she 'listed you already? You're for it, and I'll not hinder her. But, mind you, the rough digging done, the work is mostly hers."

"What work are we now preparing?"

"I'm late with the digging. A slow spring, and the snow lying most of March. This I'm thinking is for cabbage. Peter Ross at the station has the plants. He'll be on Sunday. The taties are in, and the inguns, and a row of beans and peas——"

A full-throated mellow call made him turn to the house. The tall woman was on the step of the door, her head back and her hand patting her open mouth, and from her long throat poured a syncopated volume of sound clearer and mellower than any cock's clarion.

"The Irish farm-wife calling the men from the field," explained her husband. "I've heard it as far as the Sanctuary, and the wind that way it got Craik. This way we answer it."

He took the fork from Diego, lifted it as if to resume digging, opened his hands and let it drop flat; kicked at it contemptuously, turned his back on it, and walked away towards the house. Diego followed, laughing, and his aunt's chuckling laughter made a rich echo. This was another household from that one at the head of the glen. It had been a full house once, empty enough now, but the ties that had been tied by love in this house still held fast to four sons and two daughters scattered over a warring world.

Diego cannot remember the meal they had that day, chicken or mountain mutton. But it was a good meal, for he never got a makeshift meal in that house. As Big Ellen said, "Hamish, the creature, likes his diet, and, sure, 'tis the only comfort he has." From the very beginning Diego gave up thinking of food as an inimical necessity. He ate continently of what his aunt placed before him, and damned the consequences, and as a result, naturally enough, the consequences were not untoward.

That day's table talk he remembers particularly, for it rounded off the knowledge of the Harper clan he had acquired from Henrietta. His aunt moved about the table and in and out the back-kitchen, ate a little, and moved about again; and her talk flowed. He never saw her eat a hearty meal. Milkless tea and plain bread-and-butter were her staple, though she might taste with some relish of the Irish dish that her husband liked best of all, well-cured bacon boiled with white cabbage, and potatoes in their jackets.

"You were up the loch a-ways, Don?" she remarked, and did not wait for his affirmative. "You were, and saw Lodge Affran. What did you think of it?"

"It is an ugly house, Aunt."

"Outside and in and in more ways than one, you mean. And you spoke your piece to the Major-General." She would know even that.

"A few words, Aunt."

His uncle turned head to him. "There was no need," he said. "It wasn't about yesterday he wanted to see me."

"What about, then? Come on, Cuchulain! You needn't try to hide it."

"What's the good trying?" he said resignedly. "It was about the entail. He said to me, 'McLeod, I am breaking the entail and you had better look for another place.'"

"Just so! We don't need another place, but we'll let that be. Don Diego, did you keep your temper?"

"Madam Harper saw that I did."

94

"'Tis a habit she has, yesterday and to-day and to-morrow, but not every morrow, I am afraid. If you saw the Lodge close at hand I knew you'd step inside, and say your few words stiff as a ramrod, adding insult to injury like as not. But red Ann would not let you. Who else did you see?"

"The first person I saw was a tall man, strong-featured, walking the lawn with a lame leg." He was following her own idiom.

"That was Arthur the Major. He was at Dunkirk, game leg and all."

"Not at Dunkirk he got that leg," amended her husband.

"Amn't I after saying so? He got that from a catawampus or something in Black Africay. He couldn't run as fast as the catawampus. Up the catawampus! But give him his due, he was at Dunkirk."

"Much has happened since," hinted Diego.

"Meaning, what has he done since? Lions don't shoot back same as Nazis——"

"Shame on you, Big Ellen!" protested Hamish. "A weak heart he has. I noticed that on the hill."

"You did, and maybe he has, but not so very weak, Cuchulain. He is a stronger man than his brother, but he'd be just as autocratic, and with much more bite to him. And what is more, he has no loyalty to the High-lands, and if he got Glen Affran he'd be an absentee landlord in foreign parts, and we know what the absentee landlord did in ould Ireland. Anyway, the absentee saved Ireland from the fault of the Highlands, and that's a mistaken loyalty. We had no hesitation in shooting the Scotch land-agent, poor fellow. Didn't you ever hear of the Missionary Father preaching against the evils o' strong drink? ''Tis drink,' says he, 'that gets the poor Irish tenant-farmer behind-hand with his rent; 'tis drink that gets him thrown out on the roadside; 'tis drink that puts him behind a hedge a gun in his hand, to shoot the Scotch agent coming home from a ball; and worst of all, 'tis drink that makes him miss him.' Ay so! And supposing the entail is not broken, and supposing the Major gets Glen Affran, what is he going to use for money?"

"The General has plenty," said Hamish.

"He has so. He has money to burn by dint of marrying and burying two women who had it and nothing else. And supposing the General's private wealth goes somewhere else——?"

"There's still the estate," said Hamish.

"And a fine big estate it is: fifty thousand acres of grass and heather and rock—and humans thin on the ground. There's the big house up there with five idle people in it and five more to look after them, and there are the two of us here at Loch Beg, and old Donald Gunn over at Strath Dearg, and the township of Craik with two hundred old ones and childre. And that is the wealth o' Affran Glen."

"You're forgetting the deer, woman!"

"The deer surely, and a covey of grouse down below, and a salmon in Affran Water; but where's the wealth in deer and grouse and salmon these days? Isn't the place ate alive with rates and taxes? What was it like even in the cheap old days before the General married money? And what will it be like again if his money goes somewhere else? And where will his money go, tell me that?"

Her husband would not answer any of these questions, and she did not press him, but moved about the table deep-humming a running ripple of song that Diego had not heard before.

> "As I walked down through Galway City,
>   The hour of ten on a summer night,
>   Who did I see but a Spanish Lady
>   Combing her hair by candlelight."

"Ay! and I'm often thinking of a certain Spanish lady, and her red hair held down by its green ribbon, and she twisting an old man round her fingers—and for what? Maybe she's too well liked in that house by some, and maybe others think she's playing a game and playing it too well! And maybe the General's money is the stake they're all playing for!"

"Scandal you're talking now——"

"So I am. What I'm saying is that our Major-General has them all tied to his money-bags in the hollow of his hand, and likes it fine."

"He keeps them in every comfort."

"And they dislike being kept, but they like their comforts better than they like their dislikes, for they come of a class that has lost, and long lost, the way of keeping itself. And that's enough o' that. Who else did you see this morning, Don?"

"A sullen young man staring at his toes."

"That's Charles, Charlie, Tearlath—Young Affran we call him. He's half-Highland, anyway, for his mother was a Skene, and a Skene once chiefed it in Affran. Was he in a bad temper? He was. Long may he remain that way. It will be a bad day for him, and for the Glen too, maybe, when he purrs lapping the cream in his uncle's house. I'll say nothing against him till then."

"A good boy on the hill, and active," said the hill-man.

"You trained him. It was in this house he was mostly reared, his mother dead and his father hunting wild beasts in foreign parts. He is a year older than our youngest, Larr, and they got on well together, with hidden plans of their own, and wrestling like wild cats. Do you mind, Cuchulain, when they used be reading that Neil Gunn and talking about restoring the Golden Age in Glen Affran?"

"Ay! and we called them Young Affran and his Factor."

"The dreaming young devils! And now I am at the heart of my subject. Who was the fifth person you saw this morning, my gay hidalgo?"

"Miss Henrietta Harper," said Diego smoothly.

"And she'd see you, and she'd walk with you, 'less she had a broken leg——"

"And talk with your voice, Aunt."

"Ay, would she! opening the door on all the skeletons. But herself has no skeleton yet, whatever her tongue, and she has a nice mouth too—under the paint. I'm tired talking to her about that outrageous orange, the very colour of that stain on your handkerchief when you took it out coming in the door."

Diego did not flush easily, but he flushed then. This was an unpleasant situation. The very last thing he wanted to do was to give this talking woman and quiet man a wrong impression. Silence would not help. He plucked out the handkerchief, and spread the crumpled square of it on the table. The smeared orange stain was plain to be seen. He shook his head at it.

"That is from my mouth and hers. I kissed her by surprise and she did not like it. She told me not to tell you, but you knew. I—I——" It was difficult to explain. "All right! I kissed her."

"She does open her mouth. She hurt you?"

"Something she called—something she said. And she was not a man——"

"To pierce with your—snicker snee; so you shut her mouth for her the only way you could."

"I will not kiss her again."

"What harm is a kiss?" said his uncle.

"You thought it a mortal sin the month I took to get the first kiss off you, but you became a hardened sinner after that." She considered Diego fierce-eyed, and then smiled and nodded. "Yes! I'll forgive you this time, but I'll blame you fast enough if the habit grows one-sided. You see, there is a tie between Hett Harper and this house. I am her foster-mother."

Diego knew about fosterage. It was common in certain cultures of an aristocratic bent, especially in ancient Ireland and Scotland.

"She has good blood in her," said his aunt, "and there was nothing wrong with the milk in her mouth either. Her mother died bearing her, and I was rearing Larry my young one. So I took her, and they had a breast apiece and plenty. Mind you, she is not so young and foolish as she looks. Larry was twenty-two last week and she is only two months younger. She is as much at home in this house as one of my own, and she would look upon you as a sort of a cousin and blether away to you."

"Now I understand her frankness," said Diego.

"Very well so! And I'll not any longer hinder you two bohunks going out in my bit garden and spreading manure for a patch of cabbage."

It was thus that Diego acquired a working knowledge of the Harper clan within one day of his arrival in the Glen. He would meet the Spanish lady again. He would also meet harum-scarum Henrietta, but he would not kiss her; he might spank her instead, in a cousinly way.

# CHAPTER V

## SUNDAY AT LOCH BEG

### I

DIEGO and his uncle sat each side of the peat-fire after lunch on Sunday afternoon. An April day sheeting and shining, and they had stayed indoors after returning from Mass at Craik. The fire was getting low and needed fresh peats, but they were too lazy and well fed to make a move towards the turf-box in the corner. They would wait till the woman-of-the-house came in from the byre and stirred them with her tongue. She was out there looking over her stock, and the house was unaccustomedly silent. The wag-at-the-wall clock ticktocked steadily and triumphantly in its corner by the bow window. The byre would not be silent, for Big Ellen would talk to her cows, to her fattening pig, to the shaggy pony, even to the rooster lording it over his hens. An indefatigable woman—tongue and hand—she would not take her ease till at night, in the soft pulsing glow of the peat and pine fire, she sat on her straw hassock, her hand on the arm of her husband's chair.

Diego's uncle was armoured in a dark suit of Sunday tweeds so thick and stiff in texture that the bending of knee or arm seemed to call for a noticeable physical effort. His massive neck was captive in a white collar size eighteen, and half a size too small. Though his eyes were closed and his neck-gyve propped his chin he was not asleep, for his ancient pipe was in his teeth and he remembered to keep it alive by an occasional soft puff. Sometimes Diego caught a chink of deep-set black eye glance his way, and knew that the old man wanted him to start a conversation; but Diego was given to silence too, and if his uncle wanted to talk he must provide some of it himself. All his married life he had been used to his wife's monologue, and talk, but not his own, had become a habit. But he would talk in his own slow way when his wife was abroad. He would not start, however, until Diego gave him an opening, for the young fellow might be wanting an after-meal snooze. Diego smiled, caught his uncle's half-glance and said:

"Our rough-digging is finished, Uncle?"

"Ay, is it! You did more than your share, Jamie. By May there'll be nothing to do but keep the dutch-hoe to the weeds."

"Do you have weeds?" He hadn't seen a weed lift a head.

"They come with the May sun. One bit weed that you let seed itself renews for seven years—that's the old saying. I warrant the weeds come."

"What do we do between now and May."

"Man, we're no' right started yet." He chuckled. "We plant and we sow even on, turning the soil again, and putting in the cow dung in the trenches that much and that much apart—a foot, two foot according to seeds and plants. This coming week we'll be trying our hand at a seed bed and another ingun bed, so Big Ellen tells me. You know? Taking off the top spit of soil, and spreading a thick layer of farmyard, and putting the fined soil back again, and stamping it down for the inguns. We are the great ones for inguns in this house."

"What do we plant in the seed bed?"

"If Big Ellen heard you! She is very proper in her language and another using it. She says you don't plant things in a seed bed."

"What?"

"You sow them." He chuckled again. "You sow seeds and plant plants. We'll do most of the planting, but we'll not be allowed to sow anything. She does that. She has the rotation at her finger-ends, and I can't mind two things about it. Seeds! Every dom' seed you ever heard tell of and a few only known to herself. There'll be the cabbage seed—two or three kinds—and the caulies, and the leeks and the first brocolis. We had the third brocolis for our meal the day, and the fourth will be in by May. You have to be gey careful with the rotation. If you sow beet seed before May it will bolt on you come August, and you'll not put down french beans till all danger of frost is by. I learned them two things anyway—by accident."

"A busy season before us?"

"Man, our backs'll be fair broke." He shut one eye cunningly. "When it gets past bearing I'll invent a job on the hill and be polite asking your help. An old trick of mine! But we'll have to be canny or she'll catch on, and nothing she'll say but handle the spade herself."

"But that we cannot permit?"

"Not to any great extent. She's a knowledgeable woman, and in gardening most of all. And that's a strange thing, mind you, for the Irish are no' great hands at the kitchen-garden. They grow taties and cabbages and inguns, lashins o' them, and dom the thing else. Losh! but mightn't they be right? Larry, my brother-in-law over in Cork, a grand chiel, argued it out for me. 'We select the best,' says he, 'and stick to them, and to hell with the trimmings! Good whisky, creamy porter, grass-fed butter, farmyard eggs, pasture-raised beef, mountain mutton, bacon raised on milk, and spuds, what more does a man want? Bacon and cabbage and a floury potato, there's the dish, or a steak with chips and fried inguns, and what is the rest but trimmings.' Big Ellen wouldn't agree with him at all. She's for the trimmings as well as the solids, and dang! but you get to like them—within reason, mind you. Shortly after the New Year up comes Wally the Post loaded with seed catalogues from Perth and Stirling and England itself, swearing. 'Guid be here, woman! wouldn't one be enough without breakin' my back in two places.' And after that her spare time before Lent she'll be making out her list long as your arm. Money it costs, but that's nothing. And this time my poor Wally gets a fair kink in his backbone hauling up two-three weighty parcels all the way from Craik Station, only he often waits till the Sunday and gets Peter Ross

the agent to give him a hand. There'll be the ordinar'
seed we all know—and a puckle flowers to please me—
but she's the rare one for experimenting with things
having outlandish foreign names like salsafy and scorzonera, and covy trouchuda, and kohl rabi and such,
and all the salads and flavourings. Later on in the
year she'll make up some rare dishes, tasty enough most
o' them, but one or two that'll make the eyes turn in
your head; but we'll have to eat them whatever, for
she'll stand over us, and she telling us that the foreign
people know better than us what is good for our insides.
She is the only man or woman in the Isles o' Britain
that will allow the foreigner has any gumption. Ay,
ay, man!"

He paused to relight his pipe. In length that was a
record speech for Uncle Hamish. Diego got in a word.

"Before Mass I heard the agent, Peter Ross, say he
had some plants for you?"

"Them'll be Copenhagen cabbages, solid boolies."
He glanced aside at the wag-at-the-wall. "He'll be
here with them in an hour's time, and we'll plant them
first thing the morn."

"We have visitors on Sunday?"

He nodded quickly, and a pleased gleam came from
under his heavy brows.

"Surely, surely. You saw Big Ellen at the baking
yestr'een. Sunday is her great day. I mind the old
times, and the bairns home, you couldn't stir in this
room of a Sunday evening, but on the sunny days the
young ones would have their tea down at the lochside—
in their bathing things. But not many are left now—
and no young ones scarcely. There'll be Peter Ross
and Wally the Post and Angus the Bobby and Donald
Gunn from the Strath and Long John and the Piper—
you met some o' them at the Kirk; and sometimes one
or two from the Big House, the Lady herself and Miss

Hett, and Young Affran when he's home. In the old days the young ones from the Lodge were here most Sundays, and weekdays as well."

He spoke of the old days as if a whole generation had passed. But the old days had been only three or four years ago, and the young ones were still young—if in life. These few years had made the world old and weary and insane, and opened a chasm that sundered everything but memory.

"Yon was a fine gentlemanly thing you did at the Kirk, Jamie," said his uncle, "kissing Mistress Ann's hand and arming her up the aisle."

"Only an old custom, Uncle."

"And gallant. Man! didna the Madam look extraordinar' fine in that lace shawl over the comb in her hair?"

"That was the Mass mantilla of the Basque women," Diego said, and did not add that she looked fine. She did and he knew it, and had a touch of nostalgia.

The three from Loch Beg had gone to Mass in a tub-cart behind the fifteen-hand pony. The pony had not been clipped, and was winter-shaggy from forelock to fetlock. Mass was at eleven, and they set out shortly after ten, between showers, and Diego wondered if they could do the four or five miles to Craik within the hour, for the pony's legs looked only fit for slow plodding. But Aunt Ellen, at the reins, jerked its head up, hit it a smart wallop across the rump with the rein's end, and the result nearly jerked Diego's head off, for the pony shot off as from a catapult, its leg-posts moving with remarkable celerity, and the clack of its hooves castanet-like.

They got to Craik a full half-hour before Mass-time, but they were not first on the ground by any means. The chapel yard, within its low stone wall, was the weekly meeting-place of the Glen, and the

McLeods' friends came round them and were introduced to Diego. Uncle Hamish said, "Jamie don't know the language to speak it," and his friends turned from their Gaelic to a correct English in their own idiom.

The yard and long, low, small-windowed building reminded one more of a sheepfold than a church. And, indeed, as a sheepfold it had been built in penal days. The laird, then a Skene and a Catholic, had built it, and when questioned by the established authority as to what he dared to build in a Papist glen he had replied, "I dare to build a sheepfold, would you dare to question my right to build it on my own ground?" And it was built, and became a fold for the lambs and sheep of the Church.

Five minutes before Mass-time the big open car from Lodge Affran drove up. It held the General and his lady, two female servants and an old gardener man. Diego, remembering his manners and the customs he was bred to, had the door open and a hand to the lady before the General could move. She touched his fingers as she stepped down, and he brought his lips to her hand, and again one finger twitched. The soldier pivoted out briskly, looked across at them with expressionless eyes, pouted his lower lip, and stumped away top-heavily.

"My husband, he is Presbyterian, Señor Diego," said the lady. "He departs now to a place set apart to pray to his own God, which is not ours, as I think."

"May I be permitted?" He tendered her his arm.

She put her black-gloved hand on his sleeve, and they went across the gravel and under the low lintel and up the narrow aisle side by side, her black mantilla over the green comb making her almost as tall as he was. She was slender and shapely in a long black dress under a long black cloak, and the dress gleamed with black sequins. The mantilla and the coral comb and one live red tendril of hair above the clear cream-tinted, black-eyed, heart-shaped face made her strange and exotic in that Highland glen. And she was beautiful; not bonny, not even lovely, just beautiful, which comes close to the tragical. Some days ago Diego did not think that, but now he knew. The aura of her personality enveloped him, and he hoped she did not feel his quickened pulse through his sleeve.

At each side of the aisle was a row of plain high-backed benches with knee-rests, and at the second or third outside the altar rails she pressed a finger on his arm, and he stepped aside while she bent knee and slipped far into her seat. That graceful movement of the hand invited him to kneel at her side. That was a democratic little chapel. Being a chapel of the Church that calls itself Universal it should be so, as chapels should be everywhere but are not, for in practice many chapels are the final refuge of caste and class and segregation.

A bell clanged and thudded above the wooden-lined roof, and its clang was mostly of iron. Heavy boots clumped on the strip of coir matting, and the seats about them filled up. The odour of peat and home-spun was heavy but not unpleasant. Diego's aunt came in and knelt at his side, her shoulder touching his; his uncle came at her other side, spread a red handkerchief on the knee-rest and extracted a large Roman Missal from his poacher's pocket. The chapel was not half-full though the Glen was two-thirds Catholic. There were old and elderly men, many of them in the uniform of the Home Guard, and old women and matrons with their children, but manhood and adolescent youth were entirely absent. That would be so in Diego's country too, but there it would be due to the indifference of men to this Sacrifice of Peace in a world in which it could not achieve peace. Here youth and manhood were out at war to win a peace that might be lasting and would owe little to the Churches.

A bell tinkled and two boy-servers in soutanes and surplices followed by an old vestmented priest came out on the altar under its wooden baldachin. Diego had served at Mass in his boyhood, and could follow the service, word and ritual, without the aid of a missal. He knelt a little forward, elbows on the arm-rest, clasped hands under chin, and mused on the universality of the rite that was the same here as in the pampas of Paraguay. He said no prayer. He was no longer sure that there was anyone to pray to, anyone to elevate one's soul to. The things he had seen done in Spain, by both sides, in a war that was probably the last of the religious wars and probably the last of religion in that country, had withered the source of prayer in him.

His uncle, not needing glasses, was slow turning his missal, his massive head moving from side to side in time with his eyes. His aunt was slowly trickling brown beads through her clean-boned fingers, and he could catch a whispered word sometimes. He could guess what her rosary was for. She was praying for the six children gone from her wing, and if her rosary solaced herself only it served its purpose. The woman at his other side did not use missal or rosary. She knelt upright, her mantilla pulled a little forward, and her quiet gloved hands one above the other on the arm-rest before her. She was intent on the celebrant, and, no doubt, following the rite with intelligence, but what prayers, if any, she was saying Diego could not imagine. If they were merely selfish prayers, as most prayers were, they did not matter to herself or any imaginable Deity. Did she pray for a lover? She had a husband and that prayer was forbidden. Did she pray for Spain? Any gods there be had forgotten Spain. Was she praying at all? Was she a quietist, body and mind immobile, and any currents for good in this place flowing through her? Could he send a current flowing, and what current would he send? Have that personal integrity that is above mere virtue. If you have not, it will not be given you through any prayer.

At the last Gospel, the priest turned round and spoke to his flock, his back against the small marble altar. He was an old man and frail, with plenty of white hair, an ascetic brow and a sensitive lower lip. His eyes moved placidly over his dear brethren, and for a few minutes he spoke in broad-vowelled Gaelic, and then turned to the soft sibilance of Highland English. He spoke of love, not the love of man but the love of God. He spoke so feelingly that Diego knew that he loved his God. He was perplexed at man's attitude to God. It passed his comprehension why men did not love God more, and so know the only real happiness. But his evident love of God was beyond Diego's comprehension. Woman might love God in her own way, but few men could know that mystic love. Man might bow down before God, might fear Him, might sacrifice to Him, might even create Him of necessity, but only one man in ten thousand could love him. Love as man knows it does not embrace a Deity in its compass, except for the mystic. The Highland priest was a mystic, but Diego was not, and the higher ecstasy was not for him. . .

II

Aunt Ellen came in from the outside, and her husband reached suddenly for the tongs and began building up the red peats. Diego, waking out of his muse, moved hastily to the turf-box and filled a crooked arm with dark brown sods.

"Talking, were you, Cuchulain?" she said. "You're learning language all of a sudden, and steps will be taken to save my kingdom. I heard you rumbling away, and my poor Don getting in a word edgewise till ye both fell asleep. Fill the kettle for me, now."

She was wearing her Sunday dress of black taffeta with white at the collar and cuffs. The dress had a flowing line that suited her splendid figure, and the red comb in her black hair suited the carven quality of her features. Her white Sunday apron was bunched in her hands, and she began picking out brown and white eggs and laying them in a row on a ledge of the dresser.

"Thanks be, the hens lay eggs on a Sunday, even and all if a cock crowed at Saint Peter. These are for another Peter—Peter Ross. No bachelor can keep hens unless an unnatural one. Remind me of them, Cuchulain. I'll have twelve to fourteen chickens come Wednesday. The birds are in the shell I saw through the keyhole. What were ye colloguin' about while I was out?"

"Salsafy," said Diego.

"And scorzonera. Ye'll know about them the next two weeks, and no excuse to go on the hill either. Were ye talking about my Spanish lady?"

"She was right handsome the day," said Uncle Hamish.

"In her quiet quare outlandish way. Kneeling there with her black mantilla above us all, and maybe praying too. Indeed, myself often wonders if she prays at all, but sure the whole quietness of her could be a prayer that she can be quiet for a small while—if she's let." She looked at Diego fierce-eyed. "That girl had a bad time, Don Diego. She won't say much or anything about it, but she was in jail before they made a refugee out of her."

Diego said nothing. He knew something about Spanish prisons, and if the young woman had been in one she would, indeed, not talk much about it. He would not talk to his aunt about it either. This wise aunt of his was warning him that he must not invade Ann Harper's hardly-won quiet, thereby hinting that she thought him capable of trying. Probably she thought that, like most of his generation, he had lost that thing that is inadequately called the moral sense—that inner sense of personal cleanness and integrity, the very essence of the ethic without which civilisation was beginning to perish.

"Here cometh Peter Ross," said Aunt Ellen, her hand holding aside the lace window-curtain. "And down goes his back to the rise of the brae! Put the kettle on the crane, Don boy."

III

They had their full share of visitors that Sunday afternoon. The Glen was again open after a hard winter, and all the friends of the house who could ride bicycles came up to look over and talk to the son of dead Mairi McLeod. They were mostly old or middle-aged and all men. It was only in high summer that the Glen matrons would come up on a weekday for a satisfying gossip with the Irishwoman.

These men visitors had the natural good manners of an older generation, if natural is the right word. The courtesy of these men was heired from an age when every Highlandman wore arms, when every man was prepared to resent to the letting of blood the belittling word unless spoken with a smile or a hidden affection. That is why their courtesy was so natural, and their insult so unmistakable. Courtesy will not again flourish till our mentors, the poets and politicians, wear the small-sword with a purpose.

There was a great spate of talk that afternoon, but there was very little discussion about the war. Men were tired of discussing the war, and it was only referred to in sharing the news of sons and grandsons doing their duty in every corner of the world after the manner of the breed. Local affairs were talked mostly, and with a good deal of wit and incidental narrative: the affairs of the Glen in business and love, gardening a little, sheep, cattle and deer at some length, and a side-talk of certain illegal practices that had to do with salmon and smuggled whisky. But ever the talk circled back round Diego. As the guest in this community of the Glen he must be brought in to all the talk, and his Irish aunt made sure that the family friends understood that he had been whole-heartedly embraced into the family.

Diego noted that shortly after each visitor arrived he disappeared into the seldom-used parlour at the other end of the passage, and presently reappeared clearing his throat subduedly. The spirits locked away in the parlour cupboard might have paid duty to the revenue—Angus Campbell the policeman, guardian of the law, adjourned to the holy-of-holies like the others—but Diego gathered that illicit whisky was not unknown in the Glen. The duty-paid article was entirely beyond the means of the people who in ancient days had discovered uisgebaugh and idealised it and used it continently. It was their very own native drink, and no government, home or foreign, had the right to deprive them of it by a penal duty and a penal enactment. So the people of the Glen held, and many of them of a puritan cast of mind.

And then Aunt Ellen gave them tea of her great munificence; not a sit-down tea, for there was no board-space on the table loaded with a richness of cakes and buns and scones and pastries and sandwiches. The men took their tea sitting about the fire, or leaning in the window-bay, or moving here and there to talk; and, like all men used to eating in the windy open, they ate competently, biting cleanly and dropping no crumbs; and, like all natural men, they spoke when the spirit moved them, not waiting on full or empty mouths. Aunt Ellen, talking very little for her, presided at an enormous brown teapot, and Uncle Hamish and Diego did any serving that was necessary.

"The cake in that dish is for you, Don Diego," pointed out Aunt Ellen. "'Tis light-made with a drop of cream for sandwich. Keep to it."

It was a huge cylinder of cake cut in sections. Plump old Peter Ross at Diego's shoulder bent over it.

"Fair play is a jewel, as you say yourself, Big Ellen. I had my eye on this comin' in the door."

"'Tis for a man hasn't a leather stomach, Rocky Ross."

"And haven't I to look after my own stomach six days of a week?"

"Please, Mr Ross!" Diego held the plate invitingly.

"Just the a'e piece. It wouldn't be good for you all of it. But as you say, two won't hurt me."

It was about mid-tea when the folk from Lodge Affran looked in. There were three of them, Mistress Ann, Henrietta, and young Charles; and they had walked down.

The lady was not in her Mass black; she and her niece wore their tartans and jumpers. The young man with the sullen face was in the trews of the Seaforths, and his well-cut tunic outlined his firm shoulders and depth of chest.

"A blessing on this house and on my people," said the Basque woman. "The food you eat will not curdle." She threw up her greeting arms in her fine free foreign gesture, went directly to Aunt Ellen, kissed her on the cheek, and reset the coral comb at a new angle. "That is how Señor Diego, who does not pray, has seen it worn. It is his present, yes, and the brooch. To-day, tall one, you are the queenly mother of sons, and I am jealous, for sons I crave; but the other things I crave you will give me: a cup of your brown tea of Ireland, one scone buttered, and the sandwich that is evanescent of the garlic, so that, alas! no man will want to kiss me."

Her gestures, her words, the sparkling sweep of her black eyes, showed that she was at her ease in this house amongst the men of the Glen. She went to where Uncle Hamish stood by the end-wall of the ingle, a plate in each hand, and put her hands caressingly on his sallow cheeks.

"My great father-bear is as ever guarding my sandwiches. You will not growl at me, Señor Bear?"

His deep-set eyes lit and half closed. He did not growl, he did not even speak, but if he were a cat he would be purring.

Young Henrietta whipped off her yellow silk slicker and dropped it carelessly in a corner, shouldering a big man called Long John familiarly out of her way. She took Aunt Ellen by the shoulders, drew herself up against her, and kissed her affectionately on the mouth.

"How goes it, milk-mother? I hear there is a lean bear sleeping in my very own bed?"

Aunt Ellen took the back of her hand from her mouth and looked at it.

"I wish to glory, imp, you'd be using the lipstick would stick its own place. It leaves a tell-tale stain all places—on a handkerchief sometimes."

"Goad be here!" exclaimed the startled girl. She lifted a dark curve of eyebrow whimsically in Diego's direction, and shook her flaxen hair.

"It simply cannot be done," she said.

"Your pardon, señorita?"

"Anything. The height of two peats, and let me pick only a single green gooseberry, she would take me out by the ear and show me where the gooseberry unsafe in my tum-tum had been hiding under a leaf. And I had devoured the skin too. One large tablespoon of syrup of senna. Wah!" She turned to her foster-mother. "Syrup of senna no good any more, Mother! What then?"

"My poor darling!" There was a queerly sad note in the affection of her tone. "There's your tea for you. Don Diego is feeding Donald Gunn your special jam-roll."

Diego was talking to Angus the policeman and Donald Gunn the head-stalker from Strath Dearg. Donald was a tall and wiry man of sixty, with a bush of grizzled dark hair above a lean, slit-chinned face. A quiet man and quiet-voiced. His culture was of a high order. He wrote songs in Gaelic, put music to them on his own fiddle, and read widely in two languages. He was talking to Diego about Cunninghame Graham, one of his idols. The last book that he had read was *The Conquistadors*, and he was questioning Diego about the Gauchos of Paraguay. The policeman hooded an eye at Diego and put Donald a sly question.

"Would there be any Conquistadors these days?"

"No—no! There'll be their half-bred descendants, the Gauchos that fought for Lopez against the rest of South America. The Gauchos——"

The old man's hand was hovering over the jam-roll when a hand with blood-red nails slipped under his.

"My choice, Caithness Gunn. You try the end bit. I know all about Gauchos. I met one recently."

"Ay would you, Miss Hett, if there was one about anywhere. They are daring men, I am told."

"You've said it. Flay you alive, stick you through the gizzard—or kiss you to death." She picked up another cylinder of jam-roll and moved away towards the window.

"She is a rare one, Miss Hett," said the policeman.

"She can use her tongue to hide her soundness, the little one," said Donald.

Both men had affection behind their words, and Diego was rather surprised at that. There were hundreds of young fillies like her playing at being three-year-olds in the King's Forces, but she was not dumb like some few of them.

Through the discord of sound that is the voices of men in number Diego caught the tone of Ann Harper's deep voice. His ears picked it out, and he wondered if his ears sought it. It was deeper in pitch than any voice there except one, and that was the growl of young Harper. Diego had been almost certain that the sullen young soldier would not be at home amongst the men of the Glen. Yet he was completely at home. He was naturally gruff, but he was sib somehow, and he was not condescending; and by the way the men spoke to him it was evident that he had an understood right amongst them, and indeed over them. He was grumbling frankly about incompetence in certain high places, but his grumble was a personal one, and he did not try to hide it. Simply, he had tried to get into Commando, and wanted to know why in blazes he had been rejected.

"Might be, you're ower young for the bloody work, Young Affran?" Peter Ross suggested.

"Young, you old fathead! Didn't they take Torry Campbell and he is a year younger?"

"But look at the size of Torry," said a thin bald man called Piobar Maol Tam, "and he a Campbell forbye, bred to the dirk from behind."

"Look here! I'm twenty-four and I'm not very big, but I'll throw any man in the Glen, young or old, barring Hamish here—or Long John."

"You could not throw me, young Carlos," cried Ann Harper.

"Bah!" said her young Carlos.

"You couldn't throw Larry McLeod, and he is a stone lighter," his sister told him.

"Did he ever throw me?"

"He did not, then," Larry's mother comforted him,

"ye tried each other only about a million times, and it was always a dog's fall."

He came across to Diego, refused an offer of cake, and pushed his empty cup among the plates. He was six inches shorter than the dark foreign man, and had to throw his head back to look up at him, but his gloomy eyes held, and that was a good sign.

"I understand you were in Commando, Captain?" His gruff voice held a touch of respect—or envy.

"Not able to hold it down," said Diego briefly.

"I believe you have to be tough?"

Diego could read the thought behind the words. A foreign clothes-pole could not stay the course, whilst himself—? He continued his thought in speech.

"Fit as a fiddle, a good shot with a short gun, fair to middling fencer. There's one fellow—a killer—don't know his name—they don't give names—he uses a rapier. And they turned me down! Why?" He couldn't leave his grievance alone.

"Did they not tell you?"

"Some bluff about not being able to distinguish colours."

"Red and green?"

"Only those two."

"But that is of importance. You must know your signals. The lives of your men depend on it."

"But I do not want to lead. I only want to go in and smite the devils." He lifted one black brow at Diego exactly like his sister. "You'll have a favourite weapon of your own—same as the rest?"

"We don't talk about it, do we?"

"Dam' well you don't, but we get a rumour——"

The young fellow's persistence irritated Diego. He must try and get him off the subject. He spoke slowly in a low voice.

"Colour-blindness is a fatal defect on Commando.

When volunteers are scarce in, say, ten years' time, you may get your chance and choose your weapon. Is it, then, too much I would ask of you?"

"Ask away."

"It is this. Will you, please, for the nine years you wait, try and be patient about it?"

He glared at Diego, and then some inner sense of humour came to the front. He grinned ruefully.

"All right! I am a dam' fool—and you might be one tough *hombre* yourself, and that's Spanish."

He turned on his heel and stumped away to where Ann Harper was talking to Uncle Hamish and Wally the Post.

"You adjourned the court for him," said the policeman, "but Young Affran is sound at bottom, and don't forget that, Captain."

"If I had my years back I'd do like him," said Donald Gunn. "The claymore would do me fine. I don't blame Young Affran at all."

All the men called him Young Affran. Diego was aware that the Gaels had a custom of addressing a man by the name of the land he owned or chiefed. It is a title of honour higher than any by a King's patent. General Harper owned Glen Affran but he was not called Affran; his strong-faced brother was invariably the Major; but young Charles was always Young Affran. He was the only male of the family who had grown up in the Glen, and in the ways of the Glen, and that probably explained his by-name.

IV

The evening was threatening some more rain, and none of the visitors stayed late. Donald Gunn, without a waterproof but with local tweeds oil-impregnated against showers, set off on his five or six mile tramp to

Strath Dearg; Peter Ross packed his eggs on his carrier, and set his face towards Craik Station fourteen miles away; the others followed shortly. Diego saw his aunt catch her husband's eye and gesture a head towards the outside. Diego followed him outside.

The Lodge people were in their raincoats when Hamish and Diego returned, and Ann Harper and Aunt Ellen were talking about Spanish cooking, especially the things that might be good for a Spanish man with a damaged interior. Diego noted that the accents of the two were not unlike, but of course the foreign woman would pick up the tone of the greatest talker in the Glen. He was doing it himself.

"What I'm thinking," said the big woman, "they miss the hot rod-iron they're used to—the chillies and garlic and that—and their stomachs grow soft on them."

"But no, Elene! There is the oil of the olive—that always. Later, when the things I need come out of the soil in this harshness, I will make for him what you do not see, a salad."

"Young woman, I made salads before you were born."

"But a salad! A niggard for spice, a spendthrift for oil, and a madman to mix them—that is the salad."

"Very well so!" She looked at her husband. "Cuchulain, when is the rain coming to stay?"

"The half-hour, five minutes with it—a slow drizzle."

"Then we run all the way," said the lady. "I run with great skill. One learns to run when one runs often for life. This young one, Henrietta, a butter ball would be, but I pursue her on the lawn until she falls down and weeps, and I sit on her where she will flatten. She kicks. Carlos now, he runs slowly, and you would not know he was in his own mind running to beat the brass band——"

"Put the lid on it, Ann!" growled Carlos. "Let us go."

"Sanny the pony is tackled outside," said Aunt Ellen. "The Don here will drive you up, but do not give him anything to eat in your house for another three days, mistress."

"Three days, yes! No, four! It is arranged. He is coming to his formal dinner on Thursday at seven of the clock in the evening in the best blue suit he wore at the Mass—not the dinner-jacket. The pony, it is not necessary, but you and my father-bear must be obeyed. Come, children! This house with God!"

Henrietta drove Sanny all the way to the Lodge. Diego expected a tearaway progress, but she drove considerately and well, easing the pony on the hills and keeping a firm rein against a stumble. On the first level stretch she clicked her tongue, jerked Sanny's head, applied rein's end to rump, and the pony shot off so briskly that Ann Harper, sitting opposite Diego, had to catch at his hands to keep her balance. The warm pressure of her fingers tingled through him.

One hand holding his, she leant across, her shoulder touching him, and lifted her fingers through Henrietta's fine flaxen hair.

"You will be patient with a horse and a man, my little one," she said, "for your power is coming upon you, and loveliness with it. And then—pouff! Look, Don Diego! is she not lovely?"

The girl shook her head away but not angrily.

"You dagoes will have your fun with us," she said.

"Be not angry, Don Diego," said Ann, pressing his fingers. "She did not call us dagoes with venom. Some day I will call a man—even you, Carlos—I call you *gringo*, thus, and you will feel alive but flayed; and another time I call you *gringo*, thus, and you will feel a small boy wanting a confection."

"And what the hell do you think I feel like now?" he asked her rudely.

She patted his shoulder as she would pat a hurt boy's shoulder, but he jerked it away roughly. Yes, he was rude enough to be a young man in love.

Presently, the pony coming down to a walk, he turned to his sister opposite and contemplated her. He grinned maliciously.

"Dammit, old thing!" he said. "I didn't notice it before, but the red-head is right. You are getting to be a good-looking young slut."

"You want a punch in the jaw, don't you?"

"Aiming that road. Why the devil do you make yourself up in that hellish way? You should try soap and water once in a while."

"Leave my little one alone, young barbarian!" the red-head chided. "She is of the cold northern race, and she learns slowly—but she learns."

"That's right, sister." He nodded at his sister and was bitter. "We are the stupid ones. These foreign people grow up too quickly for us—and we in the Highlands have never grown up, for we still have a foolish faith in fair proceedings. The foreigner gets us every time. We have been his prey for two centuries, for the Englishman in the glens is as foreign as Attila the Hun." He was satirical now. "And who runs the Glen these days? A Basque-Spaniard and a half-foreign Irishwoman——"

"Leave my foster-mother out of it," warned his sister.

The pony got a sudden wallop that was not all meant for itself, and went off full tilt. The Basque-Spaniard yelped, and again caught at Diego's hands. She smiled at him and put a finger to her lips.

"The foreigners in this Glen Affran—you and I, Señor Diego—we will be careful."

"The duty of foreigners always," said Diego.

Henrietta brought them round to the front of the Lodge with a final clippity-clop of hooves. The General and his brother the Major were in the sun-porch. The latter came out rather quickly for a lame man, but the General, after one lift of head, remained in his chair reading in a book. Diego was holding the lady's hand as she felt for the back step with a slender brogued foot when the soldier reached his side.

She sprang lightly to the ground and, still holding Diego's hand, placed the warm palm of the other on it. A friendly gesture, and something almost motherly in it.

"Thursday, you will remember?"

"The honour is not one I would forget. In my best blue suit at seven."

The Major looked from one to the other, and again there was speculation in his eyes.

"Is not Capitan Usted staying for supper, Ann?" he suggested.

"El Capitan is coming to dinner, it is arranged. Go with God, señor—and my thanks."

She released her hand before Diego could kiss it, and went up the two steps to the side-door, gave him her free friendly gesture, and went in to her husband who did not look up at her. The Major followed without another word or glance at Diego. That was either intentional rudeness or——!

"The old man has no dam' manners," said Young Affran, clumping solidly to the ground.

"One is not too old to take a lesson." Diego felt nettled.

The son at once bridled. "You try giving him one and see where it gets you," he said, and stumped away round the front of the house.

Henrietta, still holding the reins, was looking down at Diego.

"Fighting dogs!" she said witheringly. "Come in— come in! I'll hold Sanny till you get set. He some-times starts off and leaves you sitting when he feels a foot on the step. Not that I'd mind, only he might bust himself and the cart."

Diego slipped in opposite her. She handed him over the reins, and he waited for her to get out. She was in no hurry.

"You know about horses?" she enquired.

"A little."

"And a little about women too." She crinkled nose at him. "Pretty sleek you two foreigners in the Glen. Pretending not to see each other in mixed company—a sly glance, and your ears open, and your hands touching when you get a chance. I'm watching you."

Diego lifted the rein's end, and she hopped out nimbly through the open door. She gave him a small girl's pink tongue-tip.

"I'm watching you. Three Harpers needing a lesson, cousin Quixote!"

"Home, Sanny!" Diego said.

Sanny was in a hurry to get home to its six handfuls of oats, and Diego let it choose its own pace for all the four miles. The rain had set in steadily, but it was not much more than a heavy drizzle, and amongst the woods he scarcely felt it. The loch between the boles of the trees was dulled over, the ripples were like dark steel, and the glimpses of the hills showed the cloud curtain far down on their brows.

Was that girl right, he mused? Without being aware of it, was he taking too much interest in the Spanish lady? He had not spoken to her at all at the tea-party, but all the time he had been conscious of the live red hair held down by its green ribbon, of the smooth cream tint of her heart-shaped face, of her dark eyes under her dark brows; but what he remembered best was the fine expressive gesture of hand and head, and her touch that was electric. Hand or knee had sent a tingle through a man.

But he told himself he was only sentimentalising about her. She was of his blood, and he would like her to have strength in a strange land. That was all. He felt that she had the leading part in a drama that was working towards a climax in that stone house back there. A red-haired siren of a woman married to an old man as self-centred as an owl! And two other men in that house who would not play mouse to any owl! They were strong men and full-blooded. Her red hair would be alive for them, the depths of her voice, the way she gestured with her hands and her chin, the swing of her body as she sailed amongst the treacherous skin rugs. He could see her as he mused. And anything that happened in that house would depend entirely upon her. She held the three men in her hands, yet she was the beleaguered one. May her defences be strong in that house.

Outside the house—that was another matter. Outside the house, he himself might be concerned deeply. He would not consider how deeply. He only dimly wondered how deep the concern must bé to sap his own sense of personal integrity—that moral sense that was vanishing from the world, and that he had been lucky enough to heir from his Highland mother. An uncomfortable virtue to possess in a callous world, but the only thing worth while after all.

## CHAPTER VI

### LARRY McLEOD COMES HOME

I

It was Wednesday afternoon. Uncle Hamish was away in the heart of his deer-forest, and Diego was digging.

"I'm for a long take to-day," his uncle had said, and

remembered his honesty in time. "Not so long, but there's something we have to do I'd not care to bother you with."

"You'll be blatherin' in a minute," his wife had warned him. "Off you go, Cuchulain! Don Diego and I have to plant a row o' peas." But when he had gone she gave Diego more than an inkling of his errand. "Himself and Donald Gunn, with the Piper and Long John, will be at the back of Scurr Affran till early morning. I heard 'em at it on Sunday, and it'll take me two washings to get the reek out of Hamish's shirt."

Diego, jacket off, was preparing the ground for a longish row of peas. It looked a mile long to him, but was not more than twenty to thirty yards. The soil was in nice form after Sunday's rain and three days' warmth, and he was, not inadeptly, digging out a foot-deep trench, preparatory to forking in a layer of farmyard manure, and on top four inches of soil. Thereafter his aunt would space her seeds geometrically, and he would cover in.

His progress was neither fast nor steady, for, though he liked this business of digging, he had already adopted his uncle's method of delving for two minutes and resting one—or more. But still, the trench was lengthening out in front of him, the April sun warm on the back of his neck, the April air cooling his brow, and his mind pleasantly vacant of thought. He had already noticed that in digging one does not day-dream much, which might imply that man should not spend much of his waking time in servile work.

He did not hear his aunt coming up behind. Usually she announced her approach from the steps of the door, but here she was at his side and silent.

"Losh be here, woman!" He used his uncle's very growl. "I'll not be ready for the seed this hour."

"Diego!" she said, in such a low voice that he turned to her with a quick startle. She was standing erect, one

124

hand behind her neck as if to hold her head steady, and she was looking down the Glen road. There a man was coming on a bicycle as fast as the brae would let him.

"It is Wally the Post, Don."

"With letters for us."

"To-morrow is post day," she said quietly.

"Oh!" he said, and drove the spade savagely into the soil. This woman had four sons at the war, and a postman coming a day early——

"There is the Lodge——"

"He is coming here," she said with certainty.

"But, Aunt, any—any news would be phoned up."

"That I know, but you see, Don, I am not very brave in the bit. Wait! Wally will give us a sign."

Wally did. He pulled off his peaked cap and waved it round his head, and his high-pitched yell had a gay yip-yip at the end.

"Good man yourself, Wally!" she whispered, and sighed deeply. Her firm cheek-bones had blenched, and she put a hand towards Diego. He took her arm firmly, and gave her the prop of his shoulder.

"I'm not brave at all, boy, but don't tell Hamish on me." Her organ of a voice had a harshness in it for the first time. "I keep on steeling myself. I do be telling myself morning and night that with four sons I cannot expect to keep all or any of them. I'm of the soft Irish."

"Wo—wo—wo!" He was trying her own Irish on her. "We foreign people are at one—steel above and fire below, and a bit of foolish tenderness added to the female woman."

"Whose arm is trembling—or is it both of them?"

"Let us walk." They went arm-in-arm towards the wicket.

"'Tis not a bad thing to have a quiet foreign man about the place," said his aunt, rubbing one hand at her stiffened cheeks.

Wally was within word-reach now. He had a good bellow for a small man.

"'T's all right, B—Ellen. A letter only."

They met him at the wicket. He let his red bicycle drop carelessly, drew a long breath, and expelled it through his moustache.

"No sense at all! not the longest day I live," he grumbled. "To-morrow would do as well." He fumbled in his pocket. "The letter—'tis from Larr—it was post-marked six days ago. You'll see for yourself. Last letter you had he mentioned a bit furlough—and look at the postmark, will you, and at that word to me in the corner? 'At once, please, Mr Carpenter.' I'm no carpenter, only sometimes he'll call me 'Walrus,' and I'm no' that either. Losh! he might walk in sudden on you and the house ate empty by Hamish and the Don here."

Aunt Ellen took the envelope and glanced at it.

"Ay! it's from Larry. I'm thankful to you, Wally. You'll come in and have a dram." Her tongue was still slow.

"Ay, will I! But what's keepin' you?" He nodded at the letter. "Gi'e us your bit news."

She opened her letter, and Diego could see that it contained only one sheet with a few pencilled lines; but there were enough to restore her spirits.

"Larr sure enough! What day is it, Wally?"

"Wednesday in April, what else?"

"Fathead! I know it's Wednesday. The date I mean? He'll be the twenty-ninth."

"And that's the very day that's in it," cried Wally. "Didn't I know it? And a good thing for me I left the peats to bring that up—it came the mornin' mail. The twenty-ninth? That's the day I'm tellin' you." He extracted a big silver watch from a tight chamois bag. "He'll be arriving at Craik Station an hour from now. Are you hearing me?"

"That train is always late," Diego said.

"The coal is comin' better. Right on the crack o' time—not more than an hour late, and I'm allowing for that."

Aunt Ellen was looking at her letter and tapping one finger on her brow.

"Hamish is on the hill," she said.

"Ay! he was to meet the Piper and Long John at the Slap." Wally knew. "But I'll have him here for you after the fall o' dark. Look now! I'll be having that dram, and after—if it's no' too small—I'll push off for the station and hold Larr till the Don here——"

"Of course!" cried the Don. "I go down with Sanny." And he ran for the corner of the house. As he went he heard his aunt's voice lifted resonantly.

"Mother o' God! What have I in the house for a hungry man? Come on in, Wally, and don't be wasting my time." And from the stable, where he was getting the crupper over the pony's tail and avoiding its heels, her voice from within the house still reached him, and after a time lifted and faded away and stopped; and he gathered that, having poured Wally's dram down his throat, she had pushed him out of doors. Next moment her voice was outside the stable door.

"Is it making the harness you are? Kick Sanny in the ribs if he's holding his breath against the bellyband."

Diego dragged the pony out by main force, and his aunt had the tub-cart out of its shed and the shafts lifted. She talked over the straddle as she buckled the traces.

"Like Wattletoes you have plenty of time, but if you don't hurry up you'll be late. Put it on the third link. You'll know your cousin Larr when you see him—a mixture of myself and Hamish and a shake of yourself as well."

"Not possible, Aunt."

"A miracle, but you'll see. I'll get the gate open."

She had the gate open and Diego was about to lead the pony through when the purr of a motor came over the brae from the lochside.

"Hold everything!" Aunt Ellen was out on the centre of the road, hand already lifted.

## II

The open car came over the top and slid smoothly down the slope. Henrietta, at the wheel, was alone in it. Aunt Ellen moved clear and the car halted at her side, the wheels grating on the sandy gravel.

"Maharajah Harper's Juggernaut. Get down in front, Begum!"

"You're for the station, darling?"

"Drawer of water—my week. No lifts to myrmidons! Who is it?"

"Lassie, my brain is addled. Hold on a minute." She swept across to Diego and pulled his hand away from the bit. "Don't keep the girl waiting—I'll untackle Sanny. Tell her on the road down. The both of them suckled me at the one time. Off you go!"

Diego rounded the bonnet, and the girl had the door open. She shook her head at him solemnly.

"Kicked out already, and fleeing from wrath?"

He did not reply until she had the car going smoothly on the level.

"Your foster-brother is arriving this evening—the one you might marry."

"Larry McLeod?" Her gloved hands were steady on the wheel but her foot slackened for a moment on the accelerator.

"Just heard a few minutes ago. That is the postman ahead of us."

"Gosh! I haven't seen Larr for two years. He'll be growed up."

"And his foster-sister?"

"No one to love her for all her wiles. Larr won't like the looks of me." There was a trace of seriousness in her voice. "A serious-minded, composed sort of young customer, you could never guess what he would be saying till he opened his mouth."

"He has a sister."

"And he's the sort of brother who won't allow any dam' dago to be too familiar with her."

"An admirable brother."

This modern girl—like most modern girls—was too easy to talk to. There was no mystery about her to make men interested in anything more than flippant or, indeed, serious flirtation. He felt as familiar towards her as if he had known her for months.

"Did you ever try aloofness—as a weapon?" he asked her out of his thoughts.

"Setting yourself up as a special mentor to the dumb Harpers? You try a lesson on Spanish Ann."

"Shut up!" He poked a thumb in her corsetless ribs, and the car swerved a foot.

"Thug!" Then she laughed. "I can always touch you."

They overtook Wally the Post in a mile, slipped by and stopped. The girl gestured a hand, and Wally, apparently not for the first time, obeyed the gesture by climbing into the back seat and lifting his old cycle to rest on the running-board. The car moved on.

"Manalive, Miss Hett! You're the great one. I'll no' need to pound it down to the station. Larr is coming home—you heard?"

"Yep. I haven't seen him for two years, Wally."

"And that'll make it two years he hasn't seen you as well."

"You are no philosopher, William McKenzie," she told him in the accent of the schools. "Physical time and physiological time do not always correspond. In two years I have grown old, and Larry—I think of him as a mere boy."

"Losh!" said Wally. "But, whatever, he'll get the surprise of his life in about an hour's time. A young bit filly-foal two years ago, the hair about her eyes, and her face washed yesterday, anyway——"

"And look at the jade now!"

"I can't see where I am. You look for me, Mr Usted. Yesterday night it was, over in Long John's smithy, we were talking of the bonniest lass in the Glen——"

"Not many in the Glen, Lothario?"

"Ever in the Glen—since Mairi McLeod left it, God rest her. I'll not make your ears red, Miss Hett, by namin' our choice."

"Throw him overboard for me, Don Diego."

Diego sat forward, his back to the door, and looked at the profile of the bonniest girl ever. This blasé young modern could flush to the flattery of an old postman. But she was bonny beyond any doubt, and her golden-grey eye was lustrous. She felt his eyes on her, and the colour reached her brow.

"Blast you!" she said venomously. "Look where I'm going or I'll ditch you."

Diego chuckled, but looked ahead. Yet she did not dislike the subject Wally was on, for she spoke over her shoulder.

"Say, Father Paris, did you not consider a certain ginger-haired lady up by?"

"Oh! she's a marrit woman, and we don't consider them."

"Consider that, Señor Don Juan Diego—while you still have time."

"It is a Spanish custom," said Diego. Or it was. Until very recently, married women of Spanish blood hid the glory of their hair and kept their eyes downcast in public places, only one step removed from the days of the

130

purdah that the Moorish women brought into Spain. But Ann Harper, the Basque, was not like that. She wore a mantilla at Mass as ordained, but ordinarily she did not hide her hair or her eyes or the long curves of her sex.

The car slowed. "Here's your post offeece, Wally. Get out! Making love to me in public, a bad example to foreigners."

"He's welcome to it," said Wally.

They got to the station in good time and were warmly greeted by stout old Peter Ross. Any visitor was welcome to Peter. Craik was one of the loneliest stations in the Highlands, with only two trains a day each way and the nearest inhabited house eight miles off. And there Peter Ross lived alone, putting through his few trains and tilling his garden patch on the sunny side of the station building. But though living alone he gathered news of all the Glen and of all the stations up and down the line from Ross to Caithness.

"She's on time the day, within the half-hour—left Cairdow two minutes ago," he boasted. "Anyone coming, Miss Hett?"

"Only Larry McLeod, Peter."

"Great day, and greater news! Larry himself! There was talk of it. That's the boy, your cousin, Mr Usted. Butter wouldn't melt in his mouth, you'd think, till he opened it, and there was the big woman's voice, and the old fellow's humour and it hidden. Many's the time himself and Young Affran and a third I'll no' name put the Glen on a buzz. Do you mind the day——?"

"I am now grown up, please, Mr Ross."

"And a neat handful of young lady, praise the Lord, and an astonishment to Larry I wouldn't be surprised. Hamish didn't come down? Larr's the apple of his eye."

"He is on the hill——" began Diego, but Henrietta knew more about it.

"The worm developed a leak, Peter, and Long John is off to solder it."

"Time for him, and myself getting Young Affran to lift a yard of copper pipe out of his army stores. I warned Hamish a year past about that weak spot, and the last time we lost two gallons in the worm tub, and it the second run as well. So we used it to supple the bag of Piobar Maol Tam's pipes."

After that Peter set out to get and give the news, directly and indirectly, after the manner of his breed. In time he remarked in a tone that was a half-query:

"Ewan McInnes might be on the train too, I'm thinking," and explained to Diego. "Ewan is the law-agent and Factor for the Estate, Mr Usted."

"He is coming to-morrow morning, Peter," the girl told him. "Dirty work at the cross-roads."

"I heard a whisper o' that, Miss Hett."

"And the whisper you heard was that my damned old uncle wants Ewan to break the entail and clear all the Harpers out of the Glen."

"Ewan won't like that—he's a good Glen man himself—and it'll be a bad day when Young Affran and yourself has to leave Affran——"

"We might cut the old devil's throat first." She said that as if she meant it.

"We might—we might," agreed Peter equally, "but there's less bloodier ways to my mind."

A long whistle came shrilling up the line, and not so far away, round a curve, a white spurt of steam feathered up into the air. It kept on feathering.

"Forgi'e us our sins!" cried Peter on the jump. "Here, if I didn't forget to open the line! I'll get into the book for this."

He hastened at a waddle towards the miniature signal cabin and got busy with his levers. The open signal went down with a jerk, and the angry whistling died away with a final whine of protest.    Peter came out wiping his brow.

"That minds me o' the time we had the pother that stirred the whole line from Inverness to Lybster.   Them were the right busy days when I had a porter and a ticket-clerk—eight trains a day, four stopping reg'lar and two to set down and pick up.   It was never rightly known, but generally held that a certain young lady lifted the key and kept the train outside for eight minutes."

"She had to.   Charlie had a puncture two miles out of Craik, and while Larr and he repaired it they sent me down to hold the train—said a girl wouldn't get more than ten days for it.   We had all our money, two pounds, on Larr to win the half-mile at Helmsdale Games.   He did too, thanks to me, and I only got five bob for my share."

"It near cost me my job," said Peter.    "Dod Torrie was moved to Halkirk over it, poor fellow, and lost a girl he had up by.   Here she comes!   The carriages will be at the front."

"Go on up and look him over for yourself," Henrietta said to Diego, and walked down the platform.

III

It was an unusually long train, but there were only three passenger coaches; the rest of it was made up of heaped coal-trucks and closed waggons of military stores. The engine-driver, an irate-faced man, was leaning out of his cab bellowing at Peter and wanting to know where the air raid was.   Peter gave him a thumb over shoulder and waddled down the platform to face the Charybdis of the guard.

As Diego walked up the platform the coaches slipped ahead.  A dark young man was leaning out of a window, his glance passing by Diego to where a tall slip of a girl was moving down towards the guard's van. Before the train stopped the young man leaped down, dragged a duffel bag on to the platform, and came striding towards Diego. He was in the uniform of the Royal Air Force, and it fitted him like a glove. As the old master-novelists would put it, he was slightly above middle height, slenderly built, but of perfect proportions. He moved from the hips, and with that roll of shoulder that hill-men or seamen have, and the way he carried his hands showed a restrained inner virility. Diego knew at once, he did not know why, that he was the son of Hamish McLeod and Ellen Honora McCarthy.

He would have passed by if Diego had not stepped in front, and then he stopped with a quickness of control that poised him on the balls of his feet.

"You are Flight-Lieutenant Larry McLeod?"

He nodded, and concentrated dark and serious eyes on Diego.

"Seven pillars o' wisdom! I know who you are too." His eyes crinkled. "But dammit! I've seen you before on a peaceful occasion—one long black devil."

Diego was long and black but no devil, and he had never met or seen Larry McLeod. He shook his head.

"Silence is golden," Larry said, "but I never forget a face, as the man said. I was within ten strokes of you."

His voice was his Irish mother's, a little deeper and slower. The gravity of his face was his father's, but he was not sallow like his father. He was finely dusky, and healthy colour showed through the dusk. And his eyes were not black but brown with green tints. A dark handsome grave youth, whose head in bronze would be the head of a Firbolg.

"Let us make sure," he said, and touched a finger on Diego's breast. "Whisper! The dawn of an autumn morning, and the Channel choppy between Falmouth and Ushant. A push of ye were over the water and gave

134

the German men hell about Paimpot, and they gave it straight back with the lid off. What were left got away in a launch, and in the dawn a Stuka blew ye out of the water—simply. Six or seven men in a collapsible, and the Stuka raking them with a machine-gun, some of them dead and all of them wounded, and a long black devil working a couple of shattered oars, a wisp of a blade across his thighs and his teeth showing. I brought the bus down on the Stuka's tail sort of unbeknownst and dropped her fair across your bows. Three—no, four—four of them tried to take you by boarding, and I pancaked, my near wing almost on your gunwale. There was no need. The long black fellow took the four, one after the other, and not a motion wasted. So we gave the Stuka a burst or two to make sure, got into the air again to dog-fight, and sent a boat out from Falmouth to pick you up. It did. I didn't know at the time that the swordsman was my cousin James—Jimmy I call him. You are Jimmy Usted, aren't you?"

"I am, Larry."

"Give me a hold of your hand, then."

Their hands met, held loosely for a moment, then contacted as in an electric shock, and dropped apart. The green eyes lit.

"That's fine, cousin! How are they all up by?"

"Well—very well. Your letter came not the hour ago. Uncle Hamish was on the hill, and your mother, my aunt, is making her very high tea. I am here eight days."

"A pleasant surprise. Must have missed Mother's last letter. Say, Jimmy, there's a long-legged shemale away down there with Peter Ross?"

"Oh! some modern patrician," Diego said inspiredly. He was not going to spoil any surprise there might be.

"Just so! She has a feature or two. I must shake a paw with Peader." With his mother's warm impulsive-ness he hooked Diego around by the arm and the two went down the platform side by side.

Henrietta saw them coming and walked to meet them. She was no longer hoyden. She was a tall young gentlewoman, and prouder than Lucifer. There was not a stiff bone in her long body, and yet she walked with that touch of stiff teeter that shows infinite conceit in oneself. Her hair lay down in shining linten folds; her head was thrown back and her chin pointed at them; and she looked along her straight nose through hooded insolent golden eyes. And Diego noted for the first time that her make-up was different. She had not used any rouge, and the powder she must have used did not show on the faintly brown matt of her skin. Her mouth was no longer orange but defined delicately in a colour just one shade brighter than natural.

"Christ alive!" Diego heard his cousin whisper. "She sold herself to the devil in the King's Forces."

She stopped in a half-weary slouch in front of them, and her voice was weary with the mere necessity of being polite for a moment.

"Mr Laurence McLeod, I presume? How do you do?" She reached him her hand shoulder-high with a tired down-droop to it.

Larry McLeod just fell. He knew in his heart that this was pure fake, and possibly an inner self was only playing the game out. Yet he was not sure. His mouth was open a little, and he yielded her his hand in a helpless sort of way. And having got his hand, she jerked him forward, clasped him firmly about the shoulders, and kissed him firmly on the mouth. Diego saw his shoulders sag at that warm kiss. For the moment the youth was putty in her hands. She leant her head back and looked at him, rubbed her forefinger along his lips and examined it, and spoke to Diego over his shoulder.

"You will note for future use, señor, that my new war-paint sticks its own place." She shoved Larry away. "Does your back hairs tingle, Mr McLeod?"

"Lord'llmighty!" said Mr McLeod.

The girl swung him to her side. Diego fell in at her other side, and the three went down the platform to where Peter Ross and the guard were still altercating. Larry recovered himself.

"Oh lor'! to think of Hett Harper taking me like a new-born babe!" He turned a serious face to his cousin. "'Some modern patrician,' and there was the way paved for my downfall. Fair enough! War is now declared." He felt his mouth. "No dam' girl, sister or not, can shove my front teeth down my neck."

She shook his arm and bubbled laughter. "Oh, Larr! if you could only have seen yourself, your jaw hanging and your eyes bunging! Wait till I tell Mother. But pax-pax! I said it first. Pax for the day."

"Oh, very well—just to-day, rip."

Diego felt that his cousin was touched more than a brother should be. In his own mind he said, *You do not need any more lessons, my lady. You play as foul as any woman.*

Peter Ross and the guard had about finished their exchanges. The guard had certainly a grievance and wanted the world to know it. He knew Henrietta of old and spread his hands at her.

"I dinna ken wha to blame, but I was held for ten minutes, the brakes on on an up-grade—for no reason at all." He hit the air. "The wan day I was on time within the half-hoor and money on it. Guidsakes! Blast it a'!"

"And what's keeping you now, Robber Tait?" enquired Henrietta coldly.

"Ay! what's keepin' him now?" yelled Peter. "I opened the line for him as soon as he was in. Tak' your dom' train out o' my station, Robbie!"

The guard saw that he was outnumbered. He signalled

with his flag, using great restraint, mounted into his van with dignity, jerked the door shut savagely, and exploded his head through the open window, only to encounter a final broadside from Peter.

"Put me in the book, will you? A' right! I'll grease the track for you on the Lairg Drum, an' take my pension." He lowered his voice a little. "An' what'll you do then, Robbie, wanting them two bit parcels a week down from Loch Beg?"

The train moved, and the guard, not deigning to shout, made a dramatic gesture of eternal farewell.

"The victory remains with the aborigines," said Henrietta.

"My last argument was maybe no' fair, but it made mud of him," boasted Peter.

He turned round, squattered at Larry and pumped his hand with energy.

"Ay, Larr lad! You're welcome home. The same old Larr! Ay, man! but you're growin'. Any day now and you'll be shavin'."

"More than that, Peter. I left her down the line."

"Who?"

"The wife."

Peter examined Larry's grave face.

"Guid be here! You're no' marrit?"

"No. I mean *your* wife."

"Dom! Aughtn't I to know by this time." He sniggered reminiscently. "There was only a'e woman that near hooked me—when I was a shunter at Forres. She marrit on a spirit grocer after an' had six bairns by him."

"That's the one, Peter. The grocer is dead on her, and she says she was as nearly yours as makes no matter; and judging by one of the bairns—but hush! there are ladies present. These your parcels, Hett? Let us go. I want to see my mother."

138

They went up the Glen, Larry in the back seat. He had dumped his duffel bag in there and followed it, though Diego had intended him to sit at his foster-sister's side. He leant forward, his head over the back-rest, and one hand softly lifting through the girl's fine hair.

"Stop tickling, Larr!" But she did not shake her head away.

"Nice hirsute ornament!" He sniffed at it. "You've taken to washing and bath salts. Mind if I put a question to you?"

"I'm not confessing to anything."

"Think this one over. Could you see your way to becoming a fair to middling Roman—a Catholic, I mean?"

"Why not? Don't mind going to hell your way."

"Great! You see, my fond parents wouldn't want me to wed a heretic."

He was probably joking, but Diego could not tell that from his voice. Rather did he get the impression that Larry was touching some small secret chord. The girl threw her head back against his hand.

"I've a good mind to take you on the hop, mister, but I'll play fair for once. To-morrow evening I'll give you a chance to get smitten where you live."

"But I am now, dammit!"

"No. To-morrow evening you are coming to dinner with the Don here. You'll fall for her all right. They all do. Charlie and his officer boys, and my old man, and I do believe that the old owl has tumbled right off his perch."

"You are not referring to the old owl's wife?"

"I am."

"But, nowadays, no man loves his own wife. She is

after my time, but Big Ellen says she's nice, and she means nice."

"Nice your grandmother! Wait till you see her. You know, I tried to put my hooks into the dago here, but he fell for her even before he kissed me."

"I gathered there was a kiss—or two," he said calmly.

"One only," Diego turned to him. That kiss would keep on embarrassing him. "I had to—against her will."

"Don't worry, Jimmy!" Larry nodded. "She is playing fair and not giving me the false impression."

"I will be careful, and not again kiss her," Diego said.

"You beast! And I trying out fast colours."

"You will not kiss her again?" Larry lifted a curious eyebrow.

"No. For myself, I have found out in the words of my aunt that she is nice."

"Oh!" said Henrietta, and leant forward over the wheel to hide the flush.

"Mind you," said Larry in a rich brogue, "that is one damn'd quare reason for not kissing a purty girl. My poor, pitiful old sister!"

"Blast ye both!" said the sister, and sent the car round the curve on screeching tyres.

"My hopes are blasted, sure enough. But there's drink still." Larry threw himself back on the seat and lifted a good baritone voice in an old drinking chanty, but Diego felt that there was something behind the song that was forlorn.

> "A noggin of whisky, a rouser of rum,
>     A jug of brown ale, and again
> A noggin of whisky, a rouser of rum,
>     And laugh I at Cupid and men.
>                 Kissing men!
>     And laugh I with Bacchus again."

He sat forward and put a hand lightly on her shoulder, first saying, as to a skittish filly:

"Wo, mare! Good sister, do I gather that you do not appreciate your Aunt-out-of-Spain for more reasons than mere feminine egotism?"

"Use language, wouldn't you? You're wrong. I'd cut her throat most days, and yet, I dunno. She can get me too—any time she wants to. The kid had a hell of a time—in Spain—and things are not so easy for a foreign woman in Lodge Affran. But she is game. She is—she is—what is she, Spanish man?"

"Debonair."

"Good for you! But not always. Sometimes she has to let off steam. Lets herself go and tells us what she thinks of us cold-hearted, hidden-thoughted, second-thoughted, day-before-yesterday, day-after-to-morrow, God-fearing, God-hating, God-unloving northern bastards. If she had a gun in her hand or a knife—bang! snick! And the old owl laps it up—loves to have her in a tear that hurts her—thinks she's a masochist. Good word! And when her very adequate English fails her she switches to Basque, and it sounds exactly like first-class cussing in Gaelic. So I curse her back in Gaelic, and then we both laugh. And after that she apologises to the owl—not to us—and expresses her gratitude for what he did for her over the border. But, you know, at the back of her gratitude you sense a regret that he did not leave her to the chances of fate—or love. For, of course, she does not love him. Can you explain her to us, grandson of Spain?"

"That is a long speech," said Diego. "It is not difficult to understand her, but you make her complex. She is simple. She is a Basque, and she would be the mother of sons. Give her five or ten children——"

"You will not—not honest. The owl is an empty quiver, three times proven, if you know what I mean."

"You shameless hussy!" expostulated her foster-brother.

"Suppose she fell in love, Don—with Charles or my father or with you?"

"The Basques have a high moral sense."

Larry laughed. "And don't Dan Cupid and the devil know that that is the only sense worth tampering with. I guess I'll stay plain brother till day-after-to-morrow."

"And thereafter?"

He smoothed her hair very softly.

"Girl dear, I suffer from the serious disadvantage of having had to fight with you in my extreme youth for the better pap."

"Your mouth should be cleaner, then."

"Same to you! And you won every time. Hello! there's Wally the Post giving us a wave. Pull up, Hett?"

"No. Our mother is waiting. You wave back."

The car went through the township in a streak, hens getting out from under, for even in the Highlands hens no longer sacrifice themselves under motor wheels. Larry stood up in the car, waving to Wally and other friends, and pointing down at his abductor. A faint cheer strung out behind.

"They'll think I'm a Major-General and proud accordin'," he said.

In another quarter-hour they came honking to the gate of Loch Beg Bothy. Aunt Ellen came sailing down the path, and her son vaulted the car door. Back turned, Diego slowly pulled the duffel bag to the ground.

"Larr was not in his best form somehow," said his foster-sister. "He is a shy boy really, and you cramped his style."

"Someone did. You are coming in?"

"Not now. Bring Larry up to-morrow evening. Ann will ring."

The car moved off. Larry yelled after it, but she lifted an arm and kept going. Diego picked up the bag and went through the wicket gate. Aunt Ellen was holding her son by the shoulders and running her fierce eyes over him. She was taller than he was.

"You've grown half an inch and dam' the more, but you're tall enough. Your last suit will fit you fine. You are the spitten image of my brother Garret that I had to save the life of by marrying your da. Come on in now, the two of ye. I have the tay drawn. Hamish will be late on the hill."

"And the deil's awa' wi' the exciseman! Say, old 'umman, what have you been doing to Hett? She's no longer my sister."

"She's growed up—this week."

"I started making love to her, but she put me off with a promise of a forbidden apple."

"You'll have no time for biting it, childeen."

"Won't I? You haven't heard my news. Listen! This is not a furlough in the heart and heat o' the day, but a transfer I wangled to Tain over the hill there. And there I'll be till the apples are ripe—or till we make the onfall. Go on! be surprised for once."

"To be sure—though, mind you, in your last letter you wondered how the tyres of your old bike were standing up, and I wondered what that meant."

"No, you're not surprised, but I was, and pleasantly, to find cousin Jimmy here."

"You'll be company for each other." She turned on the step of the door and looked over her son's head at Diego. She spoke out of some deep thought of her own. "Wouldn't you be thinking that this is a dead-and-alive sort of place; a lonely lovely place, a place where life would be water in a ditch, a small quiet biteen of a hollow in the hills where life has to be lived like the grass and the heather and the water flowing its own level? But, all the same, it is in this place and places like it that life sets its problem in nakedness, and has it worked out nakedly and without distractions. It is this place where life really is. Remember that, the two of ye; and remembering it, remember another thing as well. The Usted and the McLeod and the McCarthy are a proud people. Remember who ye are!"

She turned and entered the house, and her son looked gravely at his cousin. "That's a warning, Jimmy," he said. "It is good to be home."

"You have one."

"It is yours too. Sure, some day we might make a home of our own, if it is so ordained. We'll remember who we are."

# CHAPTER VII

## DINNER AT LODGE AFFRAN

I

Larry McLeod and Diego walked up to Lodge Affran for dinner. They would not take the pony, for Larry wanted to feel the ground under his feet, but Diego had already noted that his cousin, liking the feel of the ground, did not care to delve in it. That afternoon Diego had planted plants and sown seeds, but Larry had mostly sat on a stone and smoked one of his father's new pipes; and his mother had come out and stood above him, her cool fingers running through his crisp dark hair, whereat he had purred.

Larry took a cased trout-rod for walking-stick, and they started at an easy stroll, giving themselves two hours for the four miles. Neither of them were spate talkers and, so, could be companionably silent.

It was a fine still evening after a sunny day at the very end of April, and the sun, still above the western pass, made the oval of the loch like a golden floor. Where the trees allowed a prospect, Larry's hooded flying-man's eyes sought the snow-streaked peaks above the rim of the cliff.

"That's Carn Seilig, the cairn of the hunt, lording it over there," he pointed out. "When we were boys, Young Affran and I promised ourselves to put a stone on the cairn of every peak above three thousand feet north of Glen Mor. I do not want to do that now." His voice grew a little wistful. "All I would be wanting now is a quiet place in this glen, and I am not likely to get it from our host the General, who, however, is not eternal. We used have foolish dreams, Young Affran and myself." Dreams a flying-man might have, and after—Nothingness.

"Your friend, Young Affran, went up this afternoon when you were across the water," Diego told him.

"Fine! We'll have a good chew of the rag."

In time they came to the sudden end of the wood, and looked down and across to the ugly stone house. There were several people on the lawn, and Larry, even at that distance, had no difficulty in recognising all of them.

"The Major and Hett and Young Affran—and the General and his Factor, Ewan McInnes, under the cyprus tree. A great spud, old Ewan!"

They went down the slope, through the open gates, and across the grass. The lawn had got its first mowing, and the air carried a fine faint perfume of cut grass after a day of sun. Beds of tulips blazed.

Someone saw the two coming. Young Affran lifted his voice into a clan skirl, and came hurrying across the lawn on short sturdy legs. Larry held the trout-rod out to Diego.

"Hold that, cousin! I want to find out what the years have done to this fellow. An old custom of ours."

He leaped into the air and landed softly as a cat on the balls of his feet, took two or three dancing side-steps, and went stealthily forward on his toes, his shoulders crouched and his arms wide and low. Young Affran, who was in mufti, stopped short a dozen paces away, and thrust both palms forward urgently.

"No, Larr, no! Damn it all, no!" he appealed anguishedly. "A new flannel bags and a Conon jacket— thirty-six coupons! Stop it, blast you!"

"One mouthful of grass, brother," wheedled Larry. "One touch o' Mother Earth and Antaeus-like you rise."

"But thirty-six bloody coupons, Larr? Have a heart and God love you."

"Just the a'e mouthful, my darling. Hercules is my name."

"Oh, hell!" The Conon jacket went flying. "All right, you tough! I'll make you eat mud."

The two forgot the world about them. Crouching, they circled each other, sparring like bucks, feinting this way and that, ducking away and whirling again. Suddenly young Harper charged in straight as a fighting bull, but Larry, side-stepping neatly, caught a flying wrist as it scooped, and swung his opponent off balance. But Young Affran spread his legs, came down on his feet solid as a frog, and got a hand on Larry's shoulder. They came together breast to breast.

Larry was the taller of the two, but Charles was the heavier and should have got the fall at close grips. He tried hard, lifting Larry for a cross-buttock, but Larry grape-vined him smartly and came back to the ground safely. Again they strained, grimacing in bersark fury.

Young Henrietta came at a run, yelping joyously. Her father stayed where he was, hands on hips, and laughing. The General and his Factor, sitting under the cyprus, seemed to take no notice. Henrietta circled round the vortex, holding her long skirt up with one hand, her eyes watchful.

"Watch your thigh, Larr! Charlie, you're done if he gets a hand under."

Charles, boring low, did get a thigh-grip for a second, but Larry broke it with a stiff leg jerk. They strained again, swung each other in turn, swayed, tottered, came down on their knees breast to breast, and rolled over on their sides tightly clasped. Young Affran glared up at his sister.

"Did I touch him down?" He panted.

"You did not. A dog's fall, same as always." She pulled her foster-brother loose and to his knees by the hair of the head, and Charles came to his feet above him and thumped him on the back.

"Tough as ever!" he panted.

Larry was assiduously brushing his friend's knees.

"Lord! don't say it's busted?" implored Charles.

"Two stitches, and as good as new——"

"Stitches! Oh, hell!" He shoved Larry off with his thigh and bent to examine the damage. Two dozen stitches might help a little. Diego waited for the explosion, but Young Affran, for a sullen-tempered young man, was calmly philosophic.

"Dam' fool to put them on when I heard you were home. Ah well! I saved the jacket anyway. How are you, old hoss?"

The two friends grinned and shook hands formally.

"You know my cousin, Jimmy Usted?" Larry said. "Am I supposed to know this young lady?"

Henrietta was indeed a new young lady this evening. She was wearing a long half-formal dress of light pastel blue, and it, somehow, made her delicately fragile and diaphanous. A dull-gold ribbon held her hair, her yellow-grey eyes were lustrous and a little slumbrous, and a deft touch of colour at mouth corner added beauty's serious note. At that moment Diego could not imagine anyone more attractive than this fair northern girl. She came to Diego's side, ignoring her foster-brother, hooked his arm possessively, and drew him across the lawn.

"Using me as a stalking-horse?" he enquired.

"Just that. What are you looking at—the smut on my nose?"

"Gold, amethyst, and fire! I withdraw anything I said about kissing."

"Very nice, hidalgo, but wait till you get an eyeful of Spanish Ann. She's made up gorgeous for you this evening. And there she blows!"

A deep mellow voice hailed them from the side-door of the sun-porch, and a tall lady in green swung a lissome bare arm.

"Come, my children!"

"Alas for my brief dominion!" murmured Henrietta.

"Do not struggle for it," Diego told her.

## II

Major Arthur Harper, at a glass-topped table, was shovelling ice into a tall crystal jug three parts full of golden-red liquor. He glanced up and nodded in Diego's direction. Ann Harper took Diego's hand in both of hers, and he felt the warmth of her pressure.

"But you are welcome in your best blue suit, señor. And this is your cousin?"

She went straight to Larry, took his hand and held it. She was as tall as he was, and her black eyes looked level into his brown ones.

"I am happy that you come so soon with your foreign cousin, Mr Larry McLeod. You have been known to me by the things you said and the things astonishing you did for two, six, ten years. No, two! Your father, him I love, and your great mother watches that I save my soul."

"You love my father, madam," said Larry in his cool slow draw, "but there is his son too?"

She chuckled to him, let go his hand, and lifted before his eyes a half-circle made with thumb and forefinger.

148

"Love? No! Affection — that much — for a beginning."

"Just one little small bit more, dear lady? That much?" He joined his thumb tips and made curving horns with his forefingers.

"That much, then." She moved his hands apart. "You must not ever close the circle. I close the circle for but one man—of my dreams."

"Oh lor'! pity the poor orphan! There they go already." Henrietta moved away and dumped herself in a cushioned wicker chair near the cocktail jug. Her father flicked her lightly on the ear and went across to shake Larry's hand in friendly fashion. Ann Harper came to the cocktail table, half filled a glass with the red-gold liquor, held it up to the light and added two drops.

"Go on, you niggard!" Henrietta urged. "Another tilly?"

"Your full portion, my young one. Do not hesitate or our good uncle will be on your top. At table you will be hidden behind flowers where there will be a white wine that I have but now decanted into a bottle that held the club orange."

"Good stick, Ann!"

The lady poured a full glass this time, looked at Diego and shook her head. "Not for you, señor. It is raw of Geneva. There is a red wine of Bordeaux to make blood—not the select wine, but for blood. Mr Larry, you will drink this with me." She touched her lips to the brim and he bowed over the glass as he took it. Young Affran's feet were restless on the tiles, and drew Ann's eyes. Suddenly she startled them by an agonised little shriek, and dropped on her knees at the young man's feet.

"Oh, my careless darling! Your beautiful new trousering that I pressed afresh this morning! How could you?"

"It is nothing, Ann." He tried to get his knee away from her, but she clasped him firmly at the back of the calf.

"Nothing?" Her fingers spanned the tear. "A whole decimetre! And there are stains of grass too."

"He prayed at my feet," said Larry.

"Oh, the wrestling match! The custom is of old— it is good. And my savage so-much lover bowed my nephew on his knees."

She sat back on her heels and looked up at him sorrowfully, and with her hair and her skin and her heart-shaped face she might be the Magdalene her very self.

"To-night you will place, using care, with your shoes, but not under your shoes, this that you call pants of our fine merino. I have the art to mend invisibly, and it will be new when you come again." She rose over him without apparent effort and took his hands palms upward as if he were a small boy. "Pah! they have touched earth." She smacked a palm and pointed to a ground-glass door at the side. "Go! Mr Larry, he will go too."

The two went like small boys, and Diego went with them. Inside was a cloakroom with a line of wash-basins. Larry slipped his hands through cool water, whistled a bar of a tune, and broke deeply and softly into another verse of his drinking chanty.

"A dark one, a fair one, a red-head for mine,
    And Cupid a-tipping the wink!
 Give me one, two or three, and I'll not ask for wine,
    And Hell—I'll be there—to the drink
                                For a drink!
    And Hell—they'll be there—with the drink!

"Yes, siree! Someone might be in love in this house."

Charles growled as he scrubbed his hands. "You'll be in love yourself if she wants you."

"If she wants. You heard her?"

"This much and that much——"

"Just so! That we would play some—just so much—for the sake of your soul."

"You go to hell, Larry McLeod!" Charles rubbed his hands briskly in a roller towel and hurried out of the place. He was afraid that his friend might twit him too rawly.

Larry and Diego followed, and Larry placed a hand on his cousin's arm. He spoke with his mother's voice.

"It might be a good thing that you move with admirable caution, Jimmy Usted. We be of one blood, but there is other blood in you too—and blood tells."

"Therefore I do not move at all," said Diego.

Ann Harper was sitting aside on the arm of Henrietta's chair, sipping her cocktail; and sitting thus, the dark green, heavy silk dress she was wearing outlined the swell of one thigh and showed the length from knee to ankle. It was hardly just to the fair girl that the red woman should sit thus above her, for they were a complete contrast, and the contrast did not favour the Briton. Outside on the lawn the girl had been lovely and alluring, something diaphanous about her, but now she was opaque, faded, unvital, exposed to the definite glow of the woman's beauty.

The dark green dress was without sleeves and cut square at the neck, so that it showed the small hollow at the base of the throat and the first curve of her shoulders. Her long slender arms, the slender strong column of her neck, her live red hair green-banded, the cool cream colouring of her against the dark green made her extraordinarily vivid. Henrietta at her side was just insipid. Diego could not tell if this Basque woman had used any cosmetics—but that is how they should be used. He was sorry for the Highland girl, and moved across to her side.

At that moment Major-General Harper and his Factor came in from the outside. The General, a law unto himself, was in a stiff shirt and dinner-jacket, and the smooth black outlined his heavy square shoulders and showed up the creamy-white bush of his hair. The man with him was short and plump, with a round ruddy face, grizzled hair, and prominent pale blue eyes that changed quickly from blankness to twinkling.

Henrietta slipped her glass, not yet empty, into Diego's hand. The General's unblinking expressionless eyes went over them all, his head nodded casually, and his short legs took him top-heavily across to Larry, whom he started to question—not talk to. The moment his back was turned the girl picked the glass from Diego's fingers and drained it hurriedly—too hurriedly, for some of the gulp took the wrong road. She started to strangle, tried to do it dumbly, and finished with one loud and unrestrainable whoop. The General turned quickly.

"What is wrong with the girl?"

But Diego was standing between, her glass again in his hand; and Ann, thwacking her firmly on the back, said:

"Child, if you swallow salted almond with its corners you will be sent to the nursery."

"A bloody exhibition of myself—a dirty-nosed brat of an orphan!" mumbled the girl, fumbling watery-eyed for the handkerchief Diego held out to her.

The small ruddy man was at her side, his eyes all twinkle.

"That was a right slick almond. It melted right down the lassie's thrapple. Yes, Ann, I'll ha'e another like it."

Ann was already pouring him a drink. He tossed it off in one free motion and extended his glass to be refilled.

"That was to tak' the bad taste out o' my mouth. I see Larr is back." He cocked an eye up at Diego. "This gentleman and I are due to know each other."

"Oh, the manners I am losing! This is El Capitan Diego Usted, son of a beautiful one of this glen—she is with God. Ewan McInnes, señor, is our man-of-law, our Factor in the land that breeds many deer but men so few."

The man of law shook Diego's hand warmly. At close quarters Diego saw that he was old, for his ruddy features were netted with fine lines.

"Mairi McLeod's son! I knew fine. It was in my office your mother, God rest her, got her trade, and from there she got the Secretarial post in London. I mind I sent her a wedding present of a tantalus—and a dang fulish one for South America."

"Your name is known to me, sir," said Diego, "and your tantalus—not empty—is in a house I own."

It was about then that the dinner gong boomed from the inner hall.

III

After dinner they returned to the sun-porch for coffee and liqueurs. There was a peat and pine fire in the big hall, but the vita glass of the porch held in a pleasanter and more diffused warmth.

It had been a good dinner, but, like most dinners of that class, even in wartime, there was too much of it. As Diego knew, a meal should consist of one plentiful main dish, with a salad mixed by an artist, and a light red wine from the wood.

Major-General Harper was not a good host. He was not a conversationalist. He was a questioner, and, the questioning done, he gorged at his food and ignored his guests. Diego felt that the man could not be communicated with on any mental plane. His strange vacant eyes made him as aloof as a god, and like a god he must have his pinch of incense. Denied it, he might be as merciless as Moloch.

153

The important person at the table had been the Spanish lady. With the gestures of her hands and her head and the embracing glance of her eyes she took possession of her guests from the beginning. Her red hair and cream skin borrowed whatever light there was and glowed, but at her own table one did not so much consider her as a beautiful woman to be adored as a housewife naturally lovely as a hostess. Indeed, it was difficult to realise that she was not a matron but a young and childless woman.

But there was one dominant male character in that house, Major Arthur Harper. And he was interested in the one vital woman. He kept a speculative grey eye turning from her to Diego at her side. Was he considering the possible pull of a man of her own race? Was a hidden jealousy beginning to gnaw at him? He was not old, he was a widower, he had force, and in the house was a young woman full of her sex and tied to an old man. Passion to him would be a stern thing, and even ruthless; and the incoming of a foreign rival would not make it any easier.

In the sun-parlour the General drank two cups of coffee with cream, lit a cigar, nodded towards his Factor and went outside. From the door he called to his brother, "We'll want you at the Office, Arthur." Evidently the Estate Office was somewhere at the rear of the main building.

"Let the old owl go to the devil, Dad!" growled Young Affran.

But the father shook his head, lit a pipe and went out after his brother.

Old Ewan McInnes would not be rushed. He stayed to finish a second liqueur and get his cigar drawing well.

"I'm no' to blame for this business," he said, "and don't ye think it. When it's all by, I'll have lost a good job myself."

"How long will it take, Ewan?" enquired Henrietta.

"To break an entail, my darling, takes time—and money by way of fees, Providence be thankit. Two months, anyway."

"We could do a lot in two months," said Young Affran meaningly.

"Surely! but whatever ye do, do it canny," advised the old lawyer, and turned to his hostess: "We'll be at it till midnight outby, Mistress Ann. I'll no' be seeing ye the night."

"Provision will be made, friend Ewan. The—siphon of aerated water will be in your room, on the high-up shelf of the wardrobe."

"The very thing I like for a night-cap, me being a sort of secret teetotaller," said Ewan, and went out chuckling.

Diego moved across to the glass front of the sun-porch and looked down the reaches of the loch. The light was still strong though the sun was below the notch of the pass. The evening trout were not yet rising, not a ripple moved, and the floor of the loch was laid over with a silken skin shining with a moonlike silvery glow that seemed to be evolved out of itself. Diego had difficulty in picking out the line of the shore, for the great hills were mirrored in that shining shield without any lessening of sharpness. Above the cliffs the peaks brooded in a toneless light, and one tall pinnacle, far away, streaked with the last of winter's snow, took the last of the sun in a glow of rose and orange. That shining peak and the sky still full of light made the hills and hollows below them all the more solemn and brooding.

A warm hand was on Diego's sleeve, and he knew whose the hand was without turning to look.

"It is a land in which one's heart would stay," murmured Ann Harper's deep voice.

"It is a land in which men would dream," added Diego.

"And women too. I sometimes dream of greater hills than these going up and up behind Roncesvalles."

"And you are lonely for them?"

"It is strange that I am not. Perhaps it is because of the Terror that comes between. Perhaps it is because I was young and did not know love."

"And you know love now?"

"Of that we do not speak, Don Diego," she murmured, and he felt the warning warm pressure of her fingers.

She left his side and went across to where Henrietta, replete and comfortable, reclined in a cushioned chair. She sat on the arm of the chair, pulled the girl's bare arm into her lap and began softly to stroke it; and the girl looked up at her and smiled, completely under her spell.

"It is time for my young men to talk," said the lady-of-the-house. "After food men talk amongst themselves. Talk, then, and forget that the enemy is listening!"

Larry McLeod sat on a rug at the other side of his foster-sister, resting a shoulder against her knee. She poked him off, shifted a leg, and pulled him back by the hair, so that he rested comfortably against a rounded thigh. Her hand remained in his hair.

"Talk away, my hearties," she encouraged. "There are cigars and whisky over there."

Young Charles Harper was lying flat in a wicker chair, his hands behind his head—a favourite posture of his.

"What's the good of talking?" he growled, and gestured his head towards the outside. "Our life, all life, is finished in this glen——"

"Thus he makes perpetual moan," his sister said. "His mind is turned inwards to slaughter—and abduction."

"Shut up!" snapped the brother.

"There you are! A dog in the manger." She pulled at Larry's hair softly. "As for my poor Larry here, he

156

talked so much last night that he is completely arid this evening."

"Who told you, you rattlesnake?" enquired Larry amiably.

"Our mother didn't, and you know that. My dear child, there are some three hundred humans in Glen Affran, and I'll make a near guess at what any of them is doing this minute."

"Half a crown on that?"

"Haven't got one."

"I will—is it?—stake you, my darling," said the other woman promptly.

"Thanks, Ann! You're on, Larry."

"Right. What is Long John McKenzie of Craik doing to-night?"

Diego at once knew that Larry asked that question because he wanted his foster-sister to possess half a crown. She laughed and pulled emptiness out of the air with a long arm.

"My innocent! that's your half-dollar gone wallop. Long John to the fore. He is at the bothy at the back of Scurr Affran with Hamish McLeod, Donald Gunn, and Piobar Maol Tam. The worm developed a leak, and Long John has his soldering iron, a bottle of flux, and two yards of copper piping that Young Affran here borrowed, lifted, purloined, plain stole, out of military stores."

"Blast it!" swore Young Affran. "You were supposed not to know that."

"And heaps more. They hadn't time to finish the job last night. They were down at Loch Beg before midnight, and Larry got lit up to the poetry-quoting stage with Donald Gunn—their own doggerel mostly, and pretending they'd read it somewhere. And Diego Usted cold-stone sober sang a song in Spanish that he had heard a Spanish lady sing somewhere, he said.

The Piper put music to a bit of Larry's that he liked, and practised it forty times parading up and down the pier—said it sounded better off the water. So it did too, till the forty-first time, when the Piper fell in off the deep end. And that's why Larr is wearing his old tweed suit this evening, for he went in or fell in after the Piper."

"It was the pipes I was after, not the Piper," amended Larry.

"We might have let sleeping dogs to lie," said Diego quietly.

"And then," went on Henrietta mercilessly, "Larry in his pyjamas strutted barefoot back and fore on the hearth and restored the Golden Age for the men of the Glen, the four of them with their eyes glistening——"

"Oh God!" groaned Larry. "I must have been more than lit up. Mercy—mercy!"

Henrietta chuckled, and ruffled his hair. And then Diego interceded. He had heard Larry last night, but Larry had certainly been lit up, and had moved high, wide and handsome. Now he put to Charles Harper, who looked eminently sane, a direct question, and gave him his honorary title.

"Was there ever a Golden Age in this glen, Young Affran?"

Larry it was who answered.

"Probably not. All a foolish dream, and vain as dreams."

At once Young Affran straightened up, and his gruff voice took on a vibrance. He had lived all his brief life close to this subject of the revival of the glens, and hated his co-dreamer to belittle it.

"That is not fair, Larr. You are giving your cousin a false impression, and I will not have it." He turned to Diego, and for once words came freely to him. "These are facts, Usted. The population of Glen Affran is now three hundred. One hundred and fifty years ago it was

158

three thousand. We have the records, we know the history, we know the culture, we know the laws, we know the resources. To some of us who have studied it, that period and four centuries before looked like a Golden Age for the people of this glen—and many other glens. That's all!"

"How did the people live?"

"By taking in each other's washing, as has been said in contempt. Why not? Till the lairds and the financiers made a limited liability company of Scotland, and did all the washing—and made a bloody rag of it in our generation. Took in each other's washing is right, but the laundry was a select one. There was no great dividend out of it for the managing director—the chief of the clan—only a great but honourable responsibility, so he took the easy way to wealth through sheep and deer and grouse, and discarded his responsibility for human souls. The bottom lands of Craik and Strath Dearg will grow any crop that grows in Britain. There were thousands of acres of grazing, good grazing and rough grazing and high grazing for the summer shielings. There was the fish—the salmon—and the sheep and the cattle, and the deer too. The fishing was free and more than plentiful, and though there were game laws of a sort, no swank lad need be short of a haunch, fresh or cured. Fish, mutton, beef, game, venison, eggs, milk, and butter; corn for bread and malt for the national drink, and a surplus for export in exchange for other luxuries: a silken goon, tea, a cask of wine, a book or two, and a barrel of cured herring for the salty flavour. Flax in the sunny hollows, and the hum of the spinning-wheel. Homespuns and philabeg cloth, and the clack of the hand-loom. Material things, brothers! All material things! And what did we do in winter when the Glen was closed? What the devil did it matter, closed or open. We had pipers and fiddlers and diddlers, singers and makers of song, wauking songs, love songs, war songs, songs of lament and songs of humour, makers of poems, makers of uisgebaugh, tellers of stories, and courting on the side. Christenings and weddings and wakes. Dancing at the summer shielings, games, stone-casting, hammer-throwing, tug-o'-war, shinty matches, and some more courting on the side. But why go on?"

"Why indeed?" murmured Larry McLeod gloomily.

"You have forgotten the little fighting on the side?" hinted Diego.

"Not reckless warfare because of folly—same as now. The clansmen were warm-blooded, and a man could pick a quarrel of his own choice; and that made for good manners. They were useful men of their hands, bred to claymore and broadsword and targe, and a good sworder, using his skill in the heat of fight, does not often take a killing wound. They boasted, of course, in song and story of the things they had done to the other fellow, but, as the saying goes, a man had to be killed four times before you buried him of old age. Then, indeed, it was worth while to be chief in Glen Affran, and have responsibility in council for peace and war."

A quiet heavy voice spoke from the inner doorway.

"Your heart is on your sleeve to-night, son. There will be no chief in Glen Affran any more. The Glen is finished."

That was his father. Concentrated on Young Affran, compelled by him, no one knew how long Major Harper had stood there.

"I am finished too," said the son, jerked to his feet, and poured himself four fingers of Scotch whisky.

IV

Young Affran tossed off his drink in two quick gulps, shivered to the shock, and moved across to the elephant's foot that held the walking-sticks and fencing-foils. He plucked out a foil and set the flexible blade of it to swish-swishing in short wicked cuts; and Diego noted that he had a strong arm and that his temper was still troubling him. The practice dummy on its hemispherical base stood to attention by the side of the elephant's foot. Young Affran rested the button of the foil on its breast, stepped back for distance, and began lunging and thrusting so forcefully that his blade made a half-circle and the dummy rocked back and forth. And Diego noted that he had a strong wrist lacking suppleness, and that in pronation his blade did not keep a true line. But the young fellow could fence.

He looked over his shoulder, saw Diego watching him, and frowned. And then a new thought struck him, for he grinned, plucked another foil out of the holder, strode across to where Diego leant against the sill, and tendered him the weighted pommel.

"You know this game, Usted. Show me a pass or two?"

Diego shook his head, but the hilt was under his hand, and his fingers of instinct closed on it. Young Affran stepped back out of distance. The moment Diego swung the blade to get its balance he knew that his wrist had still its suppleness but that the old essential steel was absent. Well, he would just use his skill in a few in-and-out passes and trust to luck.

"Engage!" said Young Affran, and the blades touched. The young soldier, surely, had a strong stiff wrist. But he did not attack. He was sincere in his desire to learn something from a man who might be an expert, and if this was a serious bout they should be wearing masks and jackets. So he waited on Diego's attack.

The whole thing did not take half a minute. Diego began with simple straightforward thrusts. Engage, lunge, advance, recover, retreat, parry, and again. And then, taking advantage of a wide parry after a lunge, Diego tried a *remise*, that is, a second thrust without recovering his blade on guard. The button on his foil was just touching Young Affran's breast when the parry came. That parry was a side-cut of the blade, and it had to be delivered so quickly and so forcibly that it jarred the hilt clean out of Diego's weakened grasp. The foil clattered on the tiles. No one spoke for all of three seconds, and then Major Harper's quiet voice delivered judgment smugly:

"That's the forthright British method. It serves."

Diego laughed, thrust his breast out, and flung his arms wide.

"It is death, O Master. Strike."

Young Affran picked up Diego's foil by the button.

"Sorry I was so rough, Usted—had to be or I was pinked. Try again, will you?"

"Death gives no second chance." Diego moved the hilt aside and smiled at Young Affran. "You have a strong wrist. We could try this game again and again, and still your wrist would be too strong. My compliments."

Ann Harper, leaning forward, was watching Diego with intent eyes, and there was a smile about her mouth, but she did not speak. Neither did Henrietta. But Larry McLeod did. His voice was quiet and slow and sleepy, but his nostrils were flaring, and there was a green light in the eyes staring up at Major Harper.

"Major, in a month's time your son will try my cousin again and you will thank your Maker that there is a button on one of the blades."

"Keep the button on your own blade, brother mine!" said Henrietta quickly, and shoved him off so brusquely that he sprawled. With a rustle and flounce she was out of her chair and at Diego's side. Her two hands clasped his arm.

"My turn now, gentle victim. You had a trout-rod

with you, and you and I go fishing. Look!" She pulled him round to face the glass.

The loch that had been still as a pond was no longer still, though no breath of air blew. The light, now fading, was still strong enough to show the far shore; and over all the surface of the loch the trout were rising. In some places the water seemed to be a-boil, so closely did circle join to circle; in other places the concentric rings widened out smoothly, joined another series and broke, and the reflection of the hills shivered and leaped. Thousands of fish must be darting about under that shattered silver mirror. As in all over-stocked lochs, most of the trout coming clean out were small, but here and there a big boil showed a catchable fish, and a black fin ran along the surface for a moment.

Young Affran came across. "Tell you what," he said. "I'll run the outboard down to Loch Beg and some of you can try a cast. But the coble holds only four comfortably. Are you coming, Ann?"

"Alas! but I cannot. Ewan McInnes has a secret hope that I come to his aid before he commits grievous sin by swearing." She pointed a long arm. "Henrietta, you will go to your room and change into your oldest things. Señor Diego and I will wait for you all at the boathouse. Come, señor!"

"And I'll see you don't get much time to get your dirty work in," said Henrietta, and flashed across towards the hall door.

Ann and Diego were moving side by side across the gravel when Major Harper's voice hailed them from the side-door.

"By the way, Usted, we are doing the first tramp of the season to Strath Dearg next week—Ann, Hett, and myself. Would you and Larry care to join us?"

Diego was never quite clear about Major Harper's attitude towards himself. Now, instead of answering, he looked aside at the lady, and she nodded understandingly.

"My Arturo," she said, "it is Señor Diego's meaning that you have no manners. Is it not the ladies who choose their companions for the mountains?"

"Oh, that's all right, Ann. You'll see to it?" He gestured carelessly and turned back into the sun-parlour.

"Thou cocksure one!" said Ann softly, and turned to Diego. "Señor, will your great Aunt Ellen permit me to take you into the mountains if I promise her to be very careful of myself?"

Diego chuckled. "If also you are careful of me."

"That is my meaning." She touched his arm, and the two walked shoulder to shoulder across the grass. "I was proud of you back there; you knew how to behave. Was there no—not a little—a resentment, an abasement at being disarmed by one so young? No?"

Diego laughed and wagged his lame wrist.

"He has a strong wrist, and I presented him with the parry to suit it. He had to use it, and all the credit is his. That is all."

She caught his wrist in the air, and the smooth firm tips of her fingers thrilled him.

"It is of sound bone—and strong once?"

"And will be again—perhaps."

"And then—in a month, as your cousin said—will you pin my nephew like—like a butterfly?"

"I will not. That incident is closed, Señora Ann. The boy is suffering in spirit—in heart too—and if it helps him to know that he can fence, that is good."

"I am proud again. He will never be a man distinguished; but he is not selfish, and with age will come purpose. You and I we understand each other, Don Diego." She took his arm impulsively. "You are a comfortable man to have as a guest in the house—so Elene told me—not talking, but listening to things as if

164

said wisely and not said before. You will soon come to see me again, when I send?"

"You command me, señora."

"Command I like—yes! Not men alone, but many young ones, though I command what I have. But, señor, we will not say things to each other that touch the heart, for I would not touch you deeply lest I be touched too—you are different from the others. Here now come our young ones. Go with God!"

She was a frank lady. She gave him one clear warning and another to herself. She could make him fall in love with her if she so desired, and she knew enough of herself to know that she could not help making him love her, but only so much. It is thus that dangerous love starts.


# CHAPTER VIII

## ON THE LOCH

### I

YOUNG AFFRAN's fishing-boat was a small coble of two thwarts with an outboard engine of a single horse-power. The four of them made a neat fit. As a beginner they put Diego at the stern by the tilted engine. Some days before, Uncle Hamish had taught him how to set up a rod, run a line through the rings and tie on a cast of flies; and had spent an hour with him along the margin of Loch Beg teaching him the one-two-three method of casting. But he had never landed or hooked a trout. He now protested that he did not want to fish because he could not. Charles Harper shook a finger briefly.

"Got to learn, and loch fishing is the easiest for a start."

"And you'll hook nothing under the sky," said Larry, "unless it is Young Affran's prominent off ear."

They did not start the engine. Charles and Larry each on a thwart pulled leisurely towards the southern shore where the best fishing-grounds were. Henrietta, back into her tartan skirt and high-necked sweater, sat high in the prow, balancing lissomely to the pulsion of the oars, and tied on a cast of three flies.

"We catch nothing for a while yet," she said over the rowers' heads. "You can see why."

Within fifteen or twenty yards of the boat the surface of the water was unbroken, though beyond that the trout were busy as ever leaping or sucking at white gnats netting the air or black ones floating on the water.

"Too calm," she said. "But in the twenty minutes between day and dark and for twenty minutes after we might hook an unwary feeder on a fairly long line. You'll see."

Her line was out and she was wetting it with careless and lengthening casts. She knew how to use her wrist. The line looped back gracefully, and, as if alive but leisurely, curled forward again, flattened out, and dropped caressingly on the water. Charles chose a cast for Diego from a flat aluminium box with wetted felts.

"A bloody butcher for its red tip at the tail, a silver teal and a heckham for droppers, black, red grey, silver, and a feather of jingle cock to suit all tastes." He watched Diego tie it on. "That's Hamish's own knot— you'll not slip your cast. Put your rod across and let the line out from the stern. Go on! let it out. More— more! A foolish trout might investigate it twenty yards back!"

There were no foolish trout in the loch that evening. They moved on over the ringed shining surface, not talking any more. Out there on the water the landscape took on a new aspect. The hills were more dominant and bulked bigger, and the sky was paler and higher. They were at the bottom of a bowl in the mountains, the guarding cliffs made a rim above them, and the great slopes beyond seemed to be pouring themselves down into the bowl. The only sounds were the regular check of the rowlocks and the rippling chuckle at the bow and over the oar blades.

A hundred yards from the southern side, where the pines edged the shore, the boat's nose veered off and they went on parallel to the woods. The oars slowed and slipped silently through the water, and Charles, looking up at the sky, said:

"There's a star above Carn Seilig. Reel in. You can start fishing."

Diego started to recall the ritual that Uncle Hamish had impressed on him, and tried not to be self-conscious before those two young men who would be expert anglers. The girl, one knee on the gunwale, was concentrated on her own lengthening line.

"Take your time and don't mind us," advised Young Affran lazily. "You'll not reach out to the fish for five minutes yet. That's the way! Keep it short till you have the hang of it, and then pull out another yard. Hamish has been at you. Keep an eye on Hett once in a while. Hamish taught her too."

Diego thought he was doing not so badly at getting his cast on the water, though he was not yet reaching the rings made by the rising fish. Henrietta was over them already, and suddenly her point dipped and her line tightened.

"Got him!" "Him" was a small trout. She reeled in quickly as the fish splattered on the surface, and, not waiting for the landing-net, caught her cast short and lifted the sprat inboard.

"Three ounces," she said. "We'll sacrifice him for luck."

"Watch your line!" Young Affran spoke quietly to Diego. "The water is shallowish here and you'll hook a stone while you watch her killing minnows."

Diego reeled in his trailing line and began again. He would never hook a fish, he told himself. The girl's line was out again, and in half a minute her reel whirred.

"A nice one this time! Stand out from under." That one went out and deep and stayed deep, but an expert was handling it. In two minutes it came to the surface and splattered angrily.

"Half-pounder!" said Larry. "You'll need the net."

Diego was watching interestedly and again forgot his line trailing astern with the drift of the boat. Without warning the rod was alive in his hand and an electric shock went up his arm. He felt the hard tug to the very butt of the rod, and his shoes clattered on the floor-board as he sought his balance.

"Fine! he's a good 'un," cried Young Affran. "Keep your point up, and don't let your line sag."

Diego did keep his line up, and his line did not sag. It was a stiff short line into the breast of the water, and the trout was tugging fiercely. And then the water exploded and a good fish catapulted into the air and dived again. And the line whipped loosely into the air, curled back, and noosed round Diego's neck.

"What did I do wrong?" he enquired mildly.

"My fault! You followed my advice literally and kept your little finger on the line all the time. I guess that fellow took your tail fly for keeps."

That was so. Diego loosed himself from the line and Charles tied on another butcher with two or three deft turns. Henrietta had killed her half-pounder and was into another fish already.

"By gum! they're on the take," said Larry. "We thought there wasn't a hope and that's why you two bohunks are fishing. Go on, Jimmy!" Diego was feeling quite excited now, and he wondered what was in this angling game to stir a man no longer excited by

168

war. Two fish rose to him one after the other, but he did not strike them in time.

"You'll soon learn to stiffen your grip at the touch," Charles said. "That is all you need to do."

The next fish held on, and Diego struck so hard that he lifted it a yard out of the water, but the hook did not come away. He gave that small trout all the time it wanted, keeping his tip up and letting it run on a free line. In three minutes—half a minute would have been enough—he brought it to the net belly up.

"Nice work! In time you'll learn not to punish your fish more than is necessary," Charles said.

"Four ounces—maybe six! Now you're a fisherman," Larry said.

Four ounces! That fish looked all of a pound to Diego, but when he weighed it later in his aunt's spring balance it barely touched the quarter-pound.

"This excitement is bad for me," he said. "Will one of you take the rod?"

"Get going while the going is good," said Young Affran. "You are not into the game yet."

Diego had a lively time for the next twenty minutes. He rose and missed many fish but hooked and landed a half-dozen, all small but all game. Henrietta had more than twice that number to her credit.

"The darndest luck!" said Larry. "I go fishing to-morrow."

And then on the very edge of dark Diego hooked a good fish close in. He knew it was a good one by the solid resistance to the strike. Thereafter that fish took control and did everything it wanted to except get off. First it went from there in a long curve towards Henrietta's line, and she skirled, flicked her cast to the other side of the boat and began to reel in rapidly.

"I'm afraid to advise you," Young Affran said. "Die, dog, or eat the hatchet!"

Diego stopped the fish twenty yards out and brought it in slowly in stubborn zigzags. He could feel the weight of it at the butt, and his heart was beating. It went round the boat in a grand swoop, and Henrietta had to lie flat over the bow. It went under the flat bottom and back again, and luckily the droppers did not catch. But Diego held on, and with growing confidence, for some time in that fight he suddenly discovered what the art of angling was: to get in tune with your fish.

The trout's runs became shorter. Three times it came close in. The third time it showed white, and, though there was still some fight in it, Charles slipped the net smartly under and flopped it at Diego's feet on the floorboard, where it threshed angrily till quieted by a touch of a heel on the poll. Diego's hands were trembling, and Charles had to loose the hook from the angle of the trout's jaw.

"The best fish of the night—pound and a half at least," Charles said, running his hands through the water to get the slime off.

Still neither Diego nor Henrietta were glutted. They fished on for five to ten minutes, hoping that the big ones were on the take, but not another fish rose to them. The spring night was over them now, and they could no longer see their lines. Then Young Affran pulled his oar across the gunwales.

"Session over! You'll rise nothing this side of dawn— not for another month. Like it, Usted?"

"Immensely. Thanks for the pains you took with me."

"You've got it in you. I bet a day's pay you'll fish Hamish's coble the rest of the week. The trout run bigger in Loch Beg—better feeding-ground—and they'll give you all the sport you want. Hold your line against the sky and you'll see your knots better."

Out on the water Charles Harper was no longer a sullen young man. He had shown an understanding consideration for a novice at angling, and Diego felt the first real touch of liking for him. He drew pipe from pocket and began to fill it, and Larry did likewise, first passing a packet of cigarettes over his shoulder to Henrietta. Night was about them now, a still and astonishingly balmy night for the last day of April. The girl taking down her rod was a dim silhouette in the bow of the boat, her cigarette-tip a red spark. They could no longer see the line of the shore, and twenty yards away the water faded and was gone. They seemed to float on nothingness down there in the hollow of the mountains. The faraway sky was still pale and was scattered thinly with stars, but down towards the upheaved horizon south and east it toned into yellow and pink. There the moon, near the full, would soon be above the rampart of the mountains, and against the suffused glow the peaks were stark and black and brooding. One was inclined to whisper, and when the three young people started to talk they kept their voices low.

"You opened your mouth pretty wide this evening, Young Affran," murmured Larry, but not reprovingly.

After a time Charles answered out of a muse.

"You mind the old days—the old days not so old—when we used read Neil Gunn's books?"

"Ay! *The Lost Glen*, and *Butcher's Broom* and the others."

"And this is one of the lost glens. Lord! what were we not going to do for Glen Affran? A hive of life and husbandry and culture and fun—with Jahveh put in his place apart. The men we would choose, and the women we would not have. Practical affairs like co-operative effort and water-power and light, spiritual abstractions like mysticism. And the Council that I, as laird, would preside at——"

"And don't forget I was to be your Factor at a nominal salary to save the expenses."

Young Affran laughed without mirth. "Yes, we were to live austerely, and for the sake of the Glen only. The slattern here troubled us a lot, didn't she?"

"We used to wonder whether a fellow could marry his foster-sister."

"And decided that you could marry her in a brotherly sort o' way to keep her out of harm."

"Don't mind me—you never did," said Henrietta.

"She has picked up a mind of her own somewhere along the road," said Larry. "I'm damned if I'll be that sort o' husband—to keep her out of harm's way."

"I'll decide that for you, Mr McLeod."

"Shut up, both of you!" rapped Young Affran, bent on his own way. "We two—no, be fair—we three were going to restore the Golden Age in Glen Affran. And we were very practical, we thought, and must have ten thousand pounds for a start—just a start. We couldn't get it off the county by rating, but we'd pluck it off a bush somewhere. Well! we can have the ten thousand, but we'll have no glen."

"I feel it all round me."

"You saw Ewan McInnes up at the Lodge? My uncle is breaking the entail."

"Can he?"

"With the heir's consent and a bribe of twenty-five thousand pounds he can. Know about entail, Usted?"

"Something about landed estate passing to the next of kin, Will or no Will?"

"Something like that. Will or no Will, my father is heir to Glen Affran, and it comes to me after him——"

"Don't let us worry that far ahead, old son," said Larry. "We might die any day."

"I don't care," said Young Affran strongly. "As long as life lasts I will think of the Glen, and make plans as if you and I were to live a hundred years."

"Carry on, then."

"Your father consents to the breaking of the entail?" Diego half-queried.

"For a consideration of twenty-five thousand pounds. Doing it for Hett and me probably. He spent most of his life abroad and has no particular feeling for the Glen. Twenty-five thousand would strike him as pretty good value for a moribund deer-forest eaten up with taxes."

"But, look here!" Larry cried. "Why does the General want to break the entail?"

"To sell."

"But, dammit! he doesn't need to sell."

' Not him. Just sheer cussedness. Might be vanity or pique or something. He has us in the hollow of his hand and wants to show his importance. Since this war started he has found that his importance don't fill a pint pot. He couldn't get himself dug out, you know. But he keeps on persisting for a job worthy of his metal, and he has been offered one as Governor of a couple of the Lesser Antilles out of harm's way. He'll boss negroes all right."

"And dagoes," added his sister. "But not every dago."

"You should be spanked, Hett," Larry told her.

"So there you are," said Young Affran. "The old fool is clearing out, lock stock and barrel, and is making sure I don't get Glen Affran to play with. A dog in the manger! He cuts no ice in the Glen, and he knows that I do. Our old spouting, Larr, put a bit of life in the people. They looked up and forward to us, and we are failing them. That was my swan-song to-night."

"Tell you what, Charlie!" said the outspoken girl.

"Let us cut the old devil's throat. Then you or Dad could marry the widow, and we'd have everything."

There was a hard note in Diego Usted's voice.

"Cut his throat, most certainly, but do not think to make a cat's-paw of Ann Mendoza."

"Don't I know that," said Harper. "Maybe I will cut his throat, or put a bullet in him—same as in Ireland. I have two months to do it in before the papers are signed. Oh, hell! Let us stop jawing. Change places with you, Usted?"

### III

Young Affran took the stern-seat and dropped the engine out-board. It was an old-fashioned affair, starting to the jerk of a whipcord, and it knocked and hissed emptily to several pulls. Young Affran swore, gave one furious tug, and the engine barked, spluttered, hesitated, and broke into a steady shattering purr. The boat straightened out to the rudder and went streaking down the loch.

They talked no more. Diego now understood how the affairs of Glen Affran were moving, and he was sorry for these three young people who had had their fine dreams. Dreams only? They could not be ruthless enough to make their dreams live. Killing was not in their compass. The iron of the law had broken Scotland from the '45 onwards, and the Highlands were no longer primitive enough or enough civilised to take the law into their own hands. The Golden Age could never be restored.

And these three might keep on dreaming. It did not matter. Two of them would probably be dead in war any day within a year or five years—or ten. And as for the girl? Diego rather liked the girl but was not interested in her. Was he interested in Ann Harper? No need to consider that. He himself might be dead too.

Their world was in that state where all men contemplated death close at hand, and that contemplation had different effects on different men, mostly not for their good. It would not affect Young Affran's dreams, nor would it affect Diego. If he lived, he knew that Scotland, though it appealed, was not his country. He would go back to his own hacienda of San José, but not at once. The oppressor must be beaten first, and then the old flag might again lift in Spain—the great mother country. What would Ann Harper do if the old flag flew? But he would not think of that either.

The coble went echoing through a gut between high bluffs and came out into the dim brightness of Loch Beg; and the white house glimmered against the darkness of the brae. Young Affran brought the boat round in the curve, cut off the engine, and slid softly up to the little pier.

"Here's where you drowned the music last night," Henrietta chuckled.

"You're coming up to see the old lady?" suggested Larry hastily.

"Of course."

They tied the painter to the mooring-post and went up the path in file, Charles carrying the catch in the bottom of the landing-net. They found Aunt Ellen sitting on her straw hassock under the brass lamp. She was reading. Hamish was on the hill, and she had been alone in the house for many hours. Diego felt a strange pang that she should be left alone and lonely, but he realised that this was now her life, and that she had also an inner source of life that would never fail her.

She rose to her feet and looked at them over her glasses.

"I knew ye'd be, so I had the brass lamp lighting."

"What book are you on now, milk-mother?" Henrietta reached a hand for it, but the tall woman put the book behind her back.

"It is not a book for a girl like you," she said. "I found it at the bottom of Don Diego's bag."

"Oh! That sort of book! What is it called?"

"It is called *For Whom the Bell Tolls*——"

"Pouff! Hemingway! I read it two years ago."

"Shame on you! Mind you, the lad writes well, only he shackles himself too much, and he arouses passion as if it was only a meal taken in passing." She glanced at Diego. "All the same, he gives me an impression of Spain—and its men and women—that I am glad to have. What are you doing in there, Young Affran?"

Young Affran came from the back-place carrying the catch in a basin. "Your Don Diego caught that one," he pointed out.

"Ay! I see you have the good ones on top. We'll divide them into the Highlandman's three fair halves, and send one down to Father Chisholm for his Friday's dinner." She moved towards the door. "I know why you looked in on me this late hour, and I suppose I must let you have it—you need it. Get the wine-glasses, dawtie."

She went out and came back with a tall cut flask holding a clear amber liquor. She half filled a wine-glass for the girl, half filled another and looked at Diego.

"Sample it, Don? It won't hurt you."

Diego found it an interesting drink. He got the soothing flavour of heather honey, but could not identify a pleasantly acid astringency coming through the sweetness.

"That's the sloe and its kernel," his aunt told him. "Henrietta, my darling, your eyes are smouldering, and these two boys here are in a bad temper. What is it?"

"We talked too much of the old days, Mother, and got into a killing mood."

"And that is the bad mood."

Young Affran tossed off his liquor incontinently and shook his head.

"You know what's going on, Big Ellen?"

"I do, boy. Ewan McInnes was in with me this morning and gave me a hint or two over a dram. The General is selling out, taking himself and his woman to a tropical island, and clearing us all out of the Glen."

"But can he sell, Mother?" her son asked. "Who'll buy? The royal sport is dead."

"He'll get his price. The financial classes, Jews and the rest, are investing in real estate, hoping that the ways of the pogrom shall not be fulfilled. I am sorry, but don't you three youngsters have any more foolish notions about a new life in the Glen. Glen Affran is dead, mavrone!"

"There was talk of deading the General first—and marrying his widow."

"I do not like that talk, even in fun," the tall woman said sternly. "When good things depend on the death of a man the devil has his chance. Oh! the General will die all right—the hot places kill a man quickly the second time—and his wife will marry again. But mark ye this! she will not marry a Harper again, old or young, for she'll not trust a Harper to give her the sons to rule and the daughters to bestow. You people will leave that woman alone to choose her own road. Do you hear me? You do. She would save the Glen if she could, but she can't, for the General won't die soon enough. God between us and all harm!"

## CHAPTER IX

### ON THE HILL

I

THE weather was indifferent for ten days. First came a cold snap with frequent showers of rain and sleet, and again a thin mantle of snow lay over the higher hills; a peat-fire was very welcome in the evenings; gardening —the last of the spring work—had to be discontinued; and Diego could not raise a trout in Affran Water or Loch Beg, though he tried hard. But Larry going out with a salmon-rod came back with a fresh-run salmon of ten pounds. The salmon was scarred deeply with the gaff, and no one asked him what fly he had used.

After a week the wind veered south and west and died, the cold went, great folds of white cloud came down over the hill to within a hundred feet of the valley floor, and a soft drizzle was mild on the face day after day. Down from the heart of the cloud came the strange faraway sound of running water.

And then one morning the sun was shining in Diego's window, and he looked out on a world new minted. The sky was a far-off, washen blue, and high white cloudlets sailed in from the west and faded. All the great hills sparkled; the snow was gone except for white islands in the northern folds; and thin shining torrents poured and cascaded where no water had run before.

"This is the real spring, and summer its heel," said Aunt Ellen. "We will now give my garden three days and fare-you-well."

"A pity, but I have a job on the hill with Donald Gunn," said Uncle Hamish.

"In three days when the ground is dry. Off with your coat, Cuchulain!"

So for three days Uncle Hamish and Diego wrought in the garden, in the perfume of the apple blossoms, sowing more peas and savoys and cabbages, and garden swede and beet, and the seed of such tender crops as french beans and scarlet runners that do not like late frosts. And in the evenings Diego went fishing and caught trout, and thought of himself as an angler.

"After this we'll only need to mind the rotation, and

keep the dutch hoe to the weeds," said Aunt Ellen with satisfaction.

"The dom'dest job of all," grumbled Uncle Hamish.

On Saturday Larry came home from the camp on the coast, and found himself with a job. The day was sunny and still, and he and his mother and Diego went through the five hives by the garden wall. Larry and Diego were veiled, but Aunt Ellen wore only a head-cowl to keep the bees from getting angry in her hair. Diego was inclined to dodge when they buzzed about his head, but she did not move when they poised on the tip of her nose. In time he got to like the living eager sound of the hives. His job was to scrape and wash and disinfect the floor-boards, while the other two went over the body boxes frame by frame; made sure each hive was queened; examined the new brood, some of it already capped; showed Diego a long-bodied queen at work and the minute white worms at the bottom of the cells; and removed here and there a conical projection that was the nursery of a baby queen.

"What an immense queen, that one," Diego pointed out.

"That matriarch is past her prime—four years old," Larry explained. "She needs superseding, which means death."

"We'll leave a couple of queen cells and let it swarm in June," said Aunt Ellen.

Finally they crowned the body boxes with shallow and section frames for the storing of honey, wrapped in the quilts snugly, and called it a day. Larry and Diego went salmon-fishing down Affran Water, and Diego found that he was not yet an angler.

The two-handed, rather cumbersome rod called for a new technique. Larry was patient and showed him how to get out a short cast without hooking all Scotland behind him, how to keep the butt in his groin, and work his fly at a slant down stream. But he rose no fish, and presently came to the conclusion that throwing a vain line hour after hour over disdainful salmon that sometimes leaped over it was a poor sport compared with angling smartly for trout where something was doing every minute.

Larry, throwing a looping long line that covered all the likely spots, caught two salmon. The first was a ten-pounder and he played it right out, and instructed the protesting Diego how to gaff it without endangering the cast. The fish was boring sullenly against the hook towards the tail run before Diego in a final desperation got the gaff under and the fish safely ashore.

The second fish was bigger, all of fifteen pounds. Larry played it for half a minute to make sure that it was well hooked, and then insisted that Diego take the rod. And Diego found that playing a salmon had a thrill of its own, and a thrill that no trout could give, not even a big one on light tackle. He felt the electric power and solid weight of the fish coming right through to his hands. Larry's rod was an old-fashioned greenheart, fully eighteen feet in length, with a huge wooden reel, a heavy line, a strong cast, and a big spring fly, but it could not stir that fish an inch in moments of obstinacy. The salmon simply went up and down and across the pool as it wanted. Diego's small experience with trout helped, and he did not get flustered. He kept his point up and as steady a tension on the line as he could manage, let the fish run when he had to on a whirring reel, wound it in cautiously at every opportunity, and manœuvred to keep opposite it on the bank. When it rushed him he was inclined to set backwards to recover his slack instead of working the big drum smartly, but Larry got him out of that. When it sulked nose downwards at the bottom on a sawing line, Larry routed it with a carefully thrown stone, and it exploded into the air and tried to get the cast with a wide fluke; and then it was that Diego realised the sheer power and energy of that curving angry body. He wondered how any flimsy hook and line could hold it. But hold it they did, and after twenty exciting minutes Larry gaffed it neatly. Diego wiped his brow and rubbed his aching forearms.

"To-morrow morning," said Larry, "we'll slip out before breakfast unbeknownst to Hamish, who is a bit of a Presbyterian about the Sabbath, and you'll hook your own fish and land it. Then the Glen is yours—or will be when you get blooded with your first stag."

"I may not be here then," said Diego, prodding his lean stomach where there was no ache anywhere. The tired steel in him was again being tempered into wiriness. Already he could not understand the despondency of his mood a bare four weeks ago.

On Sunday morning he hooked his own fish and played it on its side to Larry's gaff. He hooked a second and gaffed it himself after twenty-five minutes. The fish were taking and they decided to fish on until it would be too late to think of going to Mass. But when Aunt Ellen's clarion call came to them from a mile away they looked at each other and marched towards it, their long rods like lances above their heads. They went to Mass, and again Diego knelt at Ann Harper's side.

Larry had a long week-end and was not on duty till Tuesday. And it was on Monday morning, another morning full of sun, that Major Harper, Ann and Henrietta came down in the outboard-coble and proposed the tramp to Strath Dearg by the Sanctuary. Diego was quite friendly with the two ladies by this time. He had dined at the Lodge on two or three occasions, and they had been down on each Sunday. With Henrietta he was carelessly familiar as if she were actually a member of the Loch Beg family, as she virtually was. But with Ann he was still a little formal, as she was with him. There was no coldness in that formality. Not familiar and not cold, there was an old-world dignified understanding between them; and sometimes still he kissed her hand and waited for the warm pressure of her fingers. She had lovely hands, warm and shapely and not too small; and she used an expressive gesture with thumb and middle finger, and her little finger had a way of twiddling whimsically.

"We do not carry our stomach with us," she said. "I mean that we do not carry them on your shoulders. Yesterday I told Donald Gunn that we were to come if the sun shone. Have we your permission, Elene?"

"And Donald borrowed a salmon off me same as yourself," said Aunt Ellen. "He has a secret way of his own cooking it, poor old bachelor! Off with ye, then!"

So they marched in light order, carrying steel-shod crooks of hazel or holly. Diego slung on his uncle's stalking-glasses; and Ann Harper had a small rectangular parcel hanging at her hip. They went down to the foot of Loch Beg and crossed Affran Water by a wooden bridge wide enough to carry a pony with loaded panniers. From the bridge they took a short-cut over the shoulder of a slope where bracken was beginning to curl its fronds, and picked their way down across a peat-moss. It was here that Uncle Hamish cut his peats, and Larry pointed out to Diego the straight-sided banks at the edge of the moss.

Beyond the moss they entered a fold in the hills, and opened out a long leisurely meandering valley, with the verdant new grass fighting high up the slopes against the encroaching heather. There was a track winding along in the hollow with a grass-grown ridge in the centre of it and deep ruts at each side, showing that it had been a road for carts not so many generations before. It was hereabout that Major Harper called a halt. He was walking ahead of Diego, who noticed that his limp was more pronounced. He stopped and, before he spoke, drew a long breath and put a hand on his breast high-up.

"More rain to-morrow, I fear," he said.

Ann Harper, striding lithely ahead of him, arms swinging easily, and a hand sometimes thrown up to shoulder-level in a virile, full-of-life thumb-flicking gesture, turned round to face him.

"It is your leg, Arturo?"

"A fine barometer, but dam'd unpleasant," he said, stamping a heel on the ground.

Larry and Henrietta came back, and the daughter put a hand solicitously on her father's arm.

"The old limb has fallen down on the job, Hett. Doubt if I can make it round by the Strath and over the chorrie."

Ann Harper looked from him to Diego and spoke definitely. "We postpone this our walk to another time. To-day we make the fishing picnic on Affran Loch."

But Major Harper was equally definite and more reasonable. "Not at all! You mustn't let a game leg spoil the party. Old Donald will have a meal ready for you, and would be terribly disappointed. You'll get back by the chorrie, and I'll pick up the coble at Loch Beg. You'll go on and never mind me."

And as if that settled the matter he gestured them away, and went off at a steady limp on the road they had come.

"I hope it is that game leg," said his daughter doubtfully. "His old ticker is not too sound either. Shall we go on?"

"It is an order," said Ann Harper. "Follow us, my children!"

With a quick impulsive hand she swung Diego round, and the two strode off together on the grassy ridge of the track, their shoulders sometimes touching. The other two followed some distance behind. Henrietta said something about a chicken-stealer.

"Yes! I steal for this one day," said the woman at Diego's side, throwing up a free arm. "It is what Arturo insists, for with him it is not leg or heart. It is you. But that you knew?"

"I do not know."

"He is kind." Was that satire. "He would have you saying such charming things to me in this great wilderness of hills under the sun. But you will not. No?"

"You are very beautiful," said Diego.

"But that is charming. Sometimes I feel beautiful I am so full of life, and I say things." Her hands went out appealingly. "You will not mind the foolish things I say, and you will not fall in love with me, Don Diego?"

"I shall not tell you so."

"But that is perfect. Liking me a little, myself, you will be silent so that our friendship be strong—and good. I like you too. Do you sing, Don Diego?"

"As a crow sings."

"Then sing as a crow. I must. The song you heard before and that you sang when the night was merry."

She had a deep voice, strong and a little rough, like the voice of the Basque woman used to calling beasts and men. She sang a verse of that old song that one could make gay or satiric or tragic. She made it gay with a touch of satire, and Diego croaked the short lines.

"Old grey Time, on my head, do you now sift your snow?
     Snow then! snow then.
  Kingly Death, where you lead, must I go where you go?
     Go then! go then!
  For my head is fast declining, my eyes soon lose their shining,
  While my heart, still softly warm, knows my face has lost its charm.
     So I weep then, and I sleep then."

184

"There are other songs that I know too—lulling songs —but I do not sing them yet. I may not sing them at all. It is to be seen. The Sanctuary of the deer is around two corners."

Behind them Larry's voice lifted in his drinking song, that was also satiric.

> "Take a glass or a lass, take a kiss or a cup,
>     As you choose, you cannot go wrong,
> For a glass or a lass or a kiss or a cup
>         Make joy or make Life or make Song,
>                     Gallant Song,
>     And only a theme for a song."

## II

The slopes closed in to a defile, and still narrowed to a rocky gap no wider than the track; and going through that gap they came surprisingly on a fine oval valley hollowed generously out of the hills. It was as roomy as the bowl of Craik, rich with grass and herbage, without trees, but with many clumps of grey-green willows. It was a valley where men might live in any peace there was. But there were no men or the houses of men, but in the distance were many crumbling walls. The track curved round on the right slope of the valley towards those broken walls. Ann made a flowing gesture.

"This valley which is the Glen of the Willows and that hill which is Scurr Affran, they are the Sanctuary. You will see the wild deer not here so wild."

The deer were everywhere. At first Diego did not see any, but as his eye grew accustomed to the colouring he picked them out in ones and twos and clumps. And every one of them had head lifted towards him. They were all hornless hind as far as he could judge, though there might be some young buck with knobs just a-budding. The lordly stags, young tines hot in velvet, would be aloof on the higher ridges at this season, and might not come down even to browse in this mild weather.

"They are heavy with young, the dear ones," said Ann gently, her hands moving out towards them. "In a brief time now the golden-speckled darlings will be hiding in the ferns and the willows, and we shall come and see them, but they will not be easy to see, for they hide even in their Sanctuary, and if you touch them they scream like a frightened child."

And as they went on she talked wisely and whimsically about the deer and their ways, and of the things that Hamish McLeod had told her, and of the funny stalking stories probably invented by Donald Gunn for her amusement. Soon she had the little company, now close together, in tune and laughing. The very movement of her hands folded them in, and Diego wondered whether her charm was due to art or nature, and in the end decided that it was due to both, for natural charm must be reinforced by taking thought in order to be compelling.

The hills, green and brown and grey-ribbed and sun-dazed, folded closely about them, and the track lifted more steeply and turned many corners. They kept steadily on at an even pace. Three or four weeks ago that pace would have left Diego breathless, but now he breathed keenly through his nostrils and felt the Latin whalebone back in his legs. Another month, and again he might be a fighting man.

After a time the tilt flattened out and the track swung south. The valley tipped down before them, and through an opening in the hills they saw in the distance a massive mountain towering up. It was seamed with chorries, black and red, and a startlingly-white snow ridge lay below the shattered peak.

"That's Ben Dearg the other side of the Strath," Larry

said. "This is the height of ground between Glen Sallagh and Strath Dearg, and here are the resting stones. I am having a smoke to myself."

At the side of the track a row of large stones stood out of the ragged grass. All of them were worn smooth. Larry chose one, sat down and said:

"Rest the soul of all who sat before! You see, Jimmy, in the old days a man or a fighting squad, coming up from the Glen or the Strath, took the first rest here. In the end it became a ritual, and in time the two townships used meet here on summer Sundays and have games and shinty matches and pipings and dancings on that level stretch. Never again."

"Let us not be sad for the dead," said Ann Harper. "Those before be with God."

They rested for ten minutes while Larry emptied his pipe. Henrietta produced cigarettes from a sporran at her hip, and Diego took one. He tried not to inhale, but the smoke stung his throat and he let the cigarette smoulder in his fingers. The girl looked aside at him.

"You are marching again, Don. I believe you could do Carn Seilig and snowball-fight at the cairn. Larr and I are going up. What say, Ann?"

"It is not permitted for Don Diego, for his good—not yet, but soon. We will climb with you to the top of the rough chorrie that is called Garbh Ailt, and from there you will go up to the cairn, but we will make the traverse that will bring us down above the Lodge to the Rock of Skene, where we will sit in the sun of evening, our toes a hundred metres above the loch, and wait for you two hours. Moreover, we need not any duenna, for you will be watching us all the way. But we will not watch at all."

They went on. The going was steadily downhill now, and soon they opened out another bowl in the hills where there were more broken walls at both sides of a noisy stream running crystal-clear over white and grey quartz ledges. Larry shook his head.

"All this country was peopled right down to the Strath, and from there to the main glen at Craik. Now there is only Donald Gunn, since his stalkers went to war."

"With his hounds for the deer and his dogs to shoot over," Ann said. "If I could leap time I could see Young Affran's people"—she threw up an arm—"his people and their children and the children of the children come out to wish rest to our ghosts haunting in kindness these hidden places. But I am not a prophetess, and things go against me and the young men's dreams."

She was gazing intently before her, and her dark eyes had a glow from within. She touched Diego's sleeve as if to steady her feet, and her voice was sibylline.

"Hush! did I hear children laugh? But no! Was it not water playing amongst the stones? But no, again! For that sound is strange and cold and laughs only to itself. The sound I heard was warm. But no! I will not prophesy."

"You make my heart warm," said Larry.

"It is well, then."

Henrietta's shoulders twitched as in a cold air.

"The second sight comes with a chill. Stop it, Ann!"

"I stop." She laughed deeply. "Let us be happy that some time, somewhere, children shall laugh. But goodness of God! Do they not laugh now even where slaying is."

The track swung sharply and they came suddenly on a grove of tall pines thickly planted, running right and left and closing in the view completely.

"We are about there," said Henrietta, "and so my tummy tells me. As the mother says, may God direct Donald Gunn in the use of his bastable oven."

"This is the heart of the working deer-forest," Larry told Diego. "You will behold the Strath in two minutes."

He led on westwards by the side of the grove below a high grass bank. Some hundred yards on the grove finished and the track turned the corner abruptly.

"There you are!" said Larry.

III

The Strath opened out below, and the moment they appeared a deep baying of hounds and a high barking of game-dogs greeted them. It was a wide strath, flattening out across a mile and lifting slowly in a slope of green that sent tongues and bays into the wastes of young heather going up and failing against the rocky buttresses of Ben Dearg towering its shattered peak three thousand feet above.

In the forefront of the level spread was a small loch of some fifty acres, shining blue under the high blue sky; and though the day was calm the water was wimpled here and there by vagrant eddies of air.

"That's Lochan Uan," Larry told Diego. "There are good trout in it. Donald crossed the old black stock with the Affran breed and they run a good size because of the better bottom feeding. We'll not have time to-day, but we'll try them some time."

The near side and the top end of the lochan were bordered by pasture and meadow-fields protected from the deer by high wire fences. In one pasture some sturdy Highland ponies were grazing, and in another were a black cow and a dun one, with a couple of stirks.

The track went down by the side of the grove, and there, half-way down the slope, facing the west on a wide shelf, stood Donald Gunn's bothy, a squat stone house with a slated roof and one chimney peat-smoking. It was fronted by garden patch, and some distance behind and close to the wood was a line of iron-roofed outbuildings. One of these was a kennel. In a high-

189

railed enclosure two shaggy staghounds reared up against the railings and bayed at the visitors, but not angrily, and in an enclosure beyond white-and-red game-dogs barked noisily. Many hens were picking about the yard.

The dogs had apprised Donald of his visitors' arrival. He appeared round a corner of the house, waved a hand, and came loose-striding to meet them. A side-gesture silenced the dogs. One brown dog, who had its freedom, ran ahead but was not barking.

"Oscar will never know—not after two years," said Henrietta to Larry.

"You'd lose your last half-crown on that?" challenged Larry.

"You're on! but play fair, you hound."

The brown dog, no longer young, loped leisurely until it got within some twenty yards, and there it stopped dead, one paw lifted and its head forward. And, then, a strangely agonised bark broke from its throat and it shot forward. Larry walked evenly at Henrietta's side, making no sound or gesture, but the girl did not play fair, for her hand at her side flicked finger and thumb invitingly. But the dog, ignoring that invitation, charged straight for Larry, grievous whimperings of joy torn from it.

"Good old money-maker!" said Larry.

The dog fell at his feet, twisted between his legs, ran round him, tried to reach his face; and its whimperings were almost human. It was weeping with joy.

"This is my dog, Oscar," said Larry. He was on one knee holding the dog by the top-knot. "Now then— now then, old boy! don't break your silly old heart. Take it easy! You are near the end of your road." He held a finger up. "But, sir! where are your manners? There are ladies present. Salute!"

That dog knew every word. He went straight to the

mistress of the Glen, wagged his wisp of tail and lifted head for one pat.

"You so faithful one! but you must not make me weep."

Henrietta shoved at its head affectionately. "You are too constant to be Irish, but I apologise all the same."

Larry moved a thumb. "My cousin Jimmy, Oscar." And the dog sniffed at Diego's knee, wagged a tail, and went back to its master. It was a one-man dog. Diego was not sure of its breed. It was liver-brown and curled, but not quite tall enough for the curled retriever. Yet it was too tall for a spaniel, and its lean muscular body, well-boned legs, fined-down wisp of tail, and fluffy top-knot did not ally it to any breed of spaniel that Diego knew.

"An Irish water-spaniel," Larry told him, "war-lord of the spaniel tribes. Hamish brought the stock back with him from Cork. He'll not back down to anything, dog or devil. The grandest dog there is for game by land or water, but difficult to train because of his enthusiasm. I trained this one. Come along, Oscar!"

They went down to meet Donald Gunn, and were received with native courtliness. His lean, clean-skinned face smiled happily and his dark eyes sparkled. He shook hands all round.

"You are welcome indeed, Mistress Ann." He bowed over his mistress's hand. "Ye are all welcome. Eh, man! Larr, the old dog knew you. But where's the Major?"

"He'll not be," said Henrietta. "His game leg played out on him."

"I am sorry to hear that."

"Are we not detaining you from your frugal repast, Mr Gunn?" she interrupted him.

Donald's limber shoulders jerked. "Losh, Miss Hett! Wasn't I forgetting all about the dinner? Dear, dear,

dear! Ah well! as Big Ellen says, when the taties are boiled the dinner is ready. But come away down, my friends, and there might be a bite going."

Donald Gunn's kitchen-living-room was not unlike Aunt Ellen's. It was smaller and the ceiling lower, but it had a similar open hearth, and dresser of delf, and home-hewn chairs; and there were books everywhere— read books; and his male hands had made it as cleanly neat as any female hands could. There was a fiddle in a green bag hanging on the wall. Here in this room Donald had lived alone for three years. Inside he had his books, his fiddle, and his verse; outside, his garden, his hens, his hounds, his tame beasts, and the wild red deer of the hills. Six miles away through a fold in the hills was Loch Beg Bothy; eight miles through another fold was Craik; six miles over a chorrie and a mountain shoulder was Lodge Affran; and that was all.

The rectangular deal table was covered with a white cloth, and places were laid for five people. On a crane over the fire a round-bellied pot bubbled, and a bastable oven on a brander bedded in peat-coals kept its secret under a lid crowned also with coals.

"First of all," said the host, "we'll try a drappie of Big Ellen's cordial she calls heather wine—or something neater for anyone that likes."

Ann slipped the rectangular parcel from her shoulder-strap and laid it on the deep window-sill.

"The last batch of paper backs, my Donald."

"Eh, Mistress Ann!" He rubbed his dry palms with real pleasure. "I am obliged to you. I can aye be doing with another book—and wasting your time."

The meal that Donald set them down to was as good as Aunt Ellen's any day, though no one would dare hint that to her. Indeed, she was reluctant to admit that, while his scope was limited and he had not the touch for dainties, he could almost—only almost—reach her standard in two dishes. Salmon was one and November hind the other. Salmon was main—the only dish—that day, the ten-pounder that Diego had caught yesterday. Heather wine, salmon, oatcakes, potatoes in jacket, followed by what he called cream crowdie smothered in cream, and a cup of tea also with cream. A strong man's meal. But the salmon! Apparently he had skinned it, boned it, cut it in curdy chunks, and slow-cooked it in the bastable with a gravy compounded of cream, butter, shallots, and secret flavourings. The savoury savour of it was the savour that a man recalls of the days of his youth and his mother's special dish.

He heaped their plates twice, but did not eat with them. He said that, up with the sun, he had had his principal meal hours before, and would just join them in their cup of tea. Tea was his vice—unless reading is one. Like the inveterate reader, he would keep sidling towards Ann's parcel and fingering at it, and after their second helping he carefully untied the string. He voiced his pleasure.

"My—my! You're a witch, Mistress Ann. Every single last one I marked in the catalogue. How could you ken?"

"Big Ellen told her," said Henrietta. "You and she are always talking books."

Ann Harper took control after their meal. She actually shoved Donald out of doors, and swept the two men after him with that fine free arm swing.

"You men will go about your affairs where you talk of men and dogs and deer—and women sometimes. The kettle, is it not on the crook, and Henrietta knows where the drying-cloths are, and where the dishes are set. You will be gone one hour while I do the things I did in my mother's house, and a little for the sake of this young one's soul."

The men went down to the lochan on a path between

the high wire fences. These fences were eight feet in height, but Donald said that the stag sometimes got over in winter when the snow drifted.

"In a bad winter we use the hay for the deer as well as the stock. In about six weeks from now, Don Diego, yourself and Hamish will be across for the haymaking. Hamish is the great man with a scythe. Myself keeping an edge for him, he'll cut a whole acre the length of a day. Larry here is good too, but his heart is not in it."

"I'm not a man of my hands, Donald, thank the Lord!" said Larry.

"You are then, but you are better at organising things —you and Young Affran. What life is there in the Glen wanting ye?"

Larry spoke seriously. "Donald, no more can be done for the Glen by Young Affran and me—or by you either."

"Don't we know that? The Glen is not blind or deaf. We know what's going on between the General and his Factor, Ewan McInnes. Ah well! the Glen has stood a good deal in its time."

"Can it stand much more?"

"It cannot. It cannot stand any more." He drew himself up and extended a hand. "Of all the townships that were once in the Glen there's Craik, and Craik only. What chance has it confined to its few acres and denied the river and the hill. Let it be a quick finish, then. Let the sun shine on the emptiness, and the wind blow in the desolation, and the snow drift over the old graves. Piobar Maol Tam has the beginning of a lament for it to words of mine that might some long day be popular in the Lowlands as an ancient Highland song. Leave it be now. Would ye care to try the lochan? The boat is ready."

"Not to-day, Donald. Some of us are climbing Carn Seilig.—Please yourself, Oscar."

They had come to the water-side, where a small boat was drawn up. The water-spaniel was looking up at Larry and whipping its rat-tail. At the quietly spoken words it plunged straight in, not like an ordinary dog, but deep under like an otter, and it came to the surface with the otter stroke, lifting its body half out of the water and barking joyously. It swam straight for the sedges. A mallard drake and duck rose with a squawk, and their clutch of a dozen squattered through the reeds. Larry put his little finger to his mouth and whistled shrilly on two notes. The spaniel hesitated, and stopped to tread water. Again Larry whistled, and this time the dog turned and swam back, but slowly and regretfully.

"My! You have him in hand still," said Donald.

"I can keep him out of the water, but once he's in he goes his own gait."

Some three hours later the party left the bothy for the upper and wilder reaches where the Strath narrowed to a glen. Before leaving, Donald insisted that more tea must be drunk, but in addition to tea there were buttered scones and boiled eggs. After Donald's high meal Diego could not stare an egg in the face. He sat sipping tea and nibbling a scone, and marvelled at the others wolfing boiled eggs. Healthy and vital young bodies they had, and for a moment he felt strangely old.

Donald, after the Highland custom, saw them a mile on the road to the foot of a stony rise where the Strath finished and the rocky bluffs on either hand came close down to the torrent feeding Lochan Uan. There was only room for a narrow but used track on the left bank. There they shook Donald's hand and promised to come again soon.

"Do you mind the old days, Miss Hett, when yourself and Larr and Young Affran used to come up for the night?" he remembered wistfully. "Fishing till dark and promising to get up with the dawn for the early ones."

"That was a long time ago, Donald—three, four years. We'll make another night of it soon, and again you won't be able to get us up before breakfast."

Larry said good-bye to his dog. Kneeling on one knee before it, he pulled its top-knot gently and held a finger up. "I'll be back, Oscar. Look! soon. I'll be back. Go on now! Donald is going."

Donald walked away slowly, and the dog, making no protestations, walked behind his heels, but its head and tail were down.

"Love it is an unhappiness," said Ann Harper deeply. "It is not fair. I do not know what it is. I do not want to know."

IV

They went up a stony rise close to the torrent for half a mile. The track was a good one and man-made, and at its narrowest would accommodate a loaded pony. At the head of the rise they turned a corner, and there, another half-mile ahead, they saw the chorrie they had to climb. It was a steep torrent of rocks pouring from the throat of Carn Seilig. The conical peak rose to the left of it to a blunt point on which the pinhead of a cairn stood out above a ridge of snow.

"The wild hielands, Jimmy!" said Larry, "and that's our goal up there."

The half-mile between them and the chorrie was as stern a gorge as Diego had ever seen, even in Spain. The bluffs had heaved themselves erect into shattered cliffs, black and grey and rusty red; and the floor of the gorge consisted of tilted shelves of broken strata. Down the middle of it the Garbh Ailt—the rough stream—boiled and eddied, and the track wound cunningly this way and that to take the shelves at the easiest slant. Whoever had made that pony-track had taken pains with it. There was no verdure anywhere, and the sun, now three hours after its height, did not shine further than half-way down the northern wall.

At the foot of the chorrie they halted. The track ran left across its front, and went steeply up over a pass; and at the other side of the track the stream torrent came dashing down a full hundred feet in a white apron.

"High Glen Seilig is over there," Larry told Diego. "A good glen for stalking, with an easy pass round the mountain to the Lodge. Here we take a short cut."

The chorrie was so steep that it frightened Diego. He had to throw his head back to look up the thousand feet of it. A man standing erect might touch the face of it with his outstretched hand in the steeper tilts. But it was quite climbable, for it consisted of a jumble of red and green spotted basalt boulders one above and behind the other, all firmly wedged and offering a secure grip. It would be a simple clamber for a rock man, but Diego did not like the look of it. He had a poor head on a height for the first ten minutes, and merely gazing up at that thousand feet of steepness made his head reel already.

He said nothing. Larry and Henrietta, used to any sort of rock face, would not understand his squeamishness. Ann Harper clapped her supple hands, threw them high and yodelled clear and high, the cliffs about them throwing the sound back and forth.

"This is the hill I know," she cried.

"The devil does," agreed Henrietta ruefully. "I have seen her come down without once using her hands—like a wild goat from rock to rock."

"Then I lead, and make the pace that will suit Don Diego."

So Ann went first, Diego followed, Henrietta behind, and Larry bringing up the rear. For ten minutes Diego did not lift his eyes higher than Ann's legs, and of them he saw plenty. She had good legs, fined at the ankles above the flat-heeled brogues, swelling handsomely to the calves and carrying no female heaviness behind the knees. But Diego was too intent on his task to do more than admire them as a pair of workmanlike props. He made sure of his handgrips before moving his feet, and tried to keep his muscles from cramping. A man with a poor head grips so tensely, so tightens every sinew, that he wears himself out in a very short time.

Ann went on unpausing for fully ten minutes, and then vaulted easily on to a four-foot slab and sat down, her feet hanging over, and her firm breasts lifting as she breathed deeply. She reached Diego a hand and he clambered to her side. Probably she noticed that his muscles were twitching, for she tucked her arm firmly inside his, and he was glad of that arm, for the steep drop below him had a devilish drag. Henrietta came up, her mouth frankly open and panting, and leant against the rock between his knees. He felt secure now.

"You're making it, Don," she said, looking up at him over her shoulder. "You'll relax in a minute. Gosh! but I'm out of training."

Larry, breathing easily through his nostrils, came to her side, and she nudged him with an elbow.

"Mind the day I first climbed this chorrie, Larr?"

"You didn't. Tearlath and I dragged you up by main force, your eyes tight shut and your mouth full open and bellowing."

"And I still don't like it for the first five minutes."

That steadied Diego, and his head found its balance. The rest of the climb was no more than pleasantly difficult, and half-way up, when the sun again shone on him, he felt exhilarated. Close to the top a huge wedged boulder blocked the way completely, but here the top of the chorrie on the right was low and a step or two cut in it of old led them out to where another big boulder was embedded at the tip of a treacherous-looking scree. A narrow path led round the boulder, and the climbers sidled round, their backs to the stone. Diego was glad then that he had recovered his head, for the scree dipped steeply to a hundred-foot drop, and the belly of the rock was pressing against the small of his back. He held his breath and made the circuit, and a few more steps upwards and aside brought him out on the easy side of the mountain, sunlight and heather all round him.

They threw themselves down amongst the thick stems and did not speak till their breaths came easily.

"This is the parting of the ways," said Larry. "I do believe you could make the cairn, Jimmy?"

"I don't mind trying."

"But no!" said Ann. "One big effort is enough, and after that we do not climb easy mountains."

"Not so easy, old woman," said the girl. "I ain't so keen on it myself."

"You'll start on it, my darling, in just another ten minutes," Larry told her. "You're fair mountainous with fat behind the knee, and I have a duty by you."

"Indeed, but she needs the strong arm to keep her the sylph," said Ann. "You go that way and we go this."

On one hand the cone of the mountain lifted a thousand smooth feet; and on the other a foot-track in the heather went over the shoulders of the hill.

In ten minutes the two couples went their different ways. Ann called over her shoulder:

"Two hours we wait at the Rock of Skene—but longer if Don Diego charms me."

"I'll bounce a rock off the cairn at you," called back the girl.

"My poor young one!" murmured Ann. "It is cruel to make you climb, but the suet of sugar must come out of your bones."

"You have a duty by her too?" said Diego.

"While she is in my house. My heart is not cold to her, as hers is to me—not always, not often. I think your cousin—so fine and grave and humorous like his parents both—he, I think, is touched by her in a place that hurts."

"And she?"

She turned her head round at him, and her red hair tossed under its green band.

"And she! I do not know. But I will not have her hurt though she hate me. In the end, I think that she will be one with her foster-brother—if he is in life. There is the tie between them that is the strongest thing she knows, but she does not think so. I, I think for her, so for her sake I do some small wickedness—but not all for her sake. Now I talk no more until the Rock, and then you will talk."

Diego laughed. She was too like his aunt to let him do much talking.

The track they were on was easy all the way. First it led up a slope to the ridge of the Carn Seilig, and suddenly all the great hills northwards spread out before them, brown and grey and purple and smoky blue. They could not yet see the bowl of Affran Loch, for the slope down was very gradual, but they could see the lips of the guarding cliff on the far side.

They went on down the easy gradient for half an hour. Ann kept her promise and did not talk at all. She walked smoothly, untiredly, her lithe shoulders back and her head up, and her carriage was the carriage of a woman used to bearing weights on her head. But she was not all silent, for sometimes she sang a snatch of Spanish song, and one free-moving hand kept time. At the end the slope flattened out and even lifted a little against them, so that one would never suspect that there was a great chasm within a hundred paces. And thus they came to a rounded lichened mass of rock standing a man's height out of the heather.  The track curved round it on the near side.

"The Rock of Skene," Ann told him.

v

She stepped into the heather and went round to the front of the rock, Diego following her closely.  But suddenly he started back in dismay, and felt for a grip on the stone.  The edge of the cliff was only three paces off, and Ann was standing lightly on the very brink of it as if about to take the air.  Quickly she stepped back and took his arm protectingly, a little chuckle in her throat.

"I am sorry.  It is my surprise for you."

Diego straightened up and took a single step forward. He dare not take a second lest he abandonedly take a third that would reach to four hundred feet.  She swung a hand out and down.

"Behold my kingdom, but do not fall down and worship me."

He looked down and across Affran Loch.  The mountains made an immense amphitheatre before him, and the far cliff, brightly lit by the evening sun, showed black shadows in its strata.  His eyes followed the line of cliff right round to his very feet.  At the far end he saw the bluffs hiding Loch Beg and caught a distant glimpse of Glen Affran; at the near end, only a down-slanted mile away, he saw the torrent of Affran Water pouring white down the pass, and the stone house of Affran on its green tree-dotted lawn below the pine belt.  The great sweep of sombre pine-wood below the cliffs sloped down to the water's brink, and the water under the clear spring sky was blue and deeper blue, and in places purple where the deeps were; and near the far shore where there was a shallow over sand the water was silver shot with gold.

"It is only a stroll down to the Lodge," Ann said, throwing out an arm.

The track ran for twenty feet along the top of the cliff, dipped into a fault and disappeared. Beyond the fault was a jumble of pointed rocks, but the path did not reappear. Apparently it went down through the fault to the woods and on to the Lodge.

"Now we will sit here in the heather and wait," Ann said.

They sat side by side in the cushion of heather and grass between the rock and the cliff. The stone, all day in the sun, was pleasantly warm against their shoulders, and the sun of evening was pleasantly warm on their thighs. Diego felt comfortable and a little drowsy, and in other company he would have slept. But he did not sleep in that woman's company. All he wanted to do was to sit there drowsily and listen drowsily to the deep richness of her voice, and occasionally feel the touch of her shoulder and the warmth of her impulsive hand. But she did not begin to talk, and he turned his head to see if she were asleep or thinking of sleep. Her head was turned aside and tilted speculatively, and her dark shining eyes met his. She chuckled softly, deep down.

"You do not talk much, Don Diego. I said that you would talk. I am waiting."

"What would you have me talk about—your beauty?"

"But no—no! One thing only. Your own place and the life of it. Just a little! Please!"

He started uninterestedly of the house his father had left him in the metropolis of Asuncion, and how they had lived in it during the unharsh Paraguayan winters. That had been before his parents' death. He had never lived alone in it, because he had not been back. But Ann was not interested in the small city, nor in the manner of life that was there lived for three months of the year.

"What of the nine months, Don Diego?"

"There was the hacienda of San José forty miles out."

"Ah! now I know why I felt kin. I too come of land-holders. You will tell me of that very great hacienda?"

And he told her, and her deft questions got him interested and quite eloquent for a silent man. He told her of the white house, white-walled, thick-walled, deep-eaved, deep-windowed, wide-verandaed, red-roofed, with the high Moorish arch leading into the big patio where there were orange trees and palms and running water. She wanted to know of that house, how it was run, the woman in it, the half-breed servants, the cooking arrangements, the ceremonial of the house and table, the passing round of the maté gourd in the afternoons, everything.

"But, Don Diego," she said, "with that great house and the tradition that is of Paraguay you would have many brothers, and sisters too."

"I am the only child."

"But that was so lonely for you, so tragic." She frowned. "Is it that you are of a family that do not breed?"

Diego laughed at that simple frankness. "Not so. I have six uncles, and cousins by the score. My uncle Pedro who runs the hacienda for me has ten sons, and if I die his second, Juan Diaz, will have it. My mother with God, when I was born—she had an accident."

"Yes, I understand. It was a tragedy. You will go on?"

He told her of the outside then, the plantations of yerba and sugar-cane and maize and mandioca; of the far-stretching roll of the savannahs dotted with the quebracho trees down to the Paraguay River jungle where there were harmless alligators and tapirs and fierce jaguars and yards-long water-snakes; of the immense pastures inside the strong wire with the white-fronted cattle that if not fresh crossed every fourth year reverted to the old dominant long-horn type; of the horses for whose colours they had seven and forty names, alazan, bayo, cebruno, gateado, moro, osuro, rosillo, tordillo, zaino, and so on; and of the men that rode the horses so daringly but well, using the efficient short lariat instead of the spectacular long one of the North Americas; of the indomitable Gauchos of Guarani blood who with knife and cloak would face and disembowel the savage jaguar; courteous men in their own right, with a strict code that if broken brought battle with long knives used as skilfully as sabre or rapier. From them Diego learned knife-play and went on to the foil and the small sword which is erroneously called the rapier.

She half turned to him and put out eloquent hands. "But, Don Diego, with that fine house of many rooms and running water and all things, and that so immense rancho, you should be married. You are not—no—not a little?"

"Not at all," he said, laughing, "not even in the way you imply."

"That is wicked. But, it is true, you should have a wife—and children, so many sons and daughters." Her arms embraced at least twenty. "So! And houses near your wife's house with grandchildren and great-grand-children. A great, great household! The Clan, that the people of this glen speak of with sorrow."

"And who would rule in that great—great household?" he asked half-teasingly.

"Oh, but you would be so busy with your hacienda—the outside—the crops and the cattle, and the horses, and the men disembowelling jaguars and themselves, and the sport of horses and skill twice in the year—so many things. Who would rule in the house—in all the houses—but your wife, who would be a mother and grandmother at the same time? That is only reasonable, is it not?" She spoke as warmly as if it was a personal matter.

"How reasonable? Would this matriarch rule me too?"

"In her wisdom you would not know that—inside her house. But stay! You are not young any longer. Young in years, but not young. Could it be that you were not lucky in your love? Well?"

Diego spoke slowly and without any emphasis:

"I am lucky enough to be sitting here at your side in the sun, and unlucky that I sit too late."

"That saying I will try not to understand, señor," she said seriously. "While I do not think of it, tell me of your youthful loves!"

"There were some. I forget. Much has come between. My father, now with God, died young, and my mother, now with him, knowing it as his wish, sent me to Spain to find knowledge of the great Mother Race. And in Spain came the Revolution and the Civil War, and I fought for the side that had old dreams made new. Then my mother, who was not strong since me, died, and I did not go back. There was not time."

"You will go back?"

"Surely—if I live."

"Then you will go back. I see it. There was no love in Spain?"

"There was a war and the sort of love that goes with war. I preferred fighting."

"I know. You would have the code. You have a nicety from your mother. It may be only a pride of self. I do not know, but it is good. It is not Spanish. It is Basque. It is Highland."

## VI

And then, quite naturally, she drifted into talk about the Basque, and her own people. Her father was a landowner under the mountains, and so very well off that his four daughters had an Irish governess to teach them English. And that was how her very adequate English had a trace of Aunt Ellen's idiom. She regretted very much that her mother's household, while numerous in retainers, was not numerous in children—not really numerous—for she herself had but three sisters and four brothers—a mere eight. Her father and mother were dead—slain, one sister was dead she knew, and two were married, but whether now in life she did not know, and of her four brothers she knew for certain that three were dead—two in battle and one against a wall. She did not love Franco's Spain, and Diego was glad he had chosen Commando.

"We will not talk of that," she said, moving a hand rapidly. "In the end I took an old man but strong to husband, because no longer had I any courage. And here I am in this beautiful land that is dying too." She looked down at Lodge Affran and flung a hand at it. "There it is! my home. Look! there is a man on the lawn looking up at us."

The evening air was very clear and Diego had good long sight, but across the downward mile he could not say that the dot on the lawn was a man.

"It is Major Arturo," she amplified, "and he is looking up at us, his hands above his eyes."

"Do you see that—or are you guessing? I see only a black dot."

"I see. If I would take a bet like the young one you would lose five peseta—but with her you bet kisses, is it not?"

"With you I will not gamble kisses," Diego said.

"That is a compliment. You have the spy-glass. Look, and you will see!"

Diego, since the dangerous crossing of the Sierra de Gredos, knew how to use a telescope without letting the hunter see the glint of the reflector. He sidled away from Ann, lay prone in the heather, his head hidden by her hip, and took the telescope from its case. "Hold your hand so," he told her, and got the front circle resting on her thigh between her hand and her hip. He focussed slowly. It was a good instrument, as a stalking-glass must be. He got the cascade pouring down the pass, and could see the points of rock breaking the surface. He got the house and could count the panes in the window. He got the dot on the lawn.

"It is a man," he said. "It is your Major Arturo standing leg wide. He has not his hands over his eyes. He is watching steadily through field-glasses."

"I do not see the glasses. My eyes, I must have them looked at!"

Diego put the telescope on the heather, and again sat up at her side.

"I spit at you, Arturo," she said. But she did not spit. She gave no sign that she knew they were being watched. "Is it this that you would see, my brother-by-law?" she said, rested her shoulder against Diego and put a warm hand inside his arm.

"It would be more realistic if my arm was around you?" suggested Diego.

"But no!" she chuckled. "That realism is too real, and we sit thus. The good Major I do not know very well. He is of that type that can hide feeling—even that of love, almost."

"He loves you?"

"I do not know that it is love. To his children he is devoted—but completely devoted—after leaving them forsaken but so happy for twenty years, while he saw strange countries and slew beasts. To me he is all the time courteous, and will not gainsay my rule within the house. And yet! I do not know what is behind his face. So I spit. Does he now think that I would be faithless to an old—but strong—man?"

Diego laughed, and she threw her head back and aside and looked at him out of black eyes.

"That is not a thing to laugh at, señor."

But Diego still laughed, and she got angry, and then angrier. She shook his arm.

"You do not believe me. Why do you not believe me? Stop it, señor! I will not be mocked. I have a temper that causes me penance. Look! I will fall over the cliff and drag you with me."

Diego stopped then. "Your anger adds beauty to your beauty, señora. I am not sorry. You said what you cannot mean."

"I did mean it." She spoke with vehemence. "I will not be faithless. Never!"

"To an old—but strong—man?"

"I said so."

"Do you imply that if he were younger—or weaker—you might be?"

"No—no—no!" And then she threw back her head, and her hair tossed, and she laughed with Diego, her hand warm and impulsive on his arm. "But I did say that, and it was not my meaning. But how do I know?" She held up two fingers and looked at them thoughtfully. "Look! if a husband is young only he is secure, but if he is young and a weakling there comes a contempt to his wife, and such a contempt is the gateway for a new strong lover. Is it not so?"

"You so tell me. And if you have contempt for an old man—but strong?"

"We will not talk of my husband, Señor Diego."

So she did have a contempt for him. And, though she did not talk of him, he was in her thoughts, for after a silence she said with sadness:

"I cannot do any more for this glen, Don Diego."

"I know."

"Yes, you know. Everything is known in this glen,

208

where a young man's dreams were taken heed of. I tried to help and would have helped, but now it is too late. I took those two young ones, brother and sister, to my charge. To myself I said, '*I will be*—what you say—*the matriarch in the house, and when the time comes help them and your cousin to make a dream come true.*' But now I fail them in spite of all my great angers. A failure, me! I would be a very bad matriarch for the great, great household of the hacienda of San José. This glen will be sold, the dreams of youth shall go for silver, and I, I shall go to a distant island." Her voice deepened. "But, indeed, it is well that I go to a distant place with my old—but strong—husband, where I can dream my dream and hide my secret."

"In that distant place, Ann, you will be nearer to a place where I would have you."

He had kept his voice steady. She did not ask him where that place was. She took her hand from his arm, and folded it in the other on her lap.

"It is right that you call me Ann—in friendship."

"In what way I can. You know that you would be the very great matriarch in the great, great household of the hacienda of San José forty miles out of Asuncion above the river——"

"My dear! my dear!" Her shoulders rocked back and forth. "Will you too read my mind like the Irish-woman? But hush, Diego! We must not let our so fine talk go that way. It is my fault. But you will let me make this clear for you and me, and then not speak of it any more. Listen now! It could be that you and I would know love. It might be that now we love a little. You came into this place, and you were of my race, and I was proud of you so quiet and sure and not using importunities after the manner of men. It is that you are strong. And I, I have my Faith."

"I have no faith."

"But you have the nicety of mind—the code that is

not this modern no-code—the sense that is moral so that Romance shall live—the integrity that is of your own person. Am I not right?"

Diego would not admit it. He said:

"I am in your hands, woman."

"In my hands!" She held them up and looked at them. They were fine hands and strong. "I will not let you fall, for I am selfish, and will not let my dream shatter." She clapped her palms and changed her mood to lightness. "Oh! but my dreams! these I must confess once in every month to my good Father Chisholm, and take a grievous penance. Why did I make you tell me of the hacienda of San José, and risk the so grievous penance month after month?"

Suddenly and lithely she was on her feet. Diego, more slowly, got up at her side. And then a long hail came down to them from the hillside. There across the easy slope Larry and Henrietta were coming.

"Our day so fine, it is over," said Ann. She took Diego's hand in both of hers. "Thank you, Diego my friend. You will remember that we are of a proud race?"

"I will remember if you remember for me," he said with a man's selfishness.

"Then I will remember, and that is a promise between us. We come of a good stock, as your great aunt says. And remembering that, is not the summer before us— and other good days? But this day, it is over."

And that day was over. Remained only the stroll down to Lodge Affran, and dinner there, and talk that was mostly ordinary. Once, at the dinner-table, Major Harper referred to the day's outing.

"I had the glasses on the climbers," he said, "and on you two under Skene's Rock. You had a long talk."

"Most fine," said Ann easily. "Don Diego charmed me under the Rock of Skene."

"The snake-charmer!" cut in Henrietta.

"I had a glass on you too, Major Harper," Diego said.

"Oh!" His heavy brows lifted.

"You did not see. I could have stalked you to a hundred yards and shot you dead."

"Yes?"

"Most certainly."

"Then I must be very careful," he said quietly.

# PART II : THE REAPING

## CHAPTER I

### ORDERS TO QUIT

I

THIS was meant to be a not-too-long chronicle of things that happened to Diego Usted in Glen Affran one week in July. But first it was necessary to try and picture the Glen, the people who lived therein, something of the life they followed and the dreams they clung to, as well as the development of the situation at Lodge Affran working up to a climax. That might be done much more briefly than in the foregoing pages, or it might be extended—if possible—after the manner of the great woman writers of the domestic English chronicles. As it is, the foundation having been laid, more or less inadequately, let the structure of the story be raised on it.

The quiet life in Glen Affran for four weeks has been given in detail, and nothing much need be said of the equally quiet life for the next six or eight weeks. In those weeks Diego got to know the people of the Glen, and was accepted by them for the sake of his dead mother, his Highland uncle, and his Irish aunt; but he hoped that he was also a little accepted for himself alone because of something that was sib in him.

He slipped into the ways of life and thought like a duck into water. He could fish reasonably well now, knew and practised the rudiments of husbandry, understood and helped in all the practical economies of the Glen and forest, and enjoyed the talk and the recreations. And he was a particularly good listener, and, so, very acceptable amongst talkers. In short, he felt at home; probably not so much at home as he would have felt at his own place of San José. But San José was far away and he might never see it again, and here he had Glen Affran all about him.

Ann Harper and himself became very friendly, but that, of course, is an understatement. They met two or three times a week in her house or his aunt's or on the hill or at Mass, but never alone. She saw to that. She had promised to hold him up in her hands, but he often wondered how secure she thought her hold. For they were not saints, they were live flesh and blood. That is not fair to the saints, for all the really great saints—as well as most of the great sinners—are supremely of flesh and blood, and highly sexed. It takes a full man or woman to be a saint or a mystic like Augustine or Theresa.

Things happened quickly at the end. The Glen began to empty of all the young people that he knew. Larry McLeod was gone with his squadron to Northern Ireland; Young Affran was at home on embarkation leave, his battalion having been ordered abroad; Henrietta, on a sudden impulse, had applied for and got a post in the W.A.A.F. Service somewhere about North Wales—in a week she would be gone. There were left Ann and himself, the only young people at that end of the Glen, or, indeed, in all the Glen. And the summer had still many weeks to run; and the hills and their hearts called to them. Well?

Was it that he cared enough for Ann Harper to act unselfishly? Or was it that his own personal integrity was selfish? It does not matter, for the result was the same. He wrote the necessary letter, and got the reply with a promptness that was now usual but still astonishing; and the instructions in it were briefly definite. He accordingly borrowed a small suitcase from Aunt Ellen, and shoved a few things into it; and forthwith she removed and repacked them, adding two more pairs of socks and an extra shirt.

"You'll be kept a week anyway, my darlin'," she said. "Don't I know them!"

Next morning his uncle drove him down to Craik Station. Uncle and nephew understood each other now. They could go on the hill and be silent for an hour or until Diego wanted some information or Hamish had some to give; they could sit at each side of the hearth while Hamish chuckled and helped Diego to draw Aunt Ellen; and at night under the stars and on Sunday before the visitors arrived Hamish would do his own share of talking. Now, going down the Glen, he did not say a word till they came to Craik township, and he sent Sanny through there to the near suicide of a hen.

"It's not good-bye yet," he said, "and I wouldn't want them to think it."

At the station he held Diego's hand firmly. "You'll wire us the day you'll be back, Jamie? A week Big Ellen says, and I'll be down with Sanny." His black deep-set eyes searched Diego's face. "You'll be going from us, I know. Big Ellen feels it in her bones, and she's the one to know. Proud we were to have you in the house, and proud everyone to have you in the Glen, and you'll be going out now keeping your pride." His words stirred Diego, and made him glad that he had taken his own line.

## II

At Inverness Diego interviewed a Staff-Colonel, one of the new generation of colonels and captains and knights-at-arms. The day was a hot July one, and the Colonel was cool and informal in khaki shirt-sleeves, for the Army, learning to do its work comfortably, was shedding buckram.

"I report for duty, sir," Diego said.

"So I see, Captain Usted. Will you please sit down?" He turned over some papers in a buff file. "Feeling fit?"

"Quite fit, sir."

The Colonel lifted one dark eyebrow. "You would

need to be fit if you are thinking of going back to your old unit."

"I am, sir."

"We could make it easier for you—for a while—if you say so?"

"My own unit if I am found fit. If not, I shall be glad if you choose for me, sir."

He nodded a dark-grizzled but young head. "That is what I would expect from your record, Captain. We'll put you through the toughest medical board there is, and if it rates you A1 you'll do to take along. By the way, the town is rather crowded and I have arranged quarters and an orderly for you. You'll mess with my lot. Drop in early for a drink. Your orderly will show you round. Cheerio till then!"

Diego dined in Mess that evening—a frugal meal—and it was pleasant to be back again amongst soldierly men. He was treated as a guest of honour, for his reputation had preceded him and he found that it was no use decrying it as apocryphal. He sat next the Colonel and found that off duty he was a frank and easy-going Highlandman.

"Ross is my county," he said. "I have stalked the Affran beats, and your Uncle Hamish might remember me. Old Hamish, you know, is about the best forester there is, and a whale of a man besides. He totes along a good flask—duty-paid or not—and I have more than once tasted his wife's famous heather wine—Big Ellen, as she is known wherever stalkers meet. A truly remarkable woman—even if she is Irish. What?"

"A very great lady, Colonel."

"Surely! And by the way, we are appointing a new leader of the Home Guard in the Glen."

"I understand that General Harper is going abroad, sir."

"The Glen would know. And I'm dam' glad he is going. He keeps one of my boys full time answering wholly unnecessary correspondence. I'll eat my tabs if our new man writes us a letter a month. You know him?"

"I think I do, sir."

"That is he. Hamish McLeod."

Diego was surprised. The man he had in his mind was Major Arthur Harper. But he did not express his surprise. He said:

"I am sorry for your young men, Colonel."

"Go on!"

"You forget my Aunt Ellen. She will attend to the correspondence and keep at least two of your staff employed."

"Splendid! We like a bit of humour in the day's work. If the Nazis invade Hamish's territory they'll send good men—and you'll not get better—but I'll be sorry for the one interviewing Big Ellen, and I'd hate to be stalked by Hamish with malice prepense. Your very good health, Usted! You make a fellow talk."

Next morning Diego had a thickish head when he faced the medical board, and he surely was put through the mill. The doctors took a week to it. And at the end of a week they sent him back to his Staff-Colonel completely empty and thoroughly washed out. He wanted to eat a horse, but he was warned to eat little till evening and drink nothing but water.

The Colonel was affixing a fresh paper in Diego's file. He laughed and shook hands.

"You're for it, Captain. Fit as a fiddle—absolutely no trace of the old trouble. Your mind still made up?"

"Yes, sir, my old unit."

"And welcome. How soon can you go? We can't give you more than ten days to settle your affairs."

Diego hesitated, and then made up his mind quickly.

"Three days will be enough, sir."

"You're a glutton. We may take a little longer, but not much. You're staying on at Loch Beg?"

He made up his mind again. "With your permission, sir, I leave for London in two days. The address is in my file, I think, care of my Legation."

"Certainly. London it is. We don't let our good men run to seed any longer. You can't catch the north train to-day, so you'll dine with us to-night."

Thanks to his caution, he had no thick head when he joined the train next forenoon. It was a long train and crowded, but the orderly had secured him a corner seat in a first-class carriage, so that with the aid of a few journals he did not mind the many stops. But he did not read much. He mused for a long time.

III

The last time he had come up this line he had been at a low ebb, starved and frightened. But his great aunt—great in body and spirit—had at once taken charge of him, and so had his uncle in his quiet way. They had charged his consciousness with their unforced confidence; they changed his fatalistic acceptance into a real uncaringness. They made him live life at its simplest and at its best—not a servile drudgery in a lost corner of the hills, but a life that embraced the whole Glen in the spirit of an old culture, and sent its tentacles all across the world. His cure was actually faith-healing, almost miraculous, for it was almost immediate. After one day he had forgotten or ignored his malaise—but that was how miracles worked—and only yesterday the doctors could not find a single trace or healed scar of the trouble that he had been so certain would kill him. Let him accept it as a miracle, then, and give the credit, not to any gods there be, but to his Aunt Ellen.

Here he was now coming up the line again, probably for the last time. And what had life to offer him this time? Anything or nothing! He could not or would not have the one woman he wanted, and what had life to offer him with that want never to be satisfied? Not much. And yet his spirits were not at a low ebb. He was doing, to the best of his ability, an unselfish deed, and the doing of it had a fine savour. And, possibly, somewhere in the unconscious he knew that his sacrifice would bring its own reward. No doubt selfishness came in too, for selfishness always does come in—always and in everything. In abnegation after abnegation, in humility after humility, in sacrifice after sacrifice there is still a trace of pride in our abnegation and humility and sacrifice. We laugh at ourselves and take pride in being able to laugh, and laugh at that pride and are proud again, and then we wonder where in some infinite progression we at last get rid of our conceit—and we are proud that we can so wonder. Let him be a little proud, then. He could carry on now. He would go out and fight for an ideal that might be only his own. He might get himself killed neatly or wastefully. But if he survived, there, at last, was his own hacienda of San José. He stopped his thoughts there. He must not think of San José yet, for that would set him dreaming of a matriarch in that great, great household. Day after to-morrow there would be no more dreams.

Ewan McInnes, the old solicitor, joined the train at Dingwall, and after a long search found three-quarters of a seat in Diego's compartment, and at Diego's side. Diego lifted from his corner and shoved the old man into it, and was himself left on the edge of the seat.

Ewan and Diego were old acquaintances by this time. The technicalities of entail-breaking had proceeded with the usual legal leisureliness, and Ewan had been coming to the Lodge once a week, invariably calling in at Loch Beg for a crack with Aunt Ellen and a drink with Uncle Hamish.

"I hear you're for hoisting sail, Don Diego?" he said, keeping his voice low.

"In two days."

218

"The Glen will be sorry, I can tell you that, and naming no names—— Ah well! You're not the only one leaving us in the near future." He tapped the padlocked brief-case on his knees. "It is all in here. Give me three signatures to-morrow or the day after and the job is done—and a job I don't like at that."

"Three signatures?"

"Ay! the General will have Young Affran's sign-o'-hand to make siccar."

"If I were Young Affran I'd tell the General to go to hell."

"You told him yourself, didn't you, at the first off." He turned his head. "You have no' been hearing things?"

"No, nothing new."

"Just so. The lad is making a difficulty right enough, but he'll sign. The father will see to that, and what other is there to do this stage?"

"Abolish first causes."

"Ay, indeed! And Young Affran has threatened to do it—and others besides. A right pleasant pastime! But, you ken, the powers that be, the law o' the Hielands through the agency o' Angus Campbell the Bobby, might be inconsiderate enough to want to hang a body for the virtuous deed. That's the pity o't! And what's more, 'tis the wrong person that might be hanged. For I know two, three, four, six—ay, six! I know six people that'll be in the Glen the night wouldn't mind blawin' the auld boy's head into knocker-sneezin'."

"Only six?"

"At least, and I'm counting myself and yourself. Yourself, and so I'm telling you! That's right, call me a lecherous old hound." He put a hand on Diego's knee, and his voice was not much above a whisper. "You are leaving the Glen in two days, my friend, and it is the thing you have to do. You see, you have the

Glen in your pocket, as I might say, a quiet and friendly man, and you have a responsibility on you for the sake of your ain. Go you must! And I'll not go to hell either, not for a while anyway."

"Look here, Mr McInnes!" Diego spoke warmly into his ear. "I am leaving your glen in two days. I am glad of it. I would not be found dead in your glen, where a man cannot have a soul or thought of his own."

"I would not know about the soul, being inclined towards doubt, but let it go. Did you ever hear of public opinion? No one minds about it now, but it was the one great law in the Glen up to the time of the clearances and for a thousand years before. The one law worth while and the prop of society. It is the public opinion of your ain people you are up against now, and you are standing the test nain sae waur." He put his mouth close to Diego's ear, and Diego thought he was about to hear some bitter wisdom. "Come away out in the corridor wi' the broad-minded third-class fowks. I have a small flask hurting you in the ribs."

IV

Diego had not sent a wire to Uncle Hamish. He would show old Peter Ross, who had once shaken his head, that he could now walk the fourteen or so miles up to Loch Beg in three and a half hours, allowing for a ten minutes' chat with any friend he might meet on the road. But he did not walk that evening. The first person he saw on the platform at Craik was Henrietta. Of course! She was down to meet Ewan. Behind her, Peter and Wally moved off towards the guard's van—it was Wally's evening for the post.

Henrietta saw Ewan and Diego alight from their compartment up near the engine, waved a hand, and walked to meet them. She was not in her tartan and pullover, but in a light cream dress and a light blue blouse with

an open neck, and there was a blue ribbon in her fine
linten hair. She was a delicately strong, fragilely un-
breakable shaft of young womanhood; and she came at
Diego as she had come at Larry that evening he had
arrived, striding short and daintily, not quite teetering,
her throat curved back and her insolently weary eyes
looking down her nose. She stopped before Diego.

"Señor Diego Usted, I believe?"

She reached him an indolent hand from shoulder-
level, and he took her fingers firmly and bowed his lips
to their coolness.

"And the rest of it, señorita?" he said, still holding her
hand but not exerting any pull.

"Why not?" She drew him close and kissed him
firmly, briefly, on the mouth. Then she held him away,
looked closely at his lips, and was the laughing Henrietta
once more. "Foster-Ellen won't get that one. How are
you, Ewan? I wish you'd drop down dead, with your
dam' papers to light the fire under you."

"Blame me, would you?" The old man spoke tartly.
"All right! Blame away, and to hell with the Harpers!"

She saw that he was nettled. "Sorry, Ewan! But
you are coming on a useless errand. Young Affran will
not sign, and that's flat."

"Won't he now?"

"He will not." She was entirely serious. "That's
definite. There's hell to pay the last two days."

"I could come up to see, anyway, and I so far the
road?"

"Come on, then!" She swung to Diego's side, and the
three went down the platform.

"Does the Hegira start to save your soul?" she asked
Diego.

"I go to London day after to-morrow."

"I am coming with you."

"That would not help my soul."

221

"My train breaks off at Perth for North Wales, but you could take me on to Edinbro' for a jollification, and round it off in London? Who could know?"

"Am I deaf you're thinking?" enquired Ewan.

"But you've damned the Harpers already, and damned they'll be. Here's Peter with my parcels."

It took another ten minutes for Diego to give Peter and Wally his news. They were pleased that he was fit, and sorry that he was leaving, and were particularly gratified that one of their own, Hamish, was to be head of the Glen.

"But there's the Major——" Wally stopped and looked at the Major's daughter.

"Don't hesitate to shoot, Wally," she said. "Dad is not very fit——"

"Fit or not," said Ewan McInnes firmly, "there was never a Harper could touch Hamish McLeod."

"You are getting your own back, Ewan. Come on!"

They went up the Glen, the big car eating up the petrol that belonged to the Home Guard, but, then, Major-General Harper was the Home Guard. Diego sat in front with Henrietta; Ewan and Wally sat behind chatting amiably. The girl was not in a talkative mood this evening. She did not speak at all till she stopped at Wally's post office in Craik.

"I suppose you'll not give me the General's mail, you old crippler?" she said then.

"Dom't, Miss Hett! You know the regulations? In the privacy——"

"Stow it! Hamish's letter of appointment is probably in that bag."

"And what if it is? Can't the Don tell him?" He grinned. "And can't I come up the morn and ha'e a dram to the new job? And what's more, if people would mind their own business and not interfere with officials——"

The car moved on and left him. From the top of the rise Diego saw the white house of Loch Beg below the bluff.

"There's your aunt coming down to the gate already, and Hamish at the door," the girl said. "She told me to look out for you, as she had a feeling you were on the road. She knows everything beforehand. If we ever do restore the Golden Age we could introduce a bit of realism and burn her as a witch. Are you coming up to say good-bye?"

"To-morrow. You will tell Ann?" He called her Ann frankly now.

"I will. She is in one of her tempers. Poor old devil! she cannot help herself or help us, but if I were half a man I know what I would do."

"Yes?"

"I would take her away. I have no moral scruples."

"She has. She would not come."

"Ask her. I know you won't, Galahad. You'll be away day after to-morrow, and so will I. In a month she will be away. Every one of the Harpers will be out of here, and some of us holding down a job for bread and butter. That is what it has come to, Don, since you left. Your aunt will tell you, and here we are."

She barely stopped the car for Diego to get out, waved a hand generally, and went on, Ewan McInnes protesting vigorously that he wanted to congratulate Hamish.

v

Aunt Ellen held the gate open for Diego, and banged it behind him. She did not speak before she took him by the shoulders, kissed him on the cheek, and rubbed a cool palm under his ear and down his jaw.

"The clean flesh that's in it," she murmured. "Come away in, boy!"

Uncle Hamish, grave-faced, shook hands warmly. And

Diego wondered how anyone had ever considered his uncle an ugly man. In the big living-room he got the perfume of the peat afresh; the table was laid, a kettle hung on the crook, and an oven rested on a bed of peat embers; he was at home in this fine room where surcease of pain had come to him, and soon he would be leaving it for ever. He felt his first touch of lonesomeness. His aunt put him sitting in his own chair at his own side of the fire, and drew his old slippers from a corner. She spoke as if she knew.

"So it has come, Don?"

"It has, Aunt. You worked your miracle, and to-morrow is my last day in the Glen."

"It had to be. From the beginning it had to be, and there's no use me resenting it."

Uncle Hamish was in his chair feeling for a few crumbs of plug in his pockets. He did not find any.

"You will have to go on a ration, Uncle," said Diego.

"It'll be worse than that, Jamie—a black fast, I'm thinking."

"Aunt Ellen, in that suitcase over there you might find a small box of the nature of your favourite Irish sweet-meat—Peggy's Leg you call it."

"Thank you, Don," she said without her old enthusiasm. "I'll try a bit later."

Uncle Hamish looked at Diego through crinkling eyes, got to his feet and moved across to the case.

"I'll get it for her, Jamie," he said.

He took out two parcels, held one in his hand, and looked across at Diego.

"Try the other one," Diego suggested. The other one contained as many ounces of plug as a Staff-Colonel could beg, borrow or steal in Inverness.

Uncle Hamish looked at it dumbly and shook his massive head.

"That is for the Head of the Home Guard," Diego said.

Uncle Hamish started. "What's that you say, Jamie?"

"You're It. Information from Headquarters. Your letter of appointment was sent out yesterday, and is now in Wally's bag."

"Goad be here!" He looked at his wife and again shook his head. "Mind you, I'd take it, though I'm not fit for the job at my age, but I'd take it as a duty, knowing the Glen and the men to choose. But—you tell him, Big Ellen."

"You'll take it, Cuchulain, though the time may be short. But you will play the game to the end, like the man I call you after, if need be tying yourself to a post to die on your feet facing the enemy, a raven on your shoulder. Smoke up, Cuchulain! I will do the talking."

Uncle Hamish sat down and sawed plug; Aunt Ellen walked from hearth to dresser and back again, a tall caryatid come to life, her fine aquiline head thrown back on the column of her neck, and her hands still at her side. Her voice filled the room.

"I mind the fine spring evening you came in that door, my fine Spanish man. A fine spring evening before a clear night of frost, your spirit sick and your flesh weary, your mouth tight shut, and your thoughts in your eyes. Coming in to die dourly near one of your own. And, still, you were thoughtful, with your pipes and tobacco, your mother's trinkets—God rest her—beads and brooches, and the comb you set in my hair—and her wedding-ring that I have safe." She stopped, and her blue eyes stared fiercely in front of her, seeing nothing, and slowly a light lit behind her eyes. Her hands met with a clash, and her voice rolled. "By the goodness of God you will put that ring on a woman's finger, and doing it you will not be ashamed." She resumed her slow striding and went on quietly recalling. "I put you sitting down in that chair that is called Don Diego's chair now, and in an hour, though you said nothing, we knew you to the marrow of your bones. We took you into our hands, and you found your own way to our hearts. Hamish sitting there smoking his old pipe and lapping his thoughts about you, myself half-inventing an old tale to lift your heart to the turn; and your heart lifted, and there was no more trouble. You gave and received. Digging the ground with the spirit of Adam, and Eve watching you far off and lonely. Allying yourself with Hamish to make me talk easy nonsense. Going on the hills and gathering their serenity. The life of the Glen was yours, and now, after three months, the Glen is yours. Not once, Diego, did I doubt you, though my heart was often troubled. You found your own problem and faced it like a man, and you got good help, and now it is driving you out of the Glen. You are not the only one. Many a one has gone out of the Glen never to return. All our sons and daughters are gone and scattered, and if they die we will know how to bear it when the time comes. Yes, all my dear ones are going or gone, and we are going too."

She strode across to the fireside, took a folded paper from the high mantelpiece and handed it to Diego.

"That will tell you. It is in his own hand-of-write, for he wouldn't trust Ewan McInnes with it."

And while Diego read she paced slowly and hummed the most poignant—yet indomitable—of all Jacobite laments, *The Loss of Aughrim*:

> "Here's a health to you, O my King,
> The monarch of my liking!
> And a health to dear old Ireland;
> Pour blessings on her name!
> May her sons be true when needed,
> May they never fail as we did,
> For Sean Dwyer o' Glanna
> We were worsted in the game."

The communication was formal and brief.

" Major-General Charles Harper hereby informs Hamish McLeod that his employment as Head-Forester for the Glen Affran Estates will terminate a month from this date. Vacant possession of Loch Beg Bothy must be handed over at the termination of that period. Temporary arrangements as to further employment will be made by the present Factor, pending actual possession by the new owner with whose arrangements General Harper has no concern."

That could be said much more briefly and effectively: "You are out of a job in a month, McLeod, and I don't care if you get another." No word of thanks, no appreciation of good service, just a bald "clear out."

"There's the new owner," said Diego lamely, his heart empty at the thought of what this house would lose—and the Glen.

"There's the new owner surely," agreed Aunt Ellen. "I know the General has a purchaser."

"No!" cried Uncle Hamish firmly. "We will not bother with him. There's that bit place near your brother Larr's, not far from the Pass of Keimaneigh. We have gear and to spare."

"But not enough grace in my heart to grease an axle this minute. Ay, Cuchulain, you would take me back to Ireland and leave your own heart here." And again she softly raised an old song:

" My heart's in the Highlands, my heart is not here,
My heart's in the Highlands a-chasing the deer,
A-chasing the deer and a-hunting the roe—
My heart's in the Highlands wherever I go.

"And where do you think my own heart is, Cuchulain? Where but here where my children were reared, here in this glen where we helped to keep the old ways alive, and gathered friends around us without any distinction of class or creed. Where we took the last of our own and two motherless bairns—ay, and fatherless—and brought them up our own way, putting dreams and notions into their heads, and having a dream of our own that they might be leaders in a new revival. And who says that may not be? Glen Affran is not dead yet, and the situation is changing under our eyes." She clapped her hands and came to the fire in a swoop. "Mother o' God! the bottom is burned out o' that kettle, and the chicken a dishcloth. You'll eat now, and I'll talk sense for once in my life."

And whilst she got the high tea ready, and whilst they ate, she told Diego how the situation at the Lodge had developed. And as she talked she moved around the table, and back and forth between fireplace and dresser, and in and out of the back-place, and the cadence of her voice sent thrills and pangs through Diego. In memory he would hear that voice from across the world.

"Ay, Don! the situation has changed since you went to Inverness. The entail and alienation papers are all ready to sign, but they will not be signed, as old Ewan will find out to-night. But it could be that the General will have other work for him. Young Affran, home for his last week, will not sign and threatens to blow the ould devil to smithereens if he tries to coerce his father."

"Is Young Affran's signature necessary?"

"Maybe not, since he's not the heir yet, but the uncle has taken it into his head to make siccar, as Ewan says. But, and mark you this, Don! the Major has now decided that he will not sign either. And there's news for you! You'll be wondering why, and I can tell you. Because of a clause in the agreement new put in. The General, not able to boss the Glen, is making double sure that no Harper will stay behind to do it. 'Tis down in black and white. Not only must all the Harpers clear out of the Lodge within a month—which is only fair to the new owner—but they must not take up residence any place in the Glen."

"Surely he cannot enforce that clause?"

"The very thing I say," said Uncle Hamish.

"And what Ewan McInnes says as well, but there it is. The old fellow will have it in, and the Major will not sign as long as it is in. My own notion is that the Major is at last seeing the light o' day, and is making that clause an excuse. What he is afraid of is that his son will blow the uncle's head clean off before he'll let his father sign. He has threatened to do it. And there you are. Unless Ewan persuades one or the other to-night the entail stands, and he'll persuade neither, for if one is thrawn the other is twice as thrawn. And that's that."

She replenished Diego's plate, and put a hand on his shoulder.

"And that is not all, son. There's worse to follow. This very day, as a final threat, the General ordered his brother and the two young ones out of his house—house and policies and the Glen itself—and gave them two days to do it in. There was a row to raise the roof. The Major kept his temper—he always does—but he had to restrain Young Affran by main force. And Hett—'twas she told me—she used the language of a fishwife and tried to make the old tyrant's eyes blink. She didn't. And then our Spanish lady took a hand, using her hands and her voice in a last attempt to patch up things. She failed too and lost her temper—right down the drain—and told her good man what she thought of him from the day he was born till the good God rejected him; and if you ever heard the same lady tell a man what she thought of him you would be satisfied that thought had gone its limits. He got staring mad too—eyes and temper—and he called her a bad name out of the past, and a woman of many lovers. And there she smacked him full on the face. She is as strong as a slip of steel that girl, and she

229

did not hold her hand. He staggered and slipped and fell down amongst the rugs, and she added insult to injury by kicking him contemptuously in a contemptuous place. And when he got up his eyes were blinking for the first time in living memory. So Hett told me. And he raved at her about a new Will, and she turned her back and walked out on him. And that's all. So, to sum up, in two days you'll be away, and so will the three Harpers; and in a month or less we'll be out of Loch Beg, for he'll make his notice of dismissal stick; and he'll be away himself, and his wife. She'll go too, for she is loyal to her marriage vows——"

"There was no kicking in the same," said Hamish.

"But she is loyal, and he'll keep hold of her—like a spider—and suck her dry in foreign places, same as he sucked the life out of two women already." She was at the other side of the table now and looked fierce-eyed across at Diego. "Are you going up there to-morrow, Don?"

"I am, Aunt."

"You will behave yourself."

"I might not, Aunt."

"I don't mean what you mean. You are not thinking of taking up that wisp of a blade you have in your bag and spitting someone through the gizzard?"

"Is it an order?"

"No. That blade is for a sterner purpose than killing an old madman—for that is what he is."

"That is now an order," said Diego. "Will you please give me one other?"

"What is it?"

"That I take Ann out of this glen with me."

"I was afraid of that." She twisted her apron in her hands. "I am not blaming you, for men are all the same. Maybe you could persuade her to leave the Glen, but when it comes to the bit you will not try her too hard."

She swung to her husband, and she was still twisting her apron. "Cuchulain, there'll be a tragedy in the Glen if you don't watch out."

Her husband looked at her quickly and put a hand on her arm.

"Take it easy, woman!"

She threw his hand off. Her face was strangely drawn, and there was pain in her eyes. Her voice was a tone higher.

"What are you going to do about it? How are you going to guard our own?"

"I can well guard them." His voice was sure. "Leave it to me. For God's sake, Ellen——"

He was on his feet now, but she thrust him away from her.

"Leave me be, Cuchulain. I have to fight this myself. Will you two please go about your business. Go fishing. I will be all right. Go on now!"

Hamish looked at Diego and nodded his head. "There's a fish might take in Affran Water. Come on, Jamie."

But they did not go fishing. They sat down at the outside of the garden wall, and Hamish slowly filled a pipe. He shook his head disconsolately.

"She is in for one of her takings, I fear me. We'll stay here at hand, Jamie."

"What she calls prevision?"

"I'm praying the other way. It hurts her."

Diego did not pray. Selfishly enough, his thoughts went to his own problem, but they were not clear thoughts. Things had come to a crisis at the Lodge and with him. Could he or would he persuade Ann to leave the Glen with him? Having broken with that self-centred madman, her husband, was it right to let her go into exile amongst negroes and half-castes and Carib Indians? There were negroes and half-castes and Indians at San José too, but there, also, the urges of her heart were.

231

But the urges of the heart were no criterion by which to judge right or wrong! There was the moral again. Well! to-morrow he would see Ann Harper, and seeing her he might know what to say and do. And there he told himself that he was taking the weak man's way by leaving the decision to the occasion, and the decision would then be completely biased. His uncle spoke at his side.

"We will go in now, Jamie. I don't like leaving her long alone."

She was not in the living-room when they went in. Hamish went upstairs soft-footed and was back almost at once.

"She is lying down," he whispered. "She'll be all right. You and I will ha'e a dram to ourselves."

They went to bed early that night, but no one slept well. Diego heard the murmur of voices coming through two walls, and after a while there was quiet. And then in the heart of the short summer dark he was waked out of a fitful doze by the lifting of his aunt's voice. There was something hysterical about it, but his uncle's firm tones gradually subdued it. Diego heard their door open, and sprang out of bed to fumble for his own door-knob. Uncle Hamish was at the head of the stairs, a candle in his hand and a long nightshirt down to his broad bare feet.

"All right, Jamie!" he said quietly. "Something to make the body sleep. It is all over now."

Aunt Ellen's deep sane voice rolled from her room. "'Tis nothing, son. Go back to your bed. We might not sleep easy to-morrow night."

Diego went back to bed; but in the other room the murmur of voices, quiet now, went on for a long time. In that murmur he went to sleep at last, and into restless dreams.

# CHAPTER II

## QUIT IT IS

### I

Whilst they were at breakfast the following morning the phone rang, and Aunt Ellen was out in the passage before the men could move. Uncle Hamish shook his head.

"If that's the General, she'll make his eyes blink four miles off."

It was not the General. Aunt Ellen spoke in her lowest tones, but the carrying quality of her voice made every word distinct.

"Yes, my darling . . . at his breakfast and nourishing a bad humour as well . . . he is, he said so. . . . You'll have a job, but you are able for it. . . . Alone, he'll insist on that. . . . Where? . . . Oh, there! . . . Why not? as good a place as any. . . . Yes, you'll be in the public eye. . . . No, you had better not. . . . Hamish and myself will go down. . . . I'll get him."

Uncle Hamish nodded at Diego. It was easy enough to know who was at the other end of the phone and most of what she said. Diego was on his feet when his aunt's head appeared round the jamb.

"For you, Don."

"A long time you took to get the message," growled Uncle Hamish. "Mind your own business, woman!"

"What else am I doing, children?"

Ann Harper's deep voice was speaking into Diego's ear. The little familiar sibilance of it twisted his heart. She, too, had a carrying voice, and anyone in the hall at the Lodge could hear every word. But she did not try to hide her message from anyone.

"Señor Diego, it is me myself. I salute you good morning."

"Morning!" said Diego briefly.

"I am happy that you are well—so well."

"I am not."

"No!" Her voice was startled.

"You know why?"

"Oh! That I do not know. You will see me?"

"And alone, as my aunt said."

"You are being dominant, Don Diego."

"Can you say that?"

"Oh, the temper! and the sun shining." She chuckled into his ear. "I am happy that you have a small sourness in the morning. My father had——"

"I have not."

"Ah but—! Very well, my friend! I yield a little." Her voice quietened. "It will be at that place where we had our first fine talk. You will remember?"

"Señora, you and my aunt have talked so much and in so many places, how could I remember?"

"That is how men speak in the house before breakfast."

"I have broken mine."

"Then it is bad. You remember very well?"

"Skene's Rock?"

"The Rock of Skene—that is the place. The sun of evening and the world all round us. It will be seven of the clock."

"Seven, yes."

"Till then be with God—and thereafter. Please be not dominant, Diego. I am very frightened."

The phone clicked in his ear before he could say another word. He went back to the living-room, and glared defiantly at his aunt.

"Well—well—well!" was all she said.

Uncle Hamish got to his feet, his chair protesting. He was not in a good humour this morning either.

"Don't let her draw you, Jamie," he warned. "Where's that dom dutch hoe?" He made for the door, and Diego followed at his heels.

"Pictish bear and Spanish wolf!" her voice derided them. "I know, and ye know too, Cuchulain wanting his spear and the Cid his sword."

The two men worked for half an hour. Uncle Hamish plied his hoe with a savagery that showed he had a depth of temper and did not mind shearing through the white flesh of an onion. Diego worked slowly and meticulously, but after half an hour he found he could not work any longer. He dropped his hoe across a row of white turnip, lit a cigarette, and strolled away towards the shore of the loch wimpling under the sun in the dying breeze of morning. High up a lark was singing the promise of a warm day. His uncle called after him:

"You might be back for lunch, Jamie? 'Tis Friday, and only taties and trooties." That was his way of telling Diego to take to the healing hills and be in no hurry back.

Diego crossed Affran Water by the pony-bridge, went over the shoulder of the hill, and crossed the peat-bog where the bothy's winter firing stood in small stacks along the top of the cut bank. He lifted a dark brown sod, hefted it, and found it heavy and dry as bone. He had helped to cut that peat, even using the slane for a spell, spreading it with a fork, turning it later, then footing it, three sods on end and one on top like a dolmen, and finally building it into those small stacks. But he would not be here to load Sanny's panniers and build the rick at the gable-end. Where would he be—dead or——?

He struck into the Glen of the Willows and followed it to the Sanctuary under Scurr Affran. There he saw many hind with their speckled fawn trotting under their stomachs, a couple of young buck showing their first spikes, and one solitary old stag already carrying a fine stand of antlers under a sheath of brown velvet. He went on slowly by the ruined walls, up to the height of land, and down the long winding valley on the other side. And in time he came to the pine-grove, and turned the corner looking down on Donald Gunn's bothy.

In one of the wired-in meadows below the house and above the lochan three men were haymaking. Evidently some of the hay had been cut while Diego was away at Inverness, and the three men were now engaged in raking it into rows and building it up into cocks. The hounds bayed and the dogs barked, and the three hay-makers lifted heads and waved back to Diego's wave.

The three men haymaking were the tallest men in the Glen. Long John McKenzie was six and a half feet, and besides being tall was big, a massive man carrying little extra flesh, with a lion-like head of light-grizzled hair. Donald Gunn and Piobar Maol Tam were well over six feet, both lean men, but whereas Donald Gunn had plenty of dark grey hair the Piper had none at all. His tanned high-receding dome of head was as hairless as an ivory ball. That baldness had earned him one of his by-names, for *maol* means bald.

They came round Diego, prong points upright, shook his hand and hoped he had good news for them; and having got it, they were pleased that he was again sound, and sorry that he was leaving them. He would be missed from their dwindling company, but he would come again often, and be welcome, a thousand times welcome.

"We expected Hamish across," said Donald. "Are you deputising for him, Don Diego?"

Uncle Hamish had said nothing about the haymaking, and he would not, of course, leave the house on Diego's last day. Diego did not say that.

"Uncle has something on hand," he said, "and I am to try haymaking."

236

"Ay, faith!" said Long John. "You've tried everything that's going, and held it down neat and handy."

"There's the a'e thing he hasn't tried yet," said the Piper, winking, "but we can wait for that till the bit barley is cut."

II

For the next two hours Diego put his back into haymaking, raking the hay into rows with a wooden rake and building it up into small cocks with a two-pronged fork. He was handy with his hands, and soon got the trick of using the rake lightly so as not to break a wooden tooth in the grass roots, and since the turf-cutting he was adept with the fork. The sun of two days had dried the hay nicely, but it had retained some of its green colour, and the perfume of it was sweet in the nostrils. He felt the warmth of the sun on the back of his neck and on his bared arms, and soon the sweat was running into his black brows and amongst the black hairs on his breast. And with the coming of the sweat there came to him an ease of mind. Mind-worry and temper were not worth while. He would meet the occasion as it rose, and abide the issue. Meantime he would make hay.

After two hours Donald left them and went up to the house, and in a short time after that came to the door and gave them the Highland hail to the midday meal. And Diego found that he was hungry.

"Not much of a dinner, being Friday," Donald made excuses to Diego. "Long John here is a Free-Kirker, but he'll be a Christian for once. Moreover, he likes fish and I don't—not on a Friday. We'll have a drappie first."

Diego could now hold his own as a trencher-man with anyone in the Glen, and that meal was entirely to his satisfaction. Loch trout pink-fleshed, new potatoes, and freshly pulled peas, followed by a green-gooseberry tart smothered in cream—there was nothing inadequate about that meal.

It was immediately after dinner, when they were leisurely smoking, that the phone bell rang. As has been said, all the bothies were connected with the Lodge and with each other by a private wire. Uncle Hamish was on the phone, and Donald took the message. Uncle Hamish had a good deal to say.

"Yes, Hamish. . . . Just after his dinner. . . . Yes. . . . I'm listening. . . . Uh-uh! . . . Do you tell me that? . . . We'll just have to . . . right round and over the shoulder. . . . I have it . . . the two . . . uh-uh! . . . he can do it. . . . Just this minute."

Donald turned round, his eyes resting on Diego for a moment and then turning on his men.

"Hamish. He has a job for me up Glen Seilig way. He wants you two at Loch Beg just as soon as you can get there. There's no hurry on you, Don Diego, but these two young lads will have to move their shanks at the trot." He looked intently at his two friends. "Come on, heroes! and ye will remember that the Glen is at last doing some of its own work."

The two swallowed cups of hot tea, drew on their jackets, said a word to Diego, and followed Donald out of doors. From outside came their lowered and earnest voices, and Diego wondered. Were these men at last going to do some of the Glen's work? Would the clansmen again take up the old law in their hands and deal summarily with a laird who had failed them? Diego could not see them do it. There was summary law and non-law in all the world, but the glens had been cowed too long.

Donald came back and nodded at Diego. "I'm for the road, Don Diego, but you can take your own time. And I'll be obliged if you gather up the forks and rakes and put them in the shed." He moved to the fire and began to smoor it. "I might be gone a while," he explained. He drew a bed of ashes round and over the red peat-coals, and set the ends of three or four sods against the hot embers. Diego had learned how to do that nightly job in his aunt's house, and knew that the spark for a new fire would keep alive for twelve hours. In many of the Glen houses the fire had not gone out since the houses had been built.

Donald did not ask Diego to accompany him by Glen Seilig, and Diego was sorry that he did not, for it now struck him that up the Strath and over the chorrie of Garbh Ailt would be as good a way as any to reach the rendezvous with Ann at Skene's Rock. But since Donald did not ask him, Diego did not suggest it himself, for he guessed that Donald was on some particularly private errand for Uncle Hamish.

"It is not good-bye yet, my friend," Donald said. "I'll see you some time to-night. I have a book for you to remember me by."

"I do not need it to do that."

"That's it. So long, then!" He set off long-strided towards the gap at the end of the Strath, and Diego watched him go. He had slung his stalker's telescope over a shoulder, and carried a long crook under an arm.

Diego went down to the meadow and looked about him. There was still enough hay lying flat to make about two rows of cocks, and he wondered if rain would come in the night. Any time in July rain might come over the mountains with very little warning. He had plenty of time, and thought he would put up a half-row of cocks at any rate.

He stripped to the work, and in one fine sweating hour finished the meadow—two rows and one cock over. After cooling off he had a plunge in the lochan, but, even in July, found it too cold for pleasure. After that he stored his implements in the shed, talked to the dogs, put a finger through the mesh to feel a cold nose and a warm tongue, and turned his face towards the Glen of the Willows.

He actually had one foot on the pony-bridge across Affran Water when he suddenly decided that he would not cross over and face his aunt before setting out for the Rock. For the first time he did not want her indirect probing wisdom to find out the jumble of thoughts in his mind.

By this time he was familiar with every track and turn about Affran Loch. Here on the south side there was a pony-track by Loch Beg going over the bluff and twisting amongst the trees all the way to Lodge Affran. Three miles up it forked, one fork going on to the Lodge, and the other angling off amongst the trees to join the track down from Skene's Rock just below the fault in the cliff. Moreover, from where he now stood this way was shorter than by the motor road and around the head of the loch. He did not want to see anyone at the Lodge. Neither did he want his aunt to see him, but that hope was vain.

As he came to that point across the water facing the end of the house where another few strides would take him out of sight from door or window, his aunt came out on the step and looked across at him. Behind her came the figure of a young woman. Diego stopped and looked intently. Yes, that was Henrietta in her cream and blue, probably come down to say good-bye. He lifted an arm and saluted, and his aunt made a sweeping dramatic gesture that said plainly, *Go your own way*. Henrietta made no movement at all. In three strides he was out of sight.

He had ample time to get to the rendezvous before seven, and he moved leisurely along above Affran Loch. The track, silent under his feet in a mat of brown needles, lifted up and dipped down and turned this way and that among the columned pines. At no place could he see more than fifty paces ahead, and where the track wound away from the shore, so closely grew the trees, he could not see the water shining in the evening sun. The sun, tending west, was coming down into the pass at the far end of the loch. Here and there it shone aslant amongst the trees and laid a golden splash on the carpet of brown; and the reflection of light off the water sent a golden glow wavering and flowing across the trunks of the pine.

And it was there in the quietness of the pine-wood, sighing so softly and aloofly to itself, that his mind finally cleared. He knew then how much of power was in himself and what he could do with it. He knew that for that evening he could dominate Ann Harper. On this his last evening before leaving the Glen her defences would be down, and she would come to his arms if he reached them to her. He stopped in the centre of the track and looked down at his scuffed brown shoes. Yes, he could take her in his arms! He could feel her long yielding body yielding to his, feel the kisses of her mouth grown soft. He could see her coming away with him, could see her in London in their quiet and secret rooms. He could see her ruling in his house of San José? No, by God! he could not. Not in the house of San José where her clean dreams were, and if not there, then nowhere else.

He knew then, as clear as light, with the clearness of light, that he could not hurt this woman at the very centre of her life. He could not destroy the personal integrity that she had held secure amidst the terrors and degradations she had suffered in Spain when the Cause was lost amongst the Basques. He could not destroy the simple Faith that was below and was the base of the strong passion and sexual urge of the Basque woman. If he did she would be only a derelict vessel drifting where he drifted, here or in London or in the hacienda of San José.

Now, at last, he knew what he must do. He must be strong and not tender for her sake this evening. And the sooner he got this final parting over the better. He threw up his head, flicked thumb and forefinger above his shoulder, and set off briskly along the track, his arms swinging. He was even a little happy. The desolation of life had not yet come about him. He found himself whistling a tune. It was Ann's own tune, and he started to hum a verse to it.

He came, full of splendid confidence, to where the track forked, and paused to look at his watch. It was half-past six, and Skene's Rock, on top of the cliff, was only twenty minutes away. He would be there in good time. He turned into the path leading up steeply through the wood, and bent his back to the climb. Half-way up he heard a dead stick crack amongst the trees on his left, and turned his head quickly. He thought he caught a vanishing flick of brown amongst the close-set trunks. There was no sound now and nothing to see. Of course! That would be a roe deer making off, one of those lovely miniature deer so destructive amongst young plantations. He went on.

The sharp smack of a rifle from a short distance ahead startled him. He knew from experience that it was a rifle-shot, and that the rifle was of small calibre. Had someone taken a shot at that roe—or at himself? No, not at himself, for he had not heard the bullet. He knew that the General or his brother were for ever pottering about the woods with a point-twenty-two rifle taking snap-shots at roe and squirrel and hooded crows. That would be it! He went forward quickly, his eyes watchful, and wondered what the General would say to a man on his way to a rendezvous with the General's wife. He would call it an assignation in its illicit sense.

Diego would not mind. It was not an assignation, but he saw how nearly it might be, and how mean it would be.

He saw the broken rampart of stone through the trees, and came to the edge of an opening below the fault in the cliff. And there he stopped dead, the breath checking in his throat. The opening was not more than twenty yards in width, a small half-circle bounded by the trees and the cliff. Ridges of rock stood out of the matt of pine-needles. To the right, where the cliff had faulted, the track from Skene's Rock came steeply down, and the track Diego was on curved round the edge of the clearing to meet it at the side of a huge detached boulder fully eight feet high. Before that boulder, her back turned, stood Ann Harper, in her tartan skirt and green pullover, her red hair shining in the sun and the green ribbon holding it down.

She held a small rifle clasped across her breast, and at her feet, close against the boulder, lay the body of a man in grey flannels and with a mop of white hair.


# CHAPTER III

## HEGIRA

### I

DIEGO went slowly across between the ridges of rock, not thinking at all, not able to think. He wanted to move quickly, but his feet dragged in the matt of pine-needles. She did not hear his footsteps until he was at her back, but she was not startled. She turned round as with great difficulty and stared him in the face, the rifle, in clenched hands, across her breast. Her face had been always bloodless, but now her lips were bloodless too, her lit black eyes stared as if she did not know him, and every hair of her head was alive.

"My poor Ann!" whispered Diego.

At that whisper she came alive. She seemed to shrink away within herself, and her voice too was a whisper.

"Diego, is he dead?"

At her side he sat on his heels before the still figure. It was the body of her husband, Major-General Harper, and it was dead. Diego had seen many dead men, and this man was but just dead—all the colour had not yet drained out of his face below the mop of white hair. Five minutes ago he had been alive, and now life had been shattered out of him for ever. He was lying half over, and Diego saw one eye wide open and still expressionlessly staring. Yesterday he had blinked at a blow, now he would blink no more. One arm was hidden under him, the other thrown forward and clutching the stone. The jaw had not yet relaxed, and there was blood on the stone under the jaw. The irrevocability of the thing—so sudden, so appalling—came home anguishingly to Diego.

He crouched there at the woman's side, and now he was thinking clearly and rapidly. And, strangely enough, his first thought was that Hamish McLeod and his wife had failed to keep tragedy out of the Glen. He knew so exactly what had happened. Major-General Harper, that morning, had heard his wife making her appointment over the phone, and this evening he had followed her, and armed with a rifle. Yes, he would have the rifle, not she, and he might intend using it too. He had accosted her here or she had accosted him—perhaps heard him follow and waited for him behind this stone. She had a temper. There would be domination and accusation and recrimination. A mistress going to an assignation with her lover! Yesterday she had lashed out at him hand and foot. To-day she would tear the rifle out of his hands and kill him. No, not that! He was an old man, but strong. They would struggle for the rifle. Perhaps he had threatened to shoot her lover, and she had endeavoured to wrest the rifle from him. And the rifle went off between them, and he was lying there dead. She might have been the one lying dead—and better that she were.

He straightened up at her side.

"He is dead," he told her.

Her voice was just above a whisper and full of sadness.

"He was but an old man and mad. It was evil to kill him."

"It was an accident," Diego said firmly. "There was a struggle, and the rifle went off."

She nodded her head rapidly, eagerly.

"Yes! surely yes! That was the way. It must be the way."

This woman, too, had often seen death, and ugly death. She did not falter where a sheltered woman would utterly collapse. Her feet were firmly planted, and her hands firmly grasped the rifle, and in her eyes was, not madness or fear, but a sadness that was of her whole being, the beginning of a remorse that would last her life.

He put a hand out and took the rifle from her. She gripped tight for a second, and then let go, taking one step back as if shrinking from him. He looked down at the dead man for a full minute. The man was irrevocably dead. What could he, Diego Usted, do for the woman that was alive? Kill her too? No. This game of Fate—or God—must be played out. He was an old campaigner, used to crises, and his brain worked as if packed in ice. In one minute he knew what he must do. He felt no prick of conscience, though the thing he was about to do was wholly immoral. He was bent on saving this woman who had slain her husband.

By the cold northern standard that was indeed immoral, but to the Latin it was simply logical and divinely merciful.

He looked at the rifle in his hands. The dead man's finger-marks would be on it, and hers, and now his. He took off the old tweed hat that had once been Larry's, grasped the butt of the rifle through it with his left hand, drew his handkerchief from his pocket, and very carefully wiped the weapon from muzzle to butt. There were no finger-marks now, but there must be. Again he sat on his heels and laid the rifle down at the side of the dead man.

He drew in a deep breath and steadied himself for the next act. He turned the body over and pulled the hidden right arm clear. The hand was still warm and lax, but, already, it felt the hand of a dead man. In moving the body he saw the killing wound. It was under the jaw-bone, and the bullet must have gone upwards into the base of the brain. That was where a wound would be inflicted in a struggle, but it also could be a wound self-inflicted. That was the first turn of luck. But there was now a nagging small query at the back of Diego's mind: if the wound was accidental in a struggle for the rifle, would the rifle remain grasped in the woman's hands? He would not let his mind dwell on that query. He clenched his teeth and did his job thoroughly. The lax dead hands were easy to manipulate. Wrapping his own hand in his handkerchief, he clasped the fingers of the dead right hand on the stock and round the lock; he closed the fingers of the left hand on three places round the barrel; and finally closed the left hand close below the muzzle and pressed the thumb of the right hand inside the trigger. That was how a man would hold a rifle to commit suicide. And all the time he had not a prick of conscience.

He sat back on his heels considering. No! this was

not right yet. The rifle would not be held so after the explosion of the shot. But thus. With the back of his hand he flicked the rifle from the lax fingers and it lay on the stone naturally, as if it had fallen. Then, at last, he straightened up, and as he did so a harsh deep sardonic voice spoke behind him:

"Able—able! Murder to look like suicide!"

## II

As Diego whirled round he saw Ann's hand go to her mouth to suppress a scream. She had been watching Diego so intently that she too had not heard anyone approach.

Major Arthur Harper, the dead man's brother, stood up stiffly within half a dozen paces. Diego did not know where he had come from, up the path from the Lodge or through the wood, but he must have seen every damning thing that had been done. His eyes had a cold blaze, his hands were clenched, and the carved, lined face, blanched under the tan, was the colour of stained ivory. His voice was savagely sardonic.

"Once you would stalk and shoot me. You have chosen more profitable game, you dog."

Diego had never liked Major Harper, and would show that now. He took two slow strides towards him. The other did not move. He was a big, powerfully-built man, and was not afraid of this lean dark foreigner. He just lifted a clenched hand.

"No use, Usted! You will do what I tell you—both of you, murderer and accomplice. If you will consider, there is no escape." His voice was dominant now. "I am going down to the Lodge, and you will come with me. Anything you want to say you can say to Constable Campbell. Come on!"

This was the cold northerner, and he would have the

cold northern justice, which is really vengeance. Also, as a man of the north, he could dominate these two of inferior breed into obeying him. He half turned to lead the way, but Diego kept on taking slow soft strides towards him, and at once he faced round, his eyes flaring and his slit chin thrust out.

"What do you think you're doing? I'll break you in two, you dago!"

He lifted his clenched hands, but before he could make another move Diego had his wrists.

Arthur Harper was a strong man, even if he had a weak heart, though Diego, somehow, never did believe that he had a weak heart, or a game leg either. Now he used his strength to try and break explosively Diego's grip on his wrists. He could not. No one in the Glen knew that Diego had any exceptional strength, for he had never displayed it. He had come into the Glen a sick man, but he was no longer that. Now he held Major Harper's arms across his breast as if they were bound there, and slow and inexorably forced him down to his knees. It looked easy, but the man that was being forced down knew the extraordinary cumulative effect of the pressure that was so inexorably exerted against his own strength.

Diego held him there immovable and looked grimly down into his eyes, and the other's effort suddenly collapsed, and his eyes were no longer insolent.

"Easy enough to kill you, Harper, and make it look like murder and suicide. Open your mouth now, and die!"

Major Harper did not open his mouth, for he had not the final valour. Suddenly, then, Diego jerked him to his feet, loosed his arms, and struck him back-handed across the mouth.

"Go, you gringo!" Diego brought his hands to his sides, and stood there unguarded. If that man had struck him then, Diego would have killed him with his bare hands. But, indeed, the man had not the final courage that is all courage, for he turned on his heel and walked quickly towards the track. And he was not limping.

Diego went back to Ann. Her black eyes were wide on him, and her mouth a little open. He smiled for her, but she did not smile back.

"But you are a man, Diego," she said. "The other thing—it was an accident."

"Of course, my dear," he said, and put a hand on her arm.

Until then she had kept a firm hold on herself, but the moment she felt his hand she collapsed, and the collapse was complete. She did not faint. Her legs just gave way, and she fell against his shoulder; she would have sunk to the ground if he had not thrown an arm round her. For the first time he had an arm round her, and the only feeling he had was pity. There was despair in the low moan of her voice.

"Oh, Diego! my Diego! What are we to do?"

"We go from this place," he said, and, almost lifting her off her feet, drew her round the side of the boulder, away from that still figure, on to the track leading down to the Lodge. But there she pulled at his shoulder and stopped him.

"No—no—no—! not that way. They will put us in prison."

Her words gave Diego a shock. Up to now, despite the things he had done, the reality of prison had not entered his head. She was right. If Major Harper called in the police—and he must—and reported what he had seen, Diego and Ann would go to prison—and stand a trial for murder. No one would doubt the word of an officer and a gentleman against a couple of foreigners. Lovers! guilty lovers! caught trying to hide their crime in order to reap a golden harvest before a wronged husband could take steps to bestow it elsewhere as he had threatened to do! Prison it was—and worse.

"I should have killed him," said Diego desperately.

"No—no! Do not speak of killing." Her hands gripped and shook him. "Diego, you must not let them put me in prison."

"You will not go to prison, my dear," he said with a confidence that he did not feel.

"You must hide—and you must hide me too. Look, Diego! I am now all coward, there is no more in me." Her voice was shaking. "I do not fear death, but prison, yes! That I fear. I would go mad. I was in prison—many, many months—and for a little I was mad. I dream about it, and dream about it, and in my dreams I am mad again. No, not prison, Diego!"

"You will not go to prison," he said again, and now he was savagely resolved that whatever else befell her she would not go to prison.

He had heard stories of phalangist prisons that had made him realise this woman's horror. Any prison would drive her mad now. Spain-at-war had marked her body and soul. It had marked him too, and the blood he had shed at rapier point could not wash that mark away.

"But we cannot save ourselves, Diego, you cannot save me, you cannot save yourself." Even in her desperation she saw clearly. "Diego, I want to die. I want to die now."

"You will trust me," Diego said.

"My trust is in you." She turned in his arm to face him, her glowing black eyes close to his. "Diego, let us die. Let us die together." She grasped his shoulders and drew herself up against him, and her voice was siren in its appeal. "Look, Diego! I know. There is nothing more. There is nothing now for us in life. There was never anything in life for me. And now? Then let me die. Let us die together. It is easy. Look! the deep water is down there. In each other's arms. I am not afraid—I am eager. And the good Mother of God will know and get her Son's forgiveness for us; but I will lose my soul before I go mad again."

For one moment the temptation swept over him almost overwhelmingly. Anything worth while in life was over for Ann Harper. And for himself? Why, then, keep the simulacrum of life in the husk of the body? Death was an easy way out. Only for a moment did the temptation last. Death was too easy a way out, and Diego was used to playing a game to the finish. He would play this game to a finish too.

He must have time. Simply he must make time. He and the woman must remain free agents until he had time to decide the thing that they would do and keep on doing in the face of life or death. Going down to the Lodge would be fatal. Going through the woods to Loch Beg would be better, for he knew that his aunt and uncle would give them the very limit of help, but that would not give him the time he wanted. No! They must take to the hills. There was one place he could win to, and a man there that he could trust. After that——

Ann was staring up at him and moving her head sadly, for she could read, first, the softening of his mouth, and then the clenching of his jaw muscles.

"We will go," he said, loosed her hands gently but firmly from his shoulders, and swung her round on the up-hill track.

"No—no! There is no hope any way." She resisted for a moment, but he used his strength almost brutally.

"I must make time," he said angrily. "God Almighty! will you not have some sense, woman?"

She went then, but her hill-woman's legs had lost all

251

their pith. Her hopelessness, her despair, sapped the very sources of her vigour. She did not want to do anything but die. He had to help her all the way up, and, now, he was in urgent hurry. On some steep bits he had actually to lift her off her feet and charge upwards heart-burstingly. The track wound amongst big detached boulders that offered hiding-places, but hiding-places too near danger. There was only one place where they could hide for a night, perhaps two nights. And in two nights he would know.

At Skene's Rock, that fatal rendezvous, he paused for one quick survey. All the hills were vacant. There was no boat on the loch below. There was no one on the lawn fronting the Lodge. Major Harper had not had time to make that slanted mile through the wood. No one saw them yet, but soon many eyes and feet would be turned towards Skene's Rock. Now was the time to get out of sight as quickly as possible.

He put his arm firmly round Ann, lifted her so that her toes barely touched the ground, and ran her down into the shallow hollow that the moors made before they lifted into the long ridge crowned by Carn Seilig. In the hollow he stopped to get his breath back, opening his mouth wide to draw in the air as quickly as possible. One arm was aching, and his thighs were trembling, but the trip-hammer of his heart was pounding steadily. Three months ago this sudden effort would have killed him, but, now, he needed only half a minute to regain his wind, and he knew that his legs would not fail him this day or next day or any day.

He took that half-minute's rest, his eyes moving round over the slopes and peaks. They were alone up there. No man, that he could see, looked at them. Only a hill lark singing in the evening blue looked down on them, and an eagle drifting on still pinions down into far Glen Seilig. Ann Harper had sunk down in the heather, one shoulder against his knee. He looked down at her red crown. Her hair was still alive, and the green ribbon was dull in the virility of it. He put a hand softly on her head, and her head sank under it. In half a minute he lifted her to her feet and they faced the slope.

### III

"I cannot go on, Diego," she whispered, throwing out her hand in a helpless gesture. "Something has died within me—it is my whole life, I think."

"I will hold you up in my hands," he said.

"For a little while, then not again. There is blood between us now, Diego. It was not right to kill an old man, only mad."

"It was an accident."

"I know. But the blood, it is between us till we die. And look! I am not afraid to die—here in the hills— before I go mad."

There was no use trying to talk her out of this mood now. He firmed his arm round her and drew her on. He could not understand this collapse, this hopelessness. She was a Basque woman, brought up amongst the facts of life, and had seen death and ugly things. He could understand sorrow, remorse, fear, even revolt, but not despair.

They went on, but slowly. Ann's vigour showed no sign of returning. She made no effort, and if anything, she grew wearier. They had to rest often, lying off the path in the deep heather, Diego's eyes above the rough stems searching hollow and slope for signs of man. He saw no one, and later on marvelled at that. Ann's breath was coming short and shallow, and he was full of fear that she would sink into a swoon. He made her lie on her back, arms spread, and massaged across her midriff below her rounded breasts. That helped her.

In a wearily long time they got to the rock on the lip

of the chorrie of Garbh Ailt. The red ball of the sun then stood in the notch of the pass, the hills were suffused with rich orange, and the hollows shaded in gloom. Far below them the torrent poured down from Glen Seilig and the white of it was bluely cold. In another hour the half-dark of the summer night would be over them, and they must get down the chorrie while there was still light to pick a way over and among that steep jumble of stones.

The crawl down to the floor of the gorge was a slow and heart-breaking task. Henrietta had said that Ann could balance herself down that ladder of rocks without once using her hands. Now Diego had to guide her feet from step to step, clasp her fingers from hold to hold, leave her lying on her stomach over an extra-high boulder, drop below her and drag her down by the legs. And, indeed, gasping and sometimes weeping, she did her very best to help herself, but her nerve was gone. She could only just cling on while he fumbled for a place for her feet.

But they made it at last, and by that time Diego knew weariness and muscle strain. He lay prone on the rock, Ann sitting crumpled at his shoulder, his chin over the edge of a small crystal bowl in the basalt. After a time he sucked in the ice-cold water through pursed lips, and then knelt back on his heels to hold cupped hands for her to drink. He threw away the first double-handful, for he saw that there was blood on the tips of his fingers where the rocks had grazed them. She drank a little only, shivered and shook her head. And then he scooped up another double-handful and splashed it into her face, whereat she gasped and blinked and stared, but showed no spark of her temper. Then he held her firmly by a handful of her hair while he scrubbed her face and neck with his not-too-clean handkerchief. That shock and friction helped to revive her a little.

After five minutes' rest they went on down the gorge, through the gap, and into Strath Dearg. The pony-track was wide enough to take them abreast and they made better time. Ann even showed signs of a reviving strength. The half-night was over them when they came in view of Donald Gunn's bothy, and there was no moon. It faced them there on the slope, a grey shadow against the black bulk of the wood behind. The light was just strong enough to show the blackness of the door and windows. There was no glimmer of light from within, but, even here in the mountains, every window was carefully darkened with the coming of night.

There was silence all about the house, but not for long. The hounds saw them or the dogs scented them, and the night became alive with bayings and barkings. Diego fell flat on the ground, pulling Ann down at his side, and lifted a head to watch. Nothing moved at the house. The blackness of the door remained black, no man's voice hailed across the dark. Donald Gunn was not at home.

Diego had to think back. Was it only that afternoon that Donald had smoored the fire and gone off towards Glen Seilig on Hamish's errand? It seemed many afternoons ago. Why was he not home? Perhaps he had been, and had got a phone call appraising him of the tragedy. That was it! He would now be at the Lodge or at Loch Beg, and would be home later. But wherever he was, he was not hunting his Mistress Ann.

"Donald is not in," he whispered to Ann. "We will go up and wait for him."

"They will find us here too," she whispered back.

"We shall not be here."

He helped her to her feet and they went on up to the bothy. The dogs started again but stopped when the house hid the kennels. The door was on the latch, and Diego set ear to an inch of opening. There was no sound but the tick-tock of Donald's wag-at-the-wall in the kitchen. An old clock patiently ticking away physical time to itself, careless of how fast or slow went their own physiological time. It had ticked thus for fifty years and would tick for another fifty if a hand pulled down the chain once in thirty hours. If it stopped would time stop? Their time would not stop—or turn back. God! if they could only turn it back six short hours and start again.

Diego opened the door a little wider and sent his voice through. "Donald! Donald Gunn!" The dead dark inside swallowed his words. Not a mouse stirred.

Holding Ann's hand, that was not now warm with life but cold and still, he drew her along the passage to the right and through the open kitchen door. Across the floor he saw the red spark of a smouldering peat, and moved forward cautiously until he found the table and then a chair. He put Ann sitting in that chair, her arm against the table, and she sighed deeply. His eyes, used to the dark, picked out the unblinded windows, one at the front and one in the end wall. Outside them was the faint, blue, eerie glow of the summer night.

He moved across, pulled down the dark buckram blinds, and fumbled across the black cloth curtains; and now he stood in pitch blackness except for that red ember on the hearth. But he knew the internal economy of the kitchen, shuffled across to the fireplace, brushing by a chair, struck a match, and lit two tallow candles in old brass candlesticks on the mantelpiece. Donald did not use his paraffin lamp in high summer, but put aside his book when the daylight dimmed, played a tune on his fiddle and went to bed to rise with the dawn. The room glowed like a low brown cavern in the yellow light. Diego turned round to look at Ann where she sat, one elbow on the table. Her black eyes looked wearily at him out of her bloodless face, and the arm hanging at her side lifted a hand in a small helpless gesture. Diego smiled and nodded.

"Here we are, Mistress Ann. I will make us some coffee, and you will rest."

"Yes, Diego," she murmured. "I brought you no luck, my dear."

"You brought me what I would not miss, and we play this game out."

"Give me a little time, Diego."

"I am making it."

There was an old hair couch against the side wall, and he made her lie down on it, and pulled down her skirt that was stained by lichen off the rocks. Her stockings were in rags and her white skin showed through, with a red scratch here and there. She lay there very still, and her black eyes followed him as he went about the kitchen, and in her eyes, now, was not terror, but the beginning of a lasting sadness.

More than once he had helped Donald to prepare a meal and wash up after it, so he knew where the stores were kept. First he remade the fire out of the smoorings —rakings his Aunt Ellen called them—moving aside the ashes, building up the red embers with the long-thighed tongs, and propping the smouldering sods round the red core with a gap in front for ventilation. One or two long puffs of his breath and he had the flames licking. The full water-pail under a wooden lid and the kettle were below the dresser, the enamelled scone tin and the coffee canister in the wall cupboard, the knives and spoons in the table drawer, the butter, for coolness, in a covered dish in the sink, as was also a quart jug of milk with an inch of cream on top.

He made coffee, and he made it strong. He made Ann drink the first cup with very little sugar and no milk. She whispered a grateful word and sipped listlessly, but after two or three sips found that coffee was what she needed. It was very hot, but a woman can stand heat better than a man, and her cup was empty while Diego was still sipping. The second cup he half-filled with coffee and filled with cream and added two spoonfuls of sugar. She needed fuel now. He buttered a day-old scone and stood over her as she nibbled it. In the end she ate it all, and in that time he wolfed down at least six. She had more coffee and he saw the life revive in her; but as the life revived the sadness grew with it.

He knew where Donald kept his spirit cordial. He could do with three fingers but decided not to touch it, for he wanted his mind stark and calm. Alcohol in moderation livens the mind, but it also makes the mind over-sanguine as to consequences, and, presently, he wanted to stare consequences starkly in the face.

He hoped that Donald Gunn would not keep them waiting too long, for he did not want Ann to start talking wildly again. That way led to disaster. If her mind got obsessed with death she might die in spite of him, and though death might be a good thing for her, he was grimly determined that she face this thing out on her two feet.

Again they had a turn of luck. She was sipping her third half-cup when the hounds began to bay. The cup leaped out of her hands and crashed on the stone flags beyond the edge of the rug. Diego himself felt a cold thrill, and it made him speak savagely.

"Remember your breed, woman, and keep a hold on yourself this one hour. That is Donald coming. Sit still!"

IV

In a stride Diego was at the fireside and nipped out the candles between thumb and forefinger, but still the firelight made a dusky glow on the walls. His shoulder

258

brushed the jamb of the passage door, and his hand fumbled for the latch. As he opened the outer door he sank down on his knees.

Over the tops of the potato shaws in the garden he could see the white glimmer of the track going up the Strath. Nothing moved on it within reach of his vision. Whoever was coming came from the Glen of the Willows. Diego, stooping low, went quickly to the corner of the house and put a head round to look up the path coming down by the pines. Night was dark there and he could not see anything. His ears had to tell him if anyone came, and his ears did. He felt his hair lift as he heard a nailed shoe clink on stone. He listened hard. The shoe clinked again. One only was coming, and then he saw the grey shadow against the trees. And at that moment a voice spoke quietly:

"All right, Don Diego! I am alone."

That was Donald Gunn, and he had seen Diego's head before Diego had seen him. Diego straightened up and went forward to meet him.

"I knew you would be here, Don Diego," he said, and there was a quiet and stern tone in his voice.

"Ann Harper is here too," said Diego, "and she is in a bad way."

"I am not surprised. Are you?" His voice was bleak and Diego did not like it.

"You know that General Harper is dead?" he put bluntly.

"The whole Glen knows it."

The whole Glen would know, but what did the Glen know about the killing? What did Donald know? Diego sought for words to make the situation clear to this stern old man whose trust he had hoped to win. He found it difficult. But before he could choose any words Donald spoke with stern regret.

"Why did you do it, Don Diego?"

"Do what?" The query was startled out of him.

"Kill that old man. He wasn't worth while, and we thought you were."

So that was why he was stern. Diego was the killer. Did Major Harper see him taking the rifle away from Ann, or was the Major trying to shield the woman by accusing the man who had humiliated him? Diego's hands were tied—or, rather, his mouth was closed to anything but the half-lie. He told that half-lie very carefully.

"The man's death was accidental. He was armed with a rifle. There was a quarrel and a struggle, and the rifle went off. My fingers never touched the trigger."

"I believe that," Donald said. "But he is dead."

"He is, and Ann Harper is implicated——"

"That is not so," said Donald quickly.

"It is. Major Harper saw everything I did with the rifle. Ann was at my side. He called her my accomplice."

"Was she at your side when—when the General was killed?" The question was almost accusing.

"She was not." Another half-lie.

"Then she has nothing to fear."

"But she has, man! She is full of fear. Listen!" He put an urgent hand on Donald's arm and felt a muscle jerk. "She is completely broken down. Can I make you understand? In Spain she was in prison and I know what she suffered. No, I do not know. No one can know. She was out of her mind for a time. If she is put in prison now—as my accomplice—she will go mad and die. She knows it."

"She will not go to prison," said Donald confidently.

The man would not understand. Diego was sure that he had imagination, but he was being dense.

"Look here, Donald!" His voice was angry and determined. "It is necessary to hide her away for two days—till her courage returns, as it will. Then we can decide what to do."

"You are the one to decide what you will do."

"And I decide. There is that whisky bothy you have at the back of Scurr Affran. Hide us away there for two days."

He saw Donald Gunn's head shake in the half-dark.

"That bothy is known to six people in the Glen, and one of them is Angus Campbell the policeman. If he is looking for anyone, that is one of the first places he will try. The hills are not a good place to hide in if a hill-man is looking for you."

Diego drew in a long breath and straightened up.

"But we hide. It seems that you are reluctant. Very well! I take to the hills with Ann Harper, and by God! if I am driven I shall kill in earnest next time."

"You misunderstand me, Don Diego." He was coldly courteous. "I can hide you—and Mistress Ann if necessary—until you decide what to do." There was a warning in his voice now. "And when you decide you will decide for yourself alone, not for the lady. We can take care of our own in this glen."

"I can take care of my own too, and damn your glen!"

"We talk too much," said Donald quietly. "My mistress will be wondering."

Diego followed him round to the front of the bothy. From the door Donald spoke in a low but cheerful voice.

"It is Donald, Mistress Ann. Everything is fine, my dear."

"Oh, my friend Donald!" Her voice came deep and low.

The peats were flaming, and in the wavering glow they saw her sitting where Diego had left her on the couch. She had sat thus, holding on to herself, while the men were at cross-purposes outside, and that showed that some of her spirit was returning.

261

Donald lit the candles on the mantelpiece and turned to her. His lined face was very weary. She gave him one quick look, drooped her head, slipped down on her knees, and began picking up the broken pieces of china.

"My butter-fingers, Donald!" she murmured.

Donald bent at her side, took the fragments from her fingers and put them on the table. Holding her hands he lifted her gently to her feet, and, in his fine courtly way, showed his fealty by kissing her fingers.

"Have no fear, Mistress Ann. The Glen is yours."

She clung to his hands. "But I have fear, Donald. It is life that I am afraid of. The fault was in my own mind, playing with foolish dreams, so sinful, and now I am punished. Now there is nothing—nothing." She paused and went on. "Donald, you must give me time—only a little time to look at things with my own eyes, for now it is Don Diego's eyes that are looking for me. I was, indeed, wicked back there talking of death, but now I only want time to think—to hide in a corner for a little while, but with no bars."

Her mind was wholly possessed with this need to hide herself away. Donald saw that now, and Diego had had no need to give his anger a rein. The old man led her back to the couch.

"There is no cause for you to hide, my darling," he soothed her, "but I know a place where you will be safe."

"But Don Diego, he must hide too."

"His is the need to hide."

"That is so. If he is caught—no! no! I do not know Don Diego at all, Donald, and I was so certain that I did."

"So was I certain," said Donald.

"He has a force in him that I do not know, and that frightens me."

Again Diego felt a spurt of anger. He had killed no one. He had shown force with Major Harper, but

Harper was alive—blast him! He had shown force bringing this woman over the hill against her flesh and spirit, but that should not have frightened her. He had not killed anyone, and she had. Why then was she frightened of him? He spoke hotly.

"If you two would leave this dam' fool Usted——"

The phone bell shrilled on the wall. Ann sat up with a jerk, screamed, put her hand over her mouth and started to laugh. Diego knew that sort of laughter. He was angry no longer. In a stride he was at her side. He slapped her briskly on the cheek, and she caught his hand and clung tightly to it; she choked and gurgled, and Diego sat down by her and put his free hand firmly around her shoulders. She quieted then, gasping for breath, and leant against him. He felt her trembling, and knew that her nerves were gone. Donald was at the telephone, his voice low and cautious.

"Donald Gunn speaking. . . . Yes, Big Ellen . . . yes, both . . . uh-uh . . . you think so. . . . I have the place. . . . Is Hamish about? . . . Eh, what? . . . I do not understand. . . . Long John, no, I didn't see him . . . in the morning? Right!"

He hung up the phone and turned round. "Big Ellen. She knows you are here—both of you. She wants that you stay out of the way all day to-morrow—or longer—and you, Don Diego, are to take care of Mistress Ann."

"You think I am not doing that?" Diego's heart lifted. His great aunt was with him.

"I do not know what to think." Donald looked searchingly at Diego. "She wants to know where Long John is. You did not see him about any place to-day?"

"Not since he left here."

He nodded. "You wouldn't. He'll be with Hamish, who is not home yet." His tired eyes went over his mistress. "Mistress Ann, would you be able for another two miles—no hard climbing at all?"

"To the world's end, Donald, if I know where I am going." She got up from Diego's side, and her breasts lifted against her stained pullover as she drew in a deep breath.

"You are going to the safest hidie-hole in all Scotland. Give me two minutes and I'll be ready."

"I am ready," said Ann.

## CHAPTER IV

### THE HIDING-PLACE

I

THEY left the bothy in fifteen minutes. Donald Gunn, ahead, led on in his steady tireless fashion; Ann followed, and Diego brought up the rear; and Diego's legs were numb from the knees down. Strapped over his shoulder were two blankets folded in two tartan rugs. Donald carried an unlighted storm-lantern and a heavy game-bag, and the game-bag contained a day's ration. Ann Harper travelled light and she needed no help. That strange weariness, that was from the spirit, was gone, and her hill-woman's legs had recovered some of their resiliency.

The night was still half-dark, but the broken head of Scurr Affran behind them in the north-east stood up black against a white glow in the sky. That way the slow dawn was making.

Donald lit the storm-lantern when they got into the darkness of the gorge of Garbh Ailt—for it was back that road they went—and cast the light behind him to guide their steps. Some distance on he turned off the track and led over bare stone and round the belly of a rock on the bank of the torrent running fast and torn ten feet below. And, there, in the angle the lantern showed a foot-bridge going a dozen feet across at a steep upward slant. It was only a single plank with a single strand of wire for guard.

"We cross here," said Donald. "Watch your step." He went across in four easy strides, taking the sway of the plank expertly, and turned to shine the light across.

Diego put his hand on Ann's arm, but with that old impulsive gesture of hers she threw his hand off and ran so lightly across that the plank barely swayed to the easy lift of her body. Diego went across dourly, gripping the wire hard, his stomach heaving with the sickening sway under his feet.

"When that bit plank is lifted and hidden away," Donald said, "there is no way up or down to get this side of the Garbh Ailt except by jumping—and it hasn't been jumped yet."

He led on up a rough path between the cliff and the stream, and so came below the pale ghostliness that was the cascade pouring down the pass from Glen Seilig, and there he turned left into the narrow mouth of a defile going into the very jaws of the mountains. Here there was no path, but only a jumble of rounded stones that had been water-washed through thousands of years. They went carefully now, picking their steps, but not for more than a hundred yards. At a fault in the right wall of the gorge Donald swung his lantern.

"I made one or two of the steps myself," Donald said. "It is easy and not far."

They clambered up after him. As he had said, it was easy and not far. He turned a corner and stopped by a stunted mountain ash growing out of a cranny.

"Myself planted this rowan," he said, holding a low branch. "You will see why."

He pulled the branch aside. There was a rift in the rock wide enough to carry his stooped shoulders and going to a point above his head. Donald disappeared through it, and Ann and Diego followed in a crouch. The tilt was upwards and steep, but only for a few feet, then it flattened out and the rift opened into a small cavern not more than twenty feet by ten. At the far end of it the rift narrowed again and went on up into the blackness. The floor of the cave had been man-levelled with flat stones, and here and there flat-topped boulders rose out of the flags. The roof of it, sloping into a point, went into the darkness above their heads. The rock was brown in texture with bright points glistening, and there was no sign of damp.

"This is the place, hidden in the heart of the hills," Donald said. "You will not be found here, but even if anyone comes at you from below there are break-offs higher up to hide in." He swung his lantern about and was inclined to be talkative. "This place was in use one time, not in my time, nor my grandfather's time— he was the first of the Gunns to come in from Caithness way. And, indeed, this could be one of the places where Prince Chairlie hid after Culloden. The secret of the hiding-places was well kept, and so this might be one of them. And I would remind you that the Prince moved far and wide over the Highlands, thirty thousand pounds on his head, and no one sold him. Ay! and what was done once might be done again, and easier done with no regiments of red-coats searching."

Was Donald hinting that an escape was possible, with friends here and in other places ready to help? The game was still on the board.

"Look!" Donald lifted his lantern, hung it on the tine of an antler wedged into a crack, and hung his game-bag on another. "That is old—very old. The cave is bone-dry and nothing rots. Could be Prince Chairlie slept in that bed." Close to one of the sloping-in walls on a low shelf was a pile of what had been pine-fronds and bracken. Donald moved across and tried it with a hand.

"Has a spring to it yet." He reached for Diego's bundle, shook it loose, and spread one of the rugs on the pile. "You can have a rest any time you've a mind, Mistress Ann—you'll need it." He came to where the rift narrowed steeply. "This slants up straight as a rush and comes out like the hole of a fox's den close to the top of the waterfall down from Glen Seilig. You can see the daylight through it, and a blink of light comes slanting down, as you will see, and besides it is a grand drawing chimney, as the man who cut out that knew."

Below the rift cut into the solid rock was a fireplace with low side walls of stone on which a big pot might rest. There were smoke-stains on the stone, and Donald pointed them out.

"They were there when I came on this place. I tried a couple o' divots of peat in it myself and the smoke went up like a puff. Who knows but it was used for the old trade that has gone on in the Highlands since the Picts brought it with them from Scythia. The smoke would be no more than the spume off the water falling, and it would be no trouble to run down a good supply of cooling water."

"You found this place?" Diego asked him.

"I was looking for a place like it." He smiled with some diffidence. "I'll no' be denying some of us run a small industry of our own in our own hills, same as our forefathers time out of mind. Only five or six of us know, but sometimes a body gets to know that shouldn't, and then a new place has to be looked out. That has happened only once in my time and my father's time, for there are not many who would betray, and then only by a careless word or boast at fair or gathering. But always we have a second place looked out. This is our second place, and only Hamish and I know of it—and now you. So you are safe in it, and that is what I am pointing out, Mistress Ann. Well-well! I'll be leaving you to rest." He took his mistress's hand as if she were a child and led her across to the rug-covered couch. "You must rest now, my dear, and sleep if you can. I will be back in the morning and again later. You need have no fear, for the Glen is taking care of you."

He straightened up and, without a glance in Diego's direction, moved towards the cave entrance, but paused before he disappeared to say over his shoulder: "You need not stay in here all the time; you'll be safe enough as far as the Garbh Ailt. You'll know I'm coming when you hear me whistling a bar of that tune one or the other of you is always at. God keep ye!"

"Go with God!" murmured Ann. And then they were alone.

II

She looked up at Diego, and in the dim yellow light he saw the darkness of her eyes in a white face and the weary smile about her mouth. She put a hand on the rug at her side, and he went across and sat by her. She crouched forward, her forearms resting on her knees, and swayed her body back and forth, and despite her weariness her body was lithe and supple.

"Do we start thinking now, Diego?"

"Sleep, that is the first thing."

"I am, indeed, weary, but I will never sleep again."

"I will make you sleep within this hour." He put a hand on her arm and made her stop swaying. She straightened, and her shoulder touched his. "I am set here in charge of you, and you are safe in my hands," he told her.

"For how long, Diego?"

"Do not think of time. I hold it. Before you sleep let me remind you that we have harder campaigns than this behind us. We are used to war, you and I, used to danger and the hills and all the strategy of saving our own skins for another day. That is so?"

"It is so. But in the end I failed. I failed to-night."

"You faltered only. To-morrow, many morrows, you will not fail, and we win this game."

"You will not yield, I know, but what chance——?"

"Every chance. Did I ever tell you how five of us escaped out of Madrid when that great-hearted Irishman, Ryan, was captured, and how we played hide-and-seek with death all across Spain to the coast?"

"You will tell me now, Diego, thinking to put heart in me."

And he told her how five men marked for death—an American of the North, an Englishman, a Russian, one man of Valencia, and himself—had won their way through the Sierra de Grédos and down into the mostly hostile territory between Salamanca and Valladolid, and across Leon, living on the country, foraging, stealing, fighting secretly, never showing their faces, never giving quarter, never leaving a man dead in the open. One body left in the open and the game was up in a country raised around them. So they won their slow way across the Cantabrians and down to the coast, where they lifted a fisherman's boat somewhere near Gijon in the Asturias. They hoped to make the south coast of Ireland where some of the Basques had found refuge, but they were not sailors, except the Valencian, who was a fisherman, and the winds and the drift took them past Wexford in the dark and threw them on the Welsh coast. There the Englishman took charge and brought them safely into Cardiff and so by train to London; and in London there was nothing to fear, for Diego had a good friend in his own Legation. Two of these five were dead now, and two still fighting, and himself would start again, fighting for his life and hers, to-morrow.

"And that good friend of mine is still in London," he said at the end.

"London is a long way, Diego?"

"It is shorter than the way we twisted across Spain, and no war-hostile country between. Look! it is all heather southward, I am told, to within a day's march of Glasgow, a great town where two moving quietly can be lost, and from Glasgow to London no one will stop us going by train. Remember we have friends in this glen who have friends in many glens, even in Glasgow where many Highland people live. The thing is easy."

He went on spinning words that he himself did not believe, to bring her out of the slough. But after a time she stopped him with that gesture of thrown-out palms.

"But, Diego! we would be together alone in the hills many days—and many nights."

"As we are alone here."

"But nights—and then nights."

"We would not be man and woman alone in the hills, but comrades making a bid for freedom."

"We are in this because we are man and woman, Diego. We are in this because a man is dead, and one of us killed him. That is what is between us, Diego—a tie that is also a bar of iron. Do I not see where you are leading me to? From this den to Glasgow, and from Glasgow to London, and from London—where?"

"Anywhere you like."

"To the hacienda of San José? I know. But that dream is dead. There is blood between us. Do you not see? Take me in your arms, kiss me on the mouth, have passion with me, and the embrace and the kiss and the passion are bought with blood. Be patient with me, Diego! Give me time! To-morrow I may be hard and logical, ready to grasp at life, ready to take to the hills with you, body and soul in your hands. To-night I am weary to the soul."

There was no use saying anything more. They sat there shoulder to shoulder staring in front of them, too mind-and-body weary to keep their thoughts in order. Presently she lifted her arms above her head and inhaled and exhaled a long breath that finished in a moan.

"Oh! but I am weary and I cannot think." She leant against him, her head drifted down on his shoulder, and he put a quiet arm around her. She sighed deeply and was still.

In a minute or two her head started to slip off his shoulder and he propped his black head against her red one. He got the faint scent of heather and verbena. And then at the back of his throat he voiced that soothing old lullaby that Larry used to sing—the melody without words. She stirred for a moment, and then her breath started coming soft and regularly. She was on the verge of sleep and, then, in a little while he knew that she was asleep.

With infinite care he drew away inch by inch till her body was lying down, her feet off the couch. He went on his knees then and softly removed her shoes; and she gave only the sleepy turn and murmur of a child when he pivoted her long legs on to the rug. The night was warm outside, but in here it was cool, and he groped for the blankets and draped them over her, and she turned on her side like a child to be tucked in. His hand touched hers, and, like a child, her fingers closed on his. Resting on one knee at her side he let her hold his hand. Her hand that used to be warm, and had been cold earlier in the night, was not cold now, and it grew warmer, and presently a finger slipped. He drew his hand away. She was sound asleep.

He threw the other rug over an arm and, treading cautiously, moved across to where the lantern hung on the antler near the ancient fireplace. What Donald had said was right, for looking up through the rift he saw far away a round hole of light with one faint star for a centre. The dawn was outside. He turned the lamp down to conserve oil, watched it till it flickered and went out, and turned towards the entrance. It stood out dimly, a grey angle against the dawn. This cave would not be all dark during the day. Still treading softly, he went outside and down, brushing by the fronds of the rowan, to the turn where he could see the gorge below.

The dawn had come, not here a brilliant dawn of red and gold and purple, but only a toneless light full of desolation. The walls of the gorge shut away the hills and most of the high pallid sky, and he could not see the dawn walking. There at the turn of the narrow rock-ladder he draped the rug about him after the fashion of a native poncho, and sat down, his shoulder against one wall of the fault and his feet against the other. Sleep stood afar off from him notwithstanding his bone-weariness, and thoughts would come though his mind was numb. Let him think, then.

He had come into the Glen a sick man, a man sick unto death as he had thought, but Death had not come to him. Death had come to another at a moment when he himself was full of the old tough life and a new confidence, and with that coming Death had stayed and was now dogging the footsteps of himself—and of Ann. That was stern fact. Things looked black against them. Whatever their friends might think, the public would hold that they were accomplices in murder. The old and sordid *crime passionnel* with the god Mammon urging them on! That was clear. And, therefore, the Law, once it laid hands on them, would deal adequately according to the facts presented damningly by the Prosecution. And what facts had they themselves to win them mercy, for mercy was all they could hope for? They had none that anyone would believe—anyone but a few friends: Hamish

McLeod, Ellen Honora McCarthy, Donald Gunn, and whom besides?

Diego revolted against that Law that would kill them. He revolted against the blind Justice that would deal with them blindly. If Law and Justice were like that he would have none of them. He would not trust them, he dare not trust them for the woman's sake. The woman must not go to prison. His mind was made up on that. Whatever happened himself, Ann must not be degraded into madness. As for their plans, he could not make final ones until he heard from his friends that afternoon. Uncle Hamish and Aunt Ellen and Donald Gunn would have plans—they were planning already—and he would listen to them, and then——

But he knew that, deep down in him, his decision was already made. He would make a bid for freedom, for himself and for the woman. He would not surrender with mere mercy held out to him by the hands of even his friends. That was final. Stop thinking, then. But he could not stop thinking of San José, the folded savannahs down to the river, the tall grasses and the dark bulk of the quebracho trees, the white-fronted cattle, the horses of many shades, and the Gaucho horsemen so courteous and so touchy, and the big low house, red-roofed—and no woman to rule therein. A house worth ruling in! A woman that he had found and saved because she was the only woman who would ever rule in that house! A red-haired woman, her last defences broken down, life restored to her, and life all about her. San José so far away! San José! San José! San José! . . . Did he hear someone chuckle softly? . . .

He dreamt that he had come back to somewhere from somewhere after many years, but he was still young and prepared to carry on. He landed off a small boat, and knew he was in Britain but did not know where. A muddy estuary washed a plain of grey grass out of which stood broken stones. A few, not many, people were moving aimlessly about, and looked at him with incurious eyes. He did not know whether they were men or women, so sexless were they. To one he said, "What of the war?" And the other answered, "What war?" "The war between the Nazis and the World." "Oh, that war! It is over." "Who won?" "We do not know. It finished. There was no more fighting. There was nothing. There was only this." And then Diego felt a great desolation. He was the only man alive in the world. These people, not caring any longer, were waiting listlessly for Death. . . .

III

He was waked by a hand on his foot. A man used to the open in dangerous places, he waked quietly and fully, mind and body at once aware. He was awake before his eyes opened, and they opened only to watchful slits. Donald Gunn was standing before him, his face level with his own. The day was full now, and on the hills the sun would be shining from a cloudless sky. But here the young day was sad and withdrawn, and in the shadowless light of it Donald's face looked grey and tired, and there were blue shades under his eyes. He was an old man and had had a gruelling time, but his face was finely resolute and his jaw had a firm jut. He had another game-bag slung on his shoulders.

"How's Mistress Ann?" he enquired unsmilingly. "She didn't get away on you, Don Diego?"

Not likely, but she could by stepping over his legs. Without a word he got stiffly to his feet and brushed through the rowan up into the cave, Donald coming behind. There was just enough light trickling down and up to show that she was still on the old couch, the blankets tossed off her shoulders. The mass of her red hair had a

274

dark glow in the dimness. They moved across on tiptoe so as not to waken her, for they knew how forlorn would be her waking. She was half turned over on her face and apparently sound asleep, but the moment they stood over her she turned her head up, and her eyes were open. Had she been asleep at all, or had she, also, the open-air habit of waking completely and awarely? Her black eyes looked at them without feeling, and, then, with a quick suppleness she swept the blankets off and pivoted to a sitting position on the rug. They could see the white flesh through the torn stockings.

"Be with God! Yesterday I thought—— Was it yesterday? Oh! yesterday! yesterday!" Her fingers covered her eyes and ran up through her live stirring hair. But she had complete control of herself this morning, for when she spoke again her voice was natural. "There is grit under my eyelids, and behold my hands."

"Your face could do with a bit wash too, Mistress Ann," Donald said. "There's a bowl in the rock this side the turn. But losh! I have no sense. I forgot a scrap o' soap and a towel, but this will do for the towel."

From the game-bag he took a white napkin that had wrapped warm scones, and she took it from him as she stood up from slipping her feet into her ruined brogues.

"I have gone many days without soap or towel, my friend," she said, and moved slowly towards the mouth of the cave. Her feet had not quite found their balance, but head and shoulders were well back. She would not break down again, Diego knew, and he knew that it was safe to let her go outside alone.

"She is all right, but she'll never be the same," said Donald Gunn. "You did that lady a terrible wrong, Don Diego, and she trusted you."

"As you say, Donald Gunn," Diego said steadily. "Have you any news?"

"I wasn't any place to get news. This evening." He

went across and relit the lantern, jerked his game-bag off and began arranging food on a flat-topped shelf where, no doubt, meals had been eaten before. "The other bag is for the day—the thermos will keep the coffee hot. Your breakfast is in this, and my own as well."

There was a large wicker-topped flask of hot tea, and rolled in paper against the flask, to retain warmth, were four cooked trout of good size, and a packet of sandwiches wrapped in another napkin; and there were half a dozen hard-boiled eggs. Also there were three enamelled picnic cups. He had not forgotten even the salt, but strangely enough he had forgotten knives and forks, and that remissness made him warmly angry with himself. "Dam'd auld nanny!" he growled.

"Did you sleep at all, Donald?" Diego asked gently.

"A body don't need much sleep after sixty," he said. "Here's Mistress Ann back."

Her wash in the cold basalt pool had revived her bodily, but had not lifted her mind out of its quietness. Quiet and controlled, that was what her mood was. Her face had its fine even tint of ivory, her hair was held down by a re-tying of the silk ribbon, and her eyes were calm, though there were dark lines under them. And her voice was calm too.

"Yesterday I was very foolish and in hysteria. I am sorry. It will not happen again."

"Breakfast is happening now, Mistress Ann," Donald said briskly. "You will try and eat a bite."

She was as physically fit a woman as Diego had ever met, and her young body demanded food. The three of them made a good breakfast, and ate all there was in Donald's game-bag. A talkless breakfast, for Ann kept her reserved mood and Donald and Diego had nothing to say to each other. The truth was that Donald had set Diego on a pedestal, wherefrom he had fallen down to the hurt of a woman that Donald worshipped.

276

After breakfast Donald said, "I must be leaving you in a few minutes." He looked from one to the other expecting a query as to where he was going—and what he was doing—but apparently Ann was not interested, and Diego remained obdurately silent. Donald on his feet tapped his foot on a flag. "Big Ellen in her message last night told me I was to go to the Lodge first thing this morning. I am on my way now, over the chorrie. She has something in her mind, but I don't know what it is."

"I do," said Diego harshly. "We are in her mind, the guilty ones that she will stand by. Listen, Donald Gunn! I will take an order from only one person in the Glen, Ellen Honora McCarthy."

"I am not saying anything against Big Ellen," said Donald evenly. "I'll be going now." He slung on his empty game-bag and made for the mouth of the cave, but there he turned head over shoulder.

"I will be back some time to-day, and I might have news of all that is going."

"All that is—intended?" Diego queried.

"That too. And after, Don Diego, _you_ can decide what to do, and I'll not hinder you."

He put emphasis on the _you_. Donald was convinced that his Mistress Ann had had nothing to do with the whole tragic affair, and Diego could not enlighten him.

IV

"There is now a long day before us, Don Diego," said Ann when Donald was gone.

"It will pass," said Diego laconically.

She faced him, placed a hand on his arm, and looked into his eyes.

"It will pass. All days pass, but this day I want to pass quietly, and I want you to be quiet with me."

"If you mean that I am not to trouble you, I agree. But you will make me one promise?"

"It is?"

"That you do not leave this cave or the gorge below it until Donald comes back."

"I promise. That is easy, for I am not foolish any more. Yesterday I committed a grievous sin yet to be confessed, for which I must do penance many days."

Diego could have told her that she had committed two grievous sins, killing in hot blood and despair, but he kept silent.

They did spend a quiet day, and, yet, it passed quickly enough. He left her in the cave and went down the gorge to the Garbh Ailt, first scouting the ground as he had often scouted hostile territory in Spain and on Commando. No one moved about the chorrie or above the steep bluffs breaking down into cliffs; and he went up to the cascade over the pass and had a shower-bath that made him gasp to the sting of it. He had no towel and the sun had not yet reached down this far, so he stamped about on the rock and rubbed himself briskly till he was nearly dry. He was in fine physical condition, lean and long, and with a brown hide like velvet—no longer Spanish leather. Life was at its height in him, and the Law might seek to claim it. Let the Law try!

He felt his chin. It would be blue-black in bristle, and he would look the dago desperado he was supposed to be. Well! if he had to slink through the mountains a beard might not be a bad disguise. And if, at the sacrifice of his own innocence, the woman could somehow be cleared, then he would slink alone and make London in spite of an army. All the time, in his own heart, he knew that, himself and Ann going together, they had one chance in a hundred to win clear. But, by the Lord! he would take that chance.

When he got back to the fault below the cave, Ann was sitting on a stone on the opposite side of the gorge, a rug draped round her, looking up at the face of the cliff.

The air, even in high summer, had a chill in here in this gloomy gut.

"I am waiting on the sun," she said. "It is our life."

He looked up the tilted strata and strong bosses of the cliff. The lower half was still in shadow; the upper showed glistening points in the sunlight.

"Midday before the sun reaches this far," he said.

"I can wait."

He went across, chose a rock some distance from her, and sat down, his shoulder and head turned so that his eyes would not disturb her quietness. And there they waited, not talking, thinking their own throughts and watching the sunlight creep down the cliff. When it got down to within head-height of the base, Diego went across and tried to crane up into it. He failed by some inches. Ann gave a quiet chuckle.

"A man is a giant in his own mind. You are a tall man, Diego, but not seven feet. No!"

"But I am a magician and will now bring the sun down to my own gianthood. Watch thou, O priestess!"

He held his head up, his eyes closed, and waited till he felt the glow over his dark crown and dark brows. Then he opened his eyes, and the sun, his servant, blinded him.

"Live for ever, obedient one!" he saluted.

"I will greet him too," said Ann.

She came across, the rug draping in the cunning folds that woman knows how to toss, went up two steps of the rock-ladder and turned round. The light was down to her breast. She threw back her head, closed her eyes, opened her arms wide, and let the sun pour through her. The rug fell about her feet. A tall, lovely, lissome, breasted priestess, with the red halo of her hair alive in the sun. She had found that her torn stockings were beyond repair and had rolled them tightly down over her walking shoes. Her long tapering legs, apart from a scratch or two, were creamy white and satin-smooth, smoother than most women's legs, that seldom have the texture of a man's. After a time she sat on the fallen rug and waited for the sun to come down and bathe her.

When the light reached the floor of the gorge, Diego chose a spot where the stones offered a smooth enough slope and lay down on his back. He shuffled his shoulder into ease, pulled his old tweed hat over his eyes and let the sunlight soak into him. It was life indeed. But it was a drug too, for presently he found soothing waves of drowsiness pour over him, and let them pour till he was drowned deep. And someone far off yet near crooned an old lullaby that he had heard before.

When he waked, the floor of the gorge was again in shadow and the old chill was back in the air. But Ann's rug was thrown over him, and Ann herself sat on a stone at his side, leaning forward, her arms across her knees. His hat was in her hand, and she was looking down into his eyes. She smiled at him, and her smile was no longer sad.

"I was watching over your sleeping, Don Diego. You sleep with continence, not in snores, your face calm and your mouth gentle, and sometimes your nose gives a small twitch that is the very twitch of a rabbit."

"The wolf's nose twitches too," he said.

"But no! The rabbit, but not in timidity. And once down in your throat you said, 'En garde!' Even in your dreams was war."

"I was not dreaming of war. I dreamt I was on a hillside and going over, a hill I know in dreams but not in life; and I knew what was beyond—where I was going —the roads, the houses, the people in the houses that I know only in dreams. I was looking for a woman with red hair. I did not find her."

"Some day in a dream you will find her. She will come to you in a dream, and in a dream only. Until that dream come we will be patient."

Diego, lying still, scrutinised her face. It had changed since morning. It was a quiet face still, but it was set in firmer lines, and her eyes were steadfast. *My lady*, he said in his own mind, *you have been thinking all day long and you have come to a decision. And, having decided, peace has come to you, and a courage wherein you can laugh again. But if your decision is not my decision I will fight you too.*

She felt his thoughts in his eyes, for she said quickly: "Is it not time to eat?"

"It is always time to eat," said Diego, whipping away the rug.


## CHAPTER V

## WORK FOR A CONQUISTADOR

I

It was two hours before the sunset that they could not see from this defile when Donald returned. At that time they were sitting companionably together on the bottom step of the rock-ladder, their shoulders touching. They were not talking. They knew that the time was approaching, and small talk would be no help now. They heard Donald whistle his bar at the mouth of the gorge, and Ann, like a boy, wet her lips with her tongue-tip and whistled back the next bar.

Donald moved with long easy strides over the rounded stones, and looked much fresher than in the morning. Instead of game-bag he carried a brown-paper parcel under an arm. They stood up to meet him, and he came and leant a shoulder against the rim of the fault. He did not give them time to question him, or, rather, they were slow to begin.

"I am sorry," he said, "but I cannot tell ye how things

are moving. The only persons I was allowed to speak to were Big Ellen and Angus Campbell——"

"He is the Law," said Diego.

"He is, but he did not mention your name once, Don Diego."

"Naturally. Not until he is ready."

Ann threw out her hands impulsively. "Donald, you will tell us from the beginning?"

"That will be the best way, Mistress Ann. I will tell ye what I can, and it is not much, but at the end of it I'll have an important thing to say. Listen, then! I went across to the Lodge after leaving here this morning. The Major was there, and so was Hamish. The Major wanted to talk to me, but Hamish, not lifting his voice, said 'No,' and though he did not lift his voice not even the new laird dare gainsay him. I went in then to the Estate Office, where Angus the Bobby was sitting in state, and he put me through it. You see, he is questioning everyone who was at this end of the Glen yesterday and might have seen anything. I had to tell him every place I was from the time I left the bothy until—seven in the evening. Angus was so easy in himself that I took a dig at him. 'Where's the Inspector, Angus, or are you promoted Chief Constable?' And he got red in the face. 'They'll be here when they're wanted,' he said. 'And you'll be for trouble, Angus,' I told him. 'Someone will,' he said, 'and see that it isn't your ain self by opening your Caithness mouth too wide. Get out o' here!' So out I went, a flea in my lug, and Hamish met me outside and sent me straight down to Loch Beg. Long John was sitting on the bench outside the Estate Office, waiting his turn I suppose, and down at the gate I met the Piper going up, and along by the road there was Wally the Post pedalling hard against the brae. I was hoping he'd get off and talk to me, but he was in a hurry, and went by with his hand over his walrus moustache. So I sent a swear after him and went on.

"At Loch Beg there was Big Ellen by herself wanting her colour and her face like iron. 'Are my two little ones'—meaning you, and you're no' little—'Are my two little ones safe and sound, Donald Gunn?' she wanted to know first thing. 'They were after a good breakfast when I left them,' I told her. 'The food won't curdle in them,' she said. 'You look tired, Donald. You'll rest now, for you have a hard night before you.' She made me lie down upstairs, and I was tired, and slept sound till she waked me in the afternoon. I'm as fresh as a daisy now."

Donald paused there, and Diego's mind was busy. Yesterday Donald Gunn had left his bothy at two p.m. to go up Glen Seilig. At seven General Harper was dead, and his wife was standing over him, a rifle in her hand. Was Donald anywhere about Skene's Rock then? He could not be. Neither could Long John, nor Piobar Maol Tam, and certainly not Wally the Post. Diego was used to scouting, and he had scouted the ground before and behind. He had seen no one on the moors and there was no one on the moors, or under the cliff, but Ann Harper, Major Harper, himself—and a dead man—and a roe deer. All that the constable was doing was sifting the ground seeking some corroborative evidence for Major Harper's statement that his brother had been murdered by Diego Usted with Ann Harper as an accomplice. And that was that.

Ann was speaking quietly. "That is all, Donald?"

"All I know, Mistress Ann. Big Ellen waked me and fed me and sent me here——"

"With an important thing to say to us?"

"With an important thing to say to each of ye."

"We are listening, Donald."

"They are of very great importance, Mistress Ann.

She impressed that on me. She said that as you love life and honour you would heed her."

"I heed her. I am myself again, Donald. I will do what that great woman tells me. I will do what you tell me."

She did not say that she would do what Diego Usted told her. So she had come to a decision some time that day. She would not be swayed by him. Donald was speaking.

"This is the message for you, Mistress Ann. You are to come back with me to my bothy, and there you will stay till you are sent for. I will not be there to-night, but you need have no fear. There is a change of clothes for you at the bothy, and there will be a saddle-pony in case you have to go anywhere. That's it."

"It is an order. And Don Diego?"

Donald turned to Diego, his eyes piercing. "Your message is the important one, Don Diego. She repeated it for me twice, and I do not understand it, for all the addling I gave my brains."

"Go on!" said Diego harshly. But Donald wanted to impress on him the importance of the message.

"Her voice was like a bell, her face a stone, her eyes blazing. Like an oracle she was, and proud. This is what she said. 'You will tell Don Diego Usted whose uncle is Cuchulain, and whose friend I am, that he will do this thing because it is his own right and none other's. He will go to the Lodge of Affran at the set of this sun and bring Major Arthur Harper down to Loch Beg Bothy to meet the men of the Glen. He will bring him down alive. He will not let Young Affran or Young Affran's sister come with their father. On no account will he let them, even if he has to use iron. But Major Harper he will bring down alive, and well he is able.' That's the message."

Ellen Honora McCarthy was a dramatic woman.

Diego felt a tingle in his spine and his nostrils widening, and he had to clear the knot in his throat before he could speak. But Ann spoke first. She was standing head up and her two hands covering her breasts.

"It is putting himself in the hands of his enemy, the man he bent under his hands who had hate in his eyes."

"There is Big Ellen's message," said Donald. "She would have a reason for it."

"She must have. Good Mother of God! she must have. But——" She turned and looked at Diego.

Diego kept a firm hold on himself. He thought before he answered. They were taking Ann away from him who was a killer. They were going to take care of her themselves and they had a pony ready for her in case she had to get away quickly. He saw at once that he could not interfere in this, or sway Ann. It meant that this was the finish between her and himself—for now or for ever. Let that be. In his own case he was to take Major Harper, his accuser, down to Loch Beg to meet the men of the Glen. Had his aunt imposed her will on the men to do the thing she wanted, and was he her instrument? And what would take place at Loch Beg? He did not know that. But he knew what he would do. He spoke quietly:

"I will take Major Arthur Harper to Loch Beg, and alive."

Ann spoke deeply, a thrill in her voice:

"You will do that, Diego, and well are you able."

"Is it time that I go?"

"Plenty of time yet," said Donald cheerfully. His head was down and he was opening the brown-paper parcel. "She thinks of everything, that woman. After a night in the heather she wants a man at his middling-best, and, indeed, at the time o' speaking a body might cross the street from him as it were."

The parcel contained a white open-necked shirt that

Aunt Ellen had made for Diego with her own hands from a bolt of old Irish linen. And wrapped in it was his shaving tackle, including a round hand-mirror.

He shaved there at the foot of the steps, Donald holding a cup of cold water for him. He was used to shaving in cold water. Ann took the mirror out of his hand.

"I will hold it for your eyes," she said. In the touch of her hands, in the way she held the mirror, there was a new vibrancy. But she did not hold it very steadily, and he had to move his head about to keep his face reflected. She took a great interest in his method, and moved her chin and jaw and nose in unconscious mimicry. She chuckled.

"Are you not ashamed of your face when you grimace so dreadfully?"

"You should see your own face. That woman does not think of everything, Donald. She forgot to put a new blade in this safety."

"You'll thole it," said Donald.

"A man follows his own technique in this daily or weekly business," said Ann. "I have not seen this shaving since many years, when my brother Mariono let me watch him. He shaved down one side and across and up the other side with a razor of age that he called the cutter of throats, and sometimes a muzzle-loader, so that when we were on campaign in the mountains and his beard grew, all the hairs curled one way—most amusing. Mariono is now with God, and we are in God's hands."

"And in Aunt Ellen's," said Diego. He caught her wrist. "Woman, will you hold it thus one small instant. If this was a cut-throat, where would my nose be?"

"A little shorter, and so better. Now you shave down one side, and then down the other, and then your lip which is not short, and now your chin which is of Mephistophelos—or Don Juan. Ah! you have trouble

286

with that wicked dimple. A little more! Now it is right."

She reached out her hand and smoothed his long jaw.

"It is only so smooth, but enough. Go now, small boy, and wash your face—and behind the ears."

He went to the basalt bowl at the corner, and did as he was bid. And when he lifted his head she was holding a napkin in one hand and his white shirt in the other, and the mirror under arm.

He scrubbed his face and neck briskly and reached for his shirt.

"Turn your back, hussy," he ordered her.

She turned her back dutifully. The clean ozone from the linen was about his face, but when he got his head through he saw her laughing curious eye in the mirror over her shoulder.

"It is the gorilla, Donald Gunn," she said, chuckling. "I am of opinion that there be more than thirteen hairs on his chest. Think you so?"

A strange pang went through Diego. Thus would a woman, intimate, have small sayings for the man her lover.

"I think it is good to be young and clean of heart," said Donald, "and ye are that in spite of everything."

And Diego knew that Ann, in spite of what had happened, was clean of heart.

Diego did not delay now. He pulled on his jacket over the cool-feeling shirt and picked up his hat from the stones.

"I go now." He looked full into her eyes that were full on his. Her lower lip was not quite still, though it was clenched on the upper. He spoke sternly. "We will remember our name and nation. Be with God!"

He turned and went quickly down over the rounded stones towards the Garbh Ailt. No voice followed him. At the corner he turned. She was standing erect, her

287

hands to attention at her side. Then she lifted her arm, bent it at the elbow and clenched her hand tight. Thus he greeted her in return. Thus would they hold their lives.

He turned the corner. He did not know what he was going to. He did not know how this would end. This might be the end. He might never see Ann again. Let it be so, then. If it were the end she had taken it debonairly. He would remember her so.

## II

Again Diego climbed the steep chorrie of Garbh Ailt, but this time his head did not trouble him. And again he went down the long slopes towards Skene's Rock, the orange light of sunset washing over the seas of heather all round him. There was now no ridge of snow below the cairn, and the heather was beginning to bud. Here and there in sunny hollows the bell-heather was already in bloom, and its red-magenta clusters stood out against the smoky blue of the common heath. And all the northern hills, a welter of brown and orange and purple, stood up against the saffron sky of evening. And so he got to Skene's Rock.

From the brink of the cliff outside the rock he looked down on Affran Loch that was again calm and again mirrored the hills head-down and shining. The trout were not yet rising. He looked down and to his left towards the base of the cliff, but the bulge out of the fault hid the rock and the opening where a man had been killed. His eyes went on and down and saw the ugly grey house of Affran on its green-spread. There was no one on the lawn; there was no sign of life about the house; not a chimney smoked. But Diego foreknew that he would find his man waiting there for him, and he knew that the man was his enemy.

He turned round and looked at the foot of the rock where Ann and he had talked to each other two months before, and had shown each other what was growing between them; and that thing had kept growing—and had bloomed to tragedy. In the heather close to the rock a walking-crook was lying. He took a step forward and picked it up. He knew the crook well. It was Ann's own crook, cut and seasoned by Donald Gunn, who had carved a fox's mask at the point of the hand-grip. He looked at it and wondered. How did it get here? If—! No use forming theories. It could have got here in many ways. But if she had it yesterday she must have been up here before going down to face her husband—or to meet himself.

He tucked the crook under an arm and went on down the track through the fault amongst the jumble of stones. When he got to the big boulder at the junction of the paths his desire was to hurry on without glancing round the side of it to where the dead man's body had lain. There would be no body there now, but, since there had been no rain, there might be blood-stains. He turned round. There was no blood. Instead there was a small cairn of stones to mark the spot. That cairn would stay there for a long time, and men passing would drop a stone on it, as was the custom, until in time no man remembered what the cairn marked, or until an old legend grew about it. What part would he have in such a legend?

He went down among the trees, across the head-stream of Affran Water by the foot-bridge, along the demesne wall, through the open gates, and over the lawn moving steadily, unhesitatingly, unhurriedly. Half-way across the lawn he saw that there were people in the sun-porch, but they did not see him until he was at the corner. Then, through the glass, he heard the quick scrape of a chair on the tiles, but before any other move could be made he had the side-door open and shut behind him.  Major Arthur Harper was on his feet and staring at him.

Henrietta was on her feet too, looking at him and looking behind him to the lawn, looking to see if Ann Harper was coming.  Ewan McInnes, the lawyer, sat forward in his chair near the elephant's foot that held the sticks and fencing-foils, one hand rubbing his chin, and his wise old eyes wary on Diego.  Charles, Young Affran, did not move at all.  He kept his favourite posture, resting on his shoulder-blades, his ankles crossed, and his hands behind his head.  But his sullen eyes did not stay on his toes; they lifted to Diego and stayed on him, but they grew no more sullen.  These were the four people Diego found in the sun-parlour that was still too warm after the heat of a July day, though the sun was behind the hills now, and all the Glen hushing towards twilight.  And there was a weight in that room that was not of the dying day.

Major Harper's voice was coldly matter-of-fact.

"So you've come to give yourself up, Usted?  Where's your accomplice?"

Before Diego could reply Henrietta came straight at him.  She was not in black, but in that light blue dress that suited her delicate colouring and made her fragile and diaphanous.  But she had forgotten her make-up this evening, for her face was pale and her shapely mouth had little colour.  Her eyes, however, were not wan or weary.  They were angry.  It was a real deep anger that sent the blood to the heart and lit a flare in the eyes.  Her voice was insistent and a little shrill.

"That is right!  Where is Ann?  What have you done with her?"

Diego wanted to tell her to go to hell.  She was interfering with this business that would be difficult enough without her. He tried to hush-hush her with the palm of his hand.

"I will not be shooed away," she cried at him. "You will tell me where Ann is? You have her crook in your hand."

"She is safe," Diego said then.

"Safe—safe!" She threw her hands in his face. "How can she be safe? What do you people think you are doing with her?"

"Henrietta!" Her father's voice was stern. "You will please behave yourself."

She swung round. His sternness did not cow her. No one could silence this fiery girl. She stormed at him. "I will not behave myself. Someone did not, and an old man is dead. Did you tell Angus Campbell that Ann killed her husband? Did you?"

"I merely made a statement of what I saw."

"Statement—statement! Everyone has been making statements, and no one tells me anything. Did you say in your dam' statement that you saw her kill her husband? Did you?"

"I did not, but——"

"You did not, because you could not. That woman would never kill that old man, tyrant that he was— God forgive him! My God! Poor Ann! A broken kid brought into the Glen tied to an old man, why should we hurt her? Do you think I do not know her? I hated her, I loved her, I love her now, and this shell of a house is empty without her where she ruled us all with her head and her hands. No one knows what she did for me—and for you too, Charlie——"

"Shut your trap, Hett!" her brother bade her gruffly.

"I will not shut my trap, you useless young fool! I am on her side. I will fight for her. And by God! if anything happens her out of this house I will never set foot in it again. I will go away and join Larry McLeod, and I don't care a damn whether he marries me or not."

"That will be enough, Henrietta!" Her father was more urgent than stern.

"It is not enough." She stamped her foot. "I am getting this off my chest, and no one can stop me. Very well! I'll behave myself, then, and you men will listen." Her voice quieted. "I could have killed that old man, but I did not, for I was down at Loch Beg. Neither did you, Ewan, for you were at Craik all day. But you three"—she ran her finger round the three men—"where were you? Ann did not kill her husband, but one of you three did. One of you three! I cannot point my finger at the one, but when I can, God have mercy on his soul. Now I am finished, Mr Diego Usted, and you fools can squabble to your heart's content. But watch out!"

That was amply dramatic. Her chair complained as she threw herself into it. The blood was back to her face, and her eyes, still stormy, showed hot tears. But she blinked the tears back, held her head up, and would not let her face be broken before them by grief or temper or misery or desolation or whatever it is that breaks a woman's face when she weeps.

Diego gave her his military salute as he had given it to Ann Harper, elbow bent at shoulder-level and hand tensely clenched on Ann's crook, and his heart surged in a great pride for her.

"Ann Mendoza thanks you, my cousin, and I do too," he said. "She did not kill her husband. His death was accidental and by his own hand."

"Where then——?" But her father interrupted her with a short bark of laughter and said:

"You can prove that, Usted? Until you do you are under arrest, and I am now going to ring Constable Campbell."

He took one stride towards the inner door, and Diego

took a stride too, but Young Affran, notwithstanding his posture and his chunkiness, was quicker than either of them, for there he was at the closed door and facing his father.

"By the Lord, no! No, Father! Captain Usted will not be arrested in this house." He turned head. "You have some business, Captain?"

That was Diego's cue. Up to now he was not sure how to take his bull by the horns. He said:

"I have business. I want Major Harper to come down to Loch Beg Bothy with me to meet the men of the Glen."

"Why?"

"It is an order."

Major Harper faced Diego. With his carved features and deep-set eyes he looked a man of resolute character. But his mouth and voice were sneering, and a strong man does not sneer. And his eyes were calculating.

"Is that an order from the new Head of the Home Guard?"

"It is an order."

Young Affran spoke quickly. "I will go with you, Father. After all, Hamish McLeod is Head of the Home Guard——"

His father, laughing shortly, interrupted him.

"An order from the Home Guard or an order from the Glen? I know, boy, how you and your sister have been smitten with this notion of the entity of the Glen, the soul of the Glen, the revival of some golden age or other—all that nonsense. I am now the owner of Glen Affran, and if my tenants want to see me they can see me or my Factor in the Estate Office during office hours." His voice harshened. "And the business they may see me about must be the business of the estate, not the murder of my brother."

The young man looked down at his toes, and the troubled murmur of his voice was to himself.

"If we could only keep that hellish business in the Glen——"

"We cannot and I will not. Murder has been done. Look here, Usted! My son insists that you be permitted to leave my house. Go then, and tell your uncle, my head-forester under notice of dismissal, that if he wants to see me he may see me to-morrow. That is final."

Diego kept his voice as quiet as he knew how.

"You are coming down to Loch Beg to-night, Major Harper."

Young Affran stepped forward, holding his voice too.

"Be reasonable, Usted! You heard what my father said? If the men want to see him he will see them to-morrow."

"And on estate business only," added his father.

This was going badly for Diego. There was scarcely a chance now that he could succeed in his object without a rough house, and it would be a rough house. He always hated to use his strength brutally. Now a small sword—— Wait, there was one chance. He took his bull by the horns.

"It is an order that I take Major Harper to Loch Beg. He is coming, and you are not coming with him."

"No bloody use talking to a bull-head!" cried Young Affran exasperatedly, and grew hotter. "Have we got to show you that we own this house? Right!" He strode across to the side-door and flung it open. "Come on! out you go."

And there he loosed his temper. He had been holding in a savage temper all day, and it was a relief to let it go. He stuck his chin out, strode at Diego, and clenched a strong hand above his elbow. Next instant he would have tried to swing Diego towards the door, and the rough house would have begun. Diego took his one chance. He brought his hand down on Young Affran's.

"Just a moment, Harper!"

One shred of the young man's restraint held. Diego looked down at him.

"You tell me your father will not come. That is a challenge. When you make a challenge you should risk your blood and life on it like the gentleman you are. Let my arm go!"

Diego loosed some of his own temper then. He swept Young Affran away with his held arm. He used every atom of his explosive force, for he wanted a little time. Young Affran went backwards, his feet actually off the ground; the back of his knees collided with a chair, and the chair and he went over in a cursing complicated tangle that finished with the chair on top, and his legs kicking.

Diego did not wait for the young fellow to pick himself up. He had to move quickly now. He turned and strode round Ewan McInnes, who all this time had watched and said nothing, thrust Ann's crook into the elephant's foot, and in the same motion plucked out two of the foils by their weighted pommels. They were old-fashioned foils some thirty inches in length, of a square tapering section, and with gutta-percha buttons guarding the points. A smart sliding snick with each blade in turn and the buttons went rolling. The foils were killing weapons now.

A hilt in right and a point in left, he came round to face Young Affran, who was on his feet after furiously kicking the chair into a corner. He looked at Diego with angry astonishment. He was astonished at the explosive force that had hurled him over that chair. He had known Diego only as a sick man moving lazily about the Glen, digging leisurely in Big Ellen's garden; and, no doubt, he had been certain that as a Briton he could have trundled this lean foreigner through the door. Moreover, not so long ago, he had disarmed Diego at fencing, and no doubt could do so again.

Diego gave him no time to think. He thrust the hilt into his lax hand and taunted him into tightening his fingers on it.

"Take it! The sting is in the other end—or are you a coward like your father?"

"Damn you, Usted! I could spit you for that."

Diego had his temper in perfect control, but he was on tenterhooks lest anyone should interfere between them now. No one did. Henrietta, behind a chair, did not want to; Ewan McInnes knew that now was not the time to interfere; and the father knew his son for a fencer, and if this desperado, Usted, got spitted that would be a happy solution.

Diego stepped back for distance, and brought his blade up. He spoke harshly.

"Your father is coming with me, and I will ensure it with your life. En garde! Remember the buttons are off. Engage!"

The blades clicked and grated, and in that moment Diego knew that the iron was restored to his wrist and that the suppleness was still there. Young Affran's wrist was strong too, but it was not supple, and Diego, using all his strength and suppleness, kept the wisps of steel writhing on each other. After all, the youth's heart was not in this; he was only an amateur, had never seen blood follow a prick, and, with the buttons off for the first time, he remained cautiously on the defensive. But if his confidence returned, as it would in half a minute's fencing, then Diego knew that it would take a dangerous wound to quiet him. Diego had to act quickly.

Steel writhing on steel at knee-level came up on the outer circle, and there Diego disengaged, recovered his blade smartly, and lashed at his opponent the one straight cut at the head that is permissible in Spanish fencing. It so surprised Young Affran that his parry was barely in time, and Diego had the opposing blade where he wanted it. Again, as three months ago with Henrietta's stick, he bound the blade in *flanconade*, whipped it out of Young Affran's hand and at his feet, stepped forward, set his heel close to the hilt, and snapped the blade off. He was so near that he could have run his defenceless opponent through by shortening his grip. Instead, he put the weighted pommel against his breast-bone, lifted him backwards as if he did not weigh a stone, and thrust the hilt into his hand.

"There! now you are dead, but your jaw has not fallen. Keep your tongue behind it."

Henrietta came out from behind her chair. She laughed high and shrill, with a trace of hysteria.

"There's a Spanish hidalgo for you, brother. God! have you no sense?" She charged at her brother, and impulsively plucked the foil out of his hand. "Keep out of it, you dam' fool! or I'll prick you where it does most good."

Diego turned his back on them. Major Harper had his back to the inner door, his hand on the knob at his side. Had he been thinking of retreating into the house? Too late now. Their eyes locked for a moment, and then Diego saw the man's eyes flicker. He knew, since last evening, that the final resolution was not in him. The man was aware of Diego's force and would bow before it, and yet Diego did not want to put a hand on him before his children. He took one slow stride forward to give him time. And there Ewan McInnes took the opportunity that he had been patiently waiting for. He got to his feet and came forward deliberately, half between the two. He spoke with legal deliberation.

"Let us consider. You know, Major, you are the laird of Glen Affran, and I'm thinking it would be the proper thing to investigate this—this insubordination—at its source—without hesitation or troubling about this man's overbearing methods."

"You think so, McInnes?" There was relief in his voice.

"I do. I would take prompt and drastic action and show the auld fools who is laird in the Glen. As your Factor I will go with you."

"Very good, McInnes. We'll make someone suffer for this."

The old lawyer turned to Diego, and Diego was not sure if one of those wise eyes half-hooded itself at him.

"Young man, as the laird's legal adviser it is my right to accompany him, and I need not remind you that I am a man of the Glen myself."

Diego did not hesitate. "Certainly, sir. I shall be glad if you come to Loch Beg with your client." He knew that, once there, Aunt Ellen would not hesitate to send him about his business if she did not want him.

"Let us not waste time, then," urged the old man. "We'll take the coble, and by my certes! the Major and I will put a flea in a lug or two or the night is done."

Major Harper, hatless, and not lifting an eye to his children, went out the side-door. Ewan McInnes followed him, and he did not look at them either. Neither did Diego, for he did not want to see if there was humiliation in their eyes. He just lifted a hand and went out.

IV

Diego, crossing the lawn behind the other two, heard quick light footsteps behind him, turned head, and waited for Henrietta. She caught his arm and held him. He released her hand, bent his lips to it, and gently smoothed her fingers. She shook her head sadly. She was again pale, but her eyes were no longer flaming, but wide and unhappy.

"You are hard on us Harpers, Don," she whispered.

He had no answer to that, but he only said:

"For you I am grieved——"

"Never mind me. Something is happening to-night, and Big Ellen wants to keep me and Charlie out of it."

"I know nothing."

"You would not tell me if you did. I am afraid. But that is not what I am here for." She squeezed his arm: "Don, please! How is Ann?"

"She is well. She is at Donald Gunn's bothy."

"But why did she run away? She never—she could not——"

"No. The man died by accident." He paused and went on. "She was there at the time, and your father found her, and something was said—something that brought her evil days about her. She broke down, and I took her across to Donald's to give her time to recover herself. She has done that." He put his hand on her holding fingers. "She will face the world again if she has good friends like you."

"Leave me out of it. She can look after herself, and so can I as she taught me." She shook his arm. "Listen, Don! When all this mess is cleared up, you'll take her right away from here? Do you hear me? Don't lose her. Whip her up in your arms and away." She lightened her tone. "I'll forgo my claim on you, old hoss."

"She will not let me take her," Diego said.

"Let you! Let you!" She threw away his arm. "Damn you! Forget to be a hidalgo once in a while. Good night and good luck!"

She turned quickly, and her light young feet took her running across the grass. Her stocky brother was waiting outside the door for her. Diego lifted hand to him, and his hand went up to his brow in salute. He was a better man than his father.

They went down the loch in the outboard coble, the laird at the tiller, his Factor facing him, and Diego at the bow. Not a word passed amongst them all the way down. The toneless light of the gloaming was over water and mountain, but the loch itself was shining with its own molten-silver light. The trout were again feeding, and the reflection of the hills pulsed and broke in the widening rings. But there was no thought or talk of fishing that hour.

Uncle Hamish had heard the engine, and was on the pier waiting for them. He was in his dark Sunday clothes, his massive neck in a white collar and black cravat. Was this Sunday, then, Diego wondered? No, but it soon would be, for it was now late on Saturday evening. And Diego should have been in Edinburgh on his way to London. London—and even the war—could wait. He might not see either if things went wrong to-night.

The boat came round in a curve, and Hamish caught the painter that Diego threw and whipped it round the mooring-post. Diego was at his side when he straightened up, and their hands clenched.

"Ay, Jamie lad! Glad I am you're back, and sorry for what happened."

"I am sorry, Uncle," Diego said.

"Not you need be sorry. Your aunt and myself knew you would not fail us. You had no trouble?"

"My hands had not to touch anyone," said Diego, and wondered how the bare truth could lie.

Major Harper was on the pier now. His strong voice came sternly.

"What is the meaning of this, McLeod?"

"Life or Death, Major Harper. You will find out." Uncle Hamish could silence any when he wanted to. He was giving the old lawyer a hand out of the stern.

"Glad you could come, Ewan," he said.

But Ewan wanted to make his position clear.

"I am Factor for this estate, Hamish," he said. "To-night I am the laird's legal adviser. You will remember that."

"It is your right. You are welcome."

Major Harper had chosen the line he would take. It was a strong one.

"Look here, McLeod! I will have no dictation from my employees or my tenants, and you will note that your month's notice holds good."

But Hamish McLeod had chosen his line too, and nothing under the sky would make him deviate from it. His voice was quiet but definite.

"Rid yourself of the notion that I am your employee any longer, Major Harper. And for another thing, you will be careful how you speak to me."

"Is that a threat?"

"It is a warning." He half-lifted his big curved hands and looked at them. "I threaten no man." That was Cuchulain. He would warn a man once, and after that let the man beware. The Major understood.

"Let us get this over," he said abruptly.

"Come ye up to the house," said Hamish, and went ahead. Diego brought up the rear, and a great sense of relief came over him. For thirty hours a weight had been on his shoulders, and here in his uncle's house it would be lifted from him.

# CHAPTER VI

## THE NET CLOSES

I

THERE were ten people in the big living-room—nine men and one woman; and the woman dominated eight of the men, and, presently, would dominate the ninth.

The blinds were down, the dark curtains drawn, and the brass lamp hung lighted from a cross-beam above the table. A few peat-sods smouldered into white ash on the open hearth.

Big Ellen was wearing her Sunday dress too, that black taffeta with white at collar and wrists that showed the flowing lines of her noble figure. There was a touch of red high up on the bosses of her cheek-bones, a red coral comb in her hair, and never were her eyes so bright and blue and fierce. As soon as Diego entered she swooped on him, caught him so tensely by the shoulders that her fingers hurt, kissed him hot-lipped on the cheek, and rested her cheek against his. Her cheek was hot too, and Diego, a choking sensation in his throat, pressed his face close to hers. Her voice whispered in his ear:

"Don't be troubling your head about anything, my darling. Hamish and I have it in our hands."

He could not speak for the choke in his throat. She drew him to the fireside and pressed him down into his own chair. He drew in a long breath. He was home again. There was another chair at the other side of the hearth, and the old straw hassock near it.

"You will sit there," she said, "and you will say nothing."

Sitting aside in his chair Diego could see the faces of four of the five men seated round the oval table. There was an empty chair at the head, which was opposite the bow window. Next to the empty chair on the left sat Piobar Maol Tam. His back was to Diego, and his sun-peeled bald head gleamed under the lamplight. Next him sat Donald Gunn, whom Diego had left at the cave not many hours before. His ascetic lean profile was set in seriousness. Then there was a vacant space, and another empty chair stood at the foot of the table. Beyond that Long John McKenzie sat erect, his big fists on the table, his head forward, and his eyes looking underbrowed across at Diego. Next him was Wally the Post, leaning forward, his fingers softly tapping the board, and his breath lifting his walrus moustache. And to the right of the empty chair at the head sat ruddy-faced Angus Campbell the policeman. His notebook and a file of papers were on the table before him, and he held a red pencil upright on the top page of the file. Diego knew these five men intimately. They had been his friends, and they were the leading men in the Glen. Just men all, but he did not know how they regarded that fetish called Justice. There was a restraint and seriousness about them that showed that they were sitting here on very important business.

Diego settled himself in his chair. His aunt had told him that he was to say nothing, but he was not sure that he would obey her if things took a certain course. Meantime he would keep his eyes and his ears open, and concentrate his mind on the meaning of every word and look. The first thing he noted was that the five seated men did not rise to their feet on the entrance of the new laird. They did not salute or even look at him. Did that mean that they would not acknowledge him as laird, just as they had not acknowledged his brother? It might mean something else too—that they did not like the accusations he had made. But would they know about these accusations?

Aunt Ellen did not greet Major Harper either. She welcomed Ewan McInnes, shook his hand, drew him round the foot of the table, and set a chair for him between the empty one and Donald Gunn. The old lawyer sat down not looking at anyone, though he knew everyone intimately. Uncle Hamish spoke.

"Will you be seated, Major Harper?" He gestured towards the chair at the foot of the table, and himself sat down in his own chair at the head.

Major Harper, his limp noticeable, moved round to

the foot of the table and placed his hands on the back of the empty chair. He was determined to keep the strong line he had decided on. His eyes, coldly stern, went round the oval of seated men, and the men in turn met his look with a coldness that might be disconcerting. He spoke brusquely.

"I will not be seated. This business will not take long."

Aunt Ellen had not taken a seat. Any time that her mind was on the full stretch she could not remain still. Now she moved from Diego's side to behind her husband's chair.

"Major Harper will sit when he wants to," she said, "and the business will take short or long."

"Don't interrupt me, Mrs McLeod." That was an order. "A man was sent to my house who insolently told me that I was to come down here to meet you men. That sort of message I would not ordinarily tolerate, but, on my Factor's advice, I have come down to inform you personally that I will not be dictated to. Understand this clearly." His voice slowed for emphasis. "I will not stand any dictation as to how I run my estate. That is all I have to say."

"No one would think of dictating to you that way, Major Harper," said Hamish in his quietest tone.

Ewan McInnes put two quick questions.

"Then what is the Major here for? What are you fellows here for?"

"We are making an enquiry into General Harper's death," Hamish answered for all of them.

"That is no business of yours, damn you!" The Major's voice rasped angrily. He looked across unwinkingly at Angus Campbell. "What are you doing here, Constable Campbell? Are you aware that you have a man accused of murder in this room?"

The constable moved in some discomfort, and his big face got ruddier, but his answer was cool enough.

"I am not finished my enquiries, Major Harper."

"Is it usual for a country constable to take charge of a murder case?"

"Do you call it murder?" Aunt Ellen questioned sharply.

But he ignored the dominant woman. Evidently he had made up his mind to ignore her, for he knew that crossing swords with her was simply asking for trouble. He kept his stern eyes on the policeman.

"Where is your Inspector, Campbell?"

"He'll be the morn."

"Does he know——"

Angus's face grew ruddier still, but now his sandy moustache bristled.

"He'll be here, I tell you." He slapped his file. "And until he is here I have my duty as a guardian of the law. I started last night, and to-night I hope to finish, and after that——"

But Aunt Ellen interrupted him with the flat of her hand.

"Wait, Angus!" She addressed herself to the old lawyer. "You are a man of the law yourself, Ewan, and we'll not deceive you. Angus does not represent the law here, he acts for the people of the Glen, just as you act for Major Harper, and I act for my nephew, Diego Usted. It is not Angus who is enquiring into this case to-night. It is my husband, Hamish McLeod."

"And is this his court of law?" enquired McInnes with satire.

"It is a court of law. The five men of Glen Affran round this table represent an old law, the law of the Clan, that has been in abeyance for two hundred years. In fact, Ewan, they propose to take the law into their own hands."

"Usurpation of Justice, McInnes?" suggested his client scoffingly.

"It might well come to that," half-agreed McInnes. He put an elbow on the table, held one finger up, and looked round the table. "Let me tell you how I see it. I am not minding Big Ellen's talk of courts of law, and clan justice, and men taking the law in their own hands. We all like her, but we know she comes of a people, kin in a way to ourselves, who are ower fond of taking the law into their own hands to the detriment of law and order——"

"And they have gone places while you are still stuck in the mud," she riposted.

"And we'll no' choose their gait, not yet awhile at any rate. But, having said that, I must also say that if a number of men anywhere, including their policeman-by-law-appointed, associate themselves together to investigate a matter, I cannot at the moment recall any enactment that prohibits them from doing so." He shook his finger minatorily. "But they cannot form themselves into a court of law, or enforce the law or even justice, or coerce or even call witnesses——"

"Or induce a servant of the law to produce information privately given," added Major Harper.

"Most assuredly not. The penalties are laid down and they are no' light." The lawyer's finger stood erect for attention, and he peered across at Hamish. "But there is another thing that strikes me this minute, and it is of signification. This is a country at war. This glen has a Home Guard officially recruited, and commanded by a Head officially appointed and of wide powers—how wide I do not know. Such a Head might investigate, any dom' way he liked, such a thing as the death of his predecessor. That's only my own opinion, mind you."

Diego smiled. The old lawyer, after warning them of penalties, was showing them a way out. He was a clansman too. His employer turned to him angrily, but Hamish was talking solidly.

"I was not acting as Head of the Home Guard," he said frankly, "because I did not think of it. But now you mention it, Mr McInnes, I take full responsibility for this investigation. I am investigating it in my house, and I am hoping to keep it inside the walls of the Glen——"

"Impossible, Hamish!" said the lawyer; and his client snorted.

"We'll be seeing," said Hamish placidly. "Go on, Angus!"

Angus cleared his throat importantly and began:

"Yesterday evening, at about a quarter to seven, Major-General Harper was killed below Skene's Rock. Major Harper it was that told me over the phone. I went up at once." He tapped the file in front of him. "Last night and to-day I took a statement covering twelve hours from everyone——"

"Not everyone," interrupted Major Harper sneeringly.

"Everyone I could get hold of who was at this end of the Glen yesterday. One statement——"

"I object." Major Harper's voice was fiercely indignant.

"I second the objection," said the lawyer promptly. "These are privileged statements, Angus, and unless you have the consent——"

"He has not my consent," said Major Harper. "He will divulge nothing——"

Angus struck the file with his fist and was no longer a policeman, but a Campbell.

"Dom't! we can't get on." He sat up and glared round. "I'm going to talk my mind for a'e minute. Captain Diego Usted is my friend, as his mother was before him. He is my son's officer. He fought his best for this country, and it was a braw best, and he is ready to fight now again. And look ye! I'm doing my dom'dest and I'll keep on doing my dom'dest to prove that he had no hand, act, or part in this killing. That's for ye, and any man here can make use of it any way he likes."

Diego should be proud of that statement, but, instead, he was unhappy. For if the policeman proved him innocent he must prove another guilty. But he did not see how Angus could prove anything.

"It is a pity you spoke all that, Angus," said the lawyer with real regret. "It will be brought up against you as a prejudiced partisan."

"The very thing I am," said Angus, unrepentant.

Major Harper smacked the top bar of the chair.

"I have enough of this travesty," he said. "I forbid you to use my statement except in the proper place. Now I am going to ring up the Chief Constable."

Before he might take a stride Hamish was on his feet. His voice was ominously quiet.

"I cannot compel you to talk, Major Harper, but I can and will compel you to stay in this room till this is finished. Sit down, man! Sit down!"

Their eyes locked, and Diego knew whose eyes would waver. But the wise old lawyer broke the deadlock. He tapped the seat of the empty chair next him at the foot of the table.

"Under duress, Major. I have a note of it. In my advisory capacity I ask you to wait so that any future action we take may be fully informed."

"Very good, McInnes!" The Major sat down. Hamish resumed his chair and nodded at Angus.

"The responsibility is mine," he said. "All of ye will now listen, and the statements will be put before ye for consideration. I might say, Mr McInnes, that the statements were made without what you call collusion. They were made separate, and no man listening here at this minute knows what is in another man's statement."

"You know?"

"And that is why I am putting them before you. Now, Angus, for a start you will tell us what my wife, Ellen, had to say?"

So Aunt Ellen had made a statement! Diego could not see why. Angus, clearing his throat, was about to put on his glasses when Aunt Ellen, standing between him and her husband, put a hand on his shoulder.

"Save your voice, Angus. I'll say my piece for you."

"Right you are, Big Ellen! I'll keep a check on you."

II

Aunt Ellen spoke in her flowing easy way, her eyes half-closed, looking at things as they had passed yesterday.

"This is it. All day yesterday myself was not outside this house and its curtilages. In the morning, after breakfast, Hamish and Diego were in the garden hoeing, and my inguns suffered for it. After a while Diego dropped his hoe and took to the hill, going over the shoulder towards Glen Sallagh. Hamish stayed by the hoe, mostly resting, till dinner-time at midday, and after that took himself off, and he will tell you where he went. I then phoned up Henrietta, and she came down here to me at three o'clock. She was here at six when the two of us saw Diego go up at the other side of the water. He was going towards Affran Loch, and waved to us. I knew that he was going up to Skene's Rock to say goodbye to his friend Ann Harper. The appointment was made openly on the phone that morning. Henrietta was here still at eight o'clock when Hamish phoned down to me from the Lodge that her uncle was dead; and I kept her here with me all night, restless where she had often slept in my arms. Therefore she had no hand, act, or part in her uncle's death. That is my statement."

"So it is—with a flourish or so," agreed Angus.

There was nothing in that statement, Diego considered.

309

Apparently it had been made to give Henrietta a perfect alibi. It even looked as if the alibi had been arranged beforehand! But surely that was impossible? There would be no alibi for himself or for Ann Harper? There could not be.

Angus turned over the single sheet that contained Aunt Ellen's brief statement, and placed his hand on the next. Apparently he had arranged his papers in a certain order, or, more probably, they had been arranged for him.

"I have here Major Arthur Harper's statement——"

"I warn you not to read it, Campbell," threatened its author.

"There is law behind that, Angus," cautioned the lawyer.

"Wait!" cried Aunt Ellen in a new voice. "There should be no need to read that statement. The enquiry might finish here." She went to the policeman's shoulder, turned over three sheets, and plucked them clean out of the file.

"Goad be here!" cried the astonished policeman.

Aunt Ellen walked behind Wally and Long John, and stood looking down at Major Harper. He would not look up at her, but kept his eyes on his hands resting on the edge of the table. She laid the sheets down within an inch of his fingers.

"That is your statement, Major Harper. Withdraw it, and we keep this bad business inside the Glen."

He turned head to his Factor. "What do you call this, McInnes?"

"A highly indictable offence to my mind: suborning to compound a felony. But you are answering the lady, Major?"

"This is my statement." He put his hand firmly on the sheets. "It holds."

There was an urgent appeal in Aunt Ellen's voice, and there was now no colour at all in her face.

"Listen to me, Major Harper! I am not asking you to withdraw it for the sake of Diego Usted or for the sake of Ann Harper. I am urging you to withdraw it for the sake of the House of Affran, for your son's sake and for your daughter's sake."

The man was so determined to accede nothing to this woman that he did not take time to consider. He tapped the papers, and his voice sounded reasonable.

"This is a fair statement of the situation and the facts as I knew and saw them. It is more than fair, for it is prejudiced on the side that you wish it to be." He straightened up as if a sudden thought had struck him. "It is so fair that I no longer object to its being read here amongst my tenants. You have my permission to read it, Constable Campbell." He pushed the sheets up the table and the constable gathered them in.

Aunt Ellen sighed deeply, and her voice was deep too.

"I spoke too soon. The investigation goes on. Once again I will speak to you, sir, and then you will listen, and then you will listen too late. Go on, Angus!"

She came round the table to Diego's side, and put a hand on his shoulder. He felt her hand tremble. She was a changed woman now. She was more sibylline than ever. She had tried and failed to swing the case her own way, and now one felt that she was the instrument of Fate, and that she knew where Fate was leading. Her voice, when she spoke, had a metallic quality, as if it was an instrument used by someone else.

III

Angus read Major Harper's statement slowly and clearly. Diego settled down in his chair and listened carefully, but he also kept an eye on the faces he could see round the table. The men of the Glen behaved admirably, not interfering, not interrupting, not showing any prejudice one way or another. Only once during the reading did Donald Gunn throw up his head, and once Long John clenched his fists tightly. It was evident that a good deal of the statement had been elicited by question and answer.

"I was at Lodge Affran on Friday," read Angus. "I did not once leave the house until after lunch. At lunch there were my brother the General, his wife, my two children, and myself. Ewan McInnes was not at lunch as he had gone down to Craik township on estate business shortly after breakfast. After lunch I left the Lodge. That was about two p.m. The day was very fine and my leg was not troubling me, so I decided to try a turn round by Glen Seilig to see how the stags were coming along.

" I crossed Affran Water by the bridge at the corner of the demesne wall, went up by the stream and by the pony-track into the top end of Glen Seilig, and returned by the ridge that is known as Drumdyre, and so again to the side of Affran Water some distance above the foot-bridge. That was a long tramp, and took some hours. I do not know the exact time, but it was after six o'clock when, approaching the foot-bridge from the other side, I saw my brother Major-General Harper come across. He went quickly along the track that goes by the south side of Affran Loch and forks up to Skene's Rock a mile away. He was carrying the point-twenty-two rifle that he usually carries to shoot vermin.

"After some consideration I decided to follow him. I did not like him going hurriedly in that direction armed with a rifle, even if he usually carried one—as I do too. I had no rifle with me on that occasion. I do not think it is necessary to give my reasons for following him. Well, then, it was because of a serious quarrel between my brother and his wife, that morning immediately after breakfast. At that time my brother's wife, Ann, rang up Diego Usted at Loch Beg Bothy. I assumed it was Diego Usted. She spoke to him by name. There was nothing secret about the message. All of us heard her—her husband, my children, and myself. She arranged to meet him that evening at seven o'clock at Skene's Rock. It was she that fixed the time and meeting-place. I gathered that it was their final meeting to say good-bye as, I understood, Mr Usted was leaving the Glen next morning. The two were very good friends, but nothing more as far as I know.

"My brother objected very strongly to his wife meeting this man. He forbade her to go. She said that she was going to say good-bye to a very dear friend where all the world could see them. Naturally they were very friendly, being two foreigners in the Glen and allied by race. My brother lost his temper, he often did. He accused her, without reason in my opinion, of being Diego Usted's mistress. She laughed and said that she would not quarrel with him any more. Yes, they had quarrelled frequently of late. She had a hot temper, an impulsive temper but not a bad one, in fact a rather lovable temper, and my brother was often intolerantly unbearable. He then threatened to follow her to what he called an assignation, and kick her lover over the cliff at Skene's Rock. She said that in that event she would lose her temper very surely and he would remember how she could kick too. He then threatened her with the alteration of his Will, and said that his solicitor was in the house for that very purpose. She said that was well, for the devil might at any moment tempt her to become possessed of two dead women's shoes. She then left the room hurriedly, for her temper was growing warm. My children and Ewan McInnes were present at the time, and can vouch for the accuracy of this."

At this point Ewan McInnes stirred in his seat and

looked aside curiously at his client. Angus went on reading.

"Because of that quarrel and of what my brother had said I followed him. I did not want him to encounter his wife and Captain Usted with a rifle in his hand. He did not like Captain Usted.

"My brother was some distance ahead and I did not keep him in view, as the path twists a good deal. It was some time before seven, but I did not look at my watch, that I heard the rifle-shot. It was the only shot I heard. I hurried forward and came to the edge of the small opening where the track goes up the cliff to Skene's Rock. Not more than three or four minutes would have elapsed from the time I heard the shot until I came to the edge of the opening. I saw Ann Harper standing by the big boulder at the side of the track. She had my brother's rifle in her hand, or, rather, I recognised it later as the one he had carried. At her shoulder stood Diego Usted, and at their feet lay the body of my brother.

"Diego Usted bent over the body but did not touch it. He then stood upright, and he and the woman spoke, but I was too far away to hear what was said. He took the rifle from her hands, using his tweed hat to hold it, wiped it clean of all finger-marks, laid it down by the side of the body, and clasped the dead man's fingers round the lock and barrel in several places; and finally flicked the rifle away to lie naturally amongst the stones.

"I then went across the opening and made my presence known. After what I had seen, I accused the man and woman of being accomplices in murder. I said that they must consider themselves under arrest, and must accompany me back to the Lodge, where I intended to ring up the police station. Diego Usted, using physical violence, threatened to kill me and make it look like murder and suicide. He was stronger than I was and could have killed me, I believe. But I did get away and hurried

314

to the Lodge. About half-way down I met Hamish
McLeod coming up. I told him of my brother's death
and instructed him to go on and detain or keep under
observation Ann Harper and Diego Usted. He went on,
and I went down to the Lodge, where-I found my son
Charles. From there I phoned Constable Campbell.
Accompanied by my son, I then returned to the scene
of the death and found Hamish McLeod there alone. I
asked him where the others were, but he did not answer.
I did not press him, for I knew that one of the two was
his nephew. My son and I waited there till Constable
Campbell arrived, when I told him briefly what I knew.
I now amplify that in this statement. Before the Constable arrived Hamish McLeod had departed, not telling
us where he was going.

(Signed) Arthur Harper, Major (Retired)."


IV

Major Harper was the first to speak.
"I insist that that is a fair statement of what I knew
and saw."
"And what you heard too," said the lawyer crisply.
"Many things in it could be decently omitted in a statement of that sort."
But Diego had to admit that as regards the things he
himself knew the statement was fair and showed no
prejudices. The only thing that struck him was that the
Major was not clear about his times. He had stated that
he had seen Diego at Ann's side when he had arrived
at the edge of the clearing. In that case he must have
been more than three or four minutes away when the shot
was fired. But that was only a small point.
Aunt Ellen did not think highly of that statement, or,
rather, she thought the devil was in the making of it.
She swept to her husband's side, and her outflung hands

demanded attention. Her fierce blue eyes blazed in he white face, and there was a pitiless quality in the metallic tones of her voice. She could swing English.

"So that is what Major Harper calls a fair statement! I represent Diego Usted here to-night, and also I represent Ann Harper, and I will now point out to you how fair that statement is to them. It is surely clear. It is conscientious. It is what I would call a hanging statement. In it is the lead that the Prosecution should follow, the hinting of motive and opportunity so beloved by your courts of law and order, the damning of two young people. You will not meet my eye, good Major. But I can see you in the witness-box under examination by a clever criminal Counsel. He will draw out of you—oh! so much against your will—the cat-and-dog relations between husband and wife, the dislike between the husband and Diego Usted, the too-warm friendship between two foreign people related in race—a race noted for passion and ruthlessness. The accusations of an old husband and a General besides against a foreign young wife and her foreign young lover will be very damaging in the hands of your clever Counsel. The warm temper that slapped him down amongst the rugs and prodded him with a toe will be unbridled and vindictive. And that incident so damning will be corroborated by so many witnesses. The friendship, the meetings in this house, the meetings in her own house, the tramps on the hills, and the last shameless assignation, all will be corroborated. And for a final motive there was the threat of an altered Will. I can assume, Ewan McInnes, that there was an original Will?"

"Certainly," answered Ewan McInnes, and added a cunning secondary clause, "you can assume anything you like, my dear woman."

"And he left most of his wealth to his wife, the poor infatuated old man?"

"I will not answer that, of course."

"You might, then. Under oath in your own courts of law you will have to answer it, and the answer will be, yes. And, anyway, you will admit that there was a threat to make a new Will?"

"I will admit that, since it is in Major Harper's statement. It should not be."

"And therefore the old Will must have been in the wife's favour? And you have answered my question, Ewan."

"I have," he said warmly, "and it's a dom' good thing for some of us earning our bread-and-butter that you did not take to the law in the days of your youth—like young William."

"And another thing, Ewan, you were at the Lodge to draw up that new Will?"

"That also is in Major Harper's statement, but I was there primarily on other business."

"To be sure. The breaking of entail. The entail and the Will, and both of them have double edges, as I will show you. Did you draw up the new Will, Ewan?"

He hesitated before he answered. "Wills of that sort call for voluminous notes, Portia."

"Then the old Will holds?"

"If probated."

"And you will have to produce your notes in court?"

"If called upon to do so."

"Thank you, Ewan." Again she had got her answer indirectly. He had taken notes for a new Will, but it had not been made, and the old Will held good. Diego could have sworn that the canny old lawyer chose that method of giving her the information she wanted.

"And there are two things I can tell you about your notes, Ewan," went on Aunt Ellen, "but I'll tell you only one of them just now. That thing is self-evident.

The proposed new Will would leave nothing to Ann Harper unless she cared to claim her widow's mite——"

"You are assuming a lot, Big Ellen?"

"What I assume will be proved in court—if this case goes to court. And there you have the motive for the sudden death of General Harper—indeed you have two motives."

"Two?"

"I will give you only one. The motive your clever Counsel will make so clear. The motive of the guilty lovers to abolish the husband before the new Will is made. Why, any sort of Counsel worth his salt will point out that the assignation for Skene's Rock was publicly made in order to induce the husband to interrupt it, that after it was made he was taunted into interrupting it, and that he set furiously out to interrupt it. Skene's Rock is in the public eye, sure enough, but the rock at the foot of the cliff cannot be seen from twenty yards off. It is a grand rock for a man—or a woman— to hide behind, pounce out on an old man, slay him with his own gun, and make the slaying look like suicide."

Ewan McInnes slapped the table explosively, and his voice was unusually stern.

"Big Ellen, I withdraw anything I said about your being a clever pleader for your friends. You are only putting a noose round the necks of Ann Harper and Diego Usted."

Diego had to admit that the lawyer was right. His aunt was making the case damnable against Ann and himself. But she was not perturbed by the stern reprimand.

"The wicked creatures! I can see them hang. What I am doing, Ewan, is to show the things that must develop from this clever statement Major Harper has made."

"These things are the concern of Justice," said Major Harper firmly. "Personally I regret that they are so damning."

"My God!" she said in awe. She turned abruptly to the policeman. "Who is next on the list, Angus?"

"Donald Gunn is next," said Angus, turning over his file.

Donald Gunn straightened up, rubbed his long hands down over his dark grey hair, and the long breath he exhaled was very nearly a groan.

"Very well, Angus!" he said resignedly. "I will speak my piece for you and regret some of it to my dying day." He looked up at Big Ellen and shook a sad protesting head.

"Go on, Donald!" she ordered. "You will hide nothing to-night."

The blood of the fighting Caithness clan stirred in Donald. "If Don Diego Usted killed a man yesterday," he said fiercely, "it is a pity he did not kill two——"

But Donald had not time to say more.

The door opened quietly and Ann Harper came in. Every man rose to his feet, and Major Harper was the last to do so. Diego's heart lifted into his throat and then sank away hollowly. They were both in the net now.


# CHAPTER VII

## THE NET CLOSES—AND OPENS

### I

THE dramatic entrance of Ann Harper looked to Diego like an unfortunate bit of stage management. Aunt Ellen was always dramatic, and it was clear that she had arranged for Ann's appearance at this ill-going enquiry. He remembered that Donald had mentioned a change of dress and a saddle-pony. And here was Ann now, just at the moment when the case was at its blackest against her and himself. That was dramatic enough, but scarcely considerate, for he could not imagine how any further statements could lighten the case against them; indeed, he did not see how any statement could have a bearing on the case. Donald could only tell how he found them and how broken the woman was. Diego looked across at the glass-fronted press where the stalking-rifles were. No! he could not get her away now. He must wait, and there was still something in this that he did not understand.

Ann Harper was here for good or ill, but she was a different Ann Harper. She was not the broken Basque refugee of the previous night, nor the subdued woman of to-day, nor the debonair girl of the evening. This was a lady of dignity, in complete control of herself and the situation. She wore her black sequined dress of satin, long-sleeved and high-necked; and on her head was her Basque mantilla with a green coral comb shining through; and one lock of her live red hair showed outside the edge of the mantilla. She was, indeed, a Spanish lady. Her face was a creamy white against which the dark brows were strongly marked, and her black eyes had deep lights in the glow from the lamp, and on her mouth, faintly red, was a smile that was equable yet gentle. She stood up very straight inside the closed door, her eyes went over the company without resting on any-one, and she lifted one graceful arm in a salute that was also a benediction.

"Be with God, my people!" she said in her low deep way. "You will please be seated."

That was a command. The men sat down, and again Major Harper was the last to sink into his chair, his eyes never leaving the woman whom he had so plainly accused of murder. Aunt Ellen was watching him. She pointed a finger at him.

"Point a finger at her, Major Harper?"

He did not. No one dare point a finger at that tall lady standing inside the door. Everyone felt that the two women dominated the room. Aunt Ellen was standing at her husband's side, a hand on his shoulder. Ann came forward, satin softly rustling, and placed a hand on his other shoulder. Those massive male shoulders were a worthy support for these two tall women. The dark eyes, again, went over the men, and her voice was low and even.

"It is well that you are here—all of you, even he that has no reason to be my enemy. I have a thing that must be said. But first I will make my apology to the men of this glen for my ill-behaving. It was that of a child distracted by grief and terror." Her free hand came forward palm up. "Once I suffered much, and again the wave that is of madness overflowed me, so that I would have drowned and died if my friends Diego Usted and Donald Gunn had not lifted me in their strong hands until the waters receded. Now I drown no more, and I face with resolution what is to befall me." She lowered her head and looked at no one. "This is what I have to say. It is that Don Diego Usted did not kill my husband. He found me standing over my dead husband, the rifle that killed him in my hands. That is all."

*It is enough*, Diego said in his own mind. Her head sank lower, and her hand tightened on Hamish's shoulder, and the shoulder ﹍med under her hand.

Major Harper brought the flat of his hand down hard on the table, and, like an echo, so did Donald Gunn. Donald had his mouth open for speech, but Aunt Ellen, with a violent thrust of her hand, silenced him as effectively as if she had thrust the words back into his throat. Her eyes were on the Major.

"Well, Major Harper?"

"You have a confession. What is the use of going on with this farce?"

"Till we get to the tragedy. We go on. I have not begun to fight yet, in the words of Paul Jones." She looked round at the men of the Glen. "Your Mistress Ann asks you to take a long jump, but you will take a hop and a step first." She put an arm round Ann's waist. "Lady Ann—or is it Saint Anne?—you will now listen, and you will not say anything for a long time."

"I have said."

"To your credit. Now you will sit and be silent. Come!" She led her by Diego to the other side of the fire that was now smouldering in ashes. There she pressed her down into the empty chair. It was the high-backed, armed chair that Ann was accustomed to sit in, and Diego knew that it had been set there waiting for her. Aunt Ellen stood over her, and briefly explained.

"We are looking into this bad business, my dear, but we have not gone far. I have told how Henrietta was here with me the afternoon of yesterday and all the night. Major Harper, in a written statement, says he saw you with the gun in your hand and Diego Usted taking it from you——"

"But that is true. He took it to remove the marks that would condemn. That was wrong, but everything was wrong from the beginning——"

"You are talking again. Now you will do nothing but listen."

"I can do no more."

She pulled her mantilla forward, and rested her head against the tall back of the chair. Not once had her eyes rested on Diego. Her face was now in shadow, and he could see her dark brows and lashes against the pale glow of her face, and her mouth looked darker in the shade. He did not want to trouble her with his eyes;

322

so he half turned in his chair and looked up at his aunt. She was standing behind Donald Gunn's chair, and a finger touched his shoulder.

"Go on now, Donald!"

"By the Lord, I will!" exploded Donald, "and high time too." A few minutes ago he hated the task before him; now he was eager for it.

II

"Yesterday from breakfast-time," began Donald in his distinct Caithness draw, "Long John McKenzie, Piobar Maol Tam, and myself were haymaking in the Strath below my bothy. We expected Hamish but he did not turn up. Don Diego Usted came instead about eleven and worked steady with us for a couple of hours, till dinner-time. Just after dinner Hamish rang me up, and gave me instructions for myself and the two men for the rest of that day. I gave the men theirs, and sent them off, and after a time set off myself towards the head of the Strath. I left Don Diego in the house. It was then two o'clock, summer time.

"I went up by the Garbh Ailt, not over the chorrie, but over the pass into Glen Seilig. In the glen I came on a hind and her fawn in a bad way. There is that jumble of sharp rocks high up on the south face, and the hind might have slipped. Anyway, her udder was torn to pieces and the poison had gone through her. She was past help and dying on her feet, and so was her fawn—a wee buck—all skin and bone. The only thing to do was put them out of pain. I didn't find that easy. They saw me before I saw them, and, dying on their feet, their feet did not fail them; they would not let me get near enough to—make sure. But I worked them hard round the way I wanted to the back of the Carn and over the ridge of Drumdyre——"

323

He paused and looked at Major Harper, who had moved in his chair.

"You would be about the Drum that time, Major Harper, but I did not see you?"

"Nor did I see you."

"You would be on the other flank. I was on the side near the Carn. At last, over the ridge, I got downwind of the beasties, and they fell in the deep heather fair exhausted. I worked in on them yard by yard, and in time got close enough up to make sure. That would be four o'clock. You did not hear a shot, Major?"

"I may have," the other replied after a frowning pause. "I do not remember."

Diego lifted his head sharply. Had Donald a rifle with him yesterday when he left the bothy? He visualised him going up the Strath. He had a stalking-telescope slung on shoulder, and that peeled holly crook of his under an arm. He had no rifle.

But Donald was going on steadily. "I put them out of pain, and their bodies will be there yet—or their bones, if the foxes and the corbies have found them. From there I worked along the ridge and down the easy drop on the far side of Skene's Rock, a long way off. There was no one at the rock then, and I did not expect anyone at that time.

"I went on a-ways, and the next time I looked there was a person perched on top of the rock—a woman, I thought, but could not be sure at that distance—all of half a mile. I dropped like a grouse behind a tussock, and put up the glasses. A woman all right. She was Mistress Ann Harper." He tapped the table for emphasis. "It was Mistress Ann herself. The glass brought her up to my nose. I looked at my watch then, and found it was six o'clock. But she should not be there till getting on for seven. All the world seems to have known that Mistress Ann was to meet Don Diego at

Skene's Rock at seven of the clock. I knew it myself. That's why I was where I was. She was on the rock an hour before her time. But, then, she was aye fond of that place, going up to sit in the sun and look down on the loch below and on all the northern world of mountains spread out bonny before her. That bit is not in my statement, Angus, but I'm just remarking it. She was there, anyway.

"My job, then, was to get nearer, and she must not see me. I did a fair bit of stalking, though I say it myself, moving this way and that way in the hollows, crawling when I had to, lying like a hare when her head turned. I made to a stone on the lip of the fault across from her and her eyes did not light on me once— and she has keen eyes, Mistress Ann, as we all know. When my chance came I slipped down amongst the rocks and worked forward till I found a good place where two pointed stones cocked together at an angle. The track down from the rock was only ten feet below me, and the rock itself was not forty paces away. And there I lay watching my mistress.

"She was sitting on top of the rock, softly tapping at it with that hazel crook I carved for her. That's all the weapon she had. She was looking out over the hills of the north, looking up the loch and down the loch, and across at Lodge Affran; and I lay still as a tod peeping between the chinks, for she could see a rabbit peeping out of a burrow. And the sun was shining bonny on the warm red gold of her hair—and that is not in my statement either. Maybe I was a peeping Tom, but a peeping Tom I had to be, but not a peeping Tom on Mistress Ann and Don Diego." His voice hardened. "I was set there to keep a watch over my mistress. I was to see that no harm came near her that evening. But, indeed, I could not hold it from her in the end, but I could not know that. I was within ten feet of the track, and if anyone came up but Don Diego I knew what to do, and I would have done it even if I had to draw sgian. Don Diego did not come. No one else came either."

He paused there, and Diego knew that the telling after that would be bitter for the old man. How could he more than corroborate what Major Harper had stated? Why did Aunt Ellen insist on this narration? Donald knew exactly what had happened, and now it would have to come out. Diego covered his eyes with his hand.

"Listen, now! At a quarter to seven—I knew that was the time to the minute, for I had a peep at my watch—at a quarter to seven I heard the rifle go off at the foot of the cliff below. That was the shot that killed General Harper, for it was the only shot fired. That is certain. It was the only shot fired. And at that time I was looking up at Mistress Ann. She was sitting on Skene's Rock, her knees up and the crook in her two hands across her shins. She did not fire that shot. SHE DID NOT KILL HER HUSBAND."

Again Donald Gunn paused. Diego kept his hand covering his eyes, and his hand was trembling against his brow. He felt strangely abased, not elated, not relieved—just abased at the thoughts he had had. He could not lift his eyes to anyone. Ann Harper was cleared, yet he could not lift his eyes to her.

Donald Gunn spoke with a gloomy protest that Diego did not understand.

"Now that I have cleared my mistress, there is no need to go on. Can't you see that, Big Ellen?"

Her voice was firm. "You will finish what is in your statement, Donald Gunn!"

"Ah well!" He sighed. "Since it is in my statement I may as well. This is it. When the shot went off I at once made up my mind to go down and see what was

326

up. I was anxious. Don Diego should be down there about now, and I did not know but that the shot might be fired at him. But one second after the shot, before I could move hand or foot, Mistress Ann dropped her crook, bounced off the rock—I thought she was over the cliff—and came tearing down the track past me to the risk of her neck. I suppose the same anxious thought was in her mind too. As soon as she went by I followed her, but there was no need to go all the way down by the track, and my orders were that I was not to show myself. Where the track curves deep in there is that jumble of tilted slabs on the outside where the cliff bulges out and breaks down. From the point out there you can see along to the big boulder at the corner, and slide down to the bottom and jump eight feet if you are in a hurry. I went out on my hands and lay flat. I could see all there was to be seen, and there was no need for me to slide and jump yet. I saw what was to be seen before Mistress Ann got to the bottom. Mark that! There was no live person in the bit of an opening between the cliff and the trees. There was a dead one. The big stone was not forty feet below me, and I saw the General's body lying at the side of it. I could only see his head and the shoulders of his grey flannels, but I knew it was the General by his white pow of hair. I saw the rifle too. The butt of it was half covering his face, and the muzzle of it slanting my way.

"There it was that Mistress Ann came round the rock from the track. She checked back when she saw the body, her hands going up to her ears that way she has. She called his name. I was not forty feet away, and with the updrift of air I could hear a whisper. He did not whisper. He did not move. He was dead. She bent down to see his face, but the butt of the rifle was in the way and she picked it up by the lock; and what she must have seen then made her straighten up, the rifle tight in her hands. And that was how the rifle was found in her hands——"

Here Long John McKenzie struck the table a ponderous blow. Everyone, except Diego, looked at him in surprise, and he smiled unashamed:

"A funny mistake I made," he said, "but it was no' so dom' funny at the time. Go on, Donald!"

"I am finished," said Donald gloomily. "That is the statement I made and signed. I told Angus that I was not prepared to carry it further. I am not. That is all."

III

"That's so," said Angus, turning back a page of his file. "There's just a'e point, Donald. I don't see here that you had a rifle with you?"

"I had no rifle with me."

"But the sick hind——"

"If I had a rifle I could have eased the hind straight off. I had to wear her down, and get in with the sgian."

Ewan McInnes leant quickly forward and turned to look at Donald.

"You asked Major Harper if he had heard the shot?" he questioned sharply.

Donald met his look coolly. "I was trying Major Harper out—God forgive me."

"Are you implying, Gunn, that I was not on Drumdyre?" enquired the Major angrily, almost blusteringly.

"I knew all the time that you were not anywhere on Drumdyre the time you said," said Donald evenly.

"Nonsense!"

"How do you know, Donald?" questioned the lawyer quickly.

"I'll tell you. There were five stag on the crown of the ridge where they could see all round them, three lying and two nibbling here and there. I had my eye on them as I stalked the hind. I was down-wind from them and they never moved. Anyone on the far side would give them his wind, and they would have moved."

"Flimsy evidence!" sneered Major Harper.

"The strongest there is, any stalker knows. So do you, sir. Moreover, when I charged the hind they saw me and made off over the ridge. Wherever you were, you were not on the ridge of Drumdyre at four o'clock."

Ewan McInnes moved his hand rapidly. "Deer have many vagaries. It is not important." He looked up at Aunt Ellen. "Well, Big Ellen! You seem to have proved that neither Henrietta nor Ann fired the fatal shot. Where do you proceed from there?"

Aunt Ellen had moved round to her husband's side. She looked at the lawyer warily.

"We could be taking another man's statement, Ewan."

"Not yet, my dear. You are forgetting that clever Counsel for the Prosecution, aren't you?"

"What of him, Ewan?"

"He'll be on his feet cross-examining your witness. You think you have cleared Ann Harper, and I hope you have—but I'm no' a clever Counsel. If I were, there's Donald before me and no one to tell him where to stop and where to go on. An honest man under oath, he'd hold nothing back, and if he tried, the clever Counsel would drag it out of him, and show at the same time what a prejudiced witness he was. You see, this clever Counsel will assume that the General did not kill himself—not after a cool and, indeed, a callous man fabricated evidence——"

"One man or two, Ewan?"

"Ay! there was Donald also. He is not above suspicion. A minute ago he gave even myself the impression that he had a rifle with him, and everyone knows how devoted he is to his mistress. To the extent of perjury? Why was he there at all? What did he know that made him be set there to protect her? Would he kill a man to protect her?" He lifted a hand to silence Donald. "We will not go into that now. I'm no' clever, myself, but I'll ask Donald to verify one thing. When you looked over the point and saw your mistress pick up the rifle, was Diego Usted at her shoulder?"

"He was not." Donald answered readily.

"He was, later?"

Donald looked up at Big Ellen, and she nodded to him.

"Later, he was," he answered then.

"The laws of evidence in the present court are too original to have any precedent," said the old lawyer satirically. "Tell me this, Donald, how long was it from the time you heard the shot until you looked over the edge and saw no one but the dead man?"

"It was not long."

"'You'll be more particular, Mr Gunn,' says our clever Counsel. Ann Harper had to come down past you and get out of sight, and you had to go down and crawl out to the point. I know the place—the stones tilted all the one way trying to tip you off to a broken neck forty feet down. Four—five minutes, Donald?"

"No, nor half."

"That can be tested. I'll just put that question another way. From the time you heard the shot until you looked over the edge, would a man have time to drop the rifle and get into the shelter of the trees?"

"He'd have to be fast."

"An obdurate witness. I'm no' fast, and I know that place, and I could do it in half the time—if I were a cool and callous man."

"I have heard you called worse," said Aunt Ellen.

The lawyer sat aside in his chair and looked at Donald Gunn's grim profile.

"So Diego Usted came to the woman's side later. Not much later?"

"Not much later," agreed Donald.

"From the trees?"

Donald nodded.

The old lawyer spoke softly as if to himself.

"Donald Gunn was forty feet above. There was an updrift of air, and he says he could hear a whisper. I wonder what whisperings he heard?"

Donald turned head, and his voice had a queer cold composure.

"You go to hell, Ewan McInnes!"

Ewan McInnes threw his hand out towards Hamish McLeod.

"Contempt of court! Your ruling, Mr President?"

Hamish did not hesitate for a moment. He made no gesture, but his tone demanded obedience.

"Donald, you will answer every question Mr McInnes puts to you."

"But, Hamish——!"

"Every question. You must trust me."

Donald looked at him steadily and nodded. "I've trusted you forty years, and I'll trust you now, though—" He turned to Ewan. "What do you want to know, you old devil?"

"Tut! tut! You see, Donald, you finished your statement so abruptly that it was evident you heard something that you did not want to repeat. Now you will tell us what you heard and saw from the time Ann Harper took up the rifle?"

"There was not much." Donald forced calmness back into his voice. "Don Diego came from the trees to Mistress Ann's side. She saw him and whispered: 'Is he dead?' I could hear every whisper. He sat down on his heels and looked at the dead man a long time, and then he rose up and said, 'He is dead.' And she

said, 'An old man and mad, it was evil to kill him.'
And after a time he said, 'It was an accident. There
was a struggle and the gun went off.' And she said,
'Yes, that must be the way.' Then he took the rifle
from her—the rest you have heard——"

There was a note of triumph—and relief too—in Major
Harper's voice.

"Ah! there you have the confession of guilt. It was
Usted murdered my brother."

"Murder, Major Harper!" protested Aunt Ellen
mildly. "Come now! would you not be merciful and
call it manslaughter?"

Diego stirred in his chair, and Aunt Ellen stopped him
from rising to his feet by coming quickly to his side and
putting a hand on his shoulder. Good Lord! was she
merely trying to save his neck by reducing the charge to
manslaughter and getting Major Harper to accede to it?

But Major Harper would have none of it.

"Manslaughter! It was murder. Don't you see?
He suggested to his accomplice: 'It was an accident.
There was a struggle. The gun went off.' And she
agreed: 'Yes, that must be the way.'" He turned to
his Factor. "Good work, McInnes! You brought that
out very clearly."

"Do you think so?" said McInnes sourly.

"What do you think yourself, Ewan?" enquired Big
Ellen in her mildest manner.

"I think that the man that killed got amongst the
trees quickly—and came back again." He leant back
in his chair and put his finger-tips together. "Big Ellen,
you will let me be the devil's advocate for two minutes?"

"And what have you been the last hour? Go on!"

"Right, then! I will put the scene before you as a
middling smart Counsel might put it in a real court of
law. There's Mistress Ann Harper sitting on top of
Skene's Rock an hour before the time. Why? To view

332

the scenery, looking up and down and round about, and especially at Lodge Affran over there. Not at all! says our smart Counsel. She is there for that hour to spy out the ground for her accomplice coming up through the woods from Loch Beg and hiding below amongst the trees. She is there with her keen sight—and her keen sight has been pointed out—to see that no one leaves the Lodge but the victim who knew where she has gone and who had been taunted into following her. If anyone else left the Lodge between six and seven, and came across Affran Water, it would be easy for her to signal with her staff from the edge of the cliff. No one came but the man she wanted."

"His brother came?"

"He told you why. But he did not come from the Lodge. He came by the side of the water and could not be seen. And that was the unforeseen thing that spoiled their guilty plans. The husband came, and was killed with his own rifle by a man forty years younger—easy work. The woman on the rock, hearing the shot, as if it were a signal, without hesitation went tearing down the track. To see who fired the shot? To see who fired a shot in a sporting estate where shots are fired at all hours of the day? Not at all, says our smart Counsel! To join her lover and accomplice amongst the trees. And to make sure that her husband was dead, this foreign woman used to blood bent over him and lifted the gun. A fatal error. Her cool and callous accomplice would not have left finger-marks on the weapon, and now he has to come from the wood and wipe hers off, and restore the marks that pointed to accidental death—or suicide. And that gave time for Major Harper to arrive on the scene. Need I go on?" He held up his finger. "And mark you! a real sign of guilt and collusion is that after the Major's intervention the guilty pair fled to the hills and disappeared for twenty-four hours. Why?

Panic—or to give their infatuated friends time to stage this mock enquiry?"

"Are you saying that Hamish and I and our friends are in the plot?"

"I don't know how many might be in it. The whole Glen might be in it. We all know the feelings of the Glen, and your clever Counsel would point out how certain men in it would seek to palliate the crime and reduce the charge to manslaughter."

"I don't like your clever Counsel, Ewan. I am right sorry I invented him."

"Haven't you a clever Counsel of your own, Big Ellen?"

"As you say yourself, he's nane sae blate."

Aunt Ellen sounded despondent to Diego. The devilish reconstruction of the old lawyer had taken the wind out of her sails.

"He had better take off his jacket, then," said Ewan. "Up to the present, all he has succeeded in doing is to transfer the actual act of killing from the woman to her accomplice. What have you up your sleeve? Do you pass on the guilt——?"

Major Harper interrupted. He was savagely triumphant now.

"This is a damn'd plot." He glared round the table. "This Irishwoman instigated you—you dam' dreamers— and you thought you could browbeat me and hoodwink an able lawyer like Ewan McInnes. I am glad we came down."

Big Ellen was looking at Ewan and the blaze was back in her eyes.

"You will forgive me for being a vengeful woman this night, Ewan?"

"It remains to be seen, Big Ellen."

Major Harper pointed an authoritative finger at the policeman. "Are you going to do your duty, Campbell?"

334

Angus Campbell was shaking his head, and his eyes were turned amazedly on Ewan McInnes.

"That's the dom'dest ever I heard!" he marvelled. "He'll be for proving myself guilty in a minute."

"Just a devil's advocate, Angus," the lawyer said.

"If you're no' Auld Clootie, Ewan, you'll be his blood-brother."

Major Harper was almost shouting. He rose to his feet.

"Campbell, I order you to do your duty."

"My duty! Oh, yes!" Campbell started but was not perturbed. He turned over a folio. "It is your turn next, Long John."

Major Harper looked down at Long John and found that Long John was looking up at him. The big man's mane of hair was actually lifting like a lion's, and his eyes were yellow like a lion's in anger. But behind that yellow glow was a gleam of satisfaction, and that satisfaction helped him to retain his temper. A big fist moved an inch.

"You'll hear me, Major Harper. Sit down!"

Major Harper sat down. "Let the farce proceed," he said subduedly.

For the last ten minutes Diego had been watching Ann with a good deal of anxiety. She had pulled her mantilla further forward and her head was down-set so that he could not see her face, but he could see that the edges of the mantilla were trembling, and that her hands were clenched tightly on her knees. She was holding herself in with all her might, but it was not grief she was holding in but a live healthy temper. If she let herself go, her chair would go over, and Ewan McInnes, sitting with his back to her, would get his ears boxed. Diego hoped she would not erupt, and at the same time he would be pleased if Ewan discovered that he was sitting on the edge of a volcano. Long John was talking.

"I will tell what I know," he said, "and I am warning Mr McInnes that I will not tell any lies."

"You misunderstood me," said Ewan, sitting up. "I was no more than speaking with another's voice. Personally I believe every word that Donald Gunn said, and I will believe you too, Long John."

"Thank you, Ewan. My mistake. This is what I have to say."

Ann's tension slacked down. Her hands relaxed, she drew in a deep breath, and lifted her head. Her eyes met Diego's, and the moment they did all the fire went out of them. Her head went back against the chair and moved disconsolately from side to side. She shut her eyes against his, and Diego saw that that strange mood of hopelessness was on her again.

Long John had a resonant voice, but rather high in pitch for so big a man. Diego rested his elbow on the arm of his chair, and again covered his eyes with his hand. And as he listened a small thread of fire went through him. By God! his great aunt was not finished yet.

IV

"As Donald Gunn told you," said Long John, "I was making hay at the Strath till dinner-time. There was himself and Don Diego and the Piper and myself. After dinner Donald took the Piper and me outside and gave us our instructions from Hamish.

"I went up with the Piper to the corner of the wood, and he went on from there into Glen Sallagh. I went into the wood and worked back towards the bothy till I had a fair view of it back and front. After a while Donald came out and went up the Strath towards the Garbh Ailt. He had no rifle with him, only his glass and his holly crook. Moreover, he hasn't a twenty-two but a four-fifty for the hart. Don Diego was still in the house.

"When he came out his jacket was off and his sleeves up, and he hung the dish-clout on the line, so I knew he had been washing the dishes we had left, and that is a thing he'd do, being a homely man. He went over and talked to the dogs, and looked down at the meadow below the house, and up at the sky. There was a couple or so rows we hadn't time to put up, and I could see that he was thinking it might rain and the hay down, and I wanted to tell him it wouldn't rain for two days anyway, the wind where it was north of west.

"But down he went and at it he went like a man in a great hurry, and I'm telling you he made the hay fly. He'd rake a row down and rake it up the other way, and put his fork under at the end and rush it before him till he had the makings of a cock, and up went the cock as if a whirlwind was at it. A right swack lad. First he shed his shirt and then his linder, and honest to God I thought he'd shed his trews—begging the ladies' pardon. But he didn't. He stripped well, with a fine barrel of a chest to him near as hairy as my own, only black. In no time at all the hay was up to the last cock, and that time he peeled off his trews, and in with him to the lochan, giving one or two skellochs to make the dogs bark. An active figure of a man he was racing up and down the shore to dry his pelt, and I said to myself I wouldn't care to face him coming at me angry like. That was a judgmatic opinion, as I found out later on.

"He dressed himself then, and the hurry went off him. He took the tools up to the shed, and went into the house and came out again with his jacket on, and spoke to the dogs, and moved up past me, and round the corner into Glen Sallagh all at his ease. I came behind, keeping a turn of the hill between. He had his foot on Hamish's bridge when he changed his mind and went up by the other side of Loch Beg. Big Ellen and Miss Hett came out, and he waved at them and went on. They

337

didn't see me. It was Hamish trained me to stalk, and I knew how to keep hid. Big Ellen kept looking for me, knowing I would not be far away, and when Miss Hett wasn't looking I showed her a hand, and her hand signalled back, and she took the girl inside.

"Don Diego went on, still easy, by the south side of Affran Loch. He was in no hurry, just daundering along, and sometimes standing in the middle of the path, one hand dunting the other as if he was having an argument with himself. It was no trouble to keep near him with the path twisting this way and that, and sometimes I took a short cut through the trees so that I was level with him. Once I was careless with my feet, and a stick broke, and I thought his eyes picked me out, but he took me for a roe, clapping his hands at me, and a fine muckle roe I'd be. After a while he livened up, and went off smart, whistling and humming a tune we all know. Mistress Ann's song we call it.

"Now this is the time." Long John's voice slowed. "It was getting on for seven. The rifle cracked against the cliff. When it cracked I had my eyes on Don Diego walking the path in front of me. He did not fire that shot. He had no gun, not a crook even. That's the statement I signed for Angus, but having listened to Donald, I can carry it further with an easy mind. But make sure of this: Don Diego Usted did not kill General Harper."

Everyone had been listening intently, and no one moved for a moment. Diego kept his hand covering his eyes, and his heart was beating hard. There was a good deal of this he did not understand. He could understand Donald Gunn being posted to protect his mistress, but he was not at all clear as to why himself had been trailed by Long John. He would not think of that now, for there was another thing that was troubling him. A chair grated and Donald Gunn was on his feet. Diego

338

lifted his eyes to him. The old man was standing very straight, his hand to the salute.

"I ask your pardon, sir. I ought to have known better."

"So ought I, Donald."

Donald looked keenly at him and nodded.

"Man, man! Now I see. It was a bad time ye had last night." He resumed his seat, not to sink gloomily back but to sit up and look calculatingly at Major Harper.

Diego ventured a wary glance at Ann. She had not changed position. Her head was against the chair, and the mantilla had fallen back a little, showing her face colourless and her eyes closed; and her lips were moving soundlessly. She was praying, not in Spanish or Basque, but in church Latin, and Diego knew the Prayer of Thanksgiving from the movements of her lips—"Vere dignum et justum est." She opened her eyes then and looked at Diego, and her face was wholly serious, as a child's can be.

"Señor, you will forgive me not at all. Not ever must you forgive me for the thing I thought."

She did not yet realise the thing he had thought yesterday evening, seeing a rifle in her hand. Her own sense of personal integrity was such that she could not imagine a dear friend thinking her capable of killing her husband, even accidentally—that "old man and mad, it was evil to kill him." If and when she found out what his thoughts had been——! The roof would fall on him. He would hope for the best and keep his thoughts off the subject lest he transfer them to her.

"The plot develops," said Major Harper harshly. He turned aside to his lawyer as if looking to him for more able advocacy. "Is it not plain? All these men are in it. Watchers lurking and sneaking everywhere. What did they expect to find?"

"Death, and they found it," said Big Ellen.

339

The Factor did not look at his laird. He tapped his finger-tips together and kept his eyes on Long John.

"Carry it a little further, Long John," he invited.

"Ay, will I! Easy for me now after listening to Donald Gunn. Don Diego went up fast towards the opening where the shot sounded from. So did I from tree to tree, and I wasn't five steps behind him when he got to the edge, and I saw what he saw: the dead man lying by the rock, and Mistress Ann standing over him, the rifle gripped in her hands. What could the Don think? What could I think? The rifle gripped in her hands, and she looking down at a man who was alive two minutes ago——"

Now it had come. For the first time Ann realised that Diego had thought her guilty of killing. He was not looking at her, but he heard the sharp intake of her breath, and out of the side of his eye saw her two hands go up to her mouth. One glance from him would be a spark to dynamite, so he kept his eyes on the embers bedded in ashes. Long John went on talking.

"Don Diego picked his way across the clearing—and the rest is as Donald told it, only he didn't make a finish. You see, I saw the Major come out of the trees a distance down, and I'll admit that what Don Diego was doing with the gun looked bad—though I'd do it myself. I was too far away to hear what was said except when the voices were lifted, and the Don didn't lift his once. I heard the Major talk of murder and suicide, and I heard him order them down to the Lodge to wait for Angus to arrest them. And it was there Don Diego started to walk towards him, soft and slow, on the balls of his feet, his head forward, and his arms loose from the shoulders. The Major threatened him with his hands, and he has good hands we know, but like the lash of a whip the Don had his wrists. And, you know, I thought the Major would just sweep him off. He didn't.

It was the most remarkable thing ever I saw. Inch by inch, drawing out ounce after ounce of strength, Don Diego put him down on his knees, and held him there helpless. I wouldn't give a buckie for his life.

"But all at once the Don lifted him to his feet and let him go, and slapped him back-handed on the mouth. The Major took it, and when Don Diego said something and pointed, the Major went. I'd be inclined to go myself, and I'll be very careful in future not to rouse a quiet man."

He looked up at Aunt Ellen and she nodded to him.

"After that Don Diego took Mistress Ann up over the cliff. He had to because she was not in a good way, but we'll say nothing about that. I followed after, for my job was to keep Don Diego in sight all that day, to see that no one got near him with bad intent. Right to Donald's bothy I followed them, and the first of it was the real hard stalking, for the Don would keep turning about and scouting. It near broke my heart sometimes not to be able to lend a helping hand, but it was in my mind that they did not want to be seen, and my instructions from Donald was that I must not be seen. At the bothy I hid in the wood watching, till Donald came and Don Diego came outside to talk to him. After that I came down Glen Sallagh to this house. Hamish was home by then, and we ate the house empty. That's it all for you."

Donald Gunn lifted a hand for attention. "Let me make a finish too. I stayed on the point of rocks till Hamish came. I didn't show myself, and I was angry with Long John, thinking he had failed in his trust. He had not, as you know. I couldn't face Hamish. So I slipped up to Skene's Rock and down along the head of the cliff to Loch Beg, where I had to tell Big Ellen what I had seen and heard. She said nothing for once, but shook her head and fed me, and sent me home."

341

"And then the woman and her husband hatched a plot," said Major Harper. "What do you think, McInnes?"

"If there was any plot it was hatched before then."

"Exactly."

But the lawyer, moving his forefinger rapidly, would no more be devil's advocate to please his client. He spoke to Long John.

"So you thought Mistress Ann killed her husband?"

"What else could I think? I know now I was a dom'd auld fool, but there was the rifle in her hand."

Ewan turned to Donald. "And you, Donald, what did you think?"

"I didn't anything at first, not even when Don Diego came from the wood; but when he spoke there was only one thing I could think. You see, I knew my mistress hadn't killed anyone, and how anyone could think—but never mind that. I knew she was guiltless, but when Don Diego said, 'There was a struggle. The gun went off,' I and Mistress Ann too had to believe that it was with him the struggle had been. Who else?"

"But if he also was guiltless, why did he say those words?"

It was really only then that Diego realised why Donald had thought him the guilty party and that Ann had shared his thought. His words had come out of a desperate search to find an excuse for the guilty woman.

But Donald Gunn had imagination too. Suddenly he struck the table.

"That was it. Don't you see? There he was sitting a long time looking at the dead man. He hadn't killed him, and he thought Mistress Ann had. He was working out how it all happened, and then he got up and made an excuse for her—an accident, a struggle, the gun going off. As plain as the cuddy's nose on my face."

342

Ewan nodded. "That might be it." He turned aside in his chair to look at Diego. "Perhaps Don Diego will verify that?"

But Diego would not verify anything. He would not speak, or meet the old lawyer's eyes. He was nearly as angry as Ann Harper. A little while ago he had felt abased thinking how he had wronged her in his thoughts. But all the time she had been wronging him in her thoughts. That explained her attitude of shrinking dismay last night. There was blood between them, and he had shed it. He felt the hot devil in him lift a head, and he lifted his own head and stared fiercely at her. She was staring just as fiercely at him. These two, instead of being grateful to each other and grateful for their escape, were foolishly angry with each other for each lacking a complete trust in the other. She pressed her lips together and loosed them in a little explosive "Bah!" And he flicked thumb and forefinger, turned his shoulder to her and his back to the room, and looked into the dying embers.

"Don Diego will explain nothing," Aunt Ellen said quietly. "He knows when to be silent."

"Very well, Big Ellen!" said Ewan. "You have some explaining to do yourself. Why did you set a guard on Mistress Ann and Don Diego? Did you know General Harper was going to die?"

"That's right, McInnes," snapped Major Harper.

"No, Ewan. I did not know that General Harper was going to die. I knew that a someone was going to die, but I did not know who. Will you explain, Cuchulain?"

"It is time I did," agreed Hamish.

Aunt Ellen came and sat on the straw hassock between Ann and Diego. "Don, give me that tongs!"

Diego reached her the long-thighed tongs from the corner of the hob, and she moved the ashes aside and built up a little pile of red coals. He rose to his feet,

343

went to the peat-box in the corner, filled the crook of an arm with black sods, and laid them down at her side. Slowly she built up the fire. Diego noticed that for once she was fumbling. Her hands were trembling on the tongs. She was still strung. Having brought Ann and himself out of danger, she did not ease off. The strain on her was only growing worse.

Hamish was talking. Speech was never easy to him, but he had read widely and, given time, could use words adequately; and also he had a remarkable memory for conversation, even to the intonation of the speaker. Diego sat down and listened, and Ann, pulling her mantilla forward, would not deign to look his way.

# CHAPTER VIII

## AGAIN THE NET CLOSES

### I

"It was my wife, Big Ellen, started me off," said Hamish. "She knew how badly things were going for the Glen, and we talked things over the night Jamie came back from Inverness—the three of us. She said to me that there would be a .tragedy in the Glen if we did not watch out, and what was I going to do about it? That put a thought in my head. I might do something. And, then, that night in her bed she had one of her takings. You know of them?"

"We all know of her previsions," said Ewan McInnes.

"You don't then, God help me!" murmured Aunt Ellen, her shoulders moving.

"It is not the second sight," went on Hamish, "for she sees nothing in the body. She just knows. All at once she knows. The thing that has not yet happened.

344

Ordinary speaking, she follows the thought in your mind and the thought no more than shaping itself—a chancy body to live with and you trying to keep something to yourself, as Jamie and I know. But the taking is different. It hurts her in her spirit. She sat up in bed and put her hand on me. I was not asleep. 'Cuchulain, there's someone dead in the Glen, and not in bed.' That's what she said, and I jumped fair on to the floor. 'Where and who?' 'No—no!' she said. 'The death has not come—it is soon. It is in the Glen, not amongst our own out of the Glen, and I do not know if it is one of our own in the Glen. I cannot see who it is, man or woman, but death and it ill-coming I see.' She lost her head for a bit then, and was cross with me. 'You are head of the Glen now,' she said, 'and you can do nothing! Can you not save one of our own for us?' I had to give her something to quiet her, and Jamie heard us, and came to his door. She talked to him and grew quiet after that. And after that I talked to her, and told her about the beginnings of a plan I had in my mind already. You see, I was certain that someone was going to die—not an ordinary death. She is never wrong when the trouble is on her. I knew that I could not save a life, but, being a sort of a Christian, one couldn't fold his hands and wait. I could only do my best to guard the lives and good name of the people that were important to us in the Glen. We talked it over together, and in an hour or two we worked out our plan. She fell asleep then. I didn't."

He paused consideringly, and went on. "As we looked at it there were six people to be watched and warded. Just six!"

"Six!" said Ewan, pondered for a second and nodded his head. "Ay! six."

Diego turned head and looked at Major Harper. He was pondering too. His heavy brows knotted, he put an elbow on the table, shaded his eyes with his hand, and stayed thus all the time that Hamish was talking.

"Ay, six! You'll see. Big Ellen was to look after Miss Hett, and that was easy, as you have learned. I put the two best stalkers in the Glen or out of it on Mistress Ann and Jamie. I knew they were meeting at the Skene's Rock—and why not they? They were good friends and kin in race, and Jamie was leaving next day, so why shouldn't they meet and say good-bye any place they wanted? All I could do was to make sure that no one of evil mind came on them. And that was why Donald, coming from the Carn, took his post by the track, and why Long John picked up Jamie at the Strath and never left him out of his sight all the day. Ye ken, for a trained stalker it is easier to stalk a man than a stag, so long as the man does not suspect. He hasn't the eyes or the ears or the nose of the beast, and in deep heather you can keep within a hundred yards of him and watch for the turn of his head. Mind you, there was a bitter hour when I feared Donald and Long John failed me. But they had not, and I'm sorry I doubted them. Still, many besides me had doubts of their own and I'm not blaming them.

"Now, we agreed that the strategic point for our purpose was between the Lodge and the Rock. As the war people say, we gradually massed our forces there or thereabouts. My charge was, maybe, in cold blood the important one—to the Glen and himself—Young Affran. Ay, Young Affran! First of all, when I went up to the Lodge the early afternoon I made sure who was in the house. The General was there, and Mistress Ann, and Young Affran, but Major Harper was not. He was heard say that he might take a look over the stags Glen Seilig way. I marked Young Affran down in his own cubby-hole, and went outside and set myself where I could see anyone leaving the house or ground—the first fork of that big cypress—*cupressus macrocarpa*—at the corner of the garden wall near Affran Water where I could see the lawn and along two sides without being seen myself. By that time I had the ground covered.

"I kept track of the time. At five-thirty of the clock Mistress Ann came out of the house and across the lawn to the gate, and went by me over the bridge swinging her crook. She was early for the Rock but I let her go, and I knew Donald would pick her up from above even if he had to crawl for it.

"Ten minutes after that came Young Affran, along by the wall and below me, making for the bridge also. He was carrying a point-twenty-two rifle."

He held up his broad hand warningly.

"Now don't be jumping to conclusions any of ye. It was the rifle that killed his uncle surely—I know it well—but Young Affran did not kill him. For I slipped down off the fork and faced him at the corner. 'Where are you off to, young fellow?' He was chagrined and at the same time inclined to laugh—half angry, half mischievous kind. 'Go to hell, Hamish McLeod!' he told me, and then he saluted me. 'Oh! You are displaying your authority, are you? Where am I going? To give a certain old party the fright of his life. Get out of my way!' 'You are not thinking of frightening him to death?' 'Why not?' And then he laughed at me. 'So you think I might blow his head off?' 'So you threatened,' I said. 'I was only a dam' fool—he's not important any more, not to me.' 'In that case,' said I, 'give me that rifle.' He wouldn't, holding it away from me. 'Wait,' says he, 'do you know what he's up to now? Those two fatheads, Ann and your bright nephew, let the world know they are meeting at Skene's Rock, and an irate husband threatens to gang along and throw Diego over the cliff. He will go, I think, but Diego might do the throwing and get himself hanged

347

handsomely for it.' 'Are you for protecting the poor foreign lad?' I said. 'No! but I'll hide and drop a bullet or two round the old owl and see how he likes being back under fire—not that he ever was.' 'Just so!' I said. 'A bullet off a rock will kill a man nice as you like, and get the joker hanged twice as handsome. Give me that rifle.' 'I'll give you the butt!' says he, mock-threatening me with it. And before he could move I had my hands over his.

"The minute he felt my hands he quietened. He saw I was serious, and himself is as sound as bell-metal underneath. 'What is it, Uncle Hamish?' He calls me that often. 'It is Aunt Ellen,' I said. 'She saw one dead in the Glen. She didn't see who it was, but we don't want it to be you or by your hands.' He took that seriously. 'Let us up,' said he, 'and make sure it is not Ann or Diego Usted.' 'No!' I told him. 'I have good men posted and we'll not clutter the ground. You and I will go back to the house, and you'll give me a drink, and I'll tell you all about it.'

"So we went into the house to that room he has at the back where he keeps his rods and tackle and his guns, especially the double three-ought-three the Glen gave him to shoot his first stag. But before we went in there I put the twenty-two on its pegs on the wall of the big hall outside. I did not stay too long, for time was getting on and I was anxious kind. I left him in his room, and as I went through the hall I looked up to where I had hung the rifle. It was not there. Young Affran had not left his room while I was there, yet the rifle was gone. And it's a queer troubling thought I had since. If I hadn't taken the rifle out of Young Affran's hands and hung it there the General would be alive now! But how do I know?

"I hurried then. I had my foot on the bridge when that single rifle-shot went off. It was a long way off—

far enough off to be at Skene's Rock. I looked at my watch. It was a quarter to seven, as Donald says. I was afraid then, and I kept hurrying my best pace up the track. I met Major Harper coming down. He said to me, 'My brother is dead. His wife and Usted killed him.' I said, 'You are a liar.' He took that and left me there. That is why the man he accused brought him to this house to-night. I will not call him a liar in my house."

Ann leant forward in her chair, her eyes blazing at Diego.

"There is a man who knows trust. We! we are nothing."

Diego sighed; he was not angry any more, but he could not think of a mild word to say. Hamish finished quickly.

"When I got to the opening below the cliff, I found the General's dead body, and the rifle was lying on the stones. It was the one I took off Young Affran. I did not know what to think. There was no one there but myself, and, somehow, I did not want to see anyone. But also I knew that there would be one man or two looking at me from the trees, so I lifted my hand and made a signal down towards Loch Beg. You know the rest."

II

Aunt Ellen sighed and looked at Diego, and he saw that, here in the crisis, she was very weary.

"It is come," she whispered. "Mother o' God! must I go on?"

Diego did not see how he could help her in any way. She would have to finish it as Major Harper had compelled her to. She rose slowly to her feet, went round to the back of her husband's chair, and placed a hand on his shoulder, but it was for her own support that she

349

placed it there. Her face was white and still, but when she looked at the down-set red-grizzled head of Major Harper her eyes half-hooded themselves, and Diego remembered that in the falcon tribe the female was the formidable. Her eyes never left that hand-supported head though she addressed Ewan McInnes.

"Where do we stand with your clever Counsel now, Ewan?"

"We'll forget that fellow," said Ewan. "He was clever too soon." He looked briefly aside at his laird, leant forward on his elbows, and made himself one with the men of the Glen. "We are met here to enquire into this sad business. Mind you, the method of the enquiry is not one I would use myself, lacking the dramatic imagination of a friend of mine, but Hamish, as Head, was right in trying to keep things within the Glen until we know where we stand." He lifted his eyes to the tall woman. "How long do you hope to keep it within the Glen, Big Ellen?"

"Tell us first where we stand now, Ewan?"

"I will. As I see it, there was no plot or collusion. There could not be. As far as you have gone you have cleared Henrietta Harper, Ann Harper, Diego Usted, and Young Charles Harper of all complicity in the death of Major-General Harper——"

"That's four, Ewan. Hamish told you that there were six."

"The fifth was the General, and he is dead."

"Ay! he was fifth, and he is dead in spite of us. He was the one that we could not save." Her eyes did not leave Major Harper, but her finger pointed to Wally the Post. "You saw the General, Wally?"

"I saw him." Wally sat up and blew through his moustache, and knew how important he was. "I'm no' trained to the stalking like the ithers, but Hamish set me where there was good cover, and that was at the far side of the bridge across Affran Water. I saw Mistress Ann pass swinging her crook, and I saw Young Affran come to the corner, and himself and Hamish bristling and going back to the house. And after that, and the time was six-fifteen by the best watch in the Glen, General Harper came across the bridge and went by me on the track to Skene's Rock. He was the man I had to follow, and I did. He was carrying the rifle that killed him——"

A movement of Big Ellen's hand stopped him.

"You will again note where the rifle was, Ewan?" she said.

Ewan nodded, and his eyes crinkled keenly at her.

"Are you telling me, Big Ellen, that General Harper killed himself?"

"I am telling you nothing, Ewan. We have dealt with five of the six people. The sixth is the dead man's brother, Major Arthur Harper." She was standing between her husband and Piobar Maol Tam, and she placed a hand on the Piper's shoulder.

"Where was Major Harper, Piper?"

The Piper was a quiet and silent man, who expressed the feelings and the depth in him through his pipes. He spoke in a slow voice, ready to cease at any moment:

"Major Harper was not in Glen Seilig nor was he over the ridge of Drumdyre. When I picked him up at three o'clock he was sitting at the top pool of Affran Water— the Linn Pool—and he sat there a long time throwing pebbles in the water. A long time. At five of the clock——"

Aunt Ellen took up the tale in a voice as slow as his own.

"—he came down under the shelter of the trees and went on by the track towards Skene's Rock. He says that in his own statement, but he is not sure about his times. He says he heard the shot, and came to the edge of the clearing to see Ann Harper holding the rifle and

Diego Usted at her shoulder. If that is so, then it is clear from what you have heard that General Harper died by his own hand—by accident or design. That is quite possible. He was in a temper and in a hurry, the rocks are treacherous, and he was a top-heavy man. A slip, a fall—and there you have a fatal accident. When Don Diego wiped the gun clean and put it in the dead man's hands, did he restore the only finger-marks that had been on it before Ann touched it?"

"Do you say that, Big Ellen?" Ewan questioned sharply.

But Big Ellen went on, her eyes never leaving the down-set head of Major Harper.

"But if General Harper did not die by his own hand, how did he die? Ann or Diego did not kill him. Who did? Did Major Harper follow his brother to the open and from the edge of it see him standing by the big stone, gun in hand, waiting for Don Diego—waiting, perhaps, to kill him? We can never know that now. He was a man centred only in himself, and that kind often seizes the prerogative of God. Did his brother—and he is self-centred too, and lived long in places where the spawn of life is not important—did he go across and try to take the gun away, and in the struggle did one of them die? And what would the man left alive do then? Get in amongst the trees, and stop to look back and make sure that no one saw; maybe, suddenly remembering that his finger-marks were on the gun. And then comes Ann Harper, and her finger-marks are now on the gun. And then comes Diego Usted, and there are no longer finger-marks—and the two are delivering themselves into his hands. All this summer he has been intriguing them into each other's company. There on the edge of the trees was he tempted to win all that he had been in danger of losing? Earlier I spoke of the motive and opportunity that Ann and Diego might have.

What about Major Harper's motive and opportunity? The new Will is not made. Ewan, you can tell from your notes how little was to go to the Harpers. Very well! Kill the brother and convict the wife, and the estate and the wealth at once are Major Harper's. Did Major Harper fall? Well, Ewan?"

Ewan pointed a finger at the policeman and asked:

"Have you statements from Wally the Post and Piobar Maol Tam?"

"They can be produced," replied Angus imperturbably.

"If necessary only," added Aunt Ellen. She went round to Angus's side, turned back his file and removed the three loose sheets that contained Major Harper's statement. Then she went round behind Wally and Long John, and towered over Major Harper. Her voice was not metallic any longer, but had a heaviness that was oracular with fate.

"I am not asking for vengeance on you, ruthless man. You would destroy your brother's wife and you would destroy my husband's nephew for your own scheme and—I think—for the sake of your son and daughter. We, too, are thinking of your son and daughter. Once before I asked you to withdraw this statement for their sakes. Now, for the last time, I again put your statement before you. You know what you have to do, and God have mercy on your soul."

She slipped the sheets on the board under his eyes, walked behind Ewan McInnes and Donald Gunn, and sat down on her straw hassock between Ann and Diego. She put her elbows on her knees and her head between her hands, but, even so, she could not hold her head from trembling. Her work was done. Ann reached out a long arm and softly stroked her hair. Diego watched Major Harper.

Major Harper looked down at the sheets below his eyes, and everyone waited for him. All these men had behaved with a quiet dignity during the long and tense hours. Now they waited silently.

At last he lifted his head, but looked directly at no one. His face was bloodless and yellow, and the strong lines of character were deeply carved in it. A strong and ruthless man? No! not strong. Ruthless only, and ruthlessness never holds the final inner strength. He placed a hand on the papers, and his voice was low and steady.

"This statement is not complete, and some of it is— unnecessary. I would wish to amend and complete it."

"When you are ready, sir," said Hamish, equally quiet.

Major Harper folded the sheets over and then over again, and rose slowly to his feet, the folded papers in his hand. He looked directly at Hamish.

"Is it permitted that I go now?"

"It is permitted."

Without another word or glance Major Harper left the house. He was not limping. Ann Harper whispered as if to herself:

"Always had I a cold fear in my heart for that one."

## CHAPTER IX

### IN DEEP WATER

I

No one moved in the room till the distant purr of the outboard engine came faintly through the blinded window. They listened till it died away between the bluffs. Then Aunt Ellen rose to her feet and, not looking at anyone, went out into the passage, leaving the door open. They heard the telephone whirr; and Diego considered that she would have to wait some time for an answer, for whoever she was ringing must surely be abed at this hour. But, strangely enough, the answer came almost immediately.

"Big Ellen speaking! That you, Tearlath? Listen! Your father is gone up in the coble. . . . Yes. . . . Ewan is staying. . . . Go down to the pier and wait for him. . . . You will give me a ring when he is there. . . . God bless you."

In the silence the men looked at the wag-at-the-wall that was steadily tick-tocking away the time, unconcerned with the drama of the night. Now it sounded very loud in the silence, as if insisting on its unconcern. Lord! how the hours had gone! And some time had still to pass. Affran Loch was four miles long, and the coble might be capable of six knots, so that more than half an hour must elapse before Major Harper reached home and before his son rang up.

Aunt Ellen had opened the outer door before coming back, and the dawn and a breath of fresh air came in with her.

"It is God's dawn and God's day, and God save us all!" she said. And then she put on a briskness that was not real. "Drink in the morning is good for no one, but if ye will go outside and give us room, Ann and I will make the thing ye need—a pot of strong black tea. Out with ye!"

Her words slacked the tension that was still in the room. Men breathed deeply, chairs scraped, and one by one the men around the table got up and went out to see the dawn. Before Donald Gunn went he turned and looked down at Ann and Diego still sitting at each side of the fire, their eyes away from each other.

"Do not be foolish now," he besought them. "The two of you—and myself as well—we could not help the thoughts we had last night."

She rose to her feet, and Diego rose and faced her.

355

The mantilla went back with a toss, and a red band of hair moved. She stood very erect, her head up, her bust standing out firmly, and her clenched hands on her hips. Her eyes were half-closed in disdain, and her voice was remote.

"We had thoughts, yes. I will not mention them, for I am deeply ashamed of the thoughts this señor had."

Diego replied with great dignity.

"If this señor mud-head had held a gun he would forgive the señora's thought."

At once she appealed to Donald, palms and eyes.

"But, Donaldo, you remember the words he said?"

"He was making excuses——"

"Excuses! I do not want excuses for myself. I should not have believed—even his words. I have prayed him not to forgive me. But God I will ask to forgive him."

"God has strong shoulders," Diego quoted Spanish at her, and she put her hand to her mouth, knowing the satire on woman that came after it.

"Tut-tut, bairns!" reprimanded Aunt Ellen. She pulled aside the curtains and jerked up the blinds, and the light of late dawn came in and paled the lamplight. "If any man thought me spirited enough to grip a gun in a madman's hands I would not be asking anyone but myself to forgive him. Turn out that lamp, hidalgo, and go out and see the sun rise. Give the girl time. The tea will be ready in ten minutes."

Diego, not again looking at Ann, turned down the brass lamp and went out behind Donald.

II

The sun had not yet risen, but the dawn light had strengthened to a rosy glow that flowed up the Glen from the east, where the sky was rich with bars of orange and red, and the peaks of the higher hills were already in the glow of the sun. The fresh breeze of morning rippled the loch, and the ripples were edged with red gold. That breeze, fresh in Diego's face, blew some of the cobwebs off his brain. He had been so concentrated on their little human tragedies that humanity loomed too big in his mind. Out here in this immense and lightsome dawn, with the mountain peaks serene in the sun, humanity was not so important. It was not of the least importance to the dawn or to the mountains. One should take life easily, but not so lightly as to deprive a man of it lightly. Life was the only thing man had opposed to the ultimate oblivion in which all life must perish. Let humanity, then, conserve that one thing and not waste millions of lives for an ideal of race that did not matter—even if it were true.

The men were in a group by the garden wall and Diego moved across to them. They opened out quietly and faced round, so that he was amongst them, and he felt that he was with them and of them. There was no need to say anything. They were all smoking pipes except Wally, and the blue smoke curled about their heads and vanished in the soft breeze. Wally usually smoked cigarettes and probably hadn't any on him. Diego opened his cigarette-case under his nose.

"You saved my life, Don Diego," he said.

"Time I saved someone's life," said Diego, and put a hand on Long John's sleeve, the sleeve of the man who had saved him. The big man chuckled.

"You're no' an easy man to stalk, Don Diego," he said.

"There were two—four—five men around me, and you were behind me for three miles of open heather, and I did not know."

"That was easy. There were tussocks everywhere and you were only afraid of being followed from far off. So any time you turned you looked right over my head."

There was something in Donald Gunn's mind that pricked him, and he wanted to get rid of it. He faced the old lawyer, who was leaning rather wearily against the wall.

"You were hard on us early on, Ewan McInnes?" he said.

Ewan nodded. "Had to be—for your own sakes. You see, this evening—I mean last evening—when Don Diego came to the Lodge I knew he was no killer, and I knew that Ann was guiltless, having heard you; and when you proved that Major Harper was lying about his whereabouts in the afternoon I knew our man——"

"But it was after that you were hard on us?"

"Because your case was not complete. I had to show you that it must be cast-iron. It was, but I did not know then what Big Ellen was driving at. I feared she was stage-playing, but she was really working up to something, getting her effects piled up so as to affect one man the way she wanted him. It was well done." He rubbed an ear meditatively. "I don't know. For the sake of the children I would like to keep it in the Glen as well as any of ye. But can we? What do you think, Constable Angus Campbell-on-the-wrong-side-of-the-law?"

"Ay, am I!" agreed Angus. "Big Ellen talked me into it. I warned her she could not keep it amongst us, but with Hamish on her side I agreed to hold my hand till the morning. A dom' good job for me Hamish has the power in his hands, for our Chief Constable is frae the Mearns, and to hell wi' the Hielands!"

Hamish planted solidly on his feet was blowing smoke confidently.

"Big Ellen is not finished yet."

"That depends on the two statements we did not hear," said the lawyer. He looked at his feet and spoke musingly. "I just would like to know what is in Piobar Maol Tam's statement?"

"Ay, would you," said the Piper gravely.

"If the General killed himself accidentally we need not trouble. If he were killed accidentally in a struggle for the rifle we could hush it up by a small bit of manipulation——"

"And what would you do if he wasn't killed that way?" enquired Wally the Post, his eyes crinkling cunningly.

"Blast it all, Posty!" protested the Piper.

"Thank you, Wally!" said the lawyer. "You have told me what I wanted to know. The killing was not accidental." He straightened from the wall and his voice was stern. "My friends, we cannot condone murder. No man, no matter who he is, no matter for whose sake, can get away with murder. You must not be swayed by Big Ellen. I am surprised at her, but then, after all, she's Irish——"

"She is," said her husband. "Would you have her anything else? She is doing this her own way, and I am seeing that she gets time."

"Certainly, Hamish! but the time is nearly up. Once the two statements are produced——"

A mellow voice hailed them from the door. It was Ann Harper's voice, and her free-swinging arm beckoned inside. She had taken off her mantilla, and her hair borrowed the light from the young day. The lawyer led the way, shaking his head doubtfully.

On the table-end the big brown teapot lorded it over many teacups and plates of buttered biscuits. The policeman's file of statements was still on the near end, and the lawyer picked it up and went to the small table in the bow window, where the light was now strong from the sun just risen. There he sat down, fitted on his spectacles, and began turning over the leaves. The policeman made no protest.

359

Ann Harper came straight to Diego, her eyes wide in her cream face.

"Señor, I am remiss. I think only of my own conceit. You will accept my thanks for your goodness to me, holding me up in your hands. Some day the forgiveness will be full." She gave him her hand and he bent his lips to it, and he felt one finger twitch.

She turned round, and the throw of her arms embraced her friends.

"You, my friends of the Glen who have guarded me, will forgive us for this thing that has befallen through our foolishness. We are punished. I am not happy. I may not be happy ever. You will please not think ill of me."

Donald Gunn, who in courtesy was often the mouth-piece of the Glen, bowed to the lady.

"Our Spanish lady would do no wrong. She is young. There is life and happiness too."

"There is death also," said Aunt Ellen heavily. "Have your tea!" Serving food to men she had always been gay, now she was deeply serious. The long night had been too much for her, considered Diego, and now instead of relief there came more strain. She laid a full cup and a plate of scones at Ewan's elbow, went to the fireside, pale in the sunlight, and sat on her straw hassock. And that was the first time Diego had seen her sit with men to be served. It was Ann Harper who attended to the needs of the men.

That tea was most grateful. Hot and strong, it touched the right place. But the old lawyer, instead of sampling his cup, kept turning over the leaves of the file. Ann at his back said chidingly:

"Friend Ewan, your tea is as cold as the stone."

"I like it cool. You know that long ago, Mistress Ann." He felt for his cup, lifted it to his mouth and took a deep gulp. And forthwith started to choke and splutter and swear.

360

"Guid God, woman! Did you want to burn the thropple out o' me?"

"Ah! it is—what is the word?—to sear, to cauterise the place wherefrom so many foul words came."

He grinned then. "You're no saint anyway, thank the Lord!" He looked at Angus Campbell over his spectacles. "Angus, those two statements are not in this file?"

Angus gestured a thumb towards Hamish, who spoke calmly.

"Big Ellen has them in a sealed envelope."

"I have," said Aunt Ellen from between the hands cupping her face. "They will be presented to you, Ewan, with the third statement yet to come."

"Dom't! You'd think I was a Lowlander among ye."

"You are not. You helped us well all the night. Wait with me now."

He turned back to the file and placed a hand on it.

"There is nothing in this. I mean, we could manage this. Not a single word to show how the General died. All these statements were made with a view to a certain contingency—but what contingency? I cannot get it somehow. It was as if someone knew something was going to happen. But——"

He stopped and looked at the clock. A full half-hour had passed since Major Harper had left for the Lodge. But from the pier to the house would take ten minutes. In ten minutes, then, Young Affran would ring. There was no need for any of the men to wait for that ring, but some inner consciousness held them from going. They stood about and smoked and looked at the clock, and had no wish to talk. Aunt Ellen sat crouched forward on her hassock, her hands cupping her chin. Her husband stood at her side, his hip touching her shoulder. Ann sat in her own chair, her hands clasped below her breast, her eyes downcast, and the green comb shining in her red hair. So they waited.

361

At the end of an hour Wally shuffled his feet and took a step towards the door.

"Ah weel! I'm for my Post Office and another day's darg. Young Affran will be away to his bed."

"No work to-day, Wally," said Long John, the Presbyterian. "This is the Sabbath."

"The Sabbath! Losh! so it is. I'll wait another minute."

And there the phone rang.

III

It was an old-fashioned instrument where a handle is turned to make a call, and whoever was turning the handle at the other end was turning it with furious insistence. Everyone drew in a sharp breath, and Ann covered her ears.

"Hamish?" said Aunt Ellen, and her voice was husky.

Uncle Hamish could move quickly when he wanted to. He left the passage door open so that all could hear.

"Hamish! You, Miss Hett! . . . What? . . . God ha' mercy! . . . Where? . . . There . . . the deep place. . . . Yes, yes! We'll be up at once. . . . Plenty of help. . . . Young Affran . . . Yes! We're coming."

He came in, his face and voice firm, not hiding anything.

"Major Harper is drowned, God have mercy on him. Not more than a hundred yards off the pier in that deep spot. Young Affran and Hett saw it happen—a heart attack it looked like, and he fell over. They went out and dived but couldn't get him, and Young Affran was nearly lost himself."

Young Affran and Henrietta had not been to bed at all. They had sensed that something dramatic was happening at Loch Beg, but how much they guessed no one knew. They sat up and waited for their father. It had been a long wait. After Aunt Ellen's call they went down to the waterside, and in the dawn-light saw the coble far down the loch and coming at its best pace. Some two hundred yards off the shore their father saw them and stood up in the stern, his hand on the tiller, and gave them a wave of the hand. It was a wave of farewell, though it looked like a cheerful morning greeting. And then something seemed to happen him—almost as if he had been hit by a bullet. A hand went to his breast, he swayed over the tiller, fell across the hood of the fly-wheel, and toppled head first into the water. He went under—and never came up again. Affran Loch has not drowned many people. It is very deep in places, and has a tradition the same as that of Loch Ness. It never gives up a body. Major Harper's body was never recovered.

The tiller of the engine was driven hard over, and the coble swooped round and straightened out to grate to a stop in the shallows half a mile away.

Young Affran and Henrietta did not hesitate. She was in the water first, tearing off her dress and kicking off her slippers. They went out to as near the place as they could guess and dived. They could not make bottom, and came up, and tried again, and yet again. By that time Young Affran, who was not as good a swimmer as his sister, showed signs of exhaustion, and she had to help him ashore, towing him the last twenty yards. He lay on the pier and she went to ring Loch Beg and summon help.

Ann Harper was on her feet, her hands in her hair.

"Oh! my poor young ones! I must go to them at once!"

Uncle Hamish took charge.

"All of ye without bikes go up in the coble, taking ropes and the tackle we want. Donald knows. I'll harness the shelt and run Mistress Ann and Big Ellen up. Get going, friends!"

"Wait!"

Aunt Ellen rose to her feet and faced round. She was no longer under strain. Her face was white and stern and composed, and her voice was under perfect control. She put a hand out.

"Wait! The drowned man will wait long enough, and the children can wait two minutes for their own sakes." She nodded at the old lawyer. "You are on the children's side, Ewan?"

"I am," he answered promptly.

"Major Harper killed his brother and would destroy two others. His children need never know. Do you agree?"

"I agree." He frowned. "It looked as if you knew what was going to happen."

"I knew. Two nights ago I knew one was going to die in the Glen, but I did not see who. Last night I saw another man dead in the Glen, and that time I knew the man. I saw him dead in deep water, his hair moving. I had no wish to kill him, but you saw him compel me here to-night, for I had to take care of my own. Both brothers are dead now, and we will think of the living and the future. You will leave this in the hands of Ewan McInnes and myself for this day. Right! Go then and say nothing!"

# CHAPTER X

## LOOSE ENDS

### I

I DO not think that there is any need to go any further with this chronicle, but my Aunt Ellen holds that I should tie my loose ends as far as I am able.

Yes, it was I, Diego, Jamie, Jimmy Usted of San José in Paraguay, who mostly wrote this lame chronicle. I have written it in the third person (after the example of a great man), but anyone who reads it will see that the story is told through the eyes of one man. It is possible that I have boasted too much about that one; and, yet, I do think that I had a little to boast about—so why not boast? Is it that I lack the British quality called of diffidence? Which quality is nothing less than a proud sort of egotism. But there is the story for what it is worth.

Though I wrote it, there are many things in it that can be ascribed to my aunt, and if it has any dramatic qualities they are her work entirely. I sent it to her chapter by chapter, and she did not think much of my story as I developed it, and made numerous suggestions, all of which I accepted with but one exception. She said my picture of herself was a complete travesty, a gross slander, and a scandalous libel; and put her pencil through whole paragraphs of typescript; but I restored every one of them, for I am determined that my picture of her shall remain as I saw it.

I wrote it here in a hospital in Cornwall in the space of three months. The luck that took me unwounded— but not unscathed—through five years of savage warfare deserted me at last. I left Glen Affran on the Tuesday following the tragedy, and within a month I was brought into Plymouth from Dieppe with a broken head and a shattered right leg. I need not tell how I got them. But my head, being hard, was not irreparably broken; and I did not lose my leg, though it will for ever be one inch shorter than the other, and so unfit me for the active service to which I was attached. But I shall be active enough, and well able to ride a horse—perhaps on the savannahs of San José. I had very splendid nursing, for the Sister in charge of me was my cousin

Mairi McLeod of the W.R.N.S. She is named after my mother with God, and is fair and lovely like her; and her sweetheart is a Naval surgeon. Now for my loose ends.

Arthur Harper, still called Young Affran, but now the only Affran, went east with his Regiment and is now in Tananarive, so there is still hope for Glen Affran—if there is hope for any place in this world where a man who lives too much by his head can spill so much blood in the name of culture and race.

Henrietta is no longer Harper. That girl, with her modern allure and apparent sophistication, had suckled her share of wisdom from her foster-mother, and I think that she found out, in her own way, the tragic thing that happened under Skene's Rock that Friday in July— the thing that the outside world never suspected. Whatever moved her, she left North Wales and joined Larry McLeod at a place called Lurgan in Northern Ireland. There they were married, and my Aunt Ellen writes me in her frank way that their first son—always a son—will be born a bloody little Orangeman in another one hundred and seventy-three days. That is a subject I do not yet know anything about.

II

Ann Mendoza, the Spanish lady, is still in Glen Affran, but not for long now. I did not see her again before leaving the Glen, and I have not seen her since. After a week I wrote her a brief letter of thanks, and hinted not at all at what I had most to thank her for. In one week there was a reply saying that, alas, there was nothing between us two that deserved thanks; but that if I was clear that I had forgiveness for her she could almost find in her heart forgiveness for me—but only forgiveness. To that letter I replied that I did not attach the least importance to this near-forgiveness, and that if anyone needed forgiveness it was a certain one who not compelling had compelled me to dream about her in a certain place in a far but friendly country. Her reply to that was not one word about dreams but many giving me full information of how affairs were moving in the Glen and at the Lodge. That I considered was an invitation to continue a friendly correspondence. But before I could reply I got myself shot to pieces.

Indeed I was in a mess when brought ashore, still unconscious, bloody bandages on my head, and my shattered leg calling for amputation. The word that went to my uncle, as next of kin, was that I was very seriously wounded. It was then that Ann wrote what was in her heart. My wounds were severe but not so serious. My thick head, tough flesh, and clean blood stood up under the strain, and in a week I was sitting up, head bandaged and leg in a cage, reading that letter. It was a brief honest letter:

"Don Diego, you may not read this in life, or it may be the last thing you read in life. But I must write it, and if you do not read it you will know in the life after what is in my heart. It is that I love you. I love you always, with my heart and my mind and my body. I hold you in my heart. I share my mind with you. It was my hope to rule within your house, to lie with you, and be the mother of your children in the great-great household of San José. If that is not to be, be with God till I come."

There and then I replied to that letter, but shakily. Our correspondence after that went the way of all such correspondence. But she often asked my pardon for the unwomanly things she had said in that letter which she had thought her last one to me.

It was only last week that she wrote her last letter from the Glen. For she would not leave the Glen until the affairs of the estate and the Will were settled according to her wishes and commands.  Among other things that letter said:

"I now tell you that I am very poor because I am very proud, for in my hands that would not then be clean I would not take the money that is mine by law, not even that portion I could take with honour.  If money can be of use, which is in doubt, let the wise spending of it be with this Glen—with Affran still young, and Larry your cousin with his son to be—Oh jealous that I am—and your Uncle Hamish the hero, and that great woman your aunt who says she is kin to me because of a scoundrelly Spanish man who fought in an old battle called Kinsale, and made young love before that.

"I—I am poor, my Diego.  I live on the charity of your uncle in whose wife's house I write this.  A noble charity! But charity!  As I write this the tall woman says, 'Is it a business letter, Spanish Lady?'  And I say, 'It is but a note to a distant friend.  Look you at what I have written!' And now she looks, her hand on my hair that is still that terrible colour you call live in certain writings that I have but peeped at.  She laughs, and says, 'I knew it was a business letter.  You do not like charity.  You want a job. Write you on to this distant friend and, who knows?—he might hear of a job that was going.'

"Now of this job——  Does my house await me?"

So in three days she will be with me.  And we make the vows we do not break, using my mother's wedding-ring.  After that!  Is it the hacienda of San José?  Not yet, though I am due an honourable discharge from Service.  I came into this war to see this war through, and, even with a short leg, a place will be found for me. I see this war through.

Afterwards—that is with God.

This, then, for the time, thanks be to the Lord God Almighty, is the

END